A PRIVATE MOMENT OF PEACE—AND PASSION . . .

She murmured a protest, but he held her fast with one hand as the other took up the rhythm of the hair brush. And slowly Leigh, too, was drawn into the spell. Her eyes closed, and she drifted against him, totally lost in his tender care.

"Oh, Leigh," he breathed, as his need grew, consuming all this morning's fine intentions in a burst of desperate yearning. "Oh, my sweet, Leigh . . ."

LET NO MAN DIVIDE
BY ELIZABETH KARY,
AUTHOR OF THE ACCLAIMED
LOVE, HONOR AND BETRAY

"Thrilling and evocative . . . a page turner written by a skilled storyteller." —Roberta Gellis

PUBLISHER'S SPECIAL
INTRODUCTORY OFFER

Money Back Guarantee!

Berkley Books is so confident that **LET NO MAN DIVIDE** will be one of the best historical romances you've ever read that we'll refund the entire cover price if you're not completely satisfied.

Here's what to do:

You must return the *entire* book, enclosing your original register receipt. Write your name and address on a separate piece of paper and enclose it with the book. This offer is limited to consumers, one refund per customer. All requests for a refund must be received *no later than March 17, 1987*.

Mail your request to: Berkley Books, Dept. SE, 200 Madison Avenue, New York, NY 10016.

ELIZABETH KARY

LET NO MAN DIVIDE

BERKLEY BOOKS, NEW YORK

Berkley Books by Elizabeth Kary

LOVE, HONOR AND BETRAY
LET NO MAN DIVIDE

LET NO MAN DIVIDE

A Berkley Book / published by arrangement with
the author

PRINTING HISTORY
Berkley edition/January 1987

ISBN: 0-425-09472-3

A BERKLEY BOOK® TM 757,375
Berkley Books are published by The Berkley Publishing Group,
200 Madison Avenue, New York, NY 10016.
The name ''BERKLEY'' and the stylized ''B'' with design are
trademarks belonging to the Berkley Publishing Corporation.

PRINTED IN THE UNITED STATES OF AMERICA

To my husband,
Tom,
who helps me with what I write
in ways he never suspects.
And
with special thanks to
my mother-in-law,
Margaret,
for her enthusiasm over my literary pursuits
and for Tom, too.

1 ❧

May 10, 1861—St. Louis, Missouri

The sound intruded on the bright spring day, cutting across the persistent whisper of the wind in the treetops and the cacophony of chirping birds. It was in variance with the placid scene of wild flowers blooming at the edges of the roadway and the redbuds' blossoms that hung like a pale purple haze across the landscape. Leigh Pennington paused uneasily to listen to it, her gracefully arched eyebrows drawn together as she tried to discern its source. The sound came gradually nearer, a swelling rhythm: like a distant drumbeat or a hundred footsteps falling together, like the rush of waves upon a shore or a cordon of marching men. Clutching the carefully packed basket of sundries she had been on her way to deliver to her fiancé at the Confederate camp on the outskirts of town, Leigh whirled to stare back the way she had come, down the country lane toward swiftly advancing ranks of Union soldiers. The dappled sunlight that filtered through the branches above cast shifting patterns against the men's dark uniforms and glinted off their polished weapons as they marched closer. The troops came like an encroaching blue flood through the tunnel of old trees that overhung the road, and Leigh realized with despairing certainty that their destination was the same as hers. The Union army was marching on Camp Jackson!

For a few seconds she stood immobile as the ramifications of what was happening washed over her. Then,

thinking she might be able to sound the alarm at the
Confederate compound, Leigh turned to run. But before
she had gone a hundred yards toward the camp in Lindell's
Grove, she was engulfed in the living current of civilians
that was surging along beside the Union troops. There
were knotted clumps of people pushing forward: men,
women, and children moving apace with the soldiers,
apparently intent on witnessing the first confrontation of
the Civil War in St. Louis. Leigh was jostled and buffeted
as groups brushed past in their haste to reach the shady
grove at the edge of town where the Confederate camp
stood. And as the crowd congealed around her, she was
helplessly swept along with them. A babble of excitement
rose around Leigh as both cheers and jeers were flung at
the grim, straight-backed soldiers. Some of the shouts
expressed approval of the Union's actions in attacking the
newly formed compound of state militia with its blatantly
Southern leanings, while other shouts were harsh indict-
ments of it. The voices clashed just as the two groups of
soldiers soon would, and as Leigh was hustled inexorably
forward, her mind was filled with thoughts of escape. She
struggled determinedly toward the relative safety at the
edge of the crowd, but the bodies were packed too tightly
and the crush had grown too dense. She watched in anger
and frustration as the basket she had packed for her fiancé,
Lucas Hale, and his brother Brandon was torn from her
grip and its contents dispersed into a sea of greedy hands.
With a swift-rising panic that took her breath, Leigh began
to understand her helplessness against the multitudes that
were gathering, and as she stood wedged in the midst of
them, she was afraid as much for those around her as she
was for herself. Caught in a haze of carnival gaiety, no
one in the crowd seemed to sense the growing danger. She
alone realized that once these Union soldiers reached Camp
Jackson, there might well be a battle in which soldiers and
civilians alike could be killed.

When Leigh reached the wide, familiar meadow, now
checkered with row upon row of canvas tents, the Union
forces were converging from several directions to system-
atically surround the field. Meanwhile, the Confederates
ran helter-skelter across the grass, snatching up arms and

ammunition, though no order to do so had been given. Before the Southerners could form themselves into any semblance of a military unit, the camp was ringed by an unbroken wall of blue uniformed men with their bayonets at the ready.

A turbulent silence fell as the last of the Northern troops assumed their positions and General Nathaniel Lyon from the Federal arsenal sent a note to General David Frost, the state militia commander, demanding Camp Jackson's surrender. In the face of the Union's far superior strength and the confusion in his own ranks, Frost had no choice. With only a few minutes' deliberation, he capitulated without a struggle.

In the crowd's reaction to the surrender, Leigh could sense a full spectrum of response, as diverse as the population of St. Louis itself. The faces around her mirrored pride, regret, disbelief, anger, and fear, each expressing the individual's principles, sympathies, and beliefs. Nor were her own feelings, profound relief that there had been no bloodshed between the opposing armies and her concern for Lucas's and Brandon's safety, any less evident than those of her neighbors. The dread she felt at the inevitability of the coming conflict scored her wide brow with worry and tightened the corners of her gently curving mouth. The war that had begun so far away at Fort Sumter had come to St. Louis, and she was torn by her own conflicting loyalties.

Though the decision to surrender had come quickly, it took a long time to muster and disarm the captured Southern troops in preparation for the march to the Federal arsenal south of the city. While they waited, the milling crowd of citizens grew restless, and speculation ran high as to the fate of the Confederate prisoners. Women wept silently, hoping for one final glimpse of their menfolk, fearful for their safety. Leigh watched too, as anxious as the others to be reassured. She had known Lucas and Brandon Hale all her life and loved them both. Only a month before she had promised to marry Lucas, and as she shielded her eyes against the brightness, she scanned the growing ranks of captured men, seeking either his gilded head or Bran's coppery hair to reassure herself of their well-being. But as hard as she searched, there was no sign of either man, and her uneasiness grew.

"Oh, Lucas, where are you?" she breathed, the whisper catching in her throat. Her concern for her own safety was eclipsed by the fear for her fiancé and his brother.

As the mustering of the Confederate troops went on beneath the scorching Missouri sun, the civilian crowd continued to swell, until the road back to the city was lined with pedestrians and clogged with carriages and carts. To pass the time, flasks and even jugs of homemade moonshine were circulated from man to man. As her attention turned once more to those around her, Leigh began to notice people armed with guns and clubs pushing closer to the line of march. The tenor of the crowd was subtly changing too, as discord and impatience became full-blown discontent. She was aware of a growing menace in the air, but she knew Lucas and Brandon's fate might well be decided in the next minutes, and she could not desert them.

Finally the troops began to move out, the Confederates leaving their compound flanked by the victorious Union volunteers. As they marched out the camp gates, catcalls and curses rose from the crowd, some meant to bait the victors and some to taunt the vanquished. Bricks, bottles, and rocks flew along with the insults, and the closely packed citizens began to surge and fall back in a writhing mass. Once again Leigh was swept along with the mob, unable to break free. Her legs moved of their own volition to keep her abreast of the flow of bodies, but with a shiver of terror she realized that anyone who fell would be hopelessly crushed under hundreds of trampling feet. Shoulders and elbows prodded and jabbed her as the people followed along beside the sober military procession. The tension, both between the soldiers and the crowd and between factions of the crowd itself, escalated with each passing moment. The din around Leigh grew louder too, building swiftly in a rush of frenzied voices. Her fear grew apace with the noise, as waves of greater and greater ferment rolled and crashed around her. Somewhere to her right the fervor grew to a deafening roar until there was the single, sharp retort of a pistol. For a moment the crowd seethed in silence, then clamored with renewed outrage. From farther down the line of march there was a blossoming of musket fire that seemed to be moving closer and closer.

Every brain simultaneously grasped the danger, and the throng of citizens erupted into a pushing, shoving mass as they fought to escape the threat of harm. All around her Leigh heard the shrill panic of women's screams and the hoarse moan of men's muttered curses. There was the surge of blood singing in her veins as she became a victim of that same mindless terror. Wildly she sought some refuge from the maddened frenzy of the crowd and the troop's sporadic firing, fighting the crosscurrents of plunging bodies. Then, driven by the horde at her back, Leigh lost her footing as stones rolled from beneath her slippered feet. She cried out in despair as the world shifted beneath her, knowing full well that a fall could mean her death. Then a large hand clamped tightly around her wrist and dragged her to safety behind the stout bole of an oak.

For a few moments Leigh gasped for air, thankful for the tree trunk at her back and the protection of a man's hard, strong-limbed form along the length of hers. His weight crushed her full skirts as he leaned even closer to shield her body with his own, and slowly Leigh raised her head to look up into the determined, high-cheekboned face of her rescuer.

She went strangely weak for a moment, whether from her narrow escape or this man's nearness she could not say. She only knew that in spite of his rugged, uncompromising features, there was something reassuring about the solid feel of him beside her and the expression in his light blue eyes.

In that moment a feeling of breathless surprise filled Leigh as she became aware of the nubby texture of his tweed lapels beneath her clutching fingers and caught the faint, clean, citrus scent that clung to his tanned skin. Inexplicably, she sensed a like response in the man beside her. As they stood pressed intimately together, some intangible charge arced between them sending hot blood coursing to Leigh's cheeks, turning them from parchment white to rosy red. Though she tried, she could not look away, and as she watched him helplessly, she saw his pupils widen until the arctic blue irises became a pale corona for some unfathomable emotion that lit the inky depths. Then abruptly his heavy eyebrows clashed above the bridge of his nose as his hands clenched tight on her arms. His lips narrowed dangerously before he spoke, and the first words he flung at her were harsh and totally unexpected.

"God damn!" he whispered. "God damn it, no!"

Stunned and outraged by his curse, neither moved, hanging suspended, untethered by reality, until the nearby crack of a musket and the splintering of the bark not a foot above their heads broke the spell that held them.

In a maelstrom of confusion, Leigh looked away, seeking to calm her ragged breathing and quiet the jarring of her heart. Beyond her rescuer's broad shoulder she could see a wounded man twisting in pain on the ground nearby. Without considering the risk, she moved instinctively to go to his aid, but the hand that had loosened its hold on her shoulders flexed again to hold her fast.

"Where the hell do you think you're going?" her rescuer snarled.

Leigh struggled and pushed against him, heedless of the gunshots erupting around them.

"For God's sake, let me go!" she shouted. "Can't you see that man is hurt? Let me go to help him!"

The tall man's hold slackened, though he held her effortlessly immobile. "Don't be a fool, woman," he hissed against her ear. "At least wait until the shooting stops. Be sensible."

The logic of his words penetrated slowly, and Leigh went still, though now the protection this man offered seemed suddenly as much restraint as shelter. She became agonizingly aware of the press of his wide chest against her and the intruding knee that had insinuated itself between her thighs. She could feel his heartbeat in counterpoint with her own and the warmth of his breath against her skin. In spite of his obvious concern for her safety and the fact that he had probably saved her life, Leigh resented his encroaching presence and the enforced intimacy. Within her there was an overwhelming need to be free of him, to be doing her part to help the injured; and she tried without success to withdraw from his touch.

The firing dwindled away at last, and when he deemed it safe, the big man shifted his weight and Leigh scrambled away. She went immediately to the wounded man fallen near them and noted, as she bent to aid him, that there were other bodies sprawled across the grass and along the roadside. With practiced hands she opened his clothes to expose a wound high in his shoulder.

"Give me your handkerchief," she ordered her rescuer. He complied wordlessly, watching in surprise as the young woman worked quickly and skillfully to staunch the blood that flowed freely from the hole in the man's shoulder. "And now your cravat," Leigh continued.

"What for?" he demanded, already loosening the black silk tie at his throat.

"I'm going to need it for a bandage," she explained. Taking the strip of cloth to bind the compress in place, she reassured her patient and moved swiftly to a woman crumpled on the ground not far away. After a cursory examination Leigh moved on, her face grim. The next injured person they came across was a girl of twelve or thirteen bleeding from a gash at her hairline. As Leigh attacked the hem of her petticoat for cloth to bind the wound, she turned to the tall man at her elbow.

"I'm going to need something for bandages, Mr. . . ."

"Banister," he provided helpfully as he turned to go. "I'll see what I can find."

Banister strode quickly in the direction of the Rebel compound, ignoring the dregs of the troops that marched past him. Surely, he reasoned, even if there were no bandages to be had at Camp Jackson, he could at least get some bedding to press into service to bind the injured.

By the time he returned, the troops were gone and most of the crowd had dispersed. He found Leigh comforting a crying child while she fashioned a sling for him from the sash of her gown.

"Thank you, Mr. Banister." She paused to send him a melting smile. "Now could you tear those sheets into strips and sit with our young friend here until his parents come to claim him?"

Banister did as he was told, watching with amazement and growing respect as the tall, auburn-haired woman

moved with calm dispatch from one group of needy to the
next, leaving comfort in her wake. By the time the child's
mother came to claim him, the first ambulances had begun
to pull up at the roadside. After that, Banister helped load
the dead and wounded into the wagons for transport to the
city's hospitals.

As her rescuer watched the last of the emergency vehi-
cles rumble off down the street, Leigh came to stand
beside him. All around them the ground was littered with
the rocks and bottles that had been thrown at the hapless
troops and with stray clothes and belongings dropped by
the crowd in the frenzy of escape. Already scavengers
were picking through the leavings, exclaiming occasionally over a fortuitous find. With the emergency over,
Leigh's energy ebbed, draining away to leave her weak-
kneed and weary. Her companion instantly recognized a
change in her and with difficulty stifled the urge to drape
a protective arm around her sagging shoulders. Instead he
offered her what encouragement he could.

"You were magnificent with the wounded, my dear,"
he told her softly, a warm smile lighting his face.

With an effort Leigh turned to him, surprised and strangely
delighted by the rich words of praise and the glow of
admiration in the depths of his pale eyes. Color mounted
to her cheeks as the current of some undefinable emotion
flowed between them. It was a sweet and nourishing force
that seemed to strengthen and renew her. All at once Leigh
was able to square her shoulders and smile back at this tall
stranger, oddly flustered by his nearness.

"I thank you for your kind words, sir," she began
formally, "for saving me from the crowd, and for helping
with the injured, though in truth you did quite as much as I
to make them comfortable."

Banister's smile deepened at her thanks, and for the first
time she noticed the deep masculine dimples that bracketed
the curve of his lips and the crinkling lines that webbed
from the corners of his eyes.

"I did what I could, miss," he demurred in an equally
proper tone, "but you are the one with real skill."

"My grandfather was a doctor, Mr. Banister," she
volunteered.

"My given name is Hayes," he corrected her, "and since we've been partners in adversity, I see no reason why you should be so formal as to call me Mr. Banister. And your name is . . ."

"Leigh, Leigh Pennington."

He offered her his arm as if they had met on a dance floor and not in the midst of a battlefield. "Well, then, Leigh Pennington, after all that's happened today, I think it would be wise for me to take you home."

She retreated a step, prepared to refuse him. What did she know about him, after all? Could she trust him? He had saved her from the crowd and then helped her with the injured, but he had also cursed at her for no apparent reason, as if she were some common woman. Besides, she had made the trip to Lindell's Grove on her own, and she was surely able to find her way home again. "That really isn't necessary," she began, ready to assure him that she was quite capable of taking care of herself, but then the absurdity of what she had been about to say struck her. Here she stood, bruised and battered, disheveled and blood-stained, her basket and bonnet gone, touting her independence to the man who had saved her life.

In the pause Hayes Banister pressed his advantage. "Even if you don't need my protection, won't you humor me? I know I haven't made the best first impression, but unless you let me see you home, I won't sleep a wink tonight wondering if you arrived safe and sound."

Leigh knew she was being manipulated and saw the glint of teasing laughter in his eyes. Still, there was no way to refuse him. Reluctantly she took his arm, and he covered her hand with his.

"I rode the horsecar partway out here, but I doubt they're running now," she began, but Banister cut in on her explanation.

"It doesn't matter; I was quite looking forward to the walk."

As they retraced Leigh's steps together, she studied her rescuer. He was an uncommonly tall man, built big and rangy, but with smooth, confident movements that belied his size. His wavy, walnut-brown hair grew thick and long on his collar and in heavy dark sideburns that traced the lines of his cheeks. They set off his strong features—a long, straight nose, a sculptured mouth, and determined chin—in the same way the curving dimples framed his smile. His forehead was high and his eyes wide set, their color as pale and cool as aquamarine. Nor was Leigh unaware of the expensive, well-cut clothes he wore, now as dirty and tattered as her own.

They chatted companionably as they walked: about his reasons for being in St. Louis and the friends she'd had in Camp Jackson. But when they arrived at the gate to the Pennington town house on Lucas Place, both fell silent.

How, Leigh wondered, staring uncomfortably at her hands, could she adequately thank a man whose quick action had saved her life? What words could express her gratitude for the help he had given her with the injured? And why did it seem so difficult to say good-bye to this virtual stranger? She raised her eyes to his face and saw that he was waiting almost tentatively for her to speak.

Then, as they hung in the abyss of their fading conversation, a woman burst from the door to the house and rushed toward them down the steps. "Leigh! Oh, Leigh! Thank heavens you're safe!" she gasped as she hugged the girl fiercely. "Oh, Leigh, I've been so worried!"

There was no question of the relationship between the two women. Each had the same rich auburn hair and the same creamy skin. Even their fine patrician features were cast in the same mold, though the younger woman's seemed set in an expression more determined and resolute than the one the older woman wore.

"I'm fine, Mother," Leigh assured her, returning the embrace.

"I've been nearly frantic since your father sent word about what happened at Camp Jackson. Though why he didn't go to search for you, I will never know." Her Louisiana drawl was shrill with concern. "And what about Lucas and Bran? Are they safe, too?"

Leigh's face clouded. "In the confusion out there I never caught sight of either one of them, but I suppose they were captured with all the rest of General Frost's command. And as for their fate, no one knows what it will be."

Hayes Banister had been taking in the joyous reunion between the two women, pleased at his part in insuring it. Then, as if suddenly remembering his presence beside her, Leigh turned abruptly.

"Mother," she began, trying to remedy her oversight, "may I present Mr. Hayes Banister from Cincinnati. It's Mr. Banister you have to thank for my safety. Hayes, this is my mother, Althea Pennington."

Her daughter's casual use of Banister's given name was not lost on Althea, and as she ran a discerning eye over the man who had given Leigh his protection, she wondered at the familiarity between them. "I thank you for seeing to my daughter's welfare, Mr. Banister. I fear she guards that precious commodity far too carelessly, as she did today, going off alone instead of waiting for Jeb and the carriage."

"I'd say Leigh was a victim of circumstances this time, Mrs. Pennington," Banister corrected her, "or she was sent to Camp Jackson by fate to look after the injured. Her skills and quick thinking may well have saved lives in the minutes before the ambulances arrived this afternoon."

"Oh, Hayes," Leigh began to demur, but Althea Pennington was pleased with his words of praise for her daughter's skill.

"Mr. Banister," she began, smiling up at him, "perhaps you would be willing to accept an invitation to supper this evening. It will only be a simple meal *en famille*, but I know my husband will be anxious to meet you and thank you for what you did to help Leigh today."

The invitation was both unexpected and welcome; he'd eaten far too many meals alone of late. Banister accepted warmly. "I'd like that very much, Mrs. Pennington."

"Good," Althea said and nodded as she ushered her daughter toward the house. "We'll see you at six o'clock."

"Until this evening, then," he replied. Hayes watched the two women enter the double doors of the handsome brick town house, then set off down Locust Street, scuffling absently through the dust.

Hayes Banister crossed the elegant lobby of the world-famous Planters' House Hotel, past the slick

horsehair couches, the milling guests, and the banks of
potted palms to the front desk. "There's a Mr. Travis
waiting for you in the Gentlemen's Ordinary, sir," the
clerk told him as he gave Hayes the key to his room.

Hayes's fingers tightened around the cool metal, and he
frowned irritably. Now that he had found something more
pleasant to occupy his mind than the business that had
brought him to St. Louis, Travis had finally deemed it
convenient to show up. Banister had been cooling his heels
for the best part of a week waiting for this meeting, and
now, though Travis's appearance was not particularly welcome, it would at least end the waiting. With a grimace,
Hayes glanced down at his clothes. Finding them as dirty
and disreputable as Leigh Pennington's had been, he decided Travis could wait for him for a change while he
made himself presentable.

It was a few minutes later that Banister found Nathan
Travis comfortably ensconced at a corner table in the
smoky, dark-paneled room that was the gathering place and
retreat of St. Louis's most influential men. It was here that
they had come for years to eat the game and other delica-
cies that the hotel menu had to offer, drink fine brandy,
and smoke their long, dark cigars as they discussed the
politics of the day. To Hayes, Travis seemed somehow out
of place in the plush, genteel surroundings. His worn black
broadcloth coat and ill-fitting trousers were in sharp contrast to the well-dressed men at the surrounding tables, and
his common manners the antithesis of those demonstrated
by the other patrons. He was, at first glance, an unremark-
able man, neither handsome nor ugly, with thin, sharply
etched features to match the long, gangly body that sprawled
in his chair. Yet Hayes was not fooled by the man's
appearance. He knew there was keen intelligence in the
coal-black eyes beneath their heavy lids, and steely strength
in his wiry form. Many years ago when he had first met
Travis, he had been taken in, but now Banister knew the
truth. Nathan Travis was anything but ordinary, for within
him burned an instinct for survival that had been honed
sharp by years of being more than what he seemed.

They had met when Banister was still living the sometimes wild and adventurous life of a river pilot, at a fuel

stop just below Memphis. The steamboat Travis owned had
put ashore with engine trouble, and while Hayes's boat
had taken on wood, cargo, and passengers, he and the
chief engineer had gone aboard to offer their services. It
had taken a fair amount of tinkering to correct the problem, but by the time the *Priscilla Anne* was ready to shove
off again, the disabled boat was running. It had been a
chance meeting that first time, and it was months before
Hayes came to realize that he and Travis were bound by
the same stringent convictions and the same need to make
things right. After that, whenever Travis turned up, be it in
Vicksburg, New Orleans, or at the Banister Shipyards in
Cincinnati, it had seemed less from fortune than from
design.

"I trust you've found the accommodations here in St.
Louis tolerably comfortable," Travis began conversationally
as Hayes pulled out a chair to join him.

"Yes, the rooms are quite adequate," he agreed, "but I
had expected to find James Eads in town when I arrived. I
was looking forward to meeting him after finding so many
of his inventions useful, first on the river and later at the
shipyards."

"He was called to Washington unexpectedly to show
the plans you came here to review to Lincoln and his
Cabinet. He's expected back any time."

"Have his drawings been accepted, then?" Banister
inquired.

Travis snickered. "The river fleet is like a bastard child;
neither the Army nor the Navy wants to claim the responsibility or bear the expense."

"Don't those men understand the importance of the
Mississippi to both the Union and the Confederacy?" Hayes
demanded.

"Easy, Banister, easy," the other man soothed. "Eventually one or the other will admit the necessity of this
project, and then it will get under way. Right now the
Navy's busy blockading the Southern ports and the Army's
trying to figure some way to keep the Rebs out of Washington. Besides, nothing like this ironclad fleet Eads is
proposing has ever been attempted. It's small wonder they're
reluctant to commit themselves."

"Well, where does the responsibility for defense of the rivers lie?" Banister wanted to know.

The other man shrugged and sat back in his chair, laying his napkin beside the empty plate.

"Traditionally, the Army has had jurisdiction over the inland waterways, but in the end it won't matter where the money comes from. This flotilla is vital to a Union victory, and once those men in Washington stop dickering over who'll pay for what, Eads's involvement in this project is inevitable. Properly educated or not, he's one of the Union's most capable engineers."

"Then why ask my opinion of his drawings?"

"Because two heads are better than one, and you do have the advantage of schooling as well as a lifetime spent around steamboats in one capacity or another. Have you had a chance to study his plans?"

Banister nodded. "There were copies at his office."

"And what did you think of them?"

"I think the plans are brilliant!" Hayes admitted, his voice deep with admiration. "Oh, there are some problems as I see it. Covering conventional riverboats with iron plating will make them heavy and slow to maneuver, and I think the sheathing on the pilot house should be made thicker since that will be the nerve center of any mission the ironclads undertake."

"Do you have any recommendations to remedy the problems you've outlined?"

"Yes." Hayes nodded and launched into a complicated explanation of the revisions he would suggest to augment Eads's original plans.

Travis listened intently, obviously pleased with Banister's carefully considered changes and his own correct assessment of the other man's abilities as an engineer. "I'd be much obliged if you could write a report outlining what you just told me. Anything we can offer those men in Washington to encourage them to make up their minds about this project will give us that much more of a head start on the Rebels."

Hayes agreed. "I just wonder if St. Louis is the place to build this new ironclad fleet. After what happened out at Camp Jackson this afternoon, it's obvious that Southern sympathy is running high, so the place is bound to be riddled with Confederate informers. The local papers seem to be full of Secessionist doctrine and—''

Travis laughed with what seemed to be genuine humor.''I think old Nathaniel Lyon has the situation well in hand. He was out there scouting Camp Jackson just yesterday, and when he saw evidence of the arms shipment they'd received from Baton Rouge, he had the evidence he needed to move on that nest of traitors.''

Hayes was stunned at the news that the commander of the Federal arsenal had been in the militia camp. ''Wasn't he shot·on sight?''

Travis laughed again. ''What those Confederates saw was Major Frank Blair's old, blind mother-in-law out for her usual afternoon carriage ride. Lyon dressed in one of her black gowns and bonnets, with a mourning veil added for good measure. Not one of those Southern boys stopped playing soldier long enough to question him.''

''The attack was well planned; I'll give him that. Frost never had a chance. But the incident afterward was tragic.''

''There will be hell to pay for that, I reckon,'' Nathan Travis conceded as he rose to go.

''You write me that report now, won't you, Banister? Leave it at the front desk addressed to Mr. Jones. And then you might as well go on home to Cincinnati.''

Hayes looked up at the enigmatic man standing over him. ''Now that I've seen Eads's plans, I have a hankering to meet the man himself.''

Travis shrugged. ''Suit yourself, Banister, but I have a feeling your involvement with Mr. Eads and his plans for the ironclad fleet is far from over.''

2 ❧

"Well, I for one think it's a disgrace that Union troops would fire on innocent bystanders!" Althea Pennington's voice rose above the sounds of the meal as she addressed the others who had gathered at her well-laid table. "And when I think that our Leigh was exposed to that kind of danger—"

"As you can see, Mother, I escaped unscathed, thanks to Mr. Banister," Leigh broke in, "but I'd hardly say that mob out at Camp Jackson this afternoon was innocent of any wrongdoing. If they had not taunted the soldiers and pelted them with anything at hand, I doubt there would have been trouble."

Her mother was outraged. "I don't know how you can say that, Leigh, when you know that awful General Lyon has been spoiling for a fight ever since he took over General Harney's command."

"Leigh's right," Hayes Banister agreed, expressing his views on the afternoon's episode for the first time. "There's no question that those troops were provoked. I realize that's small comfort to the friends and families of the dead and wounded, but it's the truth. The real tragedy is that women and children were cut down along with the perpetrators, but violence is seldom just in its choice of victims."

In the several hours since the incident, rumors about the rioting at Camp Jackson had flown through the city, and though the stories varied, most agreed that the first shot had been fired by someone in the crowd, seriously injuring one of the Union captains. The later firing had come from raw recruits pressed beyond restraint by the crowd's venom. It had spread down the line of march, feeding on its own panic and resulting in more casualties than if only seasoned troops had been used for the mission.

Horace Pennington sat back in his chair and eyed the younger man. "Do you think we've seen the last of this uproar, Mr. Banister?"

"No, sir, I'm afraid not," Hayes replied. "When I left the Planters' House, a crowd was already beginning to gather, and what with the Confederate sympathizers meeting at the Berthold mansion only a few blocks away, I imagine that the police will be hard-pressed to prevent a confrontation. I don't doubt that things could get pretty hot down at the arsenal, either. What's worse is that I believe this trouble is only a foretaste of things to come."

"You think we will have to fight to preserve the Union, then?"

"I believe, with states seceding right and left and Lincoln's call for volunteers, it's inevitable," Banister prophesied grimly.

Pennington sighed. "Well, don't you worry about things down at the arsenal, at least. General Lyon is sure to have things well in hand."

"I've heard a great deal about this General Lyon in the past few days. I believe I'd like to meet the man."

"Oh, he's dreadful!" Althea exclaimed, her brown eyes wide with horror. "He looks like a scarecrow with that scraggly red beard of his. And his manners, my dear Mr. Banister, are simply unspeakable. But then, I understand he's from New England somewhere, and what can you expect?"

"Your friend Major Crawford is from New England, too," Leigh pointed out.

"Aaron's from Boston; it's hardly the same thing at all," Althea corrected. "And for all his Abolitionist views, he's undeniably a gentleman."

"Father, what do you think will happen to the men who were captured at Camp Jackson today?" Leigh asked as the servants began to clear the table.

"You're worried about Lucas and Bran, I suppose," Horace observed, frowning. "To tell you the truth, Leigh, I really don't know. Lyon can't keep those men under arrest at the arsenal, not all seven hundred of them. He could ship them up north, but I doubt the people of St. Louis would stand for that. If he tried, there would certainly be more rioting—"

"And even more bloodshed," his daughter finished for him.

"Most likely that's right," Pennington agreed. "But don't you shortchange Nathaniel Lyon. He'll find an equitable way out of this somehow. He's a capable officer and will serve the Union well in these next months, mark my words. The Hale brothers will be safe, Leigh. Don't you worry."

As the dessert was served, a fruit compote in fine, stemmed glasses, Hayes Banister studied his dinner companions. Horace Pennington was the quintessential Western businessman: tall, broad, and ruddy with alert, green eyes. In his late fifties, he was still a strong, vigorous man, but with thinning hair and a heavily lined face that gave evidence of his years. Cut from the same cloth as Hayes's father, Pennington was a deeply moral man with the courage of his convictions behind him. His support of Lincoln and the Union in the forthcoming confrontation would be complete and unconditional, as would his loyalty to any undertaking worthy of his effort. In contrast, his wife, Althea, who must be nearly twenty years his junior, was a delicate camellia of a woman. Absolutely lovely with a deep, stirring beauty that would never grow mellow or serene, she was obviously doted on and protected by both her husband and daughter. Yet there was a quicksilver inconsistency in her that somehow resolved the disparity between her air of childish petulance and her steely willed support of the Southern cause.

And then there was Leigh, somehow the amalgam of these two people, these two personalities. She was the image of her mother with the same breathtaking beauty, yet possessed of a fresh radiance that even Althea could not claim. But there was something of her father in her too, if not in the features, at least in her expression. He had given her his height, his air of quiet resolution, and those steady green eyes. Hayes found himself studying her with determined intensity: watching her toy with her dessert, listening to her easy laugh, sensing the affection she felt toward both her parents, even when each seemed to feel something less congenial for the other. Nor could he deny the strange attraction he felt for Leigh, evident from the first moment he had held her in his arms this afternoon with the bullets flying all around them. As the dessert dishes were being cleared away, Horace spoke, breaking into Hayes's thoughts.

"I hate to leave such pleasant company," he was saying, "but urgent matters demand my attention. Stay and finish your meal, Mr. Banister, and enjoy the rest of the evening with my ladies. You seem a man of reasonable views and opinions, sir, and if your stay in St. Louis proves lengthy, I hope you find your way back to our table. And thank you for what you did for Leigh this afternoon."

Banister rose from his place to shake Pennington's hand. "Thank you, sir. I've enjoyed the meal and the company. Have care on the streets tonight; there's no telling who's abroad."

Horace acknowledged his words of warning and turned to go. "Good night, then."

"Do be careful, Horace," Althea called after him. "It's that wretched Yankee Wide-Awakes Club that takes him out on such a night when he would be far safer at home," she complained. "I wish he would stay here instead of going gallivanting with those good-for-nothing rabble-rousers!"

Banister had been in town long enough to recognize her florid description of some of the most respectable men in the city, and smiled to himself.

"How is it, Mrs. Pennington, that you can be a staunch Confederate when your husband is such a loyal Lincoln man?" he wanted to know. But instead of her mother, it was Leigh who gave him his answer.

"We live in 'a house divided,' " she said simply, but the expression of sadness in the depths of her eyes was not lost on the man across the table.

"I admit it's a trial, Mr. Banister, but neither of us can change the way we are," Althea added softly.

A pall of quiet resignation hung over the room, and Hayes felt compelled to try to mend the rift he had caused. "Are you at odds on every point?" he continued. "Do you condone the institution of slavery while Mr. Pennington opposes it? And do you believe in each state's right to sever its ties with the Union?"

Althea drew a long breath, wondering if Hayes Banister's questions lay in men's seemingly endless compulsion to discuss politics or in an honest desire to understand the conflict that was threatening to destroy not only the nation but her family as well.

"I believe that the people in any state or territory should be free to choose their course for the common good, Mr. Banister. And as for slavery . . ." She made a vague, fluttery gesture with her hands. "We own no slaves here in Missouri though it is our right to do so. All our servants are free men and women, even my maid Julia who came with me from Louisiana when I married. And that's fine for our life here. But in the South, where I was born and raised, slavery is an economic necessity. My brothers could not run their plantations without darkies, and if slavery is abolished in this country, as some think it should be, it will be the end of a life I hold most dear."

Hayes watched the older woman with new respect. In spite of her sometimes vapid pose, she defended her own position with unexpected eloquence.

Her eyes misted as she went on. "When I was a girl, we lived such a fine life: slow and genteel, with nothing more to think about than balls and barbecues. We hunted in the spring and fall and partied through the summer. In winter we would open the house in New Orleans to attend the entertainments there." Her soft, liquid drawl lent veracity to the conjured images.

"Our Southern men made such gallant cavaliers: handsome, well-spoken, and dashing. They would go to any lengths to please a lady, and those ladies, once won, would try as diligently to make their gentlemen content. Those were such sweet days, happier than any I've ever known. If the North wins this war and outlaws slavery, those days will be lost forever, exiled to memories of glories past.''

Hayes studied her face and the unmistakable sadness in the line of her mouth, nodding slowly. "I think I understand why you want to preserve a way of life that will one day be irretrievably gone. In a way I feel the same about my time on the Mississippi. The years I spent as a pilot on a steamboat are like a dream to me now. Danger, adventure, travel, and responsibility were part and parcel of the life I was living, and I loved every minute of it. For those three years I was totally alive, intensely aware of my good fortune and of living each day to the fullest. And though the steamboats are still flourishing, they're doomed and the life I remember with them. When the railroads take over this country, as they inevitably will, it will mark the end of an era.''

Both women watched him for a long moment with warmth in their eyes. It was a rare man who admitted to his feelings, and they both recognized the strength in Hayes Banister that allowed him to do so now.

It was Althea who spoke at last. "If you feel that way, Mr. Banister, why did you leave the river?''

Hayes stirred and shrugged. "The family business needed me, and I had sown my wild oats, so to speak.'' He paused tentatively, as if he meant to say more but could not find the words.

Instead he asked a question of his own. "And why did you leave the South?''

"I left because I married Horace, of course,'' Althea replied, then sat silent for a moment, taking the measure of this tall, dark-haired man before her. She saw the broad, intelligent brow and the sensitive curve of his lips balanced by the hardness of his jaw and his clear, unflinching gaze.

Slowly she nodded. "I like you, Mr. Banister. I believe there are depths and emotions in you that you contrive to keep very well hidden.''

"Mother!'' Leigh gasped with inexplicable irritation. Her mother had no right to make such a personal observation about a man they hardly knew.

But Althea turned to her daughter unperturbed. "He's a

rare man, Leigh. You would do very well indeed to remember that.''

Then, as if the exchange had never taken place, she addressed her supper guest once more. "Would you care to take coffee on the veranda, sir? It's grown intolerably warm in here.''

When they had finished their coffee, Althea rose and excused herself. "If you don't mind, I believe I'll go indoors and practice the pieces I must play next week at Mrs. Stephens's musical.''

"No, by all means, go ahead," Hayes agreed. "I for one would enjoy a concert, and with the windows open we should have very good seats for it.''

Smiling, the older woman picked up her trailing skirts and went inside, leaving Hayes and Leigh sitting on the porch steps beneath the gracefully draped wisteria vines. A few moments later the stirring strains of "Dixie" filled the air.

"Good heavens!" Leigh exclaimed with a chuckle. "I hope she isn't planning to play that at the musical, or she'll cause a riot on her own.''

Hayes listened for a minute to the familiar melody. "She does play the piano very well," he observed. "Do you play?''

"A little; not nearly as well as Mother does. Can I get you anything else, Hayes? Brandy? A cigar?''

"A bit of brandy sounds good. Would you mind if I smoked my pipe?'' he asked, taking a pouch of tobacco and a fine old briar from his pocket.

"Not at all; I like the smell of pipe smoke.''

By the time Leigh had returned with a decanter and a glass on an ornate silver tray, smoke from Banister's pipe was already wafting upward. She poured a tot of brandy in the bottom of the snifter, then settled herself on the top step beside him. Hayes studied her in silence, drawing on his pipe and taking an occasional sip from his drink. A light wind was stirring the night air, grown thick with the promise of rain, bringing the scent of lilacs to them from the garden at the side of the house. The sound of peepers filled the darkness, and a wondrous sense of contentment flowed between them. They sat quietly enjoying the music for a very long time.

"Where do you stand in all this, Leigh?" Hayes asked at last, knocking the ash from the bowl of his pipe.

She stirred slowly. "In all what?"

"Your father is a confirmed Union man and your mother an ardent Confederate. Where does that leave you?"

She leaned back against one of the tall wooden columns that supported the porch. "It leaves me in a position of great compromise," she stated flatly. Before she went on, she drew a long breath and exhaled slowly.

"When I was a child, we would go south to visit Uncle Charles and Uncle Theo at the plantations in Louisiana, and in many ways it was the kind of life Mother remembers so fondly. During those visits she reveled in the ease and gentility, in the quiet gallantry of the men and in a woman's life of position and security. But all I ever saw was the misery that was necessary to support their pleasant indolence. I watched the Negroes toil all day in the scorching sun and saw their tumbledown hovels and the whippings. Mother has always been able to turn a blind eye to suffering. I never could.

"But then, I think it's wrong to use force to preserve the Union. The Constitution was a pact, an agreement entered into freely by all parties. If the southern states want to void that agreement and secede, then I think they should be allowed to go peacefully."

"You're caught right in the middle, aren't you?" he asked gently. "What are you going to do when the war comes in earnest?"

"You mean it hasn't?" she asked and then looked away. "I'm going to nurse."

Banister nodded. "I should have expected that answer after what you did out at Camp Jackson today. I'd say if anyone has a calling for medicine, you do."

She reached across to touch his hand in a warm gesture of gratitude before she went on. "Until my grandfather died last fall, I worked with him in his medical practice. If I have any skill, it is because he was such a fine teacher." Leigh paused uncertainly, watching the big man beside her from beneath her lashes as long-buried hopes and ambi-

tions formed themselves into words for the first time. Those
hopes had been a secret deep within her for so long that it
was nearly impossible to confess them at last, but there
was something about this stranger that invited her confidences.

"After—after Grandpa died, I thought about taking the
trust fund he'd left for me to go to medical school. There
are women who've done that, you know." Her voice
gained momentum. "Women in New England and in New
York have actually become doctors. I don't delude myself
that it would be easy, but studying medicine is all I've
ever wanted to do with my life. Only now it's more
important to stay here, even if it means an end to that
dream."

Hayes's expression was intent. "Why?" he wanted to
know.

"Because in a few months they're going to need every
pair of hands to care for the sick and wounded. I realized
that today. I'll be able to use my skills; I have something
to offer."

Hayes took her hands in his as he studied her pale,
determined face. "What you have, Leigh, is far more than
your skill. You have an honest compassion for people in
need."

"Oh, Hayes, it's so kind of you to offer me words of
encouragement when . . ." Her words faltered as she met
those strange, light eyes, and before she realized what he
intended, he had pulled her across the steps toward him. In
the same fluid motion his lips descended to cover hers, and
Leigh could taste the lingering sweetness of brandy on his
mouth. A delicate, fluttering breathlessness filled her, followed by an inexplicable sense of belonging that quelled
any questions or doubts. With ingenuous ease she gave
him her response, her arms sliding artlessly around his
neck. The kiss that had begun with the simple touching of
lips deepened as his tongue savored her more and more
deeply, and there seemed nothing so right as the helpless
languor that crept along her limbs. Her world went diffuse
and unfocused around her, and she clung with growing
intensity to the strong, solid man at her side. His open
mouth moved by minutely measured degrees to her tem-

ple, then nibbled across her cheek to her throat, as if he were charting the curves and hollows to remember for all eternity. As his lips brushed her alabaster skin, her fingers stroked his hair, sensing the deep, rich color rather than seeing it, reveling in the softness and vitality of the thickly waving strands. And though she tried, Leigh could not seem to catch her breath or quiet the sudden leaping of her heart. Then his lips returned to cover hers, fierce and greedy and oddly satisfying. Of her own volition she pressed close against Hayes with a growing need to delight in the delicious sensations he evoked in her.

"Leigh," an intruding voice assailed her. "Leigh?"

"Yes, Mother?" she managed to answer as she wrenched free of Hayes's encircling arms with guilty haste.

"Are you making sure that Mr. Banister has everything he wants?" Althea called out from the front parlor. Leigh became abruptly aware that the music had stopped, and she fumbled in confusion.

"She's doing an admirable job of that, I assure you, Mrs. Pennington," Hayes spoke up, answering for her, a purely lecherous grin lighting his face.

"Very well," Althea called back and began to play again.

As the first notes of a Beethoven sonata filled the air, Leigh's thoughts roiled in confusion: outraged propriety and the belated realization of her betrothal to Lucas Hale warring with the intense pleasure and security she found in Hayes Banister's embrace.

"How could you tell her that?" she hissed, amazed that he could be so unruffled after what had passed between them. But then, she noticed, his eyes were oddly alight and his breathing did seem a little unsteady.

"What I told your mother was the gospel truth," he said evenly. "I've wanted to kiss you from the moment I set eyes on you this afternoon with your hair tumbling down and your gown stained and dirty. And now that I know you better, there are several other things—"

"Let me go!" she demanded in a whisper as she struggled against his encroaching hands, certain that if she allowed him even this slight advantage, she would be powerless to hold him off. And in making that concession, she acknowledged to herself that her desires ran perilously close to his. He had taken her by surprise at first, but now with the full weight of rationality behind her actions, Leigh knew she must resist him.

"Don't put me off, Leigh," Hayes coaxed, keeping his tone light. "You enjoyed kissing me every bit as much as I enjoyed kissing you."

"I most certainly did not!" she protested in outraged pride.

"Liar," he returned without reproach.

"And even if I did, it's not something I'm particularly proud of," she argued, unwillingly admitting that she was not indifferent to his charm. "Unmarried ladies of breeding are not supposed to enjoy any man's kisses, much less the kisses of a stranger."

"Are we strangers, Leigh? I feel as if I've known you all my life." His voice was as soft and gentle as the spring night that surrounded them, and Leigh went weak and weightless at his words. But before she could think beyond the realization that she felt the same, he continued. "Besides, that's pure bunk, fed to those susceptible, well-bred young ladies by a bunch of old biddies who've never been properly kissed."

In self-defense she turned his words against him. "The kiss you gave me was hardly proper!" she snapped, trying to muster anger and outrage to defeat him. "And besides, there's my fiancé, Lucas—"

"Lucas?"

"Yes, Lucas Hale. Surely my behavior this evening does not speak well of my loyalty to him." At the thought of Lucas, a prisoner in the Federal arsenal tonight while she was blithely kissing another man, Leigh was overwhelmed by a new wave of guilt.

"Lucas Hale? From out at Camp Jackson?" Hayes demanded. Half a dozen scraps of conversation came together as the connection between Leigh and the "friend" she had been on her way to visit at the Confederate camp began to dawn on him. "You didn't tell me you were betrothed!" Banister seemed inexplicably furious.

"Yes," Leigh answered, flushing red in the darkness.

"Yes, I am. I was on my way to see Lucas and his brother when I was overtaken by the crowd."

"Without even setting eyes on your Lucas I know his type," Hayes blustered. "I'll warrant he's one of your mother's gallant Southern cavaliers. And it's abundantly clear from your response to me that he's always been too much of a gentleman to kiss you as you deserve to be kissed."

While Leigh should have been infuriated by Hayes's assessment of Lucas Hale's abilities, it was the fact that he found her lacking that spurred her response. "How dare you complain about my deficiencies in an area where knowledge and experience mark a woman as little more than a strumpet!" she cried, leaping to her feet. "And what makes you such an expert on just how a woman should be kissed?"

"What a forward question for a well-bred young lady to ask," he observed as he rose to stand beside her on the steps. His anger had vanished as quickly as it had appeared, and he was clearly amused by her outburst. "I confess that there are some women who might express a certain appreciation for my kisses, but modesty prevents that. And to be precise, I never said you were deficient in your response to me, only untutored. It's just possible that I could be convinced to remedy that situation if given the right incentive." His dimpled smile shone in the darkness, and there was an unmistakable twinkle in his eyes.

Leigh was stunned by his blatant proposition when she had made her own position so clear: repelled, angry, and at the same time perversely curious about what he might see fit to teach her.

"You incredibly conceited, ill-bred boor!" she gasped when she had found her voice. "How dare you say such a thing to me? I want you to leave this house! Now! This minute! And don't come back. I've made more than adequate recompense for your help this afternoon. Now, get out!"

Gently but determinedly, Hayes gathered in the hand that had indicated the gate at the front of the garden as the speediest route of departure, and with it the rest of her body as well. For a moment he caught a glimpse of her

incredulous face as he lowered his mouth to claim hers.
The kiss was slow and leisurely but sultry and provocative
as well, demanding a response. It aroused in Leigh a
devastating need, white-hot and sweet, that melted her
bones and turned her knees to water beneath her. His
caressing tongue circled her lips then dipped into her
mouth, tasting again and again, until the intimate intrusion
became a thing she craved. She could feel his broad, hard
hands moving on her back, confining her but gentling her
as well. A shiver of response swept through her as she
conceded the battle to resist him.

Hayes instantly recognized her surrender, but he wanted
so much more from this woman than submission. Exercis-
ing considerable self-control, he stepped away to wait for
her reaction.

Leigh swayed unsteadily for a moment, watching him in
confusion, uncertain of his motives. Her first impulse was
to throw her arms around him and kiss him back, giving
him the response he sought. But even as she yearned to
reach out to him, she knew she could not. For Lucas and
honor and her own self-respect, she must spurn him. As
she spun away, frustration and anger flamed inside her,
fueled not only by the unwelcome emotions Hayes aroused
in her, but by the unwilling choice he was forcing her to
make. She felt his hand stroke along her bare arm as a
final assault on her senses, and in reaction she swung back
to face him, striking out blindly, with tears in her eyes.
Her palm met his cheek with a resounding smack, and they
stood for a score of heartbeats without moving.

Then with slow, deliberate motions Banister claimed the
hand she had used to strike him and brought it to his lips.
"Are you sure you want me to go?" he asked very softly.

Leigh wrenched her fingers from his grip, feeling shaken
and ashamed. "Yes! Yes, go! Get out!" she shouted,
heedless of her mother's presence in the next room. "I
never want to see you again!"

Hayes gave a curt nod and turned to address the woman
in the parlor. "Good night, Mrs. Pennington," he called
through the open window. "Thank you for a fine meal and
a pleasant evening."

He paused, watching the lovely, auburn-haired young

woman for a moment longer, with something akin to regret in his eyes. "And good-bye, Leigh," he said.

With what seemed like galling nonchalance he shambled down the steps and across the garden, letting the gate slam behind him. Before he was out of sight down the street, Althea was beside her daughter. "Why did Mr. Banister decide to leave so early?"

"I sent him away, Mother," Leigh confessed. "He—he was very forward with me."

Her mother gave Leigh a long look, noting that her lips were smudged with kisses and that her eyes were unusually bright. How well Althea knew the signs, and she recognized them in her own daughter with a twinge of mingled envy and concern. How clearly she understood the way Leigh must be feeling now.

"Somehow Mr. Banister's behavior doesn't surprise me, Leigh. He seems to be a man who goes after what he wants; nor do I think he is likely to deny himself for the sake of convention. Yet I believe he is a man capable of great tenderness and understanding."

"How can you be so sure, Mother?" Leigh asked almost wistfully.

Althea laughed. "It's the wisdom of my years, I suppose. Has Mr. Banister upset you, dear?"

The younger woman straightened resolutely. "No, Mother, I'm fine. I'm just a little tired after all that's happened today. Perhaps I'll go right upstairs to bed."

How like Horace she is, Althea found herself thinking. It was obvious that the encounter with Hayes Banister had unsettled her, but Leigh was clearly unwilling to discuss her feelings, even if it might have helped. Althea smoothed one hand along her daughter's cheek, then kissed her.

"Very well, Leigh. Good night and sleep well."

"Good night, Mother."

There was the sound of the young woman's tread upon the stairs inside, and Althea was left alone on the veranda. She stood for a very long time watching the clouds skulk past the moon, smelling the dust in the wind and wondering if there would be a storm. Concern for her husband's safety plucked at her, and she listened to the sounds in the

distance, trying to determine if they were threatening or
benign. She knew she would not rest easy until Horace
returned, and she cursed the conflict that had driven her
from her husband's bed and made them strangers.

Finally she stirred and went inside, locking the door
behind her. As she turned down the hall to the stairs, she
noticed Hayes Banister's hat hanging on the hall tree.
Taking it from its peg, she turned it over and over in her
hands, brushing the heavy felt until the nap lay smooth and
shiny. There was something she liked about the big engineer from Cincinnati, and she had hoped for Leigh's sake
that he would come to call often.

In spite of the differences between them, Althea Pennington knew her daughter well. Leigh was a straightforward, headstrong girl, and her mother feared for her as she
went out into the world alone. Leigh would never be
content in the role society prescribed for her, and she
needed a special kind of man to stand behind her in the
inevitable battles she would face. Hayes Banister was just
such a man, secure enough in his own strength that he
would not be intimidated by Leigh's intelligence and determination. Banister would be neither condescending nor
contemptuous of her ambition, would allow Leigh the
freedom to seek her own success, and would never undermine her efforts to accomplish what she must. Althea well
understood the consequences of thwarted dreams and would
not stand idly by and let her daughter face that same kind
of disappointment. Yes, she hoped that Mr. Banister would
see fit to visit again, in spite of Leigh's sharp words and
her betrothal to Lucas Hale. And now, with Hayes Banister's forgotten hat in her hands, Althea was sure he would
return.

Smiling to herself, she hung the hat back on its peg and
went into the parlor to wait for her husband.

          Back in his suite of rooms at the Planters'
House once more, Hayes Banister prowled aimlessly from
the plush parlor, through the bed chamber, into the dressing room and back again, making the circuit with long,
impatient strides. Through the open windows he could

hear the rumble of discontented voices from the men who were milling in the pool of every gas lamp on the street below. In spite of the rain that had begun to fall, the crowd had grown as he approached the hotel, and he had run a gauntlet between banks of dissidents to gain the safety of the lobby. Nor did he relish the idea of braving their unpredictable temper a second time for the sake of walking off a little restlessness. Still, he was aware of his own pent-up energies and the need for release.

Pausing at the parlor table, he uncorked the bottle of bourbon that had been provided for his use and poured a generous glassful. He took a long swallow of the whiskey, wandered to a chair at the far side of the room, and sat down, stretching his long legs before him.

The incidents of the past twenty-four hours stood out in sharp relief against the pattern of everyday life, filling his head with a jumble of impressions, observations, and feelings. Some of the occurrences were the stuff of destiny, and he knew that today's events, both public and private, could mark the beginning of something that would consume his energies for months to come and change the plans he'd made for his future. There was no doubt that the bloodshed at Camp Jackson was a promise of other, larger and more devastating battles to be fought throughout the country, and it confirmed that men were indeed ready to fight and die over the questions of slavery and union. His meeting with Nathan Travis and the report Hayes was to write for him about James Eads's proposed ironclad flotilla might well involve him in the coming war in ways that he had never considered. For a moment Banister sat stunned by the latitude of the possibilities before him. Was he prepared to meet whatever challenges the future might hold? He stared down into his half-empty glass, then tossed off the contents. Yes, by God, whatever fate had in store for him, he was ready.

Removing his coat and opening his collar against the heat in the room, he poured himself another drink. When he returned to his seat, he brought the open bottle of bourbon with him, set it on the floor beside his chair, and stretched out comfortably to contemplate the warm, vivacious woman he had met, rescued, and kissed tonight with

such delicious abandon. Leigh Pennington was unquestion-
ably the most beautiful woman he had met in months. Her
sweet oval face, pale and petal-soft, was etched so plainly
in his mind that he might have known her always, rather
than just one day. He remembered how the sunlight had
caught in her cinnamon hair as he held her this afternoon,
and the way the curves of her body had flowed beneath his
hands. He had been unwillingly captivated in that first
moment, staring into her dark eyes, the mysterious blue,
gray, green of a spruce tree in the snow. But it had quickly
become evident that there was so much more to her than a
fair face and seductive body. She had been compassionate
and gentle in tending the injured outside Camp Jackson
and both articulate and zealous in expressing her hopes and
fears for the future. Lord, she was young, Banister thought,
viewing her from the prodigious achievement of his thirty-
two years—not more than twenty-one or twenty-two. And
Leigh was still bursting with the untarnished idealism that
made her think she could challenge the world and win.

Sighing, Banister sipped from his glass. He had been
like that once too, undaunted by the cards fate dealt him,
willing to gamble everything on his own raw courage and
initiative. It was his dawning maturity and pragmatism that
made him both admire and fear for Leigh Pennington's
innocence. In retrospect, it was not difficult to determine
when his own brash idealism had been crushed by life's
realities. It had been destroyed swiftly and brutally in the
moment when Monica Morgan Bennett had denied him his
son.

Monica. Even now that name was not without its bittersweet associations. He had seen her for the first time at the
racetrack in Saratoga, where he was spending a few weeks
between graduation from Princeton and the start of his job
at the family shipyards in Cincinnati. The girl beside him
at the rail had turned to him with a question about one of
the horses, and he had found himself looking into heavily
fringed eyes that shimmered like molten gold. Dressed in a
flounced, butter-yellow gown and a wide-brimmed hat
with violet streamers, Monica had been exquisite, with her
deep sable curls and peachy skin. In that first moment he
was lost, even before he knew her name. He had squired

her around the fashionable resort for the next weeks, much
to the chagrin of her other suitors. He had taken her
boating, riding, and dancing, becoming more and more
besotted by her beauty, her soft Georgia drawl, and the
few chaste kisses she allowed him. It was only when he
finally bared his feelings for her that he learned she was
betrothed to a merchant in Vicksburg, Mississippi. He had
been nearly distraught with disappointment and jealousy
until Monica suggested a scheme to force her parents to
void the marriage contract with the older man and allow
her to marry Hayes. At the time her rather pointed questions about his family's finances and his personal prospects
had not bothered him since they seemed a factor in determining the validity of his suit. Innocently, he had outlined
the extensive Banister holdings in Ohio and shared his
hopes for the future. Convinced of his worth, Monica had
invited him to her rooms. Her plan was simple and direct:
they were to be discovered as lovers and forced to marry.
At first Hayes had resisted the dishonesty of the plan, but
when he asked Monica's father for her hand and was
refused as a "money-grubbing Yankee," he'd had no
choice but to fall in with what she'd proposed.

Even all these years later, he could remember the intoxi-
cating mixture of excitement and desire he'd felt as he
climbed the trellis to the bedroom Monica occupied in one
of Saratoga's plush guesthouses. She had been waiting for
him, dressed in a beribboned nightgown and wrapper with
her night-dark hair loose on her shoulders. Though he'd
had no experience at seducing virgins, her initial ardor
startled him, and the tongue that explored his mouth freely
was a surprise and a delight after the few chaste kisses
she'd allowed him. The feel of her small, delicate body in
his arms and the rich, musky scent of her perfume had
fired his need and shattered his self-control. He had torn at
her bows and buttons, then at his own clothes until they
moved with naked abandon to the tall four-poster bed.
There they had played with wandering mouths and hands
until Hayes was mad with wanting. Finally he had spread
her thighs and thrust deep, driven by the goad of his
ravenous desires, and in that moment he had known he was
not the first to take her sensuously straining body for his

own. But then satisfaction had run through their blood like
flame, blotting out thought, to leave them wet and panting
in the muffling stillness of the night. They had come
together twice more before dawn, and Hayes had drifted to
sleep replete with equal parts satisfaction and exhaustion.

The rest of the plan had gone as Monica had proposed.
Hayes had awakened to find Mr. Morgan standing over
them, crimson with anger and indignation. Even then the
scene that followed had held an element of comedy, with
Monica's father shouting at the top of his voice, her
mother wailing piteously, and Hayes himself, having
abruptly discovered the disadvantage of being naked in
such circumstances, fumbling to dress under the cover of
the tumbled bedclothes. Only Monica had remained calm,
her dainty features artfully arranged in an incongruous
expression of violated innocence and smug satisfaction.
Finally, with a vow to return after breakfast to press his
suit, Hayes had retreated down the rose trellis, flushed,
half-dressed and humiliated in temporary defeat. But when
he arrived at midmorning to claim Monica's hand, the
Morgans were gone.

He had taken the first train to Georgia, learning only
when he arrived at the Morgan plantation that the family
had traveled directly to Vicksburg. The wedding between
Monica and the elderly merchant was a fact by the time
Hayes reached the city on the bluffs, but he had not given
up. He arranged a meeting with Monica at a dressmaker's
shop.

"Oh, Hayes, how glad I am you've come," she had
whispered when they were alone. "Father forced me to
marry Jacob Bennett, but it's you I'll always love."

"Then come away with me, Monica," he demanded as
he drew her close. "Let me make a life for us together."

"But how can I leave my husband?" She dabbed dain-
tily at her eyes as she watched him. "My reputation would
be in ruins, and since I'm not free to marry you, I could
never be more than your mistress. And don't ask me to be
that, Hayes, please. I couldn't bear the shame."

She had wept, and his inexperienced heart had melted.
"Then what's to become of us? I love you, Monica, and I
can't do without you!"

"You could stay here in Vicksburg," she suggested sweetly, gazing up at him through her tears. "At least, I could see you once in a while."

"What kind of a life would that be, having to be satisfied with the few hours we could steal? And what would I do here? I've wanted to design and build steamboats for as long as I can remember."

"Do?" she had inquired in total confusion. "Why, you're rich, aren't you? Why must you do anything?"

He should have understood then what kind of woman Monica was, but he had been too bewitched by her beauty, too consumed by lust, too young and green to understand her motives.

"Damn fool!" Hayes whispered in the darkened St. Louis hotel room as he filled his glass again.

Instead of returning to Cincinnati and the life he'd planned, he had stayed in Vicksburg and apprenticed himself to a crusty old river pilot. Within months he had his master's papers and a position of his own on the *Priscilla Anne* out of Natchez. He bought a tract of land north of Vicksburg and built a snug, secluded cabin where he and Monica could meet without fear of discovery. The life on the river had quickly engulfed him in honest work, rough and ready companions, and the promise of adventure. And when he made port, there was Monica, at least as hungry for his body as he was for hers. In the three years the affair lasted, Hayes had dreamed of a time when Monica would agree to run away with him. But as often as he tried to convince her, Monica never weakened. Then came the day he had never been able to accept as inevitable.

Monica had risen from the bed slowly after a particularly fierce bout of lovemaking and stood watching him as she put on her riding clothes. He could remember just how he had felt as she dressed: pleasantly spent, totally sated, and vaguely resentful of her need to hurry home.

"Hayes," she had said softly, adjusting her jabot, "this is the last time I'm coming here. I don't want to see you anymore."

It had taken an eternity for the meaning of her words to reach him, and when they did, the strength had seeped out of his limbs, leaving them cold and shaking. Then he had forced himself to stand erect beside her; no man could accept this kind of rejection lying down.

"Why?" he had asked simply.

She'd looked away from his nakedness, though she knew his big body well. "I think my husband suspects I've been meeting someone, and . . ."

His hands had moved gently along her delicate jaw, turning her face to his. "And?"

"And I'm pregnant."

Hayes had been even less prepared for that revelation than he had been for the one that preceded it. He had stood without moving, looking down into her eyes, trying to understand her reasons for destroying all they had shared, especially now.

"You're a superb lover, Hayes," Monica went on, "and I hate to give up our afternoons together, but there must be no doubt in Jacob's mind about the paternity of our son. He must accept him as his heir. My husband is a very rich man, and one day all his possessions will come to this child and to me. If Jacob found proof of my association with you, all that could be in jeopardy."

Only a fraction of what she said had penetrated Hayes's chaotic thoughts, and he knew only that he must have the answer to one question before she went away.

"Is the child mine?" he whispered.

Monica had paused almost imperceptibly, but that moment had seemed infinite to the man awaiting her answer. Slowly she shook her head. "No, the baby is Jacob's."

Hayes had not been sure if her words were false or if he simply did not want to believe them.

"Your husband is an old man—" he began in a rush, full of explanations.

"He may be an old man, gray-haired and infirm, but he is far from incapable of fathering a child."

His hands slid to her shoulders, and he shook her fiercely. "Is the child mine?" he had demanded again, not knowing what answer he sought.

Monica wrenched away. "No!" she had cried. "You are not the baby's father."

Hayes sagged to the edge of the bed, his mind in turmoil. She was lying; he was certain of it. The child must be his. With sick certainty knotting his insides he had watched Monica complete her toilette. Even in his confusion he could understand why she had chosen an empty role of respectable wife and mother rather than the shame of bearing his bastard child. Monica was afraid to give up a secure life with her elderly husband for an uncertain future by his side.

"Monica, please, leave your husband and come away with me," he offered, voicing the words for what might have been the hundredth time. "I'll make a life for us together; I swear I will. In time we can arrange for a divorce, and I'll marry you gladly. Please, Monica, don't deprive me of the chance to know my own child!"

She had turned on him with teeth bared and eyes narrowed. "The baby is not yours, Hayes!" she spat. "And even if it were, I wouldn't run away with you. Jacob is far richer than you'll ever be; I'm sure of that now. Once I thought I could marry you and have not only a rich husband but a handsome one as well, but I'd never be satisfied with a man who works as a common river pilot to earn his keep. No, the baby I'm carrying is Jacob's heir and the key to my plans for the future."

Suddenly Hayes had towered over her, naked and elemental in his righteous anger. He was painfully torn between the words of entreaty that bubbled unbidden to his lips and the churning disgust he felt for the lying jade the woman he loved had proved herself to be. For the first time he understood the motives in a crime of passion—the hurt and betrayal that could drive a man to murder—and he fought his own violent emotions. Abruptly he turned away, hating himself for the trust he'd given so indiscriminately and her for her self-serving deceit.

"May you rot in hell, Monica, if you bargain my child for that old man's riches!" he said with suppressed fury.

She had stood watching him for a long moment before she dared voice a warning of her own. "And if you ever approach me, Hayes, ever cast a pall of doubt on this child's paternity, I will see that you precede me there." Her threat had echoed in the silent cabin long after she was gone, leaving Hayes in the gathering dusk with his doubts and disillusionment.

Banister fumbled for the half-empty bottle of bourbon beside his chair and drank a silent toast to Monica's son. The boy must be nearly six now, no, almost seven. How quickly the years passed! Hayes had never returned to the cabin north of Vicksburg after that day or approached Monica directly, but he made discreet inquiries whenever his boat made port. He knew when his son was born and that he was christened with another man's name. Though he had never seen the child, when he left the river to take his rightful place at the shipyards in Cincinnati, he felt he had left a vital part of himself in the river city on the bluffs.

Setting the empty glass beside the bottle on the floor, Hayes came unsteadily to his feet. He knew from experience that liquor only served to blunt the senses but did little to dull the pain, fresh and sharp even after eight years. Still, he was irritated by his own self-indulgence. From the street below his windows the clamor of voices continued, but Hayes was no longer sure where their noise left off and the roaring in his head began.

With frowning deliberation he made his way to the bedroom and prepared for sleep, determined not to waste more time with useless regrets. Yet even after he was settled comfortably between the cool sheets, thoughts of Monica and Leigh Pennington buzzed in his head. Of course, it was not fair to compare the two of them; they were as different as midnight and noon. There was not even a superficial similarity between them. One was deceitful adventuress, the other a naïve innocent. Yet his reaction had been the same when he looked at Leigh today as it had been all those years ago when he had fallen under Monica's spell. He had been aware of those same old feelings surfacing: tenderness, warmth, desire. In a slurred voice he cursed his own vulnerability, just as he had cursed it this afternoon as he held Leigh Pennington beneath the spreading branches of an oak. Somehow Hayes had thought himself immune to women, as if having survived one disastrous love affair left him invulnerable, but today he had been struck down again. He was totally captivated by Leigh Pennington, and it scared him to death.

The fact that she was engaged to marry another man did not help his state of mind. He had fought for a betrothed woman once before and lost. Yet Hayes sensed Leigh felt that same unwelcome pull, and it hurt that she had been able to spurn him in spite of it. It wasn't difficult to discern her reasons for sending him away, either. These feelings must be confusing and intimidating to her as well, especially when she was promised to another. Still, her rejection stung.

Banister burrowed deeper into his feather pillows and pulled the sheet up to his chin. Until now all women except Monica had existed on the periphery of his life. They were decorative and pleasantly enticing, but not nearly as compelling as his work at the shipyards or his life on the river. And no matter what he felt or sensed in Leigh Pennington, he was not willing to let her assume a larger role in his life. He had his report to write for Nathan Travis and the meeting with James Eads to occupy his mind, and once those things were accomplished, he would be on his way back home. It would be no hardship to avoid the beauteous Leigh until his business in St. Louis was concluded. Then he would head for Cincinnati, back to the busy, uncomplicated life he led there. The wisest course was to put the girl out of his mind. He was sure of it.

With a murmur of determination he closed his eyes and willed himself to sleep. Yet in spite of his resolves it was the spicy, orange-blossom scent, the honeyed taste and the tempting feel of the auburn-haired Leigh Pennington who filled his dreams that night and for many nights thereafter.

3 ❧

May 11, 1861

The muffled voices from the front hall drifted up to Leigh Pennington, alerting her that the visitors she was expecting had arrived. Not an hour before a slave had come from the Hales next door with a message that Lucas and Brandon had been released from the Federal Arsenal with the rest of the militia captured at Camp Jackson, and wished to see her. The unusual formality of sending a note before calling, coupled with the events of the past twenty-four hours, filled Leigh with misgivings. Why, she wondered, hadn't Lucas and Bran simply clattered in the back door and shouted her name as they had been doing for as long as she could remember? What had made them suddenly so formal?

Anxious to learn the reason, Leigh bent closer to the bedroom mirror and tried to pinch a faint flush of color into her cheeks. But in spite of her best efforts, the sleepless night she had spent was evident in her face. Still, it was small wonder that the events of the previous day had robbed her of her rest. Taut as a plucked string and trembling inside, she had lain beneath the covers the night before with her eyes tightly closed, courting sleep. Yet as hard as she tried to forget the scenes outside Camp Jackson, they had played and replayed on the insides of her eyelids. She could still smell the dust stirred by score upon score of marching feet, could hear the murmur of the crowd grow shrill with panic. She could feel her own escalating fear and could recall the overwhelming relief and inexplicable security of having Hayes Banister beside her.

Even more than the events of the day, she had tried to exclude this disturbing stranger from her thoughts, but Banister refused to be shut out. No matter how long she had lain staring into the dark, or how diligently she had schooled her thoughts to serenity, Hayes's face rose up before her: his crystal-blue eyes sparkling with laughter, his mouth curved in a teasing smile. It seemed impossible that in the short time she had known him any man could become so entrenched in her thoughts, but Banister had inexplicably become a part of her. Feeling guilty that Hayes was on her mind once more, Leigh frowned and pushed the memory away before turning toward the stairs and the lifelong friends awaiting her in the foyer.

Lucas and Bran were indeed in the hall when she reached the foot of the stairs, and without a word she hugged first her fiancé and then his brother.

"Come into the parlor," she invited when the maid had taken their hats. But once inside, the two men stood silent as if they did not know what to say to her. As she waited for them to speak, she studied them both. Lucas was by far the more handsome, a man cast from gold with sunshine-bright hair and bronzed skin. He was tall and lean with the unconscious grace of the plantation aristocracy evident in his movements. His features were classically molded, and beneath his fair arched brows his eyes shone clear, cool hazel. After years of familiarity, Leigh had never much considered her fiancé's looks, but since their betrothal she had begun to notice the envy in other women's eyes when he was beside her. Brandon Hale's features were broader and less refined than his brother's, and his hair had a rusty tinge that Lucas's did not. A spattering of freckles speckled his cheeks, and a lopsided grin gave evidence of a winning charm that warmed everyone he met. Between Leigh and Bran there had always been a special bond of mutual understanding and respect, forged when they were little more than toddlers. Perhaps it had grown from the need to band together when playing with the older boy, or because of a similarity in their characters, but whatever forged it, the link had grown stronger as they grew. Nor had Leigh's betrothal to Lucas affected it.

In the end it was Leigh who broke the silence, asking a question whose answer she both knew and dreaded. "You're both dressed for travel. Are you going away?"

Lucas came to take her hands. "We have no choice, Leigh, especially after what happened yesterday and what we were forced to do to gain our freedom."

She looked up into his somber face. "And what was that?"

"An oath of loyalty to the United States was administered this morning, and we were forced to swear allegiance to the Union or be shipped to prisons in the North!"

"And did you swear?" she whispered.

"Yes, we swore," Brandon admitted grimly.

"We all swore, Leigh," Lucas continued, "but though we said the words, no one meant them. An oath made under duress is hardly binding."

"But why are you going away? And where will you go?"

"We can't stay here, Leigh, not now, not after what's happened! Ever since the Secession Convention in March voted for Missouri to remain in the Union, I was afraid it would come to this. Both Bran and I believe in the Confederate cause, and if we do, we have no choice but to join our brothers in the South and fight for those beliefs."

"But where are you going now?" she repeated.

"We've heard that Sterling Price is recruiting troops near Jefferson City," Bran told her. "If he's not, we'll go south until we find another place to join the Confederate army."

Leigh knew Lucas could be caught up in the excitement of the moment and might act without thinking, but one look at Brandon's set face confirmed their resolve. His irrepressible grin was gone, and in its place was steely determination. And suddenly she realized there was nothing she could do to deter them.

"Now, don't you worry, Leigh. It won't take more than a month or two to convince those Yankees to let the Confederacy go its own way. Then we'll be back, and you and I can be married as we planned," Lucas assured her. His tanned face was flushed with the promise of excitement, and his eyes sparkled with a restless need to turn words into actions. This brash courage and ungovernable recklessness had always been one of Lucas's greatest failings; it had led them all into danger more than once when they were children, and Leigh was afraid. But those very traits that made her fear for his safety were the ones that would be praised, honored, and revered in a soldier. To Lucas the war would offer irresistible opportunities to prove his daring and test his romantic ideals of bravery and honor. And though Brandon's motives might vary from his brother's, he was as deeply committed to the Rebel cause.

Leigh knew it was useless to argue with either man once his course was set, but a score of questions rioted in her mind. Was it possible that the Confederacy could win its independence in a matter of months? President Lincoln had vowed never to let the seceding states leave the Union, and with men like her father, General Lyon, Hayes Banister, and her mother's friend Major Crawford behind him, could the Confederate victory come as easily as Lucas believed it would? And even if the South won, wouldn't Lucas and Bran be considered traitors if they ever returned to St. Louis? Leigh did not voice her questions, but they loomed up, a barrier to the pleasant future she had envisioned for them all. Without self-consciousness she went into Lucas's arms, seeking the reassurance and comfort he had always given so freely. Her cheek was pressed against his chest, and her hands were clamped tight behind his waist as she hugged him fiercely and tried not to cry. How precious Lucas and Bran were to her, she reflected as her tears spilled over, and how she loved them both.

After a minute or two of silence, Lucas released her and turned her wet face up to his. "Do you understand why we must go, Leigh?" he asked gently.

Mutely she nodded and dabbed at her wet cheeks with a lace handkerchief. "Yes, I understand. I guess I've known too that eventually you and Bran would have to leave. I just didn't think it would be so soon."

Lucas gave her a wry smile. "We didn't think we'd have to sneak away like thieves in the night, either. I imagined we'd march out with flags and banners waving, soldiers proud to offer their lives to the cause. But after all that's happened . . ." He shrugged.

Brandon had been standing nearby, his expression grave. "Come give me a hug for luck, Leigh. We need to put a lot of miles behind us before nightfall."

She went into his outstretched arms reluctantly, remembering all the times he'd been her champion and confidant. He was closer to her than anyone except her grandfather. "Oh, Bran," she whispered. "be careful!"

"I will, Leigh."

"And look after Lucas. It's you and I who have always been the sensible, steady ones. Don't let him take foolish chances."

She felt him nod against her hair. "Don't worry, Leigh, I will. And you'll see that Aunt Felicity takes care of herself, won't you? I hate leaving her alone in that big house. You know how frail she is."

Leigh thought momentarily of the gentle little woman who had come to raise the two Hale boys after their parents died. How hard this parting must be for her.

"I'll go over after you leave to see if there's anything she needs," the girl promised.

Bran gave Leigh one last, hard hug, then stepped away. "I want to say good-bye to your mother, too," he said, grinning one of his lopsided grins. "Where will I find her?"

"I think she's in the sitting room upstairs, Bran."

With a final squeeze of her hand, he went, closing the parlor doors behind him so Lucas and his fiancée could have a few minutes alone before parting.

He was hardly out of the room before Lucas was beside her. "I'm sorry it has to be this way, Leigh," he began. "I never thought I would be marching off to war so soon after I asked you to marry me."

"Goodness, Lucas, no one could have foreseen the tensions that have been building between North and South for all these years would erupt into war now. All I ask is that you be careful and come back to me whole and strong."

"I will, Leigh. I'll be careful; I promise you. Just

knowing you're waiting for me will be incentive to end this war as quickly as possible. I'm just sorry it will change our plans for the future."

"I daresay there will be a great many things changed because of this war," she observed. Leigh glanced away for a moment, letting her eyes rest on an ormolu figurine on the table beside them. "I think you should know," she continued, "that I intend to offer my services as a nurse at one of the hospitals here in St. Louis. No matter how quickly this war is concluded, there is bound to be fighting and men wounded—"

"You can't be serious!" Lucas broke in. "My God, Leigh! No decent woman nurses wounded men, much less an unmarried woman. Why, it's unthinkable!"

Her usually pliant mouth hardened in an expression of determination that matched his exactly. "Nevertheless, that's what I intend to do. My grandfather trained me well, and there is bound to be a need for skilled people to care for the sick and injured. Besides, you never objected when I assisted in Grandfather's office."

"That was entirely different, and then I had no right to protest," he pointed out. "There's no telling what kind of men or wounds you would be expected to tend. And besides, you would be offering aid to the enemy!"

"People in pain have no loyalties, Lucas," she pleaded passionately. "Nor could I think of someone in need as my enemy, no matter what his politics."

"Damn it, Leigh!" he thundered. "I don't intend for any fiancée of mine to nurse in some stinking hospital."

"I don't know that after today you'll be in any position to stop me!" she countered and was immediately sorry for her defiance. Lucas was going to war, and she did not want to spend their last few minutes together in dissent or send him off in anger. Still, she did not intend to change her mind. She paused, searching for the words to make him understand her need to act in a time of crisis that would demand the energies of men and women alike. "Oh, Lucas," she began again. "I always thought you understood what medicine and using my skills to help others meant to me. Just as going south to fight is something you must do, offering my skills to help the sick and wounded is something I must do!''

''It's one thing to nurse a sick relative or friend,'' he argued, ''but quite another to care for strangers.''

Tears gathered in her eyes again, whether in remorse or frustration she could not say. And though her argument had failed to move him, Lucas had never been able to resist her tears. After a moment he put his arms around her and pulled her close. He did not want to part in anger either, but he meant to have the last word.

''Very well, Leigh, do what you must, for, as you say, I will be in no position to stop you. But if you persist in this, you do it without my permission or sanction.''

Reluctantly she nodded.

They stood for a few seconds without speaking until Lucas turned her face to his. With the fingers of his left hand he skimmed her cheek, brushing aside the tendrils of silky hair with a tenderness that spoke more eloquently than words of his love and concern for her. Something deep inside her chest melted at his touch, and she was unbearably sorry for turning their last minutes together into a confrontation. Slowly he lowered his mouth to hers in a sweet, undemanding kiss. His lips were warm and smooth, soft with a longing he could not express. Leigh accepted the proof of his deep affection for her, and with newfound forwardness that belied her natural reserve she twined her arms around his neck and opened her mouth invitingly. She felt his momentary surprise before a spark of response shot through him, and he tightened his arms around her as his kiss became demanding and greedy. Compliantly she came against him, arching to mold her body to the hard contours of his. As she clung closer still, Leigh knew she was driving him beyond the well-defined strictures of propriety, but she did not care. With a thrill of pleasure she heard his breathing accelerate and felt the racing of his heart as he took liberties with her that no Southern gentleman should.

Even as his excitement grew, Lucas did not understand the reasons for the change in her. Whether it was because of his imminent departure or the tenor of the times, he did not pause to question. He only knew that Leigh was filling him with a delight that was nearly too sweet to be borne.

And as Leigh abandoned herself to Lucas, she waited with sharp anticipation for the delicious, newly discovered sensations to claim her, as she was sure they would. But there was no melting helplessness in response to his kisses, no dissolution of will in Lucas's embrace. It was undeniably pleasant to be held and kissed by this man, but something was missing, something that had come so easily, so naturally with Hayes Banister. With bitter disappointment Leigh realized that though she could accept and respond to Lucas's warm affection, she was untouched by his passion. Before the treacherous thought was fully formed, she closed her mind to it, straining closer and closer to her fiancé in active denial of the burgeoning insight.

After a time Lucas raised his head, and she saw the raging gold light of desire deep in his eyes. "Oh, Leigh," he murmured, "Leigh. I never knew—I never suspected that there was such—such fire in you. I love you, Leigh. I love you. I'm more sure of that at this moment than I have ever been before. If only there were time to make you my wife before I go—"

"And I love you, Lucas!" she cried out as if the fervor of her words could nullify the gnawing doubt she felt at her lack of response. And in her desperation the statement was as much a disclaimer of her traitorous feelings as a vow.

Lucas swept her into his arms one last time and kissed her with that same barely restrained intensity, but she was untouched by the tempest within him. Finally they drew apart, he with aching regret and she with something akin to relief.

"Bran must be waiting," he whispered against her hair. And a moment later when they opened the door to the foyer, Brandon and Althea were indeed waiting, talking together quietly. There was a final round of hugs and kisses, and then the Hale brothers were gamboling down the walk to where Plato, their manservant, was holding their horses. They waved their hats in farewell, but the gesture spoke less of the sadness of parting and more of an impatience to begin their new adventure. With tears on their cheeks, Leigh and Althea watched them go, afraid for the Hales' safety but a little envious of their freedom as well. When they were out of sight, the women returned to the house feeling empty and abandoned.

In the silent foyer Althea laid a comforting hand on her daughter's arm. "Don't worry, Leigh," she offered in consolation. "Lucas will be back soon. Bran said it wouldn't take more than a month or two to convince the Union to let the seceding states go their own way."

"I pray he's right," the young woman replied, "but I fear he's not."

"You mustn't say such things!" her mother admonished in a whisper.

"This war has been years in the making, Mother, and I doubt it will be settled in a few skirmishes." Leigh's eyes were dry as she spoke, but her voice was thick with unshed tears. A knot of black despair fed on her sudden pessimism, and the lingering doubt in Lucas's farewell sapped her strength. But Leigh stirred herself in spite of it, knowing that there was more comfort in action than in the bleakness of her own thoughts.

"I think I'll go next door and see how Felicity is faring. This parting can't have been easy for her either, and Bran did ask me to look in on her."

"Why don't you invite her for supper?" Althea called after her daughter.

Leigh followed the route she had traveled since childhood: down the side steps, through the rose arbor, and across the grass to the solid brick town house that adjoined the Penningtons' larger one. She found Felicity Hale in the small yellow sitting room off the long main hall, perched at the edge of her favorite slipper chair, her embroidery hanging lax in her gnarled fingers. When Leigh entered, the woman glanced up, her wan face worn with new lines of care and her soft hazel eyes already dark with loneliness. Without a word the younger woman came to kneel beside her, and they bent together under the weight of their fear for Lucas and Bran. For a very long time the two women held each other in silence, and though they found comfort in the contact, it could not dispel their dread of what the future might bring.

May 13, 1861

Saturday and Sunday, May 11 and 12, were terrifying days in St. Louis as the riots that began with the taking of Camp Jackson spread to other areas of the city, causing more death and destruction. Seven men were killed on the steps of the old Presbyterian church on Walnut Street, and rumors of violence were rampant. While most St. Louisans cowered in their homes, others fled south or west to escape the threat of the mobs that roamed the city. Monday brought renewed order, and by ten o'clock Leigh was in the Tenth Street waiting room of one of the city's most prominent physicians. A longtime colleague of her grandfather's, Dr. Phillips surely would know how she could go about volunteering her services as a nurse.

"Well, Leigh, how good it is to see you," the portly, middle-aged man greeted her. "And how are your parents these days?" For a few minutes they exchanged pleasantries before Phillips inquired about the purpose of her visit.

"I've come to ask your help and advice, Dr. Phillips," Leigh began steadily, though her fingers were laced tight around the handkerchief in her lap. "As you know, I worked for several years in my grandfather's medical practice before he died, and as his assistant I learned a great deal about caring for the sick."

Phillips pulled thoughtfully on his immaculately kept beard and nodded. "Yes, Simon told me on several occasions how well you were doing and how pleased he was by your concern for his patients. You had a rare opportunity to learn your skills from one of the best doctors this city's ever had. But just what is it I can do to help you, Leigh?" His expression of respect for her grandfather brought tears to Leigh's eyes, and she had to blink them away before she could answer.

"Well, sir, I thought that with the onset of war there is bound to be a need for people to tend the sick and wounded soldiers. Since I already have my medical training, I was hoping you could tell me how to offer my services as a nurse."

Shocked silence filled the examining room as Phillips sat speechless at what she proposed. "As a nurse?" he

echoed at last. "Surely you can't be serious, my dear! A
nurse, indeed. You're a gently reared young woman, Leigh,
not some common drab from the almshouse or the gutter,
forced to work in a hospital or starve. Only those unfortu-
nates and the good Catholic sisters, of course, nurse the
ill. Why should someone with your advantages volunteer
to do such a thing?"

"Isn't it a woman's Christian duty to care for the sick?"
she countered evenly, calm and confident now in the face
of his opposition.

"Yes, it is, but working in a hospital full of wounded
men would hardly be the same as tending an old auntie
with the croup!" Phillips paused, pulling his beard with
new vigor, trying to think of any rationale that would deter
the granddaughter of one of his dearest friends from considering this foolish course. In the pause Leigh found
herself comparing his argument to the one Lucas had
voiced; somehow she had expected Dr. Phillips to be more
enlightened and open-minded than her fiancé had been.
"Besides, Leigh," Phillips went on after a few moments,
"the Army has never made provisions for women on its
nursing staff. Nor is the Medical Department any more
prepared for this war than the rest of the service."

"Then wouldn't volunteers with medical training be
welcome, sir, regardless of their gender?" There was a
note of zeal in her voice as she went on. "At the rate
things are going, it won't be long before full-scale battles
are joined, and then the wounded are bound to need someone to look after them. Surely this is a time when we must
all work together to provide for the men who are going to
defend their countries."

Phillips frowned, unimpressed by her fervor. "I daresay
there will be plenty for you to do once the war starts in
earnest. It's been barely a month since Fort Sumter fell,
and in time women will no doubt get together to roll
bandages, scrape lint, and knit socks."

"Any idiot can scrape lint and roll bandages!" Leigh
cried passionately. "And my knitting is barely adequate."

"It would improve," Phillips prophesied, his round,
florid face getting redder as he met her continued opposition.

"That's not the point!" Leigh argued. "The skills I have

can save lives. I know how to treat a high fever and change a dressing. I can even set a broken bone, if need be.''

Phillips threw up his hands in a gesture of resignation, then changed his tack. "How old are you, Leigh?" he asked.

"Twenty-two."

"And are you married?"

"Dr. Phillips, you know very well—" Leigh began to protest.

"Are you married?" he repeated.

"No, not yet," she conceded.

"And do men find you attractive?"

The question flustered Leigh, and she shrugged self-consciously. "I suppose they do, but what—"

Phillips looked smug, as if he'd made his point. "No matter how good your credentials, Leigh, those three things will keep you from the position you seem so intent on having. There's not a doctor alive who would let a young, beautiful, unmarried girl near a ward full of sick men.

"Even I wouldn't take you on, but it's for your own sake that I'd refuse. In any hospital, much less a military hospital, there would be—"he groped for the right words—"indelicacies unfit for a maiden's eyes. Leigh, listen to me as you would to your own grandfather. Even if it were possible to find the kind of nursing position you want, the horror of it would be more than you could bear."

Leigh drew herself up straighter in her chair. "I thank you for your concern, Doctor," she snapped, "but I have never been squeamish."

Phillips watched her resolute face and saw his words were making no impression. The stubborn chit would not be deterred. But then neither would she find the kind of position she was seeking, and he was silently thankful for her sake.

"What do your parents say about your nursing?" he finally asked.

"I haven't told them," she admitted less defiantly.

"And Lucas Hale?"

"Lucas has gone south; it doesn't matter what he says."

Dr. Phillips blew a deep breath and continued to pull at

his beard. He had known Leigh Pennington all her life, and her bullheadedness was not new to him. He was just thankful that his son John had gotten over his infatuation with this redheaded pepperpot before he'd gone so far as to ask her to marry him. Phillips sat back in his chair and eyed his young visitor with mingled irritation and respect. No matter how inappropriate or harebrained her intentions, the girl did have spunk. If she'd only been a man, she'd make a damned fine doctor. "Well, Leigh, take my advice, since that's what you claim to have come for. Forget about nursing wounded soldiers. There are a hundred other ways to make yourself useful in this crisis. The surgeons who'll be tending the wounded won't want or need girls like you fluttering over their patients. I'm sorry, but that's the truth, plain and simple. Accept it if you can, or go talk to someone else, but in the end you'll find there's no place for you in a military hospital. Now if you'll excuse me, I have patients to see."

Before the day was out, Leigh had heard the same thing from several other doctors and two of the St. Louis hospitals. No one wanted her help. And what was worse, their reactions of dismay and shock had made Leigh begin to doubt her own resolve. Could nursing injured men be such a horrendous and difficult task that it would somehow destroy her? Was she so sheltered and fragile that she must be protected from life's hard realities? Everyone seemed to think so, everyone but Hayes Banister.

With a soft smile on her lips she contemplated the Yankee engineer, his quiet words clear and sharp in her memory: "If anyone has a calling for medicine, you do." Banister, stranger though he was, seemed to have more faith in her strength and abilities than anyone else. "What you have, Leigh, is an honest compassion for people in need." Somehow in their short acquaintance, Banister had come to understand her far better than others who had known her all her life. Perhaps that explained why she had felt compelled to tell him about her desire to study medicine, when she had never confided her hopes in either her grandfather or Bran, and why she wanted so desperately to see Banister now. As she made her way back to the carriage, an almost overwhelming urge to talk to Hayes swept over her. Then, with a pang of conscience, she remembered how they had parted on Friday evening. Surprisingly it was grief, not anger, she felt when she remembered why she had sent him away. She had told him she never wanted to see him again, but she had to admit she'd been wrong. She wanted desperately to be with him now, to be held and comforted, to be encouraged by his faith in her abilities. For a moment she considered going to the Planters' House to find him, to seek him out in spite of her best resolves and her engagement to Lucas Hale. Hayes would not scoff at her need to do something to ease the suffering the war would bring; he would understand her disappointment at being refused a chance to use her skills. But as soon as the idea formed, she rejected it. No woman who considered herself a lady could seek a man out at his hotel. And even if she were foolish enough to go there, it was entirely possible that Hayes Banister would refuse to see her. Instead, feeling lost and disappointed, Leigh made her way back to where she had left Jeb and the carriage.

They had traversed a good part of the city when she heard someone call her name. At her signal, Jeb pulled the buggy to a halt at the curb as a tall, uniformed horseman appeared from the dimness of the tree-shaded cross street. Smiling broadly, he rode toward her and doffed his hat in greeting.

"Good day to you, Miss Pennington."

"And to you, Major Crawford," she returned pleasantly though with an effort, eyeing the man who, in spite of his politics, was one of her mother's favorite callers. Nor was it difficult to discern the reason for his popularity with women of her mother's milieu. Major Aaron Crawford was a man in the prime of his life, as evidenced by his impressive physique; his rugged, sun-bronzed countenance; and his raven-dark hair and sweeping hussar's moustache dramatically tinged with silver. He was neither too old to escape a maiden's notice nor too young and inexperienced to bore those same maidens' mothers. Though Leigh knew the gossip was unfit for her ears, she had heard his name linked with several of the city's wealthy matrons in the scant year since he had come to St. Louis. And no wonder, Leigh found herself thinking as she watched the horseman beside her. Wherever he went, Aaron Crawford cut a fine figure: impeccably dressed, unfailingly polite, handsome in the classical sense, but with a military man's toughness and swagger. Yet, in spite of his many attributes, Leigh did not like him, though she was at a loss to explain her strange aversion.

As she sat back against the open carriage's plush upholstery, she was uncomfortably aware of his intense, slate-gray eyes moving over her, taking in everything from the flush in her cheeks to the fit of her new apple-green gown.

"You're looking lovely this afternoon, Miss Pennington," he observed coolly, "though I question the wisdom of being out alone after what's happened. How have you and your family fared in these last few days? We did have some reports of looting and vandalism out your way, though I've had no time to ride over and check on them myself."

"I thank you for your concern, Major Crawford, but we've been quite safe. There are certain advantages to living in 'a house divided,' " she observed ruefully. "Neither side considers us their enemies. However, Father and some of our men did chase rioters from the Hale property next door."

She saw his eyes gleam with quick intelligence and could have bitten her tongue for her unintentional disclosure about the state of things at the Hale home. For whatever else he might seem to be, Crawford was still the provost marshal and, as such, wielded substantial power now that martial law was in effect.

"Oh, have the Hale boys gone south, then?" he probed, though it was disguised as a polite observation.

"I—I'm not sure just where they are," Leigh lied, unwilling to volunteer any more than she had already unwittingly revealed.

"They were among the prisoners from Camp Jackson, though," he reasoned aloud, obviously hoping to glean more information from her, "so they both must have disregarded their sworn oath of allegiance to the Union and set out to join the Confederates."

"I don't have any idea where they've gone," she repeated with greater conviction. "Perhaps they refuged along with so many of the other Southern sympathizers."

Crawford frowned. "It's possible, but unlikely. You realize, don't you, Miss Pennington, that if Lucas and Brandon Hale bear arms against the Union, they will be considered traitors?"

Leigh could feel the color drain from her face. "I—I think your conclusion might be a trifle premature, Major Crawford."

"We shall see," he muttered darkly. "But if I have my way, any followers of Jeff Davis and his Rebel band will forfeit their property for this act of treason."

"Surely Mr. Lincoln would never sanction that!" Leigh gasped in dismay.

"No, probably not, and more's the pity! Tell me, Miss Pennington, do you think your mother will refugee south when the war comes?"

His penetrating questions about Lucas and Bran had quite unnerved Leigh, but this one that hinted at her mother's defection threatened her last bastion of security. Her fiancé and her best friend were gone, and she could not countenance the suggestion of any further disruption of her safe little world. How could this callous, prying, reprehensible man even suggest that her mother might leave St. Louis, too?

"Of course not! No! Mother's place is here in St. Louis with Father and me!" she told him fervently.

"But if she did go, would you go with her? Would you go south to marry Lucas Hale?"

His questions were relentless and painful, and even as she fumbled to answer them, Leigh tried to fathom his reasons for asking such hurtful things.

"Do you think they would let me nurse in their hospitals if I went south?" she asked, hoping to divert him.

His dark eyebrows flickered upward. "So you want to work as a nurse, do you?"

He wasn't Bran, or even Hayes Banister, but he was, for whatever reason, a willing listener, and before she could stop herself, the tale of the day's disappointments came tumbling out. Crawford sat in silence as she spoke, with surprising sympathy in his eyes.

"Be patient, Miss Pennington," he advised her. "I believe in time the Union will welcome women like you with something to offer."

Leigh took strange comfort in his words and smiled up at him, forgetting for the moment her dislike for the man. "Why, thank you, Major. Yours are the most encouraging words I've heard all day. I only want to do my part to ease the suffering this war is bound to cause."

He met her idealistic declaration with a derisive frown that immediately brought back her feelings of mistrust. "Your sentiments are so touchingly altruistic, Miss Pennington," he observed in a tone laced with a sudden cynicism that mocked her naïveté.

Abruptly the comfort she had found in his encouragement deserted her, and she was acutely uncomfortable in his presence. Why had she confided her girlish hopes to this enigmatic man? And why had she allowed him to turn her dream of helping others against her?

A bright flush stained her cheeks, and Leigh could think of nothing but escape from Aaron Crawford's jeering smile. "If you'll excuse me, Major Crawford," she mumbled in a rush, "it's getting quite late, and I really should be on my way."

He bent closer in the saddle, clearly amused by her discomfort. "Perhaps I should ride along to see that you get home safely," he suggested in taunting solicitation.

Though their longtime coachman Jeb sat in the seat before her, Leigh was undone by an indefinable menace she sensed in Aaron Crawford's manner. Still, she stood her ground, though flushed and flustered. "I'm sure I'll be fine, Major Crawford, honestly I will."

His looming face receded, but a wolfish grin remained on his mouth, an expression that said he knew all her secrets and would not hesitate to use them as he saw fit. "Then be on your way, my quixotic Miss Pennington. And give my regards to your parents, especially your lovely mother."

Strangely shaken, Leigh watched as Aaron Crawford disappeared into the tree-shrouded dimness once more. As Jeb continued toward home, Leigh was aware of a nameless dread that moved through her in primitive reaction to her encounter with the major. And all at once she wanted nothing more than to hurry home and shore up her safe, stable world, suddenly afraid of its crumbling in ruins around her.

May 16, 1861

"My dear Mr. Banister, how good it is to meet you at last!" James Eads exclaimed as he rose from the cluttered desk in the center of his study and extended his hand.

Hayes met it with his own, wringing the older man's enthusiastically and thinking that the warmth of the greeting almost made up for the days he'd lost waiting for Eads to return from Washington. "It's a privilege to meet you too, sir," he replied, "after seeing the result of your work in clearing the river channel. It is an enormous undertaking."

Eads nodded in acknowledgment. "And an unending one as well, I'm afraid."

As they stood together, with hands clasped over the jumble of notes and drawings splayed across the desk, Hayes quickly took the measure of the other man and sensed that Eads was doing the same. What Banister saw on the far side was a man of less than medium height and slight and slender build, with a pleasant, high-cheekboned face and a sparse, pointed beard. From the receding hair threaded with gray, Hayes judged Eads to be well over forty, but there was something in the alert gray eyes that hinted at a youthful spirit and boundless energy.

In the years when he had been piloting the *Priscilla Anne,* Hayes had become familiar enough with James Eads's name. The man had been a salvager then, bringing up cargo from scuttled steamboats through the use of a unique diving bell he had invented. But Eads's innovations went far beyond the perimeters of his own business to the development of a special double-hulled riverboat that could be used to raise the treacherous snags and sawyers from the river and to dredge out deeper channels as well. It was only when Hayes had begun to make discreet inquiries as he waited for Eads's return that he began to understand

how far the man had come on nothing more than his own
initiative. A ragged adolescent who sold apples on street
corners had become a man who consulted with presidents.
Eads had completed his rise from poverty and obscurity to
affluence and respectability through his own industry, without the benefit of a formal education. And Hayes found
himself in awe, not only of the plans he had drawn up for
the river flotilla but for his gumption and genius as well.

"They tell me you've had a look at my drawings for the
ironclads, Mr. Banister," James Eads said after a moment.
"May I ask what you thought of them?"

Hayes took the chair Eads offered him. "I must admit I
was very impressed."

"But?" The older man sat perched on the edge of his
chair at the far side of the desk.

"Well, sir," Hayes began tentatively, "as you may
know, my specialty at the shipyards is designing the engines to power the boats we build."

"Yes, and some of the innovations you've introduced
have been very interesting. No one builds better steam
boilers than the Banister Shipyards."

It was Hayes's turn to acknowledge the praise with a
nod of his head. "But for the ironclads you're planning,
I'd recommend the use of high-pressure inclined-cylinder
engines to give the works more protection from incoming
fire and the boats themselves greater maneuverability."

"And just how could that be done?" Eads queried, his
gray eyes narrowed in concentration.

What ensued was a deeply technical conversation between two men who shared a love of the river and a
complete understanding of the intricacies of steam locomo-
tion. Within minutes they were poring over the drawings
of the ironclads, making changes to improve the designs.
With the glee of two small boys they plotted not only the
construction but also the deployment of the river flotilla,
stumbling over each other's sentences and elaborating on
each other's ideas as they plumbed the possibilities of
these revolutionary craft. Each man found in the other a
flawless echo of his own thoughts, a perfect amplification
of his own concepts. They were two strangers bound
together by a common dream, and before the afternoon

was over, their enthusiasm had been forged into a working partnership prepared for the task ahead.

Later, as they sat drinking a companionable whiskey in Eads's parlor, basking in the fading sunlight and in the glow of their newly formed friendship, Eads turned to the younger man. "I can count on you to join me here in St. Louis when I receive the contracts for construction of the ironclads, can't I, Hayes?"

"Aren't there bound to be other shipyards that will compete for the bids?"

"Yes, but I intend to be the one to build those ships," James Eads stated with determination. "And I want your help."

"Then you shall have it, James. You need only telegraph me when you're ready, and I'll be on the next steamboat. How soon do you think that will be?"

"Construction should be under way by the end of the summer if the boats are to be ready for the new year," Eads speculated.

Banister sat back in his chair and stretched his long legs before him, feeling swept along by currents too strong to resist. "Lord, it's exciting to be a part of something like this," he murmured.

James Eads gave a short laugh, his gray eyes bright. "This is a chance to leave our mark on history, Hayes. And by the grace of God we will."

For a moment Hayes studied the amber lights in the bottom of his cut-crystal tumbler as Leigh Pennington's face seemed to form itself in the shimmering rays. With a strange sense of inevitability, he blinked the image away. "Yes," he agreed, drawing a long breath, "yes, we'll build the best damned warships the world has ever seen, and we'll do it here in St. Louis together." Then, as if the pronouncement had been a toast, Hayes drained his glass.

4

The unrelenting mid-July sun beat down on the wide, murky Mississippi River as the steamboat came abreast of the Cairo, Illinois landing. On the deck Leigh Pennington was oblivious to the glare as she shaded her eyes with a gloved hand and pressed closer to the rail, anxious for her first glimpse of the city. But except for a church spire and a treetop or two, the town itself and Fort Defiance, the large military encampment that had grown up nearby in the last months, were invisible from the river, hidden behind the steep-sided levee. Built on a triangular piece of land between the Ohio River on the southeast and the Mississippi on the west, Cairo occupied a position of such commercial importance that the obvious advantages of settlement far outweighed the constant danger of flooding. But it was only these high earthen dikes that had made the development feasible.

Leigh lowered her hand from her brow and gripped the ornate wooden balustrade on the promenade deck with impatience. Early yesterday morning she had boarded the steamboat *Carlyle* at the St. Louis landing, carrying a single carpetbag packed with her necessities: two serviceable calico dresses, her night clothes, her underwear, a second pair of shoes, and her toilet articles. In the reticule tucked safely under her arm was a return ticket to St. Louis and a letter of introduction to Colonel Oglesby, the commander at Fort Defiance, from Major Aaron Crawford.

Surprisingly, it was her adversary she had to thank for this opportunity to try her hand at military nursing.

In the several months since their conversation on the street, Leigh had continued her search for a nursing position, but to no avail. Nor had the requirements set up by Miss Dorothea Dix for the Army Nursing Corps helped Leigh's cause. She was neither over thirty nor plain, and though she was of the Protestant faith and unlikely to be seeking converts, that single advantage was quickly outweighed by her youth and beauty. Besides, Miss Dix preferred to train her own nurses to adopt a proper attitude of humility and subservience when dealing with the government doctors.

As Dr. Phillips had predicted, women's groups did begin to organize to provide for the soldiers' needs. Spurred on by the increasingly alarming reports of shortages from the military camps, the women began to knit and sew. In a patriotic fervor they produced useful items such as socks, underclothes, and sewing kits, as well as strange hats known as havelocks that were used by their recipients in inventive ways, quite unintended by their designers. Due to Army inefficiency, camps were ill supplied, and when the news of the shortages reached the towns and cities in the North, civilians began to collect money and send donations to see that their hometown boys did not go without.

Sickness, it was reported, ran rampant through the camps: typhoid and yellow fever as a result of inadequate sanitation and malaria from the camps' swampy locations. There were outbreaks of measles and diphtheria too, as country boys came in contact with these childhood diseases for the first time. Those lucky volunteers who managed to avoid the fevers and communicable diseases fell prey to the fluxes that resulted from spoiled or improperly prepared food. And in addition there were gunshot wounds, inflicted not by the enemy but by comrades ignorant of the correct use of firearms.

When the reports began to arrive, Leigh had been wild to help, but it quickly became apparent that even now no one wanted her. Then one evening she had encountered Aaron Crawford at a garden party at Henry Shaw's country home. As they waltzed, they had exchanged banalities, and then Major Crawford had begun to relate a bit of military gossip that had come to his ears.

"There's a woman at Fort Defiance who has set up her own nursing corps, it seems," he had begun lightheartedly. "She came to Cairo from Galesburg, Illinois, in mid-June with a load of supplies from her church. They tell me she took one look at the camp and refused to leave, said she'd never seen such bad housekeeping in her life, and intended to stay until things were cleaned up," Crawford related with a laugh.

Leigh had raised her sleek, auburn head at his words, suddenly taking a new interest in the major's conversation. "Do you know who she is?"

"Mary Ann Bickerdyke is her name, though the enlisted men call her 'Mother.' "

"And why is that?" Leigh prodded, her mind working swiftly though her face remained impassive.

"It's because she cares for them when they're sick, I suppose," Crawford speculated. "From all reports she's a real tartar. If she needs anything for 'her boys,' she simply takes it from Army stores. They say she wheedles men out of their packages from home and uses the gifts for her patients. And should she decide that something needs doing, she simply commandeers a platoon of men and puts them to work."

"She sounds like an extremely resourceful woman," Leigh observed.

"She sounds like a damned nuisance," Crawford returned.

Leigh hid her growing excitement behind a demure smile. "How many women does she have working with her?"

Crawford shrugged his wide shoulders, then executed a smooth turn in perfect time to the music: "I'm not really sure: a society lady from Cairo, a few camp followers. It appears she's not as selective in her recruitment as Miss Dix."

"Thank goodness for that!" his partner mumbled under her breath. Could it be that this Mother Bickerdyke was just unconventional enough to accept the help Leigh had to offer without undue concern for her "maidenly sensibilities"? The possibility seemed worth further investigation, especially after the long, frustrating months of being denied a chance to prove herself. Leigh pursed her lips thoughtfully. Was she willing to sell her soul to the devil to get her chance at military nursing? she wondered. Then, without another moment's consideration, she conceded that she was and turned wide, luminous eyes on the major.

"Aaron," she began coyly, using the unaccustomed familiarity of his first name. "If I wanted to go to Cairo to work with this Mrs. Bickerdyke, would you write me a letter of introduction to the commander of Fort Defiance?"

Leigh wondered if Major Crawford, a man with more than a little experience with women, was aware of what she hoped to accomplish. Were the motives for her sudden interest as transparent to him as they seemed to her? Would he be taken in? Leigh had never before used her wiles to get what she wanted from a man, disdaining flirtation as a weak woman's weapon, yet she had to admit that sweet smiles and tender glances did have their uses. Heaven knows, they had always worked well enough for her mother. To be honest, she did not like Aaron Crawford any better now than she ever had, but she wanted his cooperation very badly and would do what she must to insure it.

"Now, just a minute, my dear Leigh," he murmured, claiming the familiarity of her given name in return for her free use of his. "I didn't tell you about this Mrs. Bickerdyke to encourage your schemes. Volunteering to nurse under the conditions you'd find at Fort Defiance would be sheer madness!"

"Oh, Aaron, please!" she cajoled, pouting prettily and pressing her advantage.

Aaron Crawford swallowed hard, and Leigh sensed his resolves were weakening.

"In good conscience, Leigh, how can you ask me such a thing?" he demanded, frowning down at her.

"In good conscience, Aaron, how can you refuse me?" she countered. The argument was at a stalemate, and only the light glowing in Crawford's gray eyes gave a hint to its eventual outcome.

She heard him sigh in resignation before he gave her his answer. "If your father agrees to let you go to nurse with this woman at Fort Defiance, I will certainly write you a letter of introduction,'' he conceded, obviously secure in the belief that no father would ever allow his daughter to undertake such a foolhardy expedition. But in the end, Crawford had been wrong to underestimate the persuasive powers of Pennington's wife and Leigh herself.

It was at supper the following evening that Leigh had announced her intention to secure a position nursing with Mrs. Bickerdyke, and Horace Pennington's reaction had been thunderous.

"No! I won't allow it!'' he had shouted, slamming one fist down on the table with a force that set the silverware jangling. "No daughter of mine is going to traipse all the way to Cairo, Illinois, to play nursemaid to a passel of vermin-infested Army volunteers.''

Leigh had faced her father squarely, undeterred by his set face and booming voice. For the most part Leigh tried to avoid arguments, but she was quite able to defend herself when the need arose, and she was not cowed by his bluster. "Well, Father,'' she had declared with equal determination, "the only way you are going to prevent me from leaving is to lock me in my room for the duration of the war!''

"Leigh,'' Horace had said, obviously struggling for control of his temper in the face of his daughter's outburst, "surely you realize what the conditions in those camps must be. The reports we've heard can't tell the half of it. Why in heaven's name do you want to rush off into that mess when there are things right here in St. Louis you can do?''

"That's precisely why I want to go. Those poor, sick men need my help.'' Her argument was simple, direct, and irrefutable.

But still Horace was not convinced, and he glared across the table at his daughter. "No, absolutely not! I will not permit you to travel all that way to God knows what kind of accommodations to care for those damned volunteers.''

"They're your Mr. Lincoln's damned volunteers, and if I were a man wanting to serve my country, you'd have to let me go!'' Leigh shot back. "Please, Father, there's a war on, and for the moment certain conventions of behavior must be set aside. With things as they are, it would be quite proper for me to travel to Cairo and put myself under Mrs. Bickerdyke's protection.''

"And who the devil is this Mrs. Bickerdyke person? What kind of a woman is she?''

Briefly Leigh related what Aaron Crawford had told her about the tempest in hoopskirts that had been unleashed on Fort Defiance. And Horace's frown had deepened as he listened.

"So you came by these wild notions via Aaron Crawford, did you?'' Horace demanded. "Though I do agree with his politics, I'm no at all sure I would trust Crawford with the safety of my womenfolk.'' He paused and sighed. "It's true, Leigh, if you had been a son, I would have had no choice about letting you go, but you're my daughter, my little girl, and your safety could be in jeopardy if I let you go to Cairo. Oh damn, I've always been too soft with you,'' he murmured almost to himself, "letting you tag along after your grandfather, teaching you how to drive a gig.''

From across the table his daughter had watched him, her clear, green eyes meeting his, her expression implacable, as she tried to convince him that she really meant to go.

"Didn't Grandpa go east to study medicine instead of staying in Missouri to look after the family holdings as his father wanted him to do?'' Leigh had pressed him as the silence lengthened. "And didn't you go west to set up trade with the Indians when your own father had expressly forbidden it?''

Horace had nodded in resignation as Leigh continued. "If that's so, then surely you understand why I must do as I see fit! Oh please, Father—''

Then it was Althea's cool voice that filled the room. "I think we should let Leigh go to Cairo. You know as well as I do, Horace, that she has a gift for healing.''

Both father and daughter had turned to the woman at the opposite end of the table with their mouths agape. It was quite extraordinary for Althea to interfere in decisions of this magnitude. But then, these were extraordinary times.

Ignoring their stunned expressions, the older woman continued. "Your father always said Leigh had a way with

sick people that even he envied, and, Horace, you know as
well as I do that Simon was seldom wrong. He trained
Leigh and taught her everything he could about caring for
the ill. If she has the skills to ease some of the suffering
caused by this detestable war, wouldn't it be wrong to
deprive those poor men of her care? I only wish I could be
of as much use."

Leigh had never expected her mother's support in what
she planned to do, but with Althea's inexplicable defection, Horace's objections had begun to dwindle. It was
clear that he was angry about the older woman's interference, but he had never been able to deny the two of them
when they banded together against him. Eventually, reluctantly, he had given his consent. Looking back, Leigh
could not imagine what had made her mother side with her
against her father in this, nor would the older woman
discuss her reasons. But whatever it was that had brought
Althea to her point of view, Leigh was grateful.

The steamboat whistle brayed twice as the bow nestled
closer to the Cairo dock, and the young woman turned
back to her stateroom to gather her belongings. She did not
know what to expect of the city lying in wait for her
behind the steep, earthen embankment or of the military
encampment beyond it, but as Leigh hefted her carpetbag
and moved toward the gangplank, she felt more than ready
to meet whatever challenges she found in Cairo.

       Leigh hired the services of a driver and car-
riage at the landing, and they pulled up at the main gate to
Fort Defiance a short time later. She paid the driver from
the small cache of coins in her reticule and, after hearing
the price for the scant mile ride, was glad for bills tucked
safely inside her corset. With that money and the double
eagle her father had pressed on her as he bid her good-bye
at the St. Louis levee, she would have no immediate need
of funds, but at these inflated prices she would surely need
more if she meant to stay for long.

As she walked toward the sentry at the gate, she could
see the military camp sprawled out beyond him. It was a
confused jumble of canvas tents and rough-hewn buildings

that seemed to have defied any attempts at organization, populated by hundreds of men in ramshackle uniforms. And with the sight came a smell of swampy ground, horses, and excrement fermenting in the hot sun that threatened the stability of her breakfast. Stifling the urge to put a handkerchief to her nose to muffle the stench, Leigh approached the young corporal at the entrance.

"I wish to see Colonel Oglesby," she told him as she sank ankle-deep in the quagmire that passed for a road.

"I'm sorry, miss," he told her as his gaze swept appreciatively from the crown of her feathered bonnet to the newly muddied hem of her fashionable silk gown, "but no one can enter the camp without a pass."

With a flourish she removed Aaron Crawford's letter from her reticule and extended it to the sentry. "I've come to nurse with Mrs. Bickerdyke," she told him coolly. "This letter from Major Crawford in St. Louis explains that to your commanding officer."

The man made no move to examine the carefully folded document, but a smile tweaked the corners of his mouth. "Has Mother Bickerdyke seen you yet?" he asked.

"No, she hasn't. I thought it would be better to talk to the colonel first, then to Mrs. Bickerdyke," she began, ignoring the use of the woman's familiar nickname.

"Well, now, miss, that's not the way of it at all. When it comes to nurses, it's Mother Bickerdyke that calls the tune. And she don't set much store by do-gooders in their hoop skirts and feathers, either." He gave her attire another, more derisive look and added, " 'Course there is Miss Safford, but she's a pure angel. Even Mother could see that from the first."

"Well, then," Leigh continued undeterred. "Where will I find this Mrs. Bickerdyke?"

"I reckon you'll find her at her place back in town. She does most of the cooking for the sick 'uns right there."

Since she had dismissed her hired carriage, Leigh turned with carpetbag in hand and began the trek back to Cairo. She tried to ignore the mud sucking at her shoes and the ferocious sun beating down on her as she walked, but she had not gone too far when a soft female voice halted her.

"Excuse me, please, but Corporal McGuire said you had come to volunteer as a nurse."

Leigh looked up at a fragile blonde addressing her from the seat of an open carriage. "I'm headed back to Mother Bickerdyke's kitchen with the empty pots from breakfast," she went on. "If you'd like a ride back into town, you're welcome to it."

The girl's smile was wide and welcoming, and Leigh met it with her own. "Thank you, I'd like that," she replied, tossing her bag into the back and climbing into the buggy unassisted. "My name's Leigh Pennington. I've come from St. Louis to nurse at Fort Defiance if Mrs. Bickerdyke will let me."

Up close Leigh could see the blonde was half child, half woman, not a day over eighteen and slight for her age. In the bright sun her pale hair glinted like a thousand moonbeams, and in spite of her squint against the glare, her cornflower-blue eyes seemed to dominate her heart-shaped face. She hardly seemed to fit Dorothea Dix's requirements for a nurse either, and Leigh's flagging spirits immediately rose.

"I'm Delia Dobbins from up near Springfield," she volunteered, turning to cluck at the horses. "So, you came all the way to Cairo because you think you want to be a nurse."

"I know I want to be a nurse," Leigh corrected her determinedly.

"Well, you've hardly picked a very likely place to start," Delia warned.

"Why? Doesn't Mrs. Bickerdyke need any more nurses on her staff?"

"Staff?" Delia laughed as she turned to glance at the other woman. "We're hardly a staff. We're just a few women trying to see to the sick: keep them clean, see that they get proper food, change their dressings if need be. With conditions as they are, we can't do much more than that."

"I thought that things had improved dramatically since Mrs. Bickerdyke's been here."

"Oh, they have," Delia assured Leigh, "but for the most part it's been like trying to drain the sea with a sieve.

There's no question that Mother B. has made a huge difference in the time she's been here. The medical tents are far more comfortable, and the sick have clean clothes and linens. The sanitation and cleanliness are very much improved.''

Leigh eyed the blond girl speculatively at the last statement, unable to comprehend what things must have been like before the Bickerdyke woman's arrival. Even from the front gate the stench of the camp had been overpowering.

"She sees that the sick get special food, bought from a fund set up by General Prentice at her insistence,'' Delia continued, enumerating the woman's Herculean accomplishments.

"Is it true that she commandeers the packages the men are sent from home?'' Leigh broke in.

Delia giggled and nodded, turning suddenly quite chatty. "At first she had to badger the men into it, but when they saw all the good she was able to do with what they got, they gave in peaceably. And in return she's teaching the camp cooks how to make salt pork and hardtack palatable.''

Leigh shook her head in amazement. "She sounds like a positive whirlwind!''

Delia gave another delighted laugh that sparkled like crystal in the wind and set her soft curls dancing. "A 'cyclone in calico' one of the doctors called her after their first run-in. Nor was he the last doctor she's taken to task.''

"But how did you get involved in all this, Miss Dobbins?'' Leigh wanted to know.

"Oh, call me Delia, please. My brothers both signed up in the first call for volunteers, and since there were only the three of us on the farm and no family for me to stay with, I came along with them. The Third Illinois made me the daughter of the regiment, a mascot sort of, and when Mother B. came to Cairo in June, she just took me under her wing.''

Delia slowed her horse to let an ammunition wagon lumber past, and Leigh took the opportunity to study the town spreading out before her. From the lip of the levee Cairo had seemed an inauspicious knot of buildings collected like residue in the bottom of a teacup, but now as they drew closer, she could see a bustling main street with a grid of side streets laid out to the east and west. There was building going on everywhere, and the fresh-sawed beams stood out like stark skeletons against the weathered sides of older buildings. They turned off to the left at the edge of town and passed trim houses huddled under the shady spans of old trees, finally turning into a yard hung with fresh-washed laundry. At the rumble of the carriage wheels a woman appeared from the cabin at the rear of the property.

"I was beginning to wonder if you'd gone for good," she greeted them in a gruff voice. "It's nearly time to take lunch back to the boys."

Delia jumped down from the carriage seat, and Leigh followed suit, realizing only when they stood side by side how small and slight the other girl really was. Then she turned her attention to the tall, imposing figure that was advancing toward them. So this was Mary Ann Bickerdyke, Leigh thought, quite able to believe all the stories she'd heard about the "cyclone in calico." The woman had a hard but kind face with a careworn expression and clear blue eyes that missed nothing. Judging from the gray-brown hair that straggled from the knot at the back of her neck, she was well into middle age but with the strength and vigor in her movements of a much younger woman. As she approached, Leigh straightened to face her squarely.

"Mother B.," Delia said in a rush, "this is Leigh Pennington. She's come from St. Louis to help us."

Without a word the Bickerdyke woman looked the new-comer up and down, taking in the feathered hat, the expensive lace gloves, and the gray silk gown with its fashionably full skirts. At last her eyes came to rest on Leigh's face, with its creamy skin and lovely aristocratic features. "And just what is it you think you can do to help us?" she asked quietly.

Leigh detected a certain unfriendliness in the older woman's tone, and color blossomed in her cheeks as she answered. "I was trained as a nurse," she stated flatly, "and I understand there are men here at Cairo in need of my skill."

"This ain't no charity ball you'd be volunteering to help with," Mother Bickerdyke snorted.

"I'm quite aware of that, madame, I assure you," Leigh countered, her tone as icy as the Bickerdyke woman's had been.

"I don't need help nursing my boys from society ladies who would faint at the sight of blood."

"I won't faint," Leigh answered.

"Have you seen gangrene or watched a man die of yellow fever?" she snapped.

"No," Leigh conceded, "but I've nursed my share of measles and pneumonia. And from what I understand, men die of those things in these camps as often as they do from other causes."

The older woman gave an almost imperceptible nod, whether in recognition of her skill or agreement Leigh could not tell. "Have you any experience with gunshot wounds," she continued, "or with broken bones?"

It was Leigh's turn to nod. "When I worked with my grandfather in his medical practice, we had some bullet wounds, but more often we saw farming or industrial accidents. And I've set a break by myself a time or two."

"Have you ever done washing or cooking for sick men?" There was no change of expression on Mary Ann Bickerdyke's stern face.

"No," Leigh replied truthfully, "but I'd be willing to learn how."

"They're as important here as all the rest."

"Yes, ma'am, I realize that."

Mother Bickerdyke paused to let her eyes sweep over the young woman once more. "Why did you come here?" she wanted to know.

The skepticism in the question was not new to Leigh. "I came because I have skills to offer, and I was too young and pretty to get a position in any of the St. Louis hospitals." She voiced the indictment with a slight raise of her head, as if daring the older woman to challenge it.

For the briefest instant the suggestion of a smile tugged at the Bickerdyke woman's lips as she turned away. "In an hour or so we're due back at the camp with the soup I've been brewing. You're welcome to come if you want to, and we'll try you out," she called over her shoulder. "And Delia, you show Miss Pennington where to take off that party dress and those foolish hoops."

Leigh stood for a moment after she was gone, drained by the unexpected confrontation. Then the petite blond girl was beside her, laying a comforting hand on her arm.

"Why didn't you warn me what a tigress she is?" Leigh demanded in a whisper.

Delia gave one of her silvery laughs and went to unload the pots and pans that had been emptied of porridge earlier that morning. Over the clang and clamor of the pots Delia gave her answer.

"I didn't warn you about her because I thought you could handle her yourself," she said. "And I was right!"

The temperature inside the one-room cabin that served as both kitchen and lodgings for Mother Bickerdyke and Delia Dobbins was at least twenty degrees higher than it was in the yard. And the loft above the spartan room with its stove and single cot was hotter still. As Leigh washed her hands and face in the basin of cool water provided for her, she studied her surroundings. The cornhusk pallet where Delia slept was made up in the corner, and a crate with one lone candle atop it stood alongside. The girl's meager possessions were hung on nails driven into the rafters, and a second pallet was rolled up under the open window on the end wall. Perhaps she would be offered that pallet before the day was through, she thought tiredly, if she had somehow managed to prove herself by then. Leigh sighed and questioned, not for the first time, her resolve in following the course she had set for herself. She had not expected Mrs. Bickerdyke's inquisition or the thinly veiled hostility she sensed in the older woman. When, she wondered, would she learn that people were reluctant to accept her help without questioning her motives? It seemed such a simple thing to offer all she had to give without thought of recompense, and yet that generosity was somehow suspect. Well, at least here in Cairo she was being given her chance. She would find out firsthand

if military nursing was as horrifying and difficult as everyone from Lucas to Dorothea Dix had said it would be.

For an instant Hayes Banister's smiling face flashed
before her eyes, and she could almost hear his words
ringing in her ears. "What you have, Leigh, is an honest
compassion for people in need." How often she had called
up that memory in these past weeks when she had needed
encouragement. And how odd it seemed that the words of
a stranger she would probably never see again could offer
such comfort. Once more the talisman of those softly
spoken words worked its magic, and she straightened from
the basin and dried her hands.

Untying the tapes at her waist, she dropped her hoops to
the floor with a resounding thump and divested herself of
all but one flimsy petticoat. She hung the discarded gar-
ments on an empty nail on one wall and rummaged in her
carpetbag for her blue calico gown. It was quite a bit too
long without the fullness of her underskirts to support it,
and she made a mental note to turn up the hem if she was
asked to stay. With the top two buttons of her dress left
daringly open against the heat, Leigh descended the ladder
to the cabin's main floor. Just as she reached it, another
young woman entered. She was undeniably lovely, with
lustrous dark hair and refined features. And she was hardly
in the door before Delia was making introductions.

"Mary Safford, this is Leigh Pennington from St. Louis,"
she piped up eagerly.

"I'm very pleased to meet you, Miss Pennington," the
Safford woman said, extending her hand.

"As I am to meet 'the angel of Cairo,'" Leigh returned, meeting it with her own.

Mary Safford colored prettily. "'The angel of Cairo,'
indeed!" she said with a laugh. "Whoever filled your
head with such nonsense?"

"This ain't no time for your tea-party chatter," Mother
Bickerdyke intoned from the doorway. "The soup in these
kettles is cooling while you make polite conversation."

"It's hot enough today to keep that soup boiling all the
way to the fort!" Delia declared under her breath as she
led the others outside.

In the blazing noonday sun the air in the encampment

was even more unpalatable than it had been at midmorning. For now, in addition to the other smells, there was a haze of bacon smoke that lay over the place like a greasy blue fog. The hospital tents were to the left of the fort's main road, beneath the red-brown embankment that served as ramparts for the cannon that commanded the junction of the two rivers. As she rode on the high carriage seat past the clumps of milling soldiers with their dirty uniforms and unkempt beards, Leigh kept her face carefully impassive, aware of Mother Bickerdyke riding beside her. The woman, her profile all but obscured by the shadow of the old Shaker bonnet, seemed totally oblivious to both the squalor disguised as a military camp and the reactions of the newcomer, and yet Leigh was sure those sharp blue eyes missed nothing.

The white hospital tents set off by themselves were like an island of calm in a sea of disorder. At the sound of their wheels, gaunt faces peered out of the ends of the long canvas structures, and ambulatory patients hobbled out to greet them.

"You boys a mite hungry?" the Bickerdyke woman asked, clambering down from her perch. "You, John, and you, Ted, you feel up to helping me with these kettles?"

"We sure do, Mother. Be right there," someone called out.

Feeding everyone was the first order of business, and Leigh, Delia, and Mary set out to see to those unable to feed themselves while Mother Bickerdyke ladled out soup for the rest.

The canvas tents themselves were clean and neat, though the facilities were primitive at best. Most of the men had cots made up with sheets, a blanket, and pillow, but a few lay on straw beds on the rough board floor. At the head of each tent was a water keg with a dipper, and midway down was another sawed half-barrel with chloride of lime in the bottom to be used for a different purpose. In spite of the disinfectant, it smelled and drew flies. The three young women moved from man to man, serving and spoon-feeding those who needed it. In the second tent Leigh came upon a young whey-faced soldier. Too weak to reach the proper receptacle, he had been sick all over his shirt and sheets.

"He's been feeling a mite poorly," the man in the next bed informed her.

"Yes, I can see that," she observed dryly, setting aside her bowl of soup and bending over the sick man. "I imagine you'll feel better once you're cleaned up and have fresh sheets to lie on, won't you?" she asked quietly.

Changing her priorities to accommodate the man's needs, Leigh went back to the carriage for a basin of water and fresh linen. The cleanup took only a few minutes, and by the time the young soldier was settled in his newly made bed, he was looking much brighter.

"If I bring you a cup of broth, would you try to eat it?" she cajoled her patient. "If you can keep it down, it will help make you stronger. Or try a bit of water, at least."

"I'd be willing to try the broth, ma'am," he agreed. Leigh turned away from the cot to get the man some soup and found Mother Bickerdyke watching her judgmentally.

After the men were fed, beds were changed and general cleaning was done with the help of the male nurses, who Leigh learned later were soldiers on parole from the camp stockade. It was hot, backbreaking work in the stifling tents, but afterward there was the reward of seeing the neat, freshly made cots and the grateful faces of the soldiers. Then wounds were dressed as need be, medicine administered, letters written, and stories read. Mary Safford was halfway through *David Copperfield* with the men, and as her sweet, soothing voice read Dickens's words, Leigh sat with a feverish soldier near the back of the tent. He had been too sick to eat or even drink a little of the tea Mother Bickerdyke had prepared for him. And Leigh recognized the signs of death in his pinched face. His breathing was labored and his skin waxen, but still she sat with him, sponging his arms and chest, his face and neck with cool water against the raging fever and the suffocating heat. He must be younger than she by a year or two, Leigh reflected as she bathed him, a fine-looking young man with red hair and brown eyes. Undoubtedly he was someone who had set off to war with dreams of military glory, only to be cut down by a fever no one could name.

"And my girl, Ellen," her patient said suddenly, as if continuing a conversation, "makes the best apple pie."

"Does she?" Leigh asked, moving closer.

"Won a prize at the county fair. There's nothing like Ellen's pie with a big mug of cold milk from the spring house." His voice was so low Leigh had to strain to hear it.

"I'll bet she's pretty, your Ellen."

"She surely is, with dimples on both sides of her mouth, both sides!"

Leigh smiled down at him, mistaking his consciousness as a good sign. "Do you think your Ellen would mind if I held your hand for a little while?"

The young soldier shook his head, and she took his lax fingers in her own, placing her other palm on his forehead.

"Lord, miss, you have the coolest hands," he whispered happily and closed his eyes. In another moment he was gone.

In spite of her training with Simon Pennington, Leigh had never seen someone die, and she was struck first by the suddenness of it. It was possible to know for months or years that someone was dying, but in the end the act itself took only long enough for a final breath to be expelled, a last heartbeat to flutter. A minute before, a living man had been beside her, and now she was alone. Treacherous tears simmered beneath her downcast lids, and she struggled to control them. She had been with this man in the last moments of his life, and she didn't even know his name.

Mary Safford's voice droned in her ears, and then Leigh was aware of Mother Bickerdyke standing over her. The older woman took her arm and led her the length of the tent, passing a doctor and two of the male nurses carrying a stretcher. Once outside, Leigh gasped great gulps of air, strangely aware of its volume in her lungs, its smell in her nostrils. Nor had any air ever smelled so sweet.

"Is this the first person you've seen die?" Mother Bickerdyke asked in that gruff, rumbling tone that seemed to be her normal voice.

Leigh nodded, still breathing deeply.

"Well, you're taking it better than some," she conceded.

"I'm certainly glad to hear that," the girl finally managed to reply.

"You still feeling kind of shaky?" the older woman inquired.

"No, I'm fine, really. It just came so suddenly, so finally." Leigh tried to articulate her feelings.

"It comes for all of us like that in the end," Mother Bickerdyke observed philosophically.

"It makes you very aware of your own mortality, doesn't it?"

"M-m-m-m," the woman agreed. "Now you climb up into that carriage seat and wait. It's almost time for us to go back anyway. Can you drive a buggy like this one?" When Leigh nodded, Mother Bickerdyke continued. "Good. You'll drive us back to Cairo. It'll take your mind off of what just happened. I'll go round up the others."

When they returned to Mother Bickerdyke's cabin, Leigh wanted nothing more than to take off her shoes and collapse in a corner. But the empty soup kettles were transformed almost immediately into caldrons of wash water, steaming on top of the stove. The dirty shirts, sheets, and underwear collected at the camp today needed to be scrubbed and laundered for return tomorrow, as part of an endless exchange of clean clothes and linens for dirty ones. With envy in her eyes, Leigh watched Mary Safford drive off in her own buggy, probably to a cool, soothing bath and a sumptuous dinner, she thought glumly. Then with a stubborn raise of her chin, Leigh willed away her tiredness and went back inside. This was what she had wanted, after all, she reminded herself.

All the pots, but the one full of soup left at Fort Defiance for those unable to tolerate a regular Army dinner, were filled with water and steaming on the stove. Stifling a groan of resignation, Leigh climbed up on a stool and took a wooden paddle to stir the tubs of soapy water as Delia directed her, while Mother Bickerdyke stoked the stove to even higher temperatures. All three women ran with perspiration as they worked in the steamy July twilight, and the moon was high before they finished. Leigh's hands were red and rough from the scalding water and the scrubbing, and her fingers ached with endless wringing. She was limping from too many hours in her high-heeled shoes by the time she brought the last load of wet laundry into the yard, and her back hurt from carrying the heavy baskets of clothes. But no matter how she felt, she had kept up with the other two.

"Now, if only it doesn't rain," she moaned, squinting up at the sky as she and Delia stood in the middle of the moonlit yard surveying their finished task.

Even Delia could hardly muster the strength for a laugh. "And just think, Leigh," she pointed out cheerfully, "tomorrow it all begins again."

Once inside, Delia washed the sweat from her body and climbed the ladder to her bed, but Leigh hesitated. What was she to do? Where was she to go now? She was almost too tired to care.

Sensing her dilemma, Mother Bickerdyke looked up from the shirt she was mending. "While you were hanging up that last basket of wash, I made up the second bed in the loft."

Even through her weariness, Leigh recognized the invitation and the acceptance it represented. For a moment she stood speechless in surprise, then turned toward the ladder to the loft above. Her foot was on the first rung when she heard the Bickerdyke woman speak again.

"You'll do, Leigh Pennington," she said softly. "You'll do."

A deep, warm glow of satisfaction swept away Leigh's exhaustion, and with it came an understanding of the bluff woman whose cause she was now pledged to share. This morning the hostility she had sensed had been nothing more than the protective instincts of a mother for those in her charge. Now Leigh had proven herself; she was one of them, a nurse.

Leigh smiled as she answered. "Thank you, Mother Bickerdyke, and good night."

5 ∞

November 15, 1861—Cairo, Illinois

This warm Indian summer day was to be Leigh
Pennington's last in Cairo, and she wanted to remember
the overcrowded little town at the junction of the Ohio and
Mississippi rivers as it looked now: with the muddy, rutted
main street nearly passable, with the new buildings sport-
ing their fresh coats of paint, and with a feeling of bustle
and excitement in the air. The cobalt-blue sky dusted with
pale whips of clouds and the fresh breeze blowing in
across the Mississippi heightened her appreciation, and
Leigh knew she would rather think of Cairo this way than
as it had been in the thick of summer, steaming and rank
with heat and humidity. After four months of hard work
in Fort Defiance's hospital tents, she was going home to
accept an appointment to the Army Nursing Corps and a
coveted position in St. Louis's newly opened City General
Hospital. It was only the time she had spent under Mary
Ann Bickerdyke's tutelage that qualified her as an Army
nurse, and in spite of the hard work, the long hours, and
spartan living conditions, Leigh was not sorry she had
come.

The days, weeks, and months in Cairo had passed, each
with a striking similarity to the ones that preceded it: with
breakfast, lunch, and dinner to cook and serve, with cleaning and caring for the men to fill her days, and with
endless mounds of clothes and sheets to be laundered in
the evenings. Though the work got no easier, Leigh learned

to take it in her stride, growing stronger and more confident, making the transformation from St. Louis belle to a
military nurse with an ease that surprised everyone but
herself. As Leigh learned new skills and polished old ones
Mother Bickerdyke had been infinitely patient, Mary Safford
ever encouraging, and Delia Dobbins always willing to
lighten her load with her quick humor and ready laugh.
No, Leigh was not at all sorry she had come.

Beside her Delia chatted ebulliently as they maneuvered
through the crowd. They had left their duties at the new
military hospital early with the excuse of doing a bit of
shopping, but in truth it was more the wish to spend their
last afternoon together that motivated the two young women
to plan the unaccustomed outing. During the months they
had spent together in the sweltering confines of the hospital tents and in the loft where they lay whispering their
dreams in the dark, a rich, deep friendship had grown up
between them, based in their shared experiences and mutual respect. In Delia, Leigh found a sweet, uncomplicated
friend whose infectious laughter and innate gaiety made
light of the most difficult tasks and most horrendous experiences. And in Leigh, Delia discovered the close female
companionship her life on the isolated Illinois farm had
denied her. Their friendship had become a precious and
satisfying thing, and both of them faced the wrench of
parting with the conviction that somehow, somewhere they
would work side by side again.

They had just emerged from the millinery shop onto the
rickety board sidewalks that hemmed Cairo's main street
when Leigh heard someone call her name. Surveying the
throngs out to take advantage of the fine weather, she
noticed a tall man striding purposefully toward her. In that
instant, it was only by the utmost strength of will that
Leigh managed to stifle the urge to turn and run. She could
not help but notice the way the autumn sun caught the
golden lights in his deep brown hair or the unrestrained
pleasure that sparkled in his pale eyes as he approached
her, and brilliant color rose in her cheeks. Hayes Banister
and the words he had spoken on that night so long ago had
been very much with her in the months since she had left

St. Louis, and the sight of him now sent a confusing mixture of emotions coursing through her.

"Hayes!" she exclaimed quite breathlessly. "Hayes, whatever are you doing in Cairo?"

Banister grinned and ignored the question, catching her in a bear hug and covering her half-open mouth with his own. There was in the greeting a spontaneity and welcome that spoke of past intimacy and of far more familiarity than they had ever known. For a moment, Leigh was too stunned to struggle, then the indignity of being kissed on a street corner in broad daylight by a man she hardly knew suffused her and she pushed Banister away.

"I knew it had to be you!" he declared delightedly, before she could utter a word. "No one in the world has hair quite that same color."

Leigh was as undone by his words as she was by his greeting. "I'm surprised you have any memory at all of what color my hair is!" she snapped, then flushed again, appalled that her sarcastic reply had sounded like scolding.

"Sometimes I surprise even myself at how well I remember everything about you."

His dimpled smile went crooked and wry at the admission, but there was an undercurrent of seriousness in what he said that surprised Leigh. His kiss had been too unexpected and sudden to elicit much of a response, but the tenderness in his voice sent a treacherous warmth swirling through her. Striving to regain her composure, Leigh cast about for something to say. "Goodness, Hayes," she finally managed, "I never ever expected to see you again, much less here in Cairo."

"And all along I've thought another meeting between us was inevitable," he replied, pouting, though his eyes shone with suppressed mirth.

At the memory of how she'd sent him away, Leigh's cheeks went a deeper shade of scarlet. How could he be so glib and sure about what the future might hold when she was still at a loss to explain the past?

Sensing that his teasing had gone awry, Banister's smile faded, and he gestured to the black-haired man at his side. "Leigh, may I present Nathan Travis. Travis, this is Miss Leigh Pennington, lately of St. Louis." Leigh had been so flustered by Hayes Banister's sudden appearance that she had been totally unaware of anyone else on the street, but now inbred good manners took over. She completed the introductions almost by rote.

"And may I introduce my friend Miss Delia Dobbins. Delia, Mr. Travis and Mr. Banister."

With the familiar footing of correct behavior to steady her, Leigh felt more in control and turned a curious eye on Banister's companion. Mr. Travis was nearly as tall as Hayes, but not as broad, his raw-boned body all coil and cable. There was the same stark strength in the man's jaw and cheekbones that there was in the rest of him, and his straight brows and hawk nose were equally severe. Still, his might have been a handsome face if it were lit with a smile. But judging from the narrow, sober mouth and the intensity of his coal-black eyes, there seemed no likelihood of that.

Abruptly Banister addressed Leigh, seeming content to let the newly introduced Travis and Miss Dobbins fend for themselves while he satisfied his own curiosity. "Tell me, Leigh, what on earth are you doing in Cairo?"

"I believe I asked you first," she reminded him tartly.

Hayes shrugged in resignation and began to explain. "I brought the *Barbara Dean* down last night with a load of spare parts for the ironclads stationed here at Cairo," he told her. "Since the contracts for the boats were awarded to James Eads last August, he and I have been working in partnership on the construction at his shipyard just south of St. Louis in Carondelet."

The arrival of the first of these strange-looking vessels in mid-October had caused quite a stir in Cairo. Even Leigh and Delia had taken time to climb up on the levee and watch it steam majestically down the river to its anchorage opposite Fort Defiance. Nor had the procession of six more of the boats aroused less interest. They were odd craft, to be sure, looking, with their steeply canted sides and hinged gunports, like giant metal turtle shells riding low in the water. Yet for all their peculiarities, they were impressive, innovative, and sinister looking.

"You mean you've been working in St. Louis all this time?" she asked.

Hayes nodded. "For the past three or four months."

"And since you didn't know I was in Cairo, you must not have gone by our house, not even to retrieve your hat," Leigh reasoned aloud, piqued that he hadn't made any attempt to see her.

"Well, I have been rather busy," Banister defended himself with a grin. "James promised delivery of those infernal ironclads in just sixty-five days. We've had nearly four thousand men working in shifts around the clock to get even the first one done in time. I've been literally eating and sleeping at the shipyards. This is the first time I've been away from the place since the contracts came through.

"Besides, I wasn't at all sure you would see me if I called. Would you have, Leigh?" he inquired as one of his impressive dark eyebrows quirked upward.

Leigh lowered her lashes demurely. "I don't know that there's any point in discussing it, Hayes. Even if you had come to call, I wouldn't have been home to receive you. It's a shame about your hat, though; it was a fine piece of goods, as I remember."

"That brings me back to my initial question," he put in. "What are you doing in Cairo?"

Briefly she outlined her reasons for leaving St. Louis, the satisfaction of being able to use her skills, and the vindication of having secured a position with the Army Nursing Corps at last.

"Damn fools!" Banister muttered under his breath when she was through. "At least I'm glad they've finally seen fit to avail themselves of your services. No one has more to offer to those sick men than you do, Leigh."

His confidence in her was warm and nourishing, just as the memory of his words had been in the long, barren, difficult months since that night on the porch in St. Louis. She smiled at him softly, imagining how surprised Hayes would be if she confided that she had found infinite solace in what he'd said. She would not tell him, of course, but that made the charm no less potent and Leigh no less grateful for his confidence. He had unwittingly given her a strong talisman against disappointment and despair, and her unspoken appreciation knew no bounds.

Hayes, standing beside her in the autumn sunshine, saw a subtle change in her face: a slight turn to her lips, a tender light in her eyes that made him ache with mingled desire and confusison. Leigh Pennington was a warm and beautiful woman, but even as he watched her, wanting to hold and touch her, he was intensely aware that she was promised to another man.

"When do you expect to be back in St. Louis?" he inquired, turning from the potential danger in his own thoughts. "Perhaps I'll stop by someday soon to see about my hat, now that I know you'll receive me."

"Don't presume too much from one chance meeting, Mr. Banister," Leigh warned, smiling archly. "Actually, I plan to take passage tomorrow since I must report to City General Hospital on Monday."

"We're planning to leave for St. Louis tonight," Hayes offered. "You'd be more than welcome to come with us. Can you be ready by then?"

Leigh was not at all sure she liked either the way Hayes Banister was prepared to reorder her life or the prospect of being alone with him on a steamboat. Thankful that she had a valid reason, Leigh refused him. "Oh, Hayes, I appreciate your offer, but I'm going to be on duty at the hospital all night."

"Well, I suppose we could wait until morning—"

"Oh goodness, no," Leigh protested in a flurry. "A riverboat captain could hardly delay his departure for the sake of a single passenger."

Hayes surmised the reason for her refusal, and the corner of his mouth tipped down derisively. "Since I own the *Barbara Dean*, I can't imagine that the captain would object."

"What?" Leigh mumbled in surprise.

"I own the *Barbara Dean*, out of the Banister Shipyards in Cincinnati, built as much with my own hands as time and the shipwrights would allow. I own four steamboats, but she's the cream of the crop." His pride in the riverboat was evident, and he extolled her virtues and idiosyncrasies as if she were a favorite child. "I'd been living aboard in Cincinnati, so when I came to St. Louis she came, too.

We contract for short runs by day, and she's what I come home to at night, though I've spent precious little time aboard her since August. So you see, Leigh, we can easily accommodate your schedule." His tone was light but obdurate.

"Why, Leigh, what a perfect way to travel!" Delia spoke up. "And how nice of Mr. Banister to offer you passage. After all, you were concerned about being able to get a stateroom on one of the other packets on such short notice."

Leigh was not prepared for her friend's defection and sent Delia a scathing glance. She was becoming more and more certain that she did not want to spend all those hours on a riverboat in Hayes Banister's company, much less on a riverboat he owned and operated. But Delia seem oblivious to Leigh's predicament and was instead smiling up at Mr. Travis, who, amazingly enough, was smiling back!

"Well, if you're sure it's no trouble to delay your departure . . . ." Leigh capitulated with what little grace she could muster.

"Then it's settled," Banister concluded with a victorious grin. "Would you like me to come by in the morning and help you with your baggage?"

Leigh ground her teeth in frustration. "No, thank you. I'm sure I can manage."

"Then I'll see you first thing tomorrow at the landing."

"Yes, I'll be there."

"And since you gentlemen are going to be in town tonight," Delia put in unexpectedly, "there's a dance at the town hall you might want to attend."

Leigh stared at the other girl in open astonishment. The dances were a weekly occurrence in Cairo, offering one of the few respectable diversions the soldiers from Fort Defiance had, but neither she nor Delia had ever had the time or inclination to attend.

"We'll keep it in mind, Miss Dobbins," Mr. Travis assured her, though Leigh thought him as unlikely a dancing partner as she could imagine.

There was nothing left but to say their good-byes, and Banister and Travis were hardly out of sight when Delia turned to Leigh, her face flushed and her cornflower-blue eyes as round as saucers.

"Oh, Leigh," she said breathlessly, "I think I've just met the man I'm going to marry!"

November 16, 1861

Not long after dawn, Hayes Banister emerged from the boiler room of the *Barbara Dean*, unkempt, sweaty, and covered with grease. When he had returned to the riverboat from the town, he discovered a need for repairs that would have delayed their departure from Cairo until this morning even if he had not promised Leigh Pennington passage to St. Louis. Hayes breathed deeply of the heavy morning air, thick with unseasonable humidity, and brushed the perspiration from his brow with one smudged hand. He was tired, disgruntled, and sorely in need of a bath. Nor was checking and repairing the fittings and gaskets on a steam engine the way he would have elected to spend the night.

While he had worked, Nathan Travis had gone off into the twilight to attend the town hall dance, dressed like a disapproving church deacon. But when he returned just after midnight, whistling softly under his breath, with his black coat tossed carelessly over one shoulder and his cravat askew, Travis was a changed man. As they shared a pot of strong, black coffee in the crew's quarters, Hayes had discovered the reason: Delia Dobbins. Somehow in the three or four hours they'd had together, the young nurse had plumbed a well-concealed part of Nathan Travis's personality, finding a lightness and congeniality in him that Hayes had never suspected. For those few minutes as they sat relaxing together, Travis was more garrulous and expansive than Banister had ever known him to be. But an hour later when Travis set out in a skiff for the Kentucky shore, the glow was gone from his black eyes and his grim demeanor had returned. And it was small wonder, Hayes mused. In the past three or four months he had seen enough of Travis's comings and goings to guess at his part in the war effort. The knowledge he had of the man's convictions only reinforced Hayes's suspicions. Nathan Travis was a Union spy, and wherever he was now, he was terrifyingly alone in his battle with the enemy.

Hayes stretched his cramped muscles and squinted up at the sun, just cresting the lip of the levee, and wondered how long it would be before Leigh Pennington would put in an appearance. He frowned abstractedly at the thought and leaned his elbows on the rail. What mixture of fate and coincidence had brought Leigh back into his life after all these months? God knows, it had been the truth when he told her he had been too busy in St. Louis to seek her out. His days at the shipyard had been long and hectic, and even his sleep had been caught in snatches. But there had been odd moments of leisure when he might have welcomed her company. Why, then, had he assiduously avoided anything that might have brought him into contact with the beauteous young woman who haunted his dreams?

Perhaps it had been his own perversity that prevented him from trying to see her, or the conviction that once he saw her and spoke to her and became reacquainted, he would never be able to walk away from her again. Over space and time, Leigh was with him still: her cameo-perfect features etched in his mind, her orange and spice scent an elusive memory, her ingenuous passion a thing that teased the edges of his imagination. He had not been able to forget Leigh, and in that lay a threat that tested the limits of his courage. Monica's rejection and the pain it brought had been enough to last a lifetime. And in spite of the attraction, it was obvious they both felt, he knew Leigh did not want him. She did not want him, and he would not fight and lose the same battle twice. It was as simple as that.

And yet yesterday when he had seen her on the street, his spirit had soared, leaving his doubts earthbound. She should have been less appealing in her drab, shapeless gown and shawl, with her hair twisted primly into a knot at the back of her neck, but she was not. For a few moments it had been as if he were blind to all but the sight of her, deaf to everything but the sound of her voice, his hands numbed to everything but the feel of her flesh beneath them. Seeing her had made him feel as if he were living only half a life, and he ached to make himself whole, no matter what the cost.

Hayes leaned against the rail more heavily and snorted in disgust at the trend of his own thoughts. He was a supremely rational man, he told himself stubbornly, and wasn't about to let some green-eyed chit tie him into knots. He was attracted to Leigh Pennington, as any man with eyes in his head would be, but he did have some control over his emotions. He was no longer a callow youth, a slave to his illusions and his lust. Leigh was graceful, beautiful, and sweet, but there was no reason why he had to become involved with her if he chose not to take that course. Surely he could spend the next day and a half in Leigh's company without succumbing to her charms; he could practice that much restraint, at least.

Then, Leigh herself topped the levee, the morning sun catching in her fiery hair and turning it brilliant, blazing red before she descended from the crest of the embankment into the shadows. Hayes's heart leaped at the sight, and he watched her for a long moment before he pushed away from the rail and headed toward the gangplank.

She swung jauntily down the wagon road toward the dock, a carpetbag in one hand that moved in time to her steps, a feed sack clutched in the other, an old Shaker bonnet dangling by its strings from her elbow, and a full two inches of lacy petticoats visible beneath the shortened hem of her calico gown.

"Good morning, Leigh," he called to her as he started up the slope of the old wagon trace. "Can I give you a hand with those things?"

She smiled a greeting and shook her head. "I'm far stronger than I look," she assured him. "I just hope I haven't held you up. I came here right from the hospital, but I feel terrible that you delayed your departure because of me."

"Some unexpected problems with the engine would have kept us in Cairo until this morning anyway," he assured her, coming closer. "It took us most of the night to fix them."

"Then that explains why you look like you've just escaped from a minstrel show," she teased, noting the dirt and grime on his face.

The answering rejoinder died on his lips as he came up beside her. "Leigh, you've been crying!" he blurted out as he noticed the tracks of fresh tears on her cheeks.

Leigh's expression softened at the concern in his tone. "It's been a fairly emotional hour or so," she conceded.

"Saying good-bye to your friends, you mean?"

"Yes, that, too. I've grown very attached to Delia and Mother Bickerdyke in the months I've spent here in Cairo. But we also lost one of our patients just before dawn, and that was hard to accept."

Sympathy filled Banister's pale eyes, and there was a grim twist to his mouth. "I'm so sorry, Leigh. I wish you didn't have to see that kind of thing, but since you are a nurse, I suppose there's no way to spare you—"

"But I don't want to be spared," she told him, taking exception to his well-meaning condescension. "I knew what nursing would be like when I volunteered to help here in Cairo, and I'm as prepared as anyone to deal with pain, death, and grief. Why should you want to shield me from it?"

Her answer caught him unprepared, and he was curious about just what kinds of things she'd experienced in the months since she'd left St. Louis to make her capable of such a statement. Unexpectedly, a primitive need to protect her rose up in him, and Hayes found himself wondering if the good she was able to do would ever balance the inevitable loss of her innocence. Somehow her words demanded a rebuttal, and he faced her with a frown nestled between his dark brows. "But women aren't equipped to deal with the tragedies of war," he protested.

After clinging to his words as her only solace in the dark, difficult days since she'd left St. Louis, Leigh was left feeling bereft by Hayes's defection. "And are men equipped to deal with them?" she countered as she eyed him coldly. "If I've learned one thing in these past months, it's that men feel the same things women do. The only difference is that men hold their grief inside, where it turns them hard and bitter. At least a woman knows the luxury of tears.''

Hayes had no idea how to respond to her and stood staring. Like most men of his time, he subscribed to the theory that women were weak, fragile things, to be protected and cared for at all costs. But then there was something in Leigh that suddenly reminded him of his mother, Barbara, who had taken over the shipyards when his father died, and of his sister Rose, who traveled around the country with her clergyman husband speaking for Abolitionist causes. Neither of them had ever asked for concessions to their femininity, and Leigh was not asking for any now. Uncomfortably he realized that both his mother and sister might well share Leigh's convictions and agree with her sentiments. He was used to his mother's and his sister's independence, but somehow hearing Leigh declare her own unsettled and confused him.

Unable to concede the point, Hayes wrenched the carpetbag from Leigh's hand and turned back toward the riverboat. ''Now that the engine's fixed, I think we might as well get under way,'' he grumbled.

He showed her to his own cabin on the Texas deck with its wide double berth and sumptuous appointments. ''When we use the *Barbara Dean* for short runs, we stow gear in the passenger's cabins,'' he explained as he set the carpetbag beside the bed. ''I'll be bunking next door with the crew tonight. Is there anything you need?''

Leigh took a turn around the cabin, noting the rich, masculine furnishings in warm woodsy tones and the books and drawings scattered across the built-in desk. ''I'd like to wash up first and then get some sleep.'' Hayes gave a quick nod of acknowledgment, then went, closing the door quietly behind him.

When Leigh awoke hours later, the cabin door had been propped open again to admit the faint breath of a breeze off the river and the faraway churning of a paddle wheel. Through the bed she could feel the vibration of the steam engine two decks below and sense the rhythmic motions of the mechanisms that drove the vessel forward. It was warm in the cabin, and the hazy sunlight that filtered in through the open doorway hinted that the day had turned sultry for November. She sat up and stretched lazily, pulling her loosened hair back from her face. It was months since she had slept so long or so comfortably, and she felt languorous and self-indulgent. Hospital nursing had taken her every waking moment in Cairo, and the accommodations in Mary Ann Bickerdyke's little cabin had been far from luxurious. Stretching again, she bent over the side of the bed and withdrew her serviceable forest-green wrapper from her carpetbag, pulling it on over her chemise and tying it securely before she rose from the bunk. She ambled from the bed to the doorway and glanced out across the face of the river. It was still and murky brown, with grain-stubbled fields on the bank far beyond. Before she realized Hayes Banister was sitting just outside, she had stepped into the opening to catch what she could of the logy breeze.

Tipped back in his chair with his booted feet resting on the rail and a crumpled newspaper lying forgotten in his lap, he looked comfortable and contented. "Awake at last?" he asked in a lazy tone. "I thought you were going to sleep all the way to St. Louis."

"It is nice to get a few hours of uninterrupted rest," Leigh admitted, knowing it was too late to retreat into the cabin unseen. "What time is it?"

"Almost four o'clock," he calculated, squinting up at the sun. "It will be time for dinner soon."

Since he had already seen her in her wrapper, and the months of nursing had left her with no patience for false modesty, Leigh stepped out onto the deck and leaned against the rail watching him. "You look better than you did the last time I saw you," she observed, taking in his clean-shaven face, crisp white shirt, and clinging fawn-colored trousers.

"I suppose so, since I've shaved and had a bath since then. Though I admit I did have to sneak into my cabin for some fresh clothes while you were asleep."

"While I was asleep?" Leigh echoed, irrationally irritated by the invasion of privacy.

"You never even fluttered an eyelash." Somehow it seemed only right to tell her that he'd gone back to his stateroom, but Hayes did not say that he had stood for a long while watching her sleep. Her weariness had seemed so much more obvious to him then without her natural animation to hide it, and he had been able to see the lines of care and exhaustion in her face. He had noticed how much thinner she was too, how fragile and delicate her features seemed. The toll her nursing had taken in these few months was suddenly so evident, and again he had felt an overwhelming need to protect and keep her safe. Leigh did have a calling for medicine; that had been evident from the first day he'd known her, but now he wondered at the price she was paying to follow the dictates of her conscience. Yet with the sunlight warming the tone of her skin and catching in her tumbled hair, with a smile on her lips and a glow in her eyes, she looked strong and sure and capable again.

Leigh turned her attention once more to the river, thinking it wiser to ignore his admission no matter how unsettling she found it. "A bath, now that does sound heavenly," she drawled, "and the thought of supper seems welcome, too. Just what is it you're planning to feed me?"

Hayes smiled, watching her profile appreciatively. "I heard a chicken squawking somewhere an hour or so ago, so I imagine by now she's found her way to the stewpot."

"M-m-m-m, chicken," Leigh murmured, closing her eyes, "and perhaps a bit of gravy and some biscuits."

"I think our cook can manage that if it's what you want," he said, grinning.

"And a bath with water I don't have to heat myself," Leigh went on dreamily, "enough to wash my hair, too."

"There's always lots of hot water on a steamboat. Shall I bring you the tub?"

"Oh, yes, would you? And if only I had some scented soap . . ."

"I'll see what I can do," Hayes promised and rose to go into the crew's quarters. When he returned to the deck a few moments later to give Leigh the lilac soap one of the men had been taking his wife, he found she had returned to the stateroom. He stepped into the open doorway and halted on the threshold, transfixed.

While he was gone, Leigh had taken a brush from her things and was running it through her tangled tresses in slow, rhythmic motions. Relaxed and totally absorbed in what she was doing, her eyes were closed and her lips were slightly parted as she worked. It was such a mundane, yet such an intimate act that Hayes felt like an intruder, but he could neither bring himself to turn away nor make his presence known. As if he had come on a doe feeding deep in the forest, he stood silent, caught by the sheer beauty of the scene, afraid that if he moved or spoke, the innate serenity of the moment would be lost.

Leigh's motions as she smoothed the russet masses first one way and then the other were graceful and abandoned, leisurely and sensual. In his mind, they became the even, measured movements of some exotic dance, and he stood mesmerized. Her body flowed in counterpoint to the long strokes, bending slightly sideways to let the hair tumble like a torrent of deep red across her shoulder and arm. Her profile, half-hidden by the liquid curl of hair, the grace of her sculptured features, and the gentle turning of her throat enticed him, as did the feathery wisps that clung to the hand that held the brush. He could almost feel the tickle of her hair on his skin, the coolness of the strands between his fingers, the sweet-scented silkiness against his wrists. His heartbeat went thick and labored as he watched her.

In that moment Leigh was not even conscious of his existence, yet Hayes had never in his life been more aware of any woman. He took in the sinuous curve of her body; the soft, pale luster of her skin; the tumbled masses of her cinnamon hair waving in profusion all about her. And the slumbering need that had been with him since the first moment he saw her stirred to rampant life. Without volition or conscious thought, Hayes crossed the cabin to claim the brush she wielded with such practiced care.

A soft gasp of surprise rose in her throat as his fingers closed over hers, and her eyes opened to stare into his, hot and bright with telling emotion. She moved as if to pull away, but he held her fast with one hand beneath her ribs as the other took up the motions of the brush again. He stroked at a measured pace, slow, repetitious, soothing, drawing the bristles through the russet length with infinite care. As he worked with tenderness and precision, Leigh too was caught up in the same spell that had drawn him to her. From that first day at Camp Jackson, Leigh had felt a compelling trust for Hayes, a sense of security whenever they were together, and she succumbed to that feeling of sanctuary now, gathered close beside him. A whisper of a sigh escaped her as she gave herself over to his ministrations. There was the gentle tug against her scalp, the insidious relaxation that the rhythmic strokes engendered. Her eyes slipped closed, and she drifted against him, totally lost to his tender care. His touch was gentle and undemanding, meant only to soothe and comfort her, his nearness was somehow natural and so right that she could not turn away. She sensed a reverence in the way he touched her, a glorious, masterful control that made her feel totally possessed, yet totally at ease with his possession. As he worked, Leigh gave herself over to sensation: the smooth constancy of his strokes, the slight rush and crackle as the brush moved through her hair, the penetrating warmth of his hand along her ribs. She was aware of the quiet strength in him, of her long dormant desire to be held and touched like this.

The second stretched to minutes and the minutes to time incalculable as they stood together, her body conforming to the contours of his in total relaxation, his responding to hers in age-old ways she was far too innocent to notice. Then, succumbing to temptation, Hayes raised the hand that had lain impassively along her ribs to cup her breast, balancing the weight of it in his palm, as his long fingers measured its fullness. She started against him at the touch but could not muster strength enough to twist away.

"Oh, Leigh," he murmured, as the need inside him grew, consuming all this morning's fine intentions in a burst of desperate yearning. "Oh, my sweet Leigh."

His grainy whisper sent a strange debilitating weakness creeping along her limbs, and as he lowered his head to nuzzle the sweep of her throat, languor billowed through her. Leigh caught a deep breath as she melted more intimately against him, the boundaries of their two bodies merging as they curved more and more closely together.

The brush slipped from his hand to the floor, leaving his fingers free to trace the firm, curving line of her hip and belly. Then with a shudder of delight, his big body enfolded her in a cherishing caress. His lips moved softly against her ear as he murmured words of provocation, offering her a haven in his arms and a passion that was hers to accept or deny. But though Leigh knew she should, she could muster no power to refuse him as the delicious lassitude grew.

Leigh was stunned by her uninhibited answer to his touch and intrigued by the promise of untold delight. And when Hayes turned her to him at last, she saw he was as shaken by the wondrous intimacy as she. His eyes were clouded with the intensity of the moment, heavy-lidded and strangely glazed. When his mouth came down to claim hers, the response that flowed between them was involuntary, unthinking, and almost preordained. Leigh rose up eagerly to meet his kiss: welcoming, tender, newly aware. Her mouth sought and questioned, Hayes's answered and slowly savored, until they were lost in a depth of communion that neither had ever experienced. The world could have spun to oblivion around them, and they would not have known or cared. They were totally immersed in the merging of their wills and bodies, caught in a delicate, silken snare that trapped and held them both.

Murmuring mindless endearments, Hayes slipped open the ties of her wrapper to caress the soft expanse of creamy skin, with nothing but the tissue-thin chemise to hinder him. The pressure of his hands along her ribs, moving slowly upward, kindled a glowing rush within her veins that warmed her like a long, deep swallow of the finest brandy. Sensation seared along her nerves, erotic lightning licking through her, and Leigh felt she might be cindered by all his touch evoked. His thumbs found the budding roundness of her nipples and traced slowly expanding circles that encompassed and aroused. At his touch her breasts tingled and tightened, her limbs went weak and waxen, until Leigh was hopelessly, helplessly at his command.

Hayes could feel the tempo of her desire grow in concert

with his own, sense the abandon in her movements as his hands caressed her silken flesh. This Leigh was more uninhibited and responsive, more passionate and giving, than the woman who had haunted his dreams, and he reveled in the bounteous reality. In response his hands slipped lower and his kisses deepened, claiming her lips, her tongue, her breath. Then, compelled by emotions he'd tried to deny, Hayes mouth slid from her lips to the point of her chin, then down again to the hollow at the base of her throat and the dusky valley beyond. Leigh arched and turned her head in a gesture that might have been either protest or surrender, and as she stirred against him, Hayes became unwillingly aware of what he was about to do.

He was going to take all the sweetness Leigh had to give, going to make love to her with no thought for tomorrow. He was about to make her his, though he told himself he did not want her. He was about to claim her innocence without offering anything in return. The realization stabilized his careening senses, bringing unwelcome sobriety and incipient remorse. He knew what a woman's first man meant to her. It meant an end to childhood, an end to innocent dreams. For Hayes that realization brought home the terrible responsibility of what he was about to do and a concern for the consequences of his desire. Even as his lips sought the deep, warm cleft between her breasts, he knew he could not accept her girlish passion without spoiling all that made Leigh so wondrously unique, without tarnishing her ideals and shattering her illusions.

He buried his face against her throat, and drew a ragged breath. In his own way he did care about this woman, he grudgingly conceded. He admired her commitment and compassion, her vulnerability and her strength, but if he felt those things for her, he could not take advantage of her innocence to slake his transient lust or imply a commitment to her he was not willing to make. They said that conscience was a coward's curse, and perhaps in this he was a coward. For even though he ached to make Leigh his, he lacked the courage to entrust her with his tenderest emotions or risk again the terrible hurt that loving could bring.

And if he could not give her the love that was the other half of passion, what right did he have to accept all she had to give? Besides, the bitter thought intruded, what kind of man would take such a precious gift with the knowledge it was promised to another? Rationality returned to him and with it a disappointment that slashed through him like the sharpest knife. He did not want to deny himself the delight of teaching Leigh the meaning of passion, but if he was to remain unscathed, he had no choice but to deny them both.

With difficulty he met her eyes, still soft with trust and desire. Leigh was so much less worldly than he, so unaware of her body's secrets, so totally at the mercy of the sensations he had unscrupulously evoked in her that guilt began to stir within him. Yet he had not set out to corrupt and seduce her; in truth, he had been as lost and beguiled as she. But now that some measure of sense had returned to him, it was his responsibility to guard her honor, his duty to help her understand that what had passed between them was a mistake. With a vow to treat her gently, he began a slow retreat. He raised his lips from her dewy flesh, and bit by bit his hands withdrew to the safety of her forearms.

Hayes took a long breath before he spoke. "I'm sorry, Leigh, this is not what I meant to happen when I came to bring you soap. It's just that—well, it's just that you looked so appealing, so lovely, and I—'' He took another breath, irritated at the way he was blundering through his explanation. "I guess things just got out of hand," he finished lamely.

His husky words were strange to Leigh, and she was not quite sure what they meant. She only knew that something fundamental had changed between them, that in the space of a few heartbeats Hayes had stopped wanting her. Slowly, her world was opening up again, and Leigh became aware of where her body left off and his began. Gone was the closeness that bound them, and she was staggered by the loss. Confusion descended like the darkness before a storm as she realized the impersonal hands against her arms and the candor in Hayes's tone were the antithesis of all that

had gone before. She had only vaguely understood where
the tempest of sensations had been leading them, but she
was sure this cold rationality was not the proper end to
passion.

Then, Hayes was standing her on her own feet and
stepping away. He was suddenly uninvolved and distant,
restrained and in control, and Leigh did not understand the
reason for the change.

"What's the matter?" The question seemed to linger on
her lips, and it was a full minute before she realized that
she had not spoken aloud. Then, appalled by her own
cowardice, she turned her back on Hayes, bundling the
wrapper tightly around her and crossing her arms on her
breasts as if she felt a chill. Behind her she could sense
him waiting, but she had no idea what to say to him, no
way to explain her actions or ask him about his own. How
could she rationalize her response to him when she did not
understand it herself? Regret eroded any indignation she
might have been able to muster, and a simmering resentment grew inside her with the conviction that he could
explain everything, if only he chose to do so. To bare her
naïveté and confusion was unthinkable, but Leigh needed
desperately to comprehend both her attraction for Hayes
Banister and the reason for his complete and inexplicable
rejection.

Since she could not ask the questions that burned inside
her, Leigh turned to mundane things to hide her confusion
and buy her time to think. "Will you bring me the tub and
hot water you promised me so I can get on with my bath?"

Her voice was harsh and strangely stilted, and Hayes
made a vague, conciliatory gesture. He had bungled whatever explanation he had meant to give, and there was no
reason to believe that he could do better if he tried a
second time. A frown touched the corners of his lips as he
turned to go. "One hot bath coming right up, Leigh," he
conceded, "but after supper you and I need time to talk."

Leigh stood primping nervously before the mirror in Hayes Banister's cabin on the *Barbara Dean*, patting her freshly washed hair into place and smoothing the

skirt of her wrinkled gown. She had taken the gray silk dress she'd been wearing four months before when she arrived at Cairo from the bottom of her carpetbag in the hope that it would make her feel serene and self-assured when she met Hayes for dinner this evening. Leigh had wanted to look her best when she confronted him again, but somehow the creases in the delicate fabric, the unaccustomed corset and hoops, the wide skirts and frivolous style made her feel trussed up, awkward, and uncomfortable instead.

She had no desire to spend the evening with her host on the *Barbara Dean,* and the thought of more time in Hayes's company filled her with confusion and dread. Would he make more advances when he came for her tonight, and how would she respond if he did? Hot blood flooded her cheeks when she remembered what had passed between them this afternoon, and she pressed icy hands against her face as she tried to force those unsettling minutes from her mind. But the memory persisted: of his mouth assaulting hers, of his big body curved against her own, of his hands moving across her skin, and her eager reply.

How could something as innocent as brushing out her hair escalate into such mindless, headlong passion? Why had she responded to Hayes as she had? And who would have expected her, the serious, level-headed Leigh Pennington, to be capable of such abandon? The questions went round and round in her head and still defied an answer. But above all else she wished she understood why, when Hayes could have had all she had to give, he had turned away instead. She did not delude herself that he was a gentleman; he had forfeited all claim to the title that night on the porch. But then neither had she comported herself like the lady she had been raised to be. Though she had thought of little else as she bathed and dressed for dinner, she understood neither Hayes's actions nor her own in opening herself to him. How could she have been so weak and pliable, so base and forward? And why did she find such illicit delight in Hayes Banister's arms when she was promised to marry another man?

She turned abruptly from the looking glass and went to

light a lamp, unwilling to read the answer she feared she would find in the depths of her own shadowed eyes. It was growing dark on the river, and in a few minutes Hayes would come for her. Delicious smells were already wafting up from the galley on the deck below, and her mouth watered in response.

Still, she dreaded Hayes's knock on her door. What would she say when he came for her? Should she make an apology for her wanton behavior or expect one from him for his own? There was a time when she had been curious about this thing called passion, a time when she had sought it shamelessly in Lucas's embrace. But now that she was beginning to understand the scope of physical desire and realize its power, Leigh was frightened by what Hayes had been able to make her feel. He had taken liberties with her no gentleman would take, and she had reveled in his possession, offering him even more. Though her own reactions worried her, Leigh wanted, above all, to know why Hayes had pulled away, leaving her lost and confused. How could he have such control over his desires when she could claim no constraint on her own?

A knock at the door interrupted her musings, and Leigh took a long, unsteady breath before she answered it. Hayes was indeed outside, wearing a shawl-collared vest and deep brown coat buttoned over the fawn trousers he had worn this afternoon. Leigh's gaze moved slowly up from the crescent-shaped stickpin in his immaculately tied cravat, along his strong browned throat, past the flaring curve of his mouth until she came in contact with those crystal-blue eyes. As hard as she tried, it was impossible to read the expression in their pale, shimmering depths, and she did not know what to expect of him.

"You look very nice this evening, Leigh. Are you ready for dinner?" The polite, impersonal words were somehow anticlimactic after all the time she had spent dreading this confrontation, and his cool, impassive tone gave no hint of what he was thinking.

In reply, Leigh nodded wordlessly, and with no further comment he led her down the stairs to the salon on the deck below. Normally there would be other passengers sitting at the tables, but tonight, because of the nature of Hayes's business in Cairo, the salon was empty. One lone table before the window had been laid with a linen table-cloth, fine china and crystal, heavy silver plate, and a brace of candles. They illuminated only a small section of the long room and cast flickering reflections on the glass, making the flames appear to burn from the darkened river-bank beyond the window. Hayes pulled out one of the ornate gilt chairs with its jewel-toned upholstery, and Leigh seated herself gingerly.

Once he was settled in his own chair, Hayes poured a small glass of wine for them both, then gestured for the food to be served. As Leigh had ordered, there were chicken and biscuits in a rich gravy, a dish of green beans and another of caramelized carrots, as well as a plate of bread and one of relishes. She ate hungrily, more than willing to let the sounds of the meal fill the gaps in the conversation. Hayes seemed equally content with the silence and applied himself to the dinner with enthusiasm. But at last the food was consumed and the plates were removed by an efficient Negro steward.

"Have you room for dessert, ma'am?" the servant asked quietly. "The cook's made some mighty fine apple pie, if you're interested."

His shy but friendly smile encouraged Leigh. "I do believe I could eat a little," she agreed.

"And we'll have some coffee too, Marcus," Hayes added. As the man disappeared in the direction of the galley, Hayes turned to regard Leigh intently. Now that their meal was complete, he was going to turn his full attention to her once more, and the prospect filled her with misgivings. He had said this afternoon that they needed to talk, but she dreaded the inevitable subject, the galling familiarity he was sure to express, and the shame she would feel for her own salacious behavior. More than anything, Leigh wished she could find a way to escape to her cabin, but she was positive Hayes would have an answer for any excuse she might offer.

Banister waited until the pie, cups, and a large urn of coffee had been delivered to the table before he spoke.

"I've been wondering ever since yesterday afternoon about the time you spent in Cairo. What were your duties once you joined Mrs. Bickerdyke's staff? And did nursing prove to be everything you'd hoped?"

Somehow Leigh was not prepared for that question when there were a dozen others he might have asked, and it took her a moment to change from a defensive demeanor to one that would allow her to share a bit of what her life had been like in the last months.

She began with an account of her first meeting with Mary Ann Bickerdyke and Delia, and the difficulties she had encountered during her stay in Cairo. But as she spoke, her voice warmed with memories of the men and women who had shared the stifling hospital tents with her and the victories they'd won together over dirt and disease. There were stories of courage, of the kindness of one soldier to another, and the protectiveness the nurses felt for the men in their care. For the first time Leigh had a chance to realize the good she'd done and all she'd learned from Mary Ann Bickerdyke. In Cairo, she had been so wrapped up in the effort it took to survive from day to day that she'd had little time to reflect on what she'd accomplished, but now Hayes made her acknowledge it. With little more than nods and gestures, he helped her accept the gains she'd made and showed his approval for her having had the courage to follow her dreams. He was a good listener, just as he had been on that night on the porch, and in spite of all that had happened this afternoon, there was no barrier between them. Somehow he was a part of her, a special friend where no friendship had reason to exist, a confidant when there was no reason to trust, an ally when he should have been her enemy.

Banister sat back in his chair, eyeing her through the veil of fragrant pipe smoke. "Did you get any of the casualties from Grant's battle at Belmont?" he asked to break the lingering silence.

Leigh took a sip of her coffee before she answered. "More than two hundred wounded men came back on the steamers, and we met them at the dock with any wheeled vehicle we could commandeer." She shook her head slowly at the memory. "We had everything from Mary Safford's plush

carriage to wheelbarrows, whatever we could find to transport the men, but we few women were simply not equipped
to deal with the numbers or the kinds of wounds those men
had.'' A shudder passed through Leigh, speaking far more
eloquently than words of the scene at the wharf that cold
November day. ''They overran the hospital tents at Camp
Defiance in no time, so we began to take them to the St.
Charles Hotel, half-built as it was then. At least the roof
was on, though there were rooms where the walls weren't
up, and there was no way to heat the place.''

Leigh had been staring past Hayes into the darkness, but
she shifted her gaze until it met his. ''We have to find a
better way to care for our men after a battle. It was a day
and a half before all the wounds were dressed and there
weren't nearly enough nurses and doctors. So far we've
found no comfortable way to transport the wounded either,
and there are far too few hospital beds to accommodate
them all. When the boats came in after the battle, those
who had been hurt were stacked on the decks like cord
wood: cold, uncomfortable, and untended by anyone but
their comrades.'' She paused and her gaze narrowed
consideringly. ''Couldn't a riverboat be designed to transport the wounded: one with beds, operating rooms, and a
staff of its own?''

Hayes sat up a little straighter. ''There's probably a
good idea in that, Leigh. It's something we should look
into, at least. Could you give me some suggestions about
the facilities you would need on such a vessel? Now that
things at the shipyard have slowed down a little, I think I
could find time to do some drawings of the kind of ship
you're describing.''

''Do you really think it's feasible?'' There was excitement in her voice.

''I don't know why not. There are bound to be other
battles along the river, and the casualties will need to be
moved as quickly and painlessly as possible. The Western
Sanitary Commission has been looking into the use of
special railroad cars for transporting the wounded on land.
This seems to amplify the work they've done already.''

''That any volunteer group could be organized so quickly

and so well is quite miraculous,'' Leigh commented, speaking of the movement that had begun with a meeting of women in New York and had spread like wildfire throughout the North. "The good they've done in providing clothing and supplies for the soldiers was evident in Cairo mere weeks after the group was formed.''

"It's a good thing they've taken the responsibility of providing for the wounded,'' Hayes observed, drawing on his pipe, "since the Army Medical Corps seems incapable of making any attempt to care for them.''

Leigh nodded in agreement. "The Sanitary Commission's efficiency doesn't surprise me, though. We women are capable of far more than you men will give us credit for.''

"And you not the least of them,'' he pointed out gently, with a smile in his eyes.

Leigh took a moment to bask in his praise before she turned the conversation to him. "While I was nursing in Cairo, what were you doing in St. Louis?'' The question came naturally, an outgrowth of the unexpected camaraderie that seemed to exist between them.

"I've been building the best damned warships this world has ever seen,'' he answered without false modesty. "The idea of ironclad ships came out of the Crimea, back in the fifties, but the ones we've designed and constructed are unlike anything that's ever been built before. They're fast and maneuverable. They protect their crews from incoming fire—''

"And they'll be quite effective at raining destruction on the Confederate batteries along the riverbank,'' Leigh observed with resignation in her tone.

Hayes frowned at her, easily following the trend of her thoughts. She was concerned for her Confederate, for Lucas Hale, the man whose wife she would one day be. Unexpected resentment flared in Hayes, and with it a helplessness that only added fuel to his smoldering emotions. He and Lucas were on opposite sides of this conflict, and Leigh would forever see Hayes as a threat to the future she had planned. Both as a Yankee and as a man, he was Lucas Hale's enemy.

The parlor was filled with silence again, a silence that billowed in the shadows looming just beyond the candlelight. It was a silence filled with the differences between them, the conflicts and the loyalties that kept them apart, as well as the unwelcome emotions that drew them together.

As they sat without speaking, Hayes studied Leigh across the table, feeling her disapproval, sensing the fear she must feel for the man she loved. Because Lucas Hale was fighting for the Confederacy, it was likely Leigh had no idea where he was or even if he was well and safe. How could she help but see the ships he built for the Union and the passion that had flared between them this afternoon as threats to all she held dear? But even though Hayes understood, it did not make her censure any easier to bear.

Unable to watch the accusation in her face, his gaze dropped to the hand that rested against the tablecloth. Curled in upon itself, it was tapered and long-fingered, the shape graceful and refined. But it was a broad and capable hand as well, hinting at a physical strength and stamina that he would not have expected in a woman born to a life of ease. The nails were trimmed close and the skin was red and chapped from the days she had spent in the service of others. It was a hand that could gesture eloquently as she spoke, and could no doubt sew the finest seams, but he also knew it was a hand that had offered comfort to the wounded and ease to the dying. Without volition, his own hand crept across the expanse of linen to claim hers, feeling the coolness of her fingertips against his palm, the rasping roughness of her skin against his. His thumb traced the gentle curve of her fingers from the sensitive tips upward toward the reddened knuckles, until it encountered the heavy ruby ring she wore on the third finger of her left hand. He had never noticed the ring before, never seen the bloodred stone set in an intricate gold filigree, but he immediately recognized its significance and loosened his hold on her.

His own hand contracted sharply, balling into a fist. "Why don't you tell me about Lucas Hale?" he suggested.

Leigh took a long breath as she studied him, understanding exactly what he wanted to know. "Lucas and I have known each other all our lives," she began softly. "Our families have lived next door for as long as I can remember. We grew up together, went to school together, got in scrapes together. Lucas, his brother Brandon, and I shared all our spotty childhood diseases, our birthdays, our haunts, our toys, our adventures. Lucas fought my battles for me when he could, dried my tears when I cried, carried me home when I broke my ankle jumping off the carriage-house roof the summer I was eight. He has always been there when I needed him: to get my cat out of the tree when I was too little to climb it, to kill the spiders in the attic when we went up there to play, to teach me to waltz when my mother said I was too young to learn. He's a special kind of man: honorable, gallant, brave, and good. He's all that's familiar, all that's safe and secure." She paused for a moment, then continued with marked deliberation. "Lucas is a very precious part of my life, just as I am of his. We were meant to be together always, and when the war is over, we shall be."

It was a statement that brooked no argument, yet there was a long silence as Hayes pondered her meaning. "You've made no mention of love," he pointed out quietly.

Leigh drew herself up taller in her chair. "Of course I love Lucas!" she declared. "I've loved him all my life!"

Hayes's thumb stroked the bowl of his pipe, and he considered the curve of its stem as if it held some compelling mystery. "Have you, Leigh?" he finally asked without even glancing at her. "Do you love Lucas as you did as a child, or have you come to love him as a woman?" He well knew the weight and cruelty of his words, but he could no more have stopped the question than he could have turned away without hearing her reply.

"I love him as a wife must love her husband, with tenderness and confidence and trust."

His gaze rose to her face. "There's more to a marriage than tenderness and trust." His unspoken challenge lay between them, like a serpent ready to strike. Their eyes clashed across the table, testing, measuring, daring, until he was forced to give it voice. "Do you love him with passion, Leigh, with a passion that ignites your soul?"

Leigh inhaled slowly and raised her head. "And why must a woman love her husband that way? She will still bear him children, still be able to satisfy his needs. There are more important things a wife must feel for her husband: trust, obedience, and respect. I love Lucas in that way, and together we will make a strong and enduring marriage."

"A strong and enduring marriage," he goaded her almost without meaning to. "Is that what you really want?"

"Of course it is. Yes." There was a quiver of barely suppressed anger in Leigh's voice when she replied, and he could see the color blazing in her cheeks. "I want a marriage where I can be content, a marriage where I can be at peace. A marriage should offer solace, not conflict; unity, not division. Lucas and I have always complemented each other, and he knows me down to my bones."

Hayes drew absently on his pipe and found it had gone out. With a frown he set it on the table. He was not sure just what it was he hoped to accomplish with his questions about Leigh and her love for Lucas Hale, but he could not leave the subject alone. Was he trying to convince himself of the depth of Leigh's love for Lucas so he could put her out of his mind and be free again? Did he want a reason to hope?

Before he had time to contemplate the answers to his questions, Leigh was standing over him, her flushed face set and her hands clenched together at her waist. "I've had quite enough of this inquisition for one evening, Mister Banister, so if you will excuse me, I'm going up to bed."

Hayes rose to stand beside her and, with a show of cordiality he did not feel, took her arm. "At least let me see you to your cabin," he offered.

Outside the salon the clear, crisp November moon had painted the sky a deep pewter blue and washed the decks with silvery light. Moonbeams danced across the water like a thousand spangles, laying a shimmering pathway to the bank far beyond. But even the beauty of the night could not banish the tension bubbling between these two people, and as they walked, all that was in harmony between them was the sound of their footsteps ringing on the wooden deck.

At the door to the cabin, Leigh paused as if she wanted one last word on the subject before they parted. But Hayes sensed he could claim a victory in this argument with one simple act. Smiling to himself, he swayed toward her with the sweetness of her lips his goal, but Leigh saw his ploy and stopped it with a hand braced against his chest.

Hidden in the deep blue shadow he cast against the wall, Hayes could not read or interpret Leigh's expression, so when she spoke at last, the mingled determination and entreaty in her voice surprised him. "Hayes," she began in a whisper, "promise me—"

He took a breath, strangely moved by her tone. "What, Leigh? What do you want?"

Leigh heard the tenderness and concern in his question and paused in confusion. What was it she wanted Hayes to promise? she asked herself: not to undermine her feelings for Lucas Hale; not to make her fall in love with him; not to arouse in her the dangerous, delightful sensations that could only end in her downfall? Whatever she asked would reveal far too much about her feelings for this strong, compelling stranger.

"Promise me—oh, Hayes, promise me you won't try to change the way I feel about Lucas, not until the war is over, not until he's come back safely."

Hayes could feel her eyes on him and could just barely make out the stark expression she wore. A hundred questions circled in his brain, but the tone of her voice forbade him any answers. "Leigh, I—"

Her hand caught one of his, and her urgency communicated itself to him in the most basic way possible. "Hayes, please give me your word."

As they stood side by side in the moonlight, he was painfully aware of everything about her: the scent that clung to her alabaster skin; the lush, long-limbed body inches from his own; the scope of the feelings she was capable of arousing in him. Still, he well knew the answer he should make. Why was it so hard to give her the promise she was seeking? Leigh was beautiful, desirable, unique, but he didn't want the kind of involvement she would demand, she would deserve. He wanted to be free, unencumbered, unscathed. This afternoon he could have taken everything she had to give, and he had refused her. Why was he hesitant to give her his promise now?

Yet when he spoke at last, the words were more difficult than he had supposed. "I won't try to come between you and Lucas Hale," he swore solemnly, "not now, not ever."

He waited in silence for some reply, and when none came, he continued harshly. "There, I've given my word. Does that satisfy you? Does that make you happy?" He was angry, confused, and in pain, though he didn't fully understand the reason.

Leigh's voice was as soft and cool as the November night. "Yes, Hayes, yes. It pleases me very much." She stood for another moment watching him before she turned away. Then, without another word, she went inside and closed the cabin door behind her.

6 ❦

The city had changed in her absence, changed
in ways Leigh Pennington had not foreseen. It was grayer,
grimmer, busy with an industry that reflected the stark
determination of a country at war. It was harsher, frag-
mented, divided now by things that had always been toler-
ated. It was no longer a city dependent on the trade
between the industrial North and the agricultural South for
its livelihood, and that change showed on the riverfront
and in the streets near the customs house. From the moment the *Barbara Dean* had nosed in to a berth along the
cobblestone levy late Sunday afternoon, Leigh had been
aware of the difference in the town she loved. The dark
clouds that hung low over the jutting spire of the old
French cathedral and hovered above the impressive courthouse dome gave her a sense of impending doom that
became more acute as she watched the familiar surroundings pass beyond the carriage window. In spite of her
delight at being home, nothing could divert her from the
menace that roamed the streets in the guise of Yankee
uniforms or the sinister presence that threatened the life
she remembered so well. Nursing at Fort Defiance, she
had become accustomed to seeing men clothed in military
blue, but somehow when they dotted the streets where
she'd grown up and filled the park where she had played
as a child, she felt overwhelmed by their numbers. War

had intruded on her home, and she resented both the
intrusion and the inevitable change it brought.

Nor were things within the town house on Locust Street
as she had left them, either. Horace had accepted a civilian
position with the quartermaster corps, procuring food and
supplies for the growing number of troops being mustered
through the city. In revenge for his blatant support of the
Union, Althea had taken it upon herself to make the
decision one he would heartily regret.

Only the position at City General Hospital lived up to its
promise. After the tents at Fort Defiance and the first days
in the converted hotel in Cairo, the polished floors, the
spotless kitchen, the adequate help, and the comfortable
surroundings were a welcome change. Though she missed
Delia and Mother Bickerdyke terribly, Leigh liked the
hospital and respected the chief surgeon, Dr. Hodgen. He
was an efficient, capable man, and though it was obvious
that he was not totally at ease with the female nurses in his
charge, he treated Leigh with a deference that made it
evident she had already proved her worth. To her amazement Leigh found herself considered something of a hero-
ine. To have had the courage to leave the safety of her
home before it was acceptable to do so and offer her
services as a nurse at a rough-and-ready place like Fort
Defiance was seen by her colleagues as brave and daring.
But Leigh dismissed their awe with an easy laugh and was
thankful instead for the good, basic nursing the experience
with Mary Ann Bickerdyke had taught her.

Late one afternoon not long after her return to St. Louis,
Leigh was trudging toward the horsecar with a monumen-
tal pile of linen bundled in her arms. The pipes to the
laundry room in the basement of the hospital had frozen
with the first hard frost, and, like several of the other
nurses with domestic help at home, Leigh had volunteered
to take a portion of the dirty clothes to be washed and
returned the next day.

She was just picking her way along the uneven sidewalk
on Fifth Street, wishing she had either taken fewer sheets
or accepted the help one of the orderlies had offered, when
all forward progress abruptly ceased and a familiar voice
assailed her.

"Is that really a walking bundle of clothes I see, or is there a person behind it somewhere?" Grinning, Hayes Banister peeked around the pile of wash, his silvery-blue eyes full of mischief.

There was a sudden catch in Leigh's chest at the sight of him, and she did her best to dismiss it as nothing more than a reaction of surprise. Hayes had not made any attempt to call on her since she had left the *Barbara Dean*, and she had convinced herself she was glad he was keeping his word. But now, with his deeply dimpled smile shining at her from behind the towering bundle of clothes and his vital presence making her forget the long hours she had spent at the hospital, Leigh was unconditionally glad to see him.

"Could you use a hand with this?" Hayes offered, shifting some of the weight of the clothes from her even before she'd had a chance to answer him. "Where on earth are you taking such a mountain of laundry, anyway?"

"I'm headed for the horsecar, and if you can help me get these things that far—"

Hayes began to laugh. "The horsecar? You aren't serious! They'll probably make you pay double fare for all of this!"

"Well, there was a problem with the water in the laundry at the hospital," Leigh explained breathlessly, struggling to maintain her hold on the mound of wash. "Since we'll need these in the morning, I thought if I could get everything home, I could wash them and let them dry overnight so they'd be ready to be used tomorrow."

"A noble project, to be sure," Hayes agreed, "and one I'd be willing to donate carriage fare to, at least." Taking the entire bundle from her and tucking it under his arm as best he could, he waved down a passing carriage and helped Leigh climb inside. The huge wad of dirty wash came next, followed by Hayes himself squeezing into the narrow seat. Because of what had happened on the *Barbara Dean*, Leigh now suffered momentary misgivings about being alone with Hayes, but wedged into the hired cab with the laundry piled high between them, Leigh's concern evaporated.

"You've picked such a stimulating companion for this

excursion, my dear,'' Hayes complained, peering over the top of the bundle. ''Are you sure all this isn't just a ploy to keep me at a distance?''

Leigh giggled at the thought. ''But of course it is, Hayes. I just knew you would be lurking outside the hospital today waiting for me, so I decided to bring a chaperon to keep you in your place.''

''Well, you've certainly succeeded admirably. I couldn't move a muscle even if I did have designs on you.''

''Just as I planned,'' Leigh crooned, grinning, ''just as I planned.'' There was something in Hayes Banister that never failed to garner a response in her: something vital, something exciting, something she could never bring herself to name. The air seemed to crackle with energy when they were together, with humor, with tension, with life. He filled her with conflicting emotions: a sense of security so elemental and profound that she could take refuge in its strength, and a threat to her future that took her breath when she thought of the havoc his mere presence could create.

''Now that you've been back a while, how are you finding St. Louis?'' Hayes inquired. ''Is the position at the hospital everything you hoped it would be? And how are your parents?''

She had been so caught up in her own thoughts it took Leigh a moment to answer. ''Oh, the nursing position is fine. Our facilities are so much better here than they were at Fort Defiance.''

''But?'' Hayes must have sensed the hesitancy in her voice, an underlying reserve he did not understand.

Leigh glanced out the window. Did she really want to tell her problems to this man? Somehow he seemed to invite her confidences, but could Hayes even begin to fathom how much the change in the city distressed her? Would she be able to explain about the strain between her parents and her own feelings of impending disaster whenever she heard them snarling at each other? Was he capable of the insight necessary to recognize her concerns and fears for what they were, if she did decide to open herself to him?

"I guess I just miss Delia and Mother Bickerdyke," she lied instead.

In silence the hired carriage pulled up in front of the Pennington town house, and Hayes took the laundry as far as the door.

"I thank you for your help this afternoon, Hayes," Leigh told him with a smile. "I'll admit, it might have been a real challenge to handle this laundry in a horsecar."

"But there's not a challenge of any kind you'd willingly avoid, is there?" he observed wryly, answering with a smile of his own.

"Not when it comes to the welfare of my patients," she assured him. "Mother Bickerdyke taught me that lesson very well."

Hayes acknowledged her words with a nod of his head and turned his attention to other topics. "Do you usually leave the hospital at this time of the day?"

"Yes, usually. The shift I'm working is over at four. Why?"

"Oh, just wondering, I guess."

But the next day it was evident why Hayes had asked the question, and his reasons became more obvious in the cold November and December days that followed. She found him waiting for her at the main doors of the big, marble-fronted building three or four times a week, sometimes with a hired carriage parked at the curb, sometimes with nothing more in mind than walking her as far as the trolley stop. Leigh came to welcome the sight of him leaning patiently against a lamppost, to crave the spark that leaped between them, filling her with new energy no matter how long and difficult her day had been. They did nothing more than talk when he took her home or as they stood waiting for the horsecar, chatting about mundane things mostly: about the escalating price of essentials and the steadily worsening winter weather. They discussed things at the shipyards and the hospital, the difficulty the Army was having finding good-quality supplies to feed and clothe its men, the plodding progress of the war, and the skirmishes being fought in the country to the west.

As the days passed, Leigh found herself looking forward to their meetings, the few moments of friendly companionship before she faced the deteriorating situation in the house on Locust Street. She welcomed the chance to express her opinions on the news of the day without fear of censure by one parent or the other and enjoyed listening to what Hayes had to say as well. She might even have asked him to share a meal with her family as he had months before, but she would not invite anyone to a dinner table where words were fired back and forth like salvos between armies at war. These were dark days for the city, for the country, and for Leigh herself, and the few carefree minutes she shared with Hayes Banister at the end of the day became a luxury she treasured.

As they walked toward the trolley one afternoon just before Christmas, Hayes drew her urgently into the shadowed doorway of a storefront shop. His face was tensed and serious as he stood over her, and there was a strange intensity in the depths of his blue-gray eyes. For a moment Leigh appreciatively noted the wedges of color the cold had brought to his cheeks and the few wet flakes of snow that sparkled in his hair, before concern and curiosity overwhelmed her.

"I want you to send these south for me, Leigh," he murmured, pressing several letters into her hands. "They need to go through as soon as possible." When Leigh only stood staring up at him in silence, he went on, his voice soft and persuasive. "I'm well aware that mail is smuggled through the lines, and I am quite certain you know exactly how it's done."

Leigh watched Banister in confusion, stunned by what he was asking her to do. In a city like St. Louis where loyalties were divided, much went on without the government's knowledge or sanction. As with any activity that existed outside the strictures of the law, there were risks, penalties, and dangers. Sending mail to the Confederacy was no exception, and she shook her head at first, filled with questions.

"But why are you sending letters south, Hayes? Who are these messages for?"

He scowled down at her in evident irritation, clearly unwilling to answer her. "Can you send them for me or not?"

"Yes, I can send them for you. I've sent letters of my own, and I know the courier."

"You've sent them to Lucas Hale, no doubt," Hayes accused, then glanced away.

"In the hope they would find Lucas, yes," she said, nodding. "And though the mail does go out with some regularity, you need to understand that there's no guarantee these letters will reach their destination. Or that there will be an answer."

He heard the sharp regret in her tone as she spoke the last sentence, and a frown tugged at the corners of his mouth. "I don't expect an answer," he growled. "Getting them through the lines is all that's important."

"But who are they for?" Leigh asked again.

"What the hell difference does it make to you?" Banister exploded. The words were angry and curt, and he clearly resented her questions. Then, as if regretting his sharp words, he sighed with resignation and began to explain. "My mother has some family down in Tennessee, a cousin I've always been particularly close to, a great-uncle, and some others. I promised her I'd send them Christmas greetings. They—they used to come to visit us for the holidays, and she didn't want the season to pass without someone sending word."

"But surely your mother knows of people in Cincinnati who— "

"Damn it, Leigh, if you won't help me, at least tell me where to take the letters."

"No, no, I'll take them for you. They would know you're a Yankee; it might be dangerous." She was looking past him, thinking aloud. She didn't believe the tale he'd told her about the letters being for his family, but if it was so important for him to get the messages through the lines, she would take them to the woman up on Chestnut Street herself. Without so much as a glance at the addresses, Leigh shoved the envelopes into her reticule. Beside her Hayes sagged with relief.

The wind whipped along the street, making them both shudder with cold as they huddled in the doorway and Hayes's arm tightened around her protectively. "Thank you, Leigh," he whispered against her hair. "Thank you for agreeing to get the letters through."

But Leigh did not hear his words of appreciation or feel the warmth of him beside her. Instead she was staring past him through the gathering dusk with doubt in the depths of her spruce-green eyes and a sudden chill of foreboding in her heart.

December 28, 1861

Hayes Banister noticed Leigh the moment she appeared in the doorway at the far end of the double parlor where the dancing had just begun, and, as always, something warm and exciting lit inside him at the sight of her. In a bottle-green gown of watered silk and with holly leaves woven through her garnet hair, she was a strikingly beautiful woman. The deep ruffle of ecru lace dripping from the wide neckline pointed up the creamy slope of her shoulders, and the wide, bell-shaped skirt with rows of delicate ruching gave her a regal air that made her seem aloof, yet compelling. Even from across the room Hayes felt her power to stir him, and he watched with a glow in his eyes as she stood quietly conversing with their host for this evening's festivities.

In the weeks since her return to St. Louis, Hayes had seen a good deal of Leigh Pennington. Their brief meetings had quickly become the high point of his days, and he found himself watching the clock impatiently in the afternoon, waiting for the time when he could leave James Eads's offices and walk over to the hospital. After spending twelve or fourteen hours of each twenty-four hunched over a drawing board, Hayes enjoyed the chance to escape from his assignments and get out in the air. Now that the ironclad project was nearly complete, there were other kinds of boats to design and build for use along the Mississippi: mortar barges, transports, tinclads, and rams, all meant to disrupt Confederate shipping and open the river channel to the south. It was stimulating and demanding work, but it could easily consume all of a man's time and energies. And as the days progressed, he found in

Leigh's quiet company a delightful diversion to the satisfying but solitary life he was living.

Checking the knot in his gray and white pinstriped necktie, then stroking one hand along the lapel of his frock coat, Hayes skirted the dance floor, moving purposefully in Leigh's direction. That he was drawn to her like steel to a magnet no longer troubled him. In the weeks since she had returned from Cairo, he and Leigh had become a part of each other's lives: friends and confidants, allies and coconspirators, until somehow it seemed only right that he should be able to claim a place by her side.

He greeted her with a formal bow and an extravagant compliment and received her bright smile and a deep curtsy in return. It was not until they were swirling across the dance floor a few minutes later that he noticed the almost imperceptible lines of strain around her mouth. "Is something bothering you, Leigh?" he asked with a hint of concern in his tone.

At first she shook her head and glanced away, but when he pressed her, Leigh relented and began to explain. "Mother and Father had a terrible row before we came tonight, and I'm afraid they'll continue it here."

His arm tightened around her impulsively as they executed a sweeping turn. "I don't think you need to worry, Leigh," he reassured her. "Your parents are both sensible people. They won't do anything to embarrass themselves, or you."

Leigh drew a heavy sigh. "That might have been true once, Hayes, but I'm not so sure anymore. There was a time when conflicts were settled at home, but my parents have changed since the war began, and so has the society we're living in. Once both factions in St. Louis mixed freely, but now Northerners and Southerners don't even speak when they pass on the street. And at a party like this one, given to celebrate General Halleck's appointment as Commander of the Mississippi, a Confederate can hardly feel at home. Mother didn't want to come tonight, and I can hardly blame her, but Father insisted."

The tension between Leigh's parents had been painfully evident last spring, Hayes reflected, long before the bitter battles at Bull Run and Wilson's Creek had decisively split both the nation and Missouri in two. As he considered what he knew of the older Penningtons, Hayes found himself wondering once again at all the things Leigh never talked about, never shared. How had the forces that were dividing the nation, turning brother against brother and father against son, affected the already perilous relationship between her dissenting parents? And what toll was all of this conflict taking on Leigh? If she had been torn and confused that night on the porch at the beginning of the war, what must she be feeling now? For the first time, Hayes found himself speculating about how the volatile atmosphere Leigh had lived in all her life might have tempered and shaped her personality. Did it explain why she craved safety and familiarity above all else, why she had held herself aloof and found it difficult to trust?

"I'm just afraid," Leigh continued, interrupting Hayes's thoughts, "that Mother may feel compelled to create a scene of some sort to show Father how strongly she feels about being forced to come." There was a subtle sadness in the turn of her lips, a stark resignation in her expression as she spoke, and Hayes wanted nothing more than to hold her close and make her problems disappear.

"Will you help me keep Mother out of trouble tonight, Hayes, dance with her or take her away for a cup of punch if things get difficult?" Leigh's luminous eyes were filled with entreaty.

That she would ask his help at all in such a delicate and personal matter confirmed the depth of her concern, and Hayes readily agreed. But as the evening progressed, no dire circumstances arose, and they both began to relax and enjoy themselves. It was infinitely pleasant to have the time to spend in each other's company without a freezing wind or the arrival of a horsecar to cut their visit short, utterly delightful to be able to talk and laugh together as part of a larger group, without fear of censure for their behavior. They ate supper in their host's conservatory with a dozen other young couples, then whiled away the evening dancing. Aaron Crawford claimed a waltz or two with Leigh and several with her mother; Hayes spent time with Horace Pennington, drinking good Kentucky bourbon and speculating on General Grant's spring offensive. Since

Grant was a former resident of the city, there was more than a casual interest in the military man's prowess, and as they stood watching their women whirled around the floor by other partners, Pennington expressed the somewhat unpopular view that Grant knew what he was doing.

"I was right about poor General Lyon," he declared, finishing off the last of the whiskey in his glass, "and I'm right about Grant, too. There's very little comparison between a man's ability to sell real estate, or even firewood, and his ability to lead an army of men. Grant's tough and ruthless; he's single-minded and shrewd. His leadership is just what the Union needs to win some good, solid victories."

When the dance was over the women were returned to an alcove near the front windows where the two men waited. For a few moments they all stood together, Althea and Leigh fanning themselves and sipping punch, recovering from their exertions on the dance floor. But as the musicians struck up the first bars of the next selection, General Halleck came toward them across the room and stopped before the older woman.

"Mrs. Pennington," he addressed Althea with the slightest of bows, "I have been admiring you from afar all evening, and I hope you will consent to dance this waltz with me."

Halleck was the highest-ranking Federal officer in the West, and Althea immediately saw her opportunity to embarrass both this pompous Yankee general and revenge herself on her overbearing husband. Not pausing to consider the consequences or the censure her actions might bring, Althea seized the chance to make her feelings about the Union patently obvious. With her sweetest simle on her lips and a reckless gleam in her eyes, she drew herself up to her full height and affected her thickest Louisiana drawl. "Ah declare, General Halleck, though Ah'd rather dance with a pig than a Yankee general, it just so happens that Mr. Banister has already claimed this dance."

For a moment everyone within earshot stood with mouths agape as Althea Pennington faced down the furious Federal officer. Her support of the Confederacy was well known throughout the community, but no one had suspected she would do anything to show her hatred of the Union so blatantly. Then Hayes, instantly deciding the best way to defuse the situation was to do exactly as Althea said, offered her his arm and led her onto the dance floor.

Horace sputtered an apology for his wife's behavior, but the affront to the general had been a grave one, and there were really no words to make the situation less difficult or embarrassing than it was. With his face crimson and his mouth set in an angry line, General Halleck beat a hasty retreat, and on the other side of the room another lady quickly accepted the invitation Althea had refused.

Once the tempo of the party picked up again, Horace Pennington began to mutter, half to himself. "Why does she do things like that to me? Why does she have to be so damned defiant?"

Filled with concern, Leigh laid a comforting hand on her father's sleeve. "You knew Mother didn't want to come tonight. Why couldn't you just let her plead a headache and stay at home instead of demanding she accompany you?"

Horace's mouth narrowed angrily, but there was resignation in the way his shoulders sagged. "Have you taken her side, too, Leigh? Have I lost your love as well?"

Leigh's eyes burned with unshed tears as she tried to reassure him. "You haven't lost my love, or Mother's either, but none of us can go on as we are. You know how she hates the work you're doing for the Union, yet you continue with the Quartermaster Corps as if what she thinks doesn't matter."

"A man must do what he feels is right," Horace defended himself. "You above all others should understand that, Leigh. My loyalty is to the Union, to the abolition of slavery, to Abraham Lincoln."

"And what of your loyalty to your wife?"

"It's she who owes her loyalty to me, her loyalty and her obedience. I can't abide any more defiance or tolerate her harping."

"And what will you do, Father, to stop her?" Leigh demanded. "Will you abandon your work for the North or be less vocal in your support? Can't you let her know that what she thinks and feels is at least as important as your political views? Because if you can't or won't make any concessions, I think you're going to drive her south, back to where she can live her life without this constant conflict.''

"I'll see her in hell before I'll let her go south," Horace blustered.

"I think perhaps she's already in hell," Leigh snapped, turning his words against him, "and so, for that matter, are you."

She spat the condemnation defiantly, but with a feeling of defeat, then swept across the room with no clear idea of where she was going. She needed quiet, sanctuary, a place to be alone and regain her composure after the unpleasant scene in the parlor.

Hayes watched her go with concern in his eyes, a concern that was seen and carefully noted by Althea Pennington. "You care for my daughter, don't you, Mr. Banister?" she observed quietly.

Hayes swept her into a graceful turn, using the time to frame an answer. "Yes, ma'am, I do care about Leigh, and I hate to see what you and Mr. Pennington are doing to her."

Brilliant color rose in Althea's cheeks. "What goes on in our house is no concern of yours, Mr. Banister," she warned. "Besides, I love my daughter and would never do anything to hurt her."

"Do you love her? I find that hard to believe after the little scene I just witnessed."

"Horace forced me to come tonight; I was only paying him back for what he'd done," the older woman defended herself. "Can't you see that?"

"What I saw was a selfish and vindictive act, meant to hurt people you claim to love," Banister replied, his silvery blue eyes flinty.

"That's not true!" Althea began, but Hayes cut her short.

"It is true, and I think you know it. I'm only beginning to understand what scenes like that do to your daughter, and it's clear to me, Mrs. Pennington, that you haven't a clue to how much arguments between you and your husband affect her."

"Leigh understands how difficult it is for me to live with what Horace is doing to support the Union." Althea continued as if she had not heard him. "She knows how I feel when I realize he's trying to destroy my brothers and the way of life I love."

"Yes, she's aware of how you feel," he conceded, "and she understands that your husband is only trying to live by his own convictions. Leigh's a very understanding person, and in this case it's tearing her apart!"

Althea took the measure of his words, weighing them against her own perceptions of the daughter she loved. That there was more truth in what he said than in her angry protests was painfully evident.

Her face had softened with regret when she spoke again. "You do care for Leigh, don't you, Mr. Banister? You care for her very deeply."

Hayes saw the change in her expression and felt a certain grim satisfaction that she was acknowledging the consequences of her actions. "I value Leigh's friendship very much," he admitted carefully.

"Ah, her friendship, is it?" A knowing look lurked in her eyes. "Well, then, Mr. Banister, I'm glad you are her friend. Leigh needs friends right now, friends she can talk to and confide in. That's never come easy for her, and with both her grandfather and Bran gone—"

Hayes's brows drew together. "Bran?"

"Brandon Hale, Lucas's brother. Surely she's mentioned him to you. He was her best friend when they were all growing up."

"Not Lucas?" His tone was puzzled.

"Lucas? No, never Lucas." Althea shook her head. "There might have been a time when he was her hero, and they always got on well, but it was Bran who was her special friend. And I think she misses him terribly since he's gone off to war."

Hayes digested the information in silence. "And which is most important to a woman, I wonder, a friend or a lover?" he mused at last.

"I think a man who could be both a friend and a lover would have a distinct advantage, Mr. Banister, don't you?"

A swell in the music swept away any answer Hayes

might have given, but he was still pondering Althea Pennington's pointed observation when he went to look for her daughter some minutes later.

Leigh did find the solace she was seeking in the book-lined study at the end of the hall. After she had closed the tall double doors behind her to guarantee privacy, she moved across the room toward the fire burning in the grate and stretched her cold, trembling fingers toward the blaze. Silent tears seeped down her cheeks as she stood drinking in the fire's warmth while the scene that had taken place in the parlor only moments before played and replayed before her eyes.

Her parents were going to destroy each other; that fact was now painfully clear to her. Their behavior tonight gave evidence that the antagonism growing between them was no longer limited to the confines of their home. Surely such a public declaration of their marital difficulties boded ill for their future together. Yet she could not believe that the reason for their hostility lay only in their differing political opinions. Such vehemence, such bitterness, such pain must have its roots in something more basic than the questions that divided the nation. It must go far deeper than the conflicts over slavery and union to have instilled such hatred in people who had once been deeply in love.

If the stories her grandfather had told her were true, the marriage between Horace Pennington and Althea Mattingly was indeed based in love. Because the Mattinglys, an old plantation family, had refused to consider a trader, a Northerner, a humble doctor's son, as worthy of Althea's consideration, Horace and Althea had eloped after knowing each other for a very short time. But when Leigh's parents had returned to the Mattingly plantation from a six-month-long honeymoon in Europe, Althea had already been great with child, and her family had been forced to be more accepting. If they had not welcomed the young St. Louis businessman into their midst, they had at least instilled a sense of the trust they were placing in him by granting him their youngest daughter's hand.

But though the strong physical love the couple shared had been evident from the start, the unification of their personalities had been turbulent and stormy. Both Horace

Pennington and his bride were stubborn, and bitter battles
ensued when they did not agree. Yet as violent as their
fights were, they were soon made up and forgotten. When
she was a child, it had always confused Leigh that her
parents could be shouting at the top of their voices one
minute and snuggled in each other's arms the next. And
though it was years before she understood all the implications, Leigh had always blamed herself for her parents'
problems, and for her untimely birth forcing them into a
marriage that neither of them might otherwise have considered. Her grandfather had tried to reassure her, but she had
never totally believed his explanations.

Instead, when the shouting started, Leigh would retreat
to her room with the door tightly closed to shut out the
ruckus, or to the genteel atmosphere at the Hale house
where no one ever raised his voice. Nor was she ever quite
sure, when all was quiet at last, if both her parents would
be there together, or if their loud, upsetting arguments
would finally succeed in destroying the security the childish Leigh had craved.

Now, with the war to further separate and divide them,
her childhood fears seemed to be coming true. Althea and
Horace no longer made up between the battles, and whatever the basic differences between them had been during
the turbulent years of their marriage, those differences had
taken on new and terrifying proportions.

Leigh turned from her dark contemplation at the sound
of the door to the study opening, and briefly Aaron Crawford
was silhouetted against the brightness and the noise of the
party.

"I've been waiting to have a few words alone with you
all evening," he began, crossing the dimly lit room to
where Leigh stood before the fire. "It seems you've been
so busy since you returned to St. Louis, I haven't had a
chance to talk to you."

"I don't have much time beyond my nursing duties. I
work all day and try to write letters for my patients in the
evening so that their people will have at least some idea
what's happened to them."

"Leigh Pennington, altruism personified." His tone

mocked her. "Is this devotion to nursing one of the things you learned in Cairo from the Bickerdyke woman?"

"It's a lesson Mother Bickerdyke is well qualified to teach, I think," Leigh observed.

"Did you learn a great deal besides that while you were at Fort Defiance?"

"Yes, Aaron, a great deal. I'm glad I had the chance to go."

At the trend in the conversation, his smile became hard and predatory. "I'm pleased to hear you feel such gratitude; I only hope you aren't averse to showing a little appreciation for the opportunity I gave you."

"Show my appreciation?" she asked. "Whatever do you mean?"

"I think you are quite aware of what I mean, Leigh, so let's not mince words when our time together is bound to be short." Like the good military man he was, Crawford had maneuvered for the best position, flanking her and cutting off her route to the door.

Leigh was quickly becoming aware of his intent, and with a swirl of apprehension she realized the form he meant his reward to take. "Aaron, I do thank you for the help you gave me in securing the position at Fort Defiance," she began, belatedly trying to back away, "but I assumed the good I could do for those poor soldiers would be payment enough for any favor." At the time she had asked him for the letter of introduction to Colonel Oglesby, she had sensed that the service was not without its price, but in the ensuing months she had forgotten that she owed Crawford any debt.

"You're really quite naïve, my dear, if you believed that your gratitude was all I wanted. And now I think the time has come to collect on my favor."

Leigh tried to think of some way to put him off, but his slate-gray eyes were fastened intently on her lips, and his arms were closing about her. With her uneasiness growing, she remembered all the whispers she'd heard about his reputation, about the liberties he had taken with other women. Determinedly she placed her palms against his chest and bent back in an attempt to avoid him. "Aaron, please," she gasped, "please don't do this."

But his mouth was descending to devour hers, and his hand had come up to cup her breast, claiming it as if he had a perfect right to hold and fondle her as he chose. His mouth was hot, moving over hers in a burning violation, and Leigh tried to squirm away. Still Aaron held her fast, and his kisses became harder and more demanding, as if her struggles to escape excited him.

"Sweet, sweet girl," he murmured, crushing her close. "So young, so soft, so lovely, the very essence of your beautiful mother."

Crawford's breath was heavy with the smell of whiskey and stale tobacco, and his musky scent threatened to overwhelm Leigh. Incensed by his words and the liberties he was taking, she fought to turn her head away. In painful retribution for denying him her lips, he took sharp little bites of the silky skin along her throat, making her twist even more violently against him. Panic leaped inside Leigh as the discomfort grew. "Aaron, stop! Please stop; you're hurting me," she protested in desperation.

Then abruptly she was torn from Aaron's arms by a force that was overwhelming strong, but surprisingly gentle. She was grasped around the waist and swept behind a taller, broader body, and it was a moment before she realized that her salvation had been accomplished by someone with more than a little experience in the capacity of her rescuer.

"What the hell are you doing here?" Crawford growled, angry at having been deprived of the woman he had long been stalking.

"Defending the lady's honor, it seems," Hayes Banister snarled back. The two men stood facing each other for a long moment on the verge of the most primitive and basic combat known to any species: a contest for the possession of a desirable female. Their eyes were locked as each took the measure of the other, their feet set as if claiming some intangible plot of ground, their shoulders hunched with readiness as each waited for the other to make some aggressive movement. Hostile vibrations quivered between them, and it seemed only a matter of seconds before they would come together in a violent clash that would owe much to some primitive need to claim and defend and little to any guise of civility man had forced on his baser emotions.

Leigh sensed the coming confrontation and threw herself between the two predatory males. "Stop it!" she hissed at each man in turn. "Stop behaving like beasts!"

Still they stood glowering, as if her words had made no impression. Each sensed in the other a primary threat to the possession of this woman, but beyond the question of possession was a challenge issued on another level that touched the essence of their masculinity.

Leigh felt the conflict between them keenly and, though she did not fully understand its scope, tried to reach them both again. "I want you to stop this now! I won't be fought over like some tart in a saloon!"

For a moment longer they held their fighter's poses, and then, almost imperceptibly, the tension began to ease. Their faces were still flushed and set in unyielding lines, but their shoulders had begun to relax and their fists to uncurl.

Leigh took a long, shaky breath, wondering what she would have done if they had not responded to her words. It had seemed as if they were both quite willing to tear each other apart in her behalf, and the thought of what might have happened made her shudder. Resolutely she turned to Aaron Crawford. "I think you'd better go now, Aaron. Whatever you believe I owed you for favors past must by now have been repaid in full. And I would appreciate it if in the future you stay as far away from me as possible."

She could sense that Hayes was about to make a statement of his own to reinforce the strength of hers, and she reached behind her to catch his hand, hoping to forestall any threats he might be rash enough to make. Leigh did not want these men fighting over her, and she was determined to prevent a confrontation at all costs. For the moment it seemed that she might succeed, if only Hayes heeded her warning. Somehow the strength of her grip must have conveyed her meaning, and with evident difficulty he managed to bridle his tongue.

In the silence that followed her dismissal, Crawford made a stiff bow. "If that is what you wish, Leigh, it will be no hardship to stay away." Then making a sharp military turn, he headed toward the door and closed it noisily behind him.

With knees gone weak, Leigh turned back to the man who had once again saved her from harm. Above her his face was as still as granite: stern, harsh, and forbidding. His behavior a few minutes before gave evidence of a part of Hayes that she had never seen, a dangerous, ruthless part that was the antithesis of the gentle man she had come to know in these last weeks. It was apart from the rational engineer who solved problems with cool logic and separate from the tender lover she had glimpsed that afternoon in his cabin on the riverboat. This man was a stranger to her, and though she welcomed the help he had been able to give in dealing with Aaron Crawford, he frightened her.

As if becoming aware of her apprehension, Hayes's face suddenly softened. "Are you all right, Leigh?" he asked solicitously. "Did that bastard hurt you?"

She welcomed the change in him, the return of the caring man she knew. Wearily she leaned against his chest and accepted the security his encircling arms afforded. "I'm glad it's over, but I'm sorry I was so naïve. When Aaron told me about Mary Ann Bickerdyke and agreed to write me a letter of introduction, I guess I knew the letter had strings attached. I just put the whole situation out of my mind, thinking that whatever happened, the opportunity to prove myself as a nurse would be worth it. And, you know, in a way it was. I'm finally doing what I've wanted to do all my life."

"I'm just glad," Hayes murmured with a hint of humor in his tone, "that I was here so you were not forced to pay a higher price than Crawford's service warranted."

Leigh acknowledged his words with a nod and snuggled closer. It was so nice just to lean against him, Leigh found herself thinking, so nice to have his arms around her. She was aware of him towering above her, of the breadth of his body conveying strength and safety. She liked the crisp, starched shirtfront beneath her cheek; the warmth of his hands at her waist; the citrusy scent that seemed to cling to his clothes and skin. Contentment seeped through her, and she indulged herself in a few moments of tangible security to help her recover from the unsettling interview with the Yankee major.

Hayes was even more aware of Leigh than she was of him, and he held her gently, as if she might crumple beneath his touch. The emotions that had torn through him when he opened the door and found her struggling in Aaron Crawford's embrace had been frightening in their intensity, and he would have gladly torn the major limb from limb if he'd had the chance. He had been filled with a fury he had never known: half protective, half defensive, totally possessive of this complicated woman who huddled in his arms.

She was so soft, he thought dazedly, so wondrously soft beneath his hands. He buried his lips in her cinnamon hair and breathed deep of her spicy essence. Without volition, his senses began to expand and spiral as he became more and more attuned to everything about her. His fingers were splayed against the rich silk at the back of her bodice, and the warmth of her rose up against his palms. In his mind he saw other times when he had held her: that night on her porch with the scent of lilacs in the air, the afternoon on the riverboat when he could have made love to her. The taste of her kisses seemed fresh on his lips as he remembered, and the sound of her whispered endearments were loud in his ears. The memory of those moments stirred him, and he felt his body harden in response. Through the mists of reverie, the need to turn the past into present grew strong within him, and he ached to revive those memories in Leigh, too. But now a promise barred his way.

It was a promise that no longer seemed as valid as when she had demanded and he had freely given it. Yet it was sufficient to keep him from turning her face up for his kiss, to keep his hands from caressing her. If he allowed himself even the slightest touch against her skin, the slightest taste of her sweet, pink mouth, he knew he would be helpless to curb his own desire. And that would make him no better than Crawford, consumed and besotted by his lust. He was her friend, and as a friend he must protect her, from unscrupulous men like Aaron Crawford and from that undisciplined, unscrupulous part of himself.

Hayes had come to know Leigh well in the past weeks,

to begin to understand and treasure her. He had seen her with the shine of laughter in her eyes, dried her tears when something hurt or touched her, felt a wondrous communion of spirit flow between them. At first he had hoped to find the friendship between them enough to satisfy whatever alchemy had existed from the first, but tonight he had discovered that mere friendship was not enough. What he felt for Leigh was primitive and pure, sexual and strong. He wanted her, yet because he had given his word and won her trust, he could not act on those deeper emotions. He was lost, compromised, defeated, and there was no way to change either what he wanted or what he had denied himself.

Before he could be tempted to act on the feelings growing within him, Hayes gently drew away, becoming suddenly conscious of the time they had spent together alone in this dimly lit room and the possible consequences to her reputation. "Leigh," he said softly. "Leigh?"

She smiled up at him through her lashes, and though he wished with all his heart to read something more in her luminous, spruce-green eyes, they shone with gratitude alone. "Thank you, Hayes, for everything you did: for cooling Aaron's amorous advances, for being here when I needed you."

And thank you for being my friend. Though the sentiment was left unspoken, it loomed between them, a barrier impossible to scale or destroy. Hayes studied her face for a long moment, seeing the pale ivory glow of her skin in the firelight, sensing the faith she had placed in his honor. Then abruptly he turned away so she would not realize the terrible bleakness that overwhelmed him.

"You're welcome, Leigh," he said.

7 ❧

There were tears on her cheeks when Leigh stepped out the front entrance of the hospital, and as soon as she saw Hayes waiting in his usual place beneath the street lamp, she rushed toward him as if homing to solace and shelter. Heedless of the people passing on the sidewalk, Hayes put an arm around her, but he was not prepared for the depth and intensity of the grief he saw in her face. "What is it, Leigh?" he murmured. "What's the matter?"

"Lucas," she whispered, the word muffled against his shoulder. "Oh, Hayes, it's Lucas."

Banister didn't wait for more explanations, but flagged down a passing horsecab and handed Leigh inside, turning to give the driver the Penningtons' address before he climbed in beside her.

"Oh, Hayes, no please!" she implored him in a horrified whisper. "I can't face my parents and Felicity Hale just yet. I don't know how I can break such news to them. Please, please take me somewhere to get control of myself before I have to go home and tell them what's happened."

One look at her ravaged face and brimming eyes convinced Banister of the sincerity of her plea. "I can take you to the *Barbara Dean,* if that's all right," he offered.

She nodded mutely, and Hayes changed his instructions to the driver. Once he was inside the carriage, Leigh crept across the leather seat to nestle unselfconsciously beside him, seeking security and comfort in Hayes's arms. She nuzzled against his woolly lapel and seemed to welcome the rasp of the rough material against her skin, seeking in some desperate, primitive way to ease her pain through contact with his stronger, surer presence.

The strangled sounds of her weeping filled the interior, and Hayes held her close, understanding instinctively that she needed this immediate release of tears far more than any words of consolation he might offer. When her initial grief was spent, there would be a time for condolences and questions, a time when she would need a less basic kind of comfort.

When they reached the levee, Hayes paid the driver and began to lead Leigh across the cobblestones to where the *Barbara Dean* was berthed for the night. In the deepening twilight the wind licked along the water's edge, and a sleety rain had begun to spatter against the stones, making the way slippery and treacherous. Seeing Leigh's difficulty on the uneven footing, Hayes swept her up in his arms with an ease that belied her height and weight, and carried her to his cabin. Once he had set her on her feet beside the bed, he slipped the buttons of her short paletot from their holes and motioned her to a seat on the edge of the bunk. Then, removing his own overcoat and jacket and loosening his necktie, Hayes sat down beside her and began to chafe her icy hands. He could sense how lost and shaken Leigh was, feel how violently she was trembling. The dazed expression in her eyes was the same one he had seen in his mother's the day his father had been killed in an accident at the shipyard, and he knew that initially physical contact was the most effective kind of consolation. So he simply held her for a very long time. His voice was a monotonous counterpoint to the sobs that were wrenched from her throat, his rhythmic stroking in variance with the uncontrolled shudders that moved through her, his hand a lifeline wrung again and again in an agony of grief. For a time it seemed that Leigh would never stop her weeping, but eventually she quieted, leaning trembling and spent against his shoulder. He held her for a few minutes more, then disentangling himself from her grip, went to add more wood to the stove in the corner of the cabin and pour a glass of brandy from a bottle in the cupboard beside the desk.

"Drink this," he urged, bending over her. "It will help, at least a little."

Leigh took the glass, put it to her lips, and took a sip of the liquor, hissing deep in her throat as she swallowed. Hayes pressed another longer draught upon her and another, until all the brandy had been drunk. Within a few minutes he could see that the alcohol had begun to have its desired effect, and Leigh seemed somewhat calmer.

"Can you tell me what's happened?" he asked, as he knelt beside her, taking her hands in his again.

Leigh drew a wavering breath, but for the first time since she had left the hospital, her eyes were dry. "I was making my final rounds before I left and stopped by to check on a new patient sent over from the Confederate prison down Fifth Street where Lynch's slave pen used to be. We get men from there when they need more nursing than the other prisoners can give them or when an amputation is necessary. The Confederate seemed to recognize my name, and he asked me if I was acquainted with a Lucas Hale, who'd signed up with Sterling Price in the first days of the war."

"Was he from Lucas's unit?"

Leigh nodded. "All this time I haven't had a clue to where Lucas and Bran ended up. They left suddenly, right after the capture of Camp Jackson, and I haven't heard a word from either of them since.

"I asked the prisoner for word of Lucas: how he was, if he was at least getting enough to eat. A strange look came over the man's face then, and though he tried to put me off, I pressed him. 'I'm plumb sorry to tell you this, Missy,' he said, 'but Lucas Hale was killed in the battle at Wilson Creek, killed in the same charge as Nathaniel Lyon. And a fair trade that was, I reckon, a brave Confederate boy for that miserable Yankee general.' " Leigh paused and took another uneven breath. "I asked him if he was sure about what had happened, and he said—he said he had helped Bran and Plato, their servant, bury Lu–Lucas—"

Leigh's tears came again, only this time they were angry

tears, harsh with disillusionment and despair. "Oh, Hayes, all these months and I didn't know; I didn't even know he was dead."

In the dim light the wetness sparkled on her lashes and traced shimmering pathways down her cheeks. Hayes pulled her fiercely against him, his face contorted with sympathy. "I'm sorry, Leigh," he whispered. "Oh, God, I'm so sorry."

"The man—the man said Lucas was at the front of the second charge up Bloody Ridge, right at the front, full of bravado, shouting at the top of his voice. That's so like Lucas, always taking chances. Always. I tried to warn Bran the morning they left. I told him that Lucas would have more courage than sense when it came to soldiering, more courage than sense, just like he did when we were children. Still, I knew the warning was futile. Lucas never listened to anyone, much less Bran or me. Lucas was— Lucas was . . ." Her voice trailed off, muffled against Hayes's shirtfront.

Banister moved from his knees to the bed beside her, shifting to brace his shoulders against the headboard and pulling her with him until they half sat, half sprawled across the velvet coverlet. There was comfort in their physical closeness, a rightness in the way their long-limbed bodies flowed together. Leigh lay along his chest, her face hidden against his shoulder, and as she wept, he could feel the wetness of her tears on his skin, feel the brush of her lips against his throat as she whispered a name that was not his own. Hayes's heart ached for her as he pulled her close, knowing the depth of what she'd lost. Lucas had been her lifelong friend as well as her fiancé. He had been the larger part of the future she was planning, her promise of the security that seemed so essential to her well-being. Now Lucas was gone, his life carelessly spent on a battle-field miles and months away. And with his passing went all Leigh's hopes and dreams for the future.

Hayes shifted on the bed and hugged Leigh tighter. He was sorry for her, sorrier than he could say. Leigh deserved happiness, not despair, companionship, not loneliness. She should have any man who could make her happy; she should have Lucas Hale if she wanted him!

But now that Lucas was gone, some insidious voice inside Hayes whispered, now that Lucas was dead, there was nothing to stand between Leigh and him, if he should decide he wanted her. The thought circled through Banister's brain as he considered the possibilities before him, and then he realized what he was doing. He was making carnal plans for a woman who had trusted him and sought comfort in his arms. He was plotting to take advantage of a person who saw him as nothing more than a friend. His own insensitivity appalled Hayes, and he scowled in self-disgust. To consider such a thing when words of sympathy were fresh on his lips branded him as a hypocrite and opportunist, but the thought would not be denied. He cared for Leigh, Hayes admitted in resignation, cared for her in a very different way than he had ever cared for any other woman. He valued her thoughts and opinions, enjoyed her intelligence and humor, found her body enticing and delightful. And beyond that was the thing he'd sensed from the first moment he saw her, the thing he'd confirmed in the weeks since she'd returned from Cairo: Leigh was a part of him, someone who complemented him and made him whole. Lucas Hale's death had forced him to realize the scope of his feelings for the woman by his side, but that realization was tempered with guilt and confusion.

"Damn, damn," he whispered angrily, not even realizing he spoke the words aloud.

Leigh raised her head in surprise and dashed away her tears with one hand. "Hayes? What's the matter?" she whispered back, wanting, even in her grief, to offer him what comfort she could.

The emotions in his eyes were impossible to fathom, but Leigh thought she understood the brooding expression that narrowed the corners of his mouth. "Oh, Hayes, please don't grieve with me," she pleaded. "I need your strength and friendship so much right now."

As she spoke, Leigh pressed one work-roughened hand to his cheek, and when she felt him move against her palm, she brushed her mouth across his lips. It was only the slightest of kisses, but she discovered a profound consolation in the simple intimacy. A flicker of warmth flared within her chest, a spark of feeling to fill the aching void Lucas's death had left inside her. She retreated in wonder as her fingers molded to the shape of his jaw, then she slanted her lips across his again, seeking greater warmth and solace. Their deepening kisses fanned the ember inside until a satisfying glow moved through her blood. Hayes's nearness and the tenderness he offered her were an anodyne for the terrible pain of her loss and a temporary diversion from the responsibility of breaking the news of Lucas's death to the others who would grieve as deeply as she. In a few minutes she would go, Leigh promised herself, in a few minutes she would confront her parents and Felicity Hale, but for now she needed the comfort only Hayes Banister seemed capable of giving.

Outside, the sleet slashed at the windows as the darkness deepened, and the *Barbara Dean* moved sluggishly against the current, buffeted by the fierce wind whipping down from the north. But inside Hayes's cabin the fire crackled and the lamps glowed, banishing the cold and the darkness, creating a haven of warmth and security. Tumbled across the bed, the man and woman lay together, giving and receiving the most basic kind of consolation, savoring the salt taste of tears and the sweetness of brandy as their mouths melded together. For Leigh the growing intensity of their kisses kept reality at bay, but Hayes was all too aware of the time passing, too aware of the effect holding and kissing Leigh was having on him, too aware that these intimacies stretched the boundaries of friendship to breaking.

"Don't you think we should get up and take you home?" he murmured, against her lips.

"Not-yet, Hayes. Oh, don't make me go yet," Leigh whispered almost desperately. "Let me stay a few more minutes, please?"

Whether she wanted to remain in his arms to avoid acknowledging Lucas Hale's death, or because of the delight swelling between them, Hayes did not know. But before he could consider her reasons more carefully, Leigh's half-opened mouth moved over his once more, and any reservations he might have had were obliterated in a rush of devastating sensation. Their tongues swirled in the depths of each other's mouths, and their bodies strained ever closer.

Hayes gave himself over to satisfying her needs and kissed Leigh as if he would never stop, totally consuming her consciousness, driving thought, regrets, and grief from her mind. Even through the despair of losing Lucas, her body responded to his, and Leigh willingly surrendered to the physical side of her nature. Nothing existed now but Hayes: no death, no loss, no responsibility. She wanted him to go on holding her, pleasing her, bringing forgetfulness. And she selflessly sought the same for him.

Hayes's heartbeat tripped erratically as Leigh's hands slipped over him, sliding up inside his untucked shirt, moving in a caress that was innocent and gentle, but tantalizing as well. Her fingers were cool against his flesh, but their touch was like flame to kindling, and he was consumed by a yearning he was helpless to deny.

The other times desire had flared between them, he had been the one in control. The night on the porch and that afternoon on the riverboat he had been the one to press on or hold back. Now it was Leigh who had seized the dominant role, and he wondered if she understood her power or the ruthless strength of the thing she was unleashing upon them. The feel of her hands moving on his body, the abandon in her kisses were pushing him toward a point where he would be incapable of restraint, and he tried one last time to turn away.

But Leigh had already made her decision. In the name of oblivion, she welcomed his passion and met it with her own. Her hands moved steadily upward over his ribs, brushing the smooth nipples hidden in the tangle of curly hair on his chest. When he groaned mindlessly at the contact, she returned to touch them again, smiling to herself, both curious and strangely delighted by the thing she had discovered. With deliberate provocation she continued her exploration, then touched the lobe of his ear with her tongue and felt his body quicken beneath her. There was an exalting power in being able to garner a response from him, and while she reveled in the sweet forgetfulness he offered, the seeds of some deeper understanding were sown within her.

His body had stirred erotically as they kissed and hardened at Leigh's untutored touch, so that now Hayes was a man aggressively ready to take his pleasures. With a single motion, he rolled over, pressing Leigh back onto the bed, claiming her as his. For the briefest instant he hestitated, and when he saw only welcome in her eyes, he willfully lost himself in her. Once before he had refused to show her the wonders of physical love, but now he wanted nothing more than to initiate her to the world of delight. Then he had not wanted to admit what the last days had proved: that he loved Leigh, that the idea of a commitment no longer frightened him. He wanted to be her first man, her last man, the only man Leigh Pennington would ever know.

Hayes opened the bodice of her gown with trembling hands, and her breasts seemed to billow above the lacy top of her chemise, a fetching display of her abundant charms.

Murmuring words Leigh could not hear, he buried his mouth against her throat, then traced scalding designs downward toward the apex of her breasts. Through the sheer chemise he teased her nipples, moistening the fabric until it was translucent, circling and sucking the rosy buds beneath until they blossomed with sensation. Tremors flowed along her spine and down her limbs as Hayes moved over her, and she hugged his dark head closer, urging him on. Her world contracted as they twined together until nothing and no one but Hayes existed.

His hands sought the strings of her whalebone corset, finding the tie at the waist and spreading her stays. As the constriction eased, Leigh drew a breath and felt all at once abandoned and free. She arched her back, filling her lungs with air, letting a feeling of wanton liberation flood through her body. Twining her arms around Hayes, she sought his mouth for another lingering kiss and reveled in the eagerness of his response. Then the tapes at her waist were loosened too, and Hayes was impatiently pushing her heavy skirts, petticoats and corset aside.

Somehow in their tussling his shirt had come undone, leaving studs pooled beneath them on the coverlet and with a murmured promise, he slid the fine linen garment down his arms. Pausing now and then to fondle her, he wriggled out of his other clothes until he lay beside Leigh with her batiste-covered curves pressed to his hard, bared torso. Hayes had expected a retreat now that the protection of their clothes had been swept away, and he steeled himself to accept her recoil gracefully if she turned from him, but instead of making a retreat, Leigh's hands moved over his body, touching, exploring, making him ache with longing.

Then, all at once, Hayes began to understand the scope of what Leigh wanted. In the dark face of death she was flaunting man's only chance for immortality, savoring the very essence of life instead of acknowledging death. She had run from her grief to the depths of their passion, seeking deliverance in their intimacies, forgetfulness in their mutual desire. And, as he lowered his mouth to hers, Hayes recognized the inexorable trap in his own emotions. For whatever her motives were in abandoning herself to him, he was seeking only Leigh.

Then they were both lost to thought, caught up in the most intense and mindless of all man's endeavors. Her underclothes were drawn from her body, and her skin bathed in a wave of worshipful kisses. Leigh reveled in the touch of his mouth and hands upon her flesh, delighted in the feel of his muscles stretching and flexing beneath her fingers. As he skillfully made love to her, Leigh became aware of many things: of the gentle murmur of his muffled endearments, of the vitality of his tousled hair, of the rugged strength of his chest and shoulders, of the masculine tang of his skin. Every impression was engraved upon her memory, every bit of her awareness consumed by the act of making love. Then the peripheral sensations drifted away, and she knew only his stroking hand between her thighs, the spiral of excitement as he drew upon her breasts. Her eyes closed, and her body stilled its movement as she savored the wondrous pleasure that was dissolving her very being. She held her breath, poised and waiting, every gram of concentration on the delight that Hayes had wrought. Then came the need for something more, something that was not hers alone to enjoy, and when she moved her hips against his in mute evidence of her need, Hayes came to her joyously, eagerly joining his body with hers.

The pain that came with the first thrust was unexpected

and sharp, and she stiffened, twisting helplessly against him.

"Easy, easy, Leigh," he whispered in a voice raw and grainy with desire. "I'm sorry I hurt you; I thought you knew I would." There was a momentary pause, and she could feel his breath fan against her throat before he continued in that same husky whisper. "It will be better next time, I promise you, my sweet."

Then, as if he had no choice, he began to move within her, stroking gently but pressing deep. She was shocked by the intimacy of his penetration, the abandon in his movements, but from some primitive well of understanding came the urge to open herself to him. What was happening between them was something that went beyond the physical union of their bodies, and Leigh strove to understand the mystical bond being forged between them. Then Hayes was moving more quickly, his breathing harsh and ragged, until he shuddered to straining stillness and spilled his essence into her.

For a moment he hung above her on trembling arms, a morass of emotions in the depths of his eyes, and finally, with a sigh that seemed to come from his very soul, he withdrew to lie beside her. Curving protectively, he splayed the fingers of one hand across her waist in a gesture of ultimate possession.

As they lay side by side in the stillness, she could hear the harshness of his breathing, feel the jarring of his heart. Overwhelming tenderness for this man who had come to her in passion and consolation welled through her. His gentleness, his patience, and his understanding of her loss were so evident in his actions that she was stunned by the extent of his concern.

Fresh tears singed her lowered lashes and slid slowly into her hair to mingle with the ones she had cried for Lucas. Today she had shed tears for the two men who held claim to her emotions, and as she wept for Hayes's warmth and compassion, she became agonizingly aware of the other half of what she'd done. In seeking solace from her grief in Hayes's ardor, Leigh had sullied and betrayed the memory of Lucas Hale.

At that moment Hayes was beyond guilt, but Leigh was not, and it devastated her. The forgetfulness she had been seeking had proved transitory at best, and in the aftermath of their lovemaking, Leigh was forced to acknowledge her own weakness. Now, in addition to facing the loss of the man she loved, came the burgeoning realization that she had sullied his memory by giving the honor she had promised Lucas to another man. The sweetness and pleasure Hayes had provided had defiled her feelings for Lucas far beyond any comfort this joining might have given her. She had found shame, not consolation, pain, not peace in Hayes's arms. Even now, Hayes was a threat to Lucas, an unwitting despoiler of the sacred word Leigh had given her fiancé all those months and months before. Her own appalling lack of temperance overwhelmed her in ways the news of Lucas's death had not, and she knew she had disavowed Lucas in death as she had refused to do in life. And worse, no matter what she did, she could never make it up to him.

Leigh turned on her side and curled in upon herself, huddling just beyond the arc of Hayes's embrace, staring sightlessly across the room as waves of self-loathing rushed over her. She had betrayed Lucas, betrayed him at a time when he and all they had meant to each other should have been foremost in her mind. In turning to Hayes for comfort, she had sullied Lucas Hale's memory, nullified the love he had given so unstintingly. Instead of hoarding every memory of Lucas as something impossible to replace, she had denied their value, cheapened the respect and honor Lucas had always showed her.

With the realization of what she'd done, of what she'd betrayed, of what she'd become, Leigh was devastated. She was an empty, discarded husk of a woman, devoid of pride and self-respect. She was a tramp, a harlot, a whore, bartering her body for something as fleeting as a moment's oblivion. As she lay in the thundering silence, her misery grew, and Hayes, lying so close beside her, could not help but sense her feelings.

"Leigh," he whispered. "Leigh?" And when she gave him no reply, he continued. "Leigh, do you hate me?"

His voice was like the rustle of dead leaves in the silence that filled the cabin.

She stirred sluggishly and coiled closer, his quiet words adding a new dimension to her guilt. Now she was hurting Hayes too, and she knew she could not let him bear this burden in her stead. No matter what had happened or his part in it, she owed Hayes the truth at least. "No, Hayes," she admitted as a paralyzing lethargy seeped through her limbs. "I hate myself for letting this happen, not you."

There was a pause while Hayes measured the scope of his own remorse. "This wasn't your fault, Leigh," he told her. "You were hardly thinking clearly. I should have known; I should have held back." Regret and resignation mingled in his leaden tone, and pain shredded the usually deep timber of his voice.

More tears pooled in her eyes as Leigh turned to look at him. "Oh, Hayes, no. This is what I wanted. You did nothing more than what I asked." She knew there must be something else she could do to spare him, but she could not bring herself to talk more about what they had done or admit the depth of her shame.

"I want to get dressed and go home now," she said finally, granting no absolution, harshly condemning herself without any hope of mercy. "Surely my parents are wondering where I am, and I still have to tell them about—about Lucas."

In brittle silence they dressed and found a carriage: Leigh wretched and dry-eyed, Hayes guilty and grim. They sat for the duration of the ride as if they were at opposite ends of the world instead of at opposite ends of the carriage seat. Nor had they spoken or reached any resolution between them when the coach pulled up before the Pennington town house on Locust Street.

"Leigh, I'm sorry," Hayes began, feeling the need to apologize at least, but her frozen expression cut him short.

"There is nothing, nothing you can say that will change what just happened between us. It was my doing, totally mine. You have nothing to be sorry for." She spoke without even looking at him. "I just want to put this whole incident behind me, put everything behind me. I just want to forget."

All she could think about was the horror of going inside
and breaking the news of Lucas's death to people who
loved him more than she. Leigh had to relieve herself of
that burden at least, and then, absolved of that responsibility, in the solitude of her room perhaps she could come to
terms with the rest.

There was a long pause before Hayes answered her.
"Very well, Leigh. I'll see you in a couple of days when
you're thinking more clearly."

"No!" She swung around to stare at him. The thought of
discussing what had happened, even at some time in the
future, sent her into panic. "No, I don't ever want to see
you again! Never! Never!

"Leigh, you don't mean that. You're upset and—"

"I do mean it, Hayes." Her voice began to fray. "I
promise you. Don't ever come near me again."

He made a slight conciliatory gesture. "Leigh, there are
things we must discuss, consequences—"

"No! No!" His insistence drove her to action. Without
waiting for him to open the carriage door Leigh reached
across to twist the handle and clambered out over his long
legs.

"Leigh!" His voice was filled with entreaty she could
not allow herself to acknowledge as he followed her as far
as the wrought-iron gate.

"Leigh, please," he tried one last time. But she was so
caught up in preparing herself for the ordeal to come that
his words barely reached her.

The brick town house loomed before her: the flight of
stone steps leading to the arched double doors; the windows glowing invitingly, lit from within; the upper floors
shrouded in sleeting darkness. Yet there was no welcome
for her here tonight. This house had always been a sanctuary, but not now. For the first time in her life she was
reluctant to pass through the heavy, etched-glass doors; down
the spare, impersonal hallway into the commodious parlor.
For the first time in her life she was afraid to face the
people within. They were people who loved her: her parents and Felicity Hale. But now she had proved herself
unworthy of their love—or Lucas's either.

How would she find words to tell them what she must?

What could she possibly say that would ease their grief?

She fought her own overwrought emotions for calm, reached deep inside trying to summon strength. She was aware of Hayes standing just beyond the gate, but there was nothing more she could say to him. She had to concentrate on the task before her, on that alone.

She squared her shoulders, drew a deep, cold breath of air into her lungs, and resolutely started up the steps to the door. She was going inside. If she was to regain her self-respect, she had no choice.

8 ⌖

January 16, 1862—Alton, Illinois

What the devil was this all about? Hayes Banister wondered as he followed Nathan Travis into an innocuous clapboard hotel nestled beneath the towering, milky-hued bluffs at the edge of Alton's bustling waterfront. Why had Nathan brought him to the busy river town twenty-three miles upstream from St. Louis, and just who was it that wanted so badly to see him?

It had been early afternoon when Hayes received Nathan Travis's note, and he left Eads's offices immediately, bound for the Planters' House Hotel. With the paper still crumpled in his hand, Hayes had stood in the doorway to the Gentleman's Ordinary trying to penetrate the pale gray filigree of smoke that drifted above the tables. Finally he located the man he was seeking, sprawled in his chair with a negligence that totally belied the urgency of his summons. As Hayes made his way across the room, he felt the same surge of relief at the sight of his friend that he had experienced when he recognized Travis's scrawl on the message a few minutes before. Somehow Travis had returned from his mission to the hills of Tennessee, hale and hearty in spite of the sporadic skirmishing that would surely have turned friends into enemies and made every stranger suspect.

Yet as Hayes pulled out a chair on the other side of the table, his face gave away none of the concern he had felt on the other man's behalf. "This had better be good,

Travis, to drag me away from the office in the middle of the day," Hayes grumbled.

"It's pleasant to see you again too, Banister," Travis said, raising his half-empty glass in greeting. "It is important, I assure you, but don't sit down and get too comfortable. There's someone who wants very badly to see you, and I agreed I'd make the introductions." As he spoke, Nathan took a handful of coins from his pocket and counted out the price of the drink.

Hayes had frowned darkly as he waited, wondering what was going on. Who was it that wanted to see him? And why couldn't the man show himself in St. Louis's finest hotel? Hayes was wary of the tone of Nathan's invitation, but he was curious enough to accompany him in spite of it.

For the most part he trusted Travis, though until that night in Cairo, when Nathan had confided his burgeoning feelings for Delia Dobbins, Hayes had not considered him a friend. In the days before the war their paths had crossed from time to time as they went about their business on the river, but it was only in the past year that Banister had seen the other man with any frequency. First, Travis had brought the request from the War Department to review James Eads's plans for the ironclads. Then, once Hayes had come to St. Louis, he had shown up in the city to pass the time between his mysterious visits downriver. Nathan Travis had never played coy with Hayes about his activities behind the Confederate lines, nor had he questioned Banister's trustworthiness. From their first meeting all those years ago, it had been evident they shared the same view of slavery and were willing to risk their lives to see Negroes smuggled north to freedom. There had never been a need for the two of them to discuss their loyalties or their beliefs since it was obvious that they both subscribed to Abolitionist causes. But it was only lately that Hayes had begun to glean any insight into the other man's personality, or for their acquaintance to approach the realm of friendship.

Now, as they stood before a door on the second-floor landing of this seedy Alton hotel, the trust Hayes had put in Nathan Travis was being put to the test. Travis knocked

twice on the scarred wooden panel and waited. From the
far side of the door there was the faint creek of floorboards
protesting under a man's weight; then the barrier swung
open. Silently, Travis stepped aside and motioned Hayes
into the darkened room. For an instant Banister hesitated,
looking at the other man with questioning eyes. Travis
nodded once, then with a hand on Hayes's shoulder guided
him through the doorway and closed the panel from the
outside.

Even in the unlighted hallway it had been brighter than
it was in the shuttered hotel room, and it took Hayes's
eyes a moment to adapt to the dimness. As he did, he
became aware of the figure standing in the deeper shadow
beside the bed, sighting at him down the smooth bore of a
pistol. It was a moment before Hayes could raise his gaze
from the cold steel barrel to the face of his host, but when
he did, Banister caught his breath with recognition and
surprise. The man holding the revolver was purported to
be Secretary of War Cameron's man in the West, Albert
Pincheon.

Stepping away from the wall Pincheon circled Banister
slowly, like a lion scenting his prey. A frisson of uneasiness skittered along Hayes's nerves, but he stood his ground
as the bearded man studied him judgmentally.

"How long has it been since I've seen you, Banister?"
Pincheon asked at last, setting his pistol aside and offering
his hand in a gesture of cordiality. "Six years, maybe
seven?"

Hayes recalled the incident as if it were yesterday.
"Closer to eight, I expect—not since I delivered that
young couple and their sick child to you just south of
Chicago." The family had come aboard the *Priscilla Anne*
just below Memphis: a woman with cavernous eyes, a
baby half dead of some fever, and a man with the marks of
shackles worn into his ankles and wrists. Hayes shuddered
with the memory; it was one of the things about those
years that haunted him still. "I went back to work at my
family's shipyard in Cincinnati shortly after that."

Pincheon nodded. "Yes, I know."

Pincheon had always known more about him than Hayes
would have liked, and he was assailed by vague feelings of

violation now. Beyond the realization that this man undoubtedly knew everything he had done these last months
was the even more unnerving fact that the reputed head of
spies for the Union in the West wanted to see him.

"Won't you have a seat, Banister?" Pincheon offered,
indicating a chair by the table at the far side of the room.
"Can I offer you a drink or some coffee?"

Hayes accepted a seat and declined the offer of refreshment. Pincheon nodded again. He was a man without the
ease of social graces, and once he'd discharged his pre-
tense at hospitality, he stormed ahead to the reason he'd
had Hayes brought to Alton.

"Banister, I know that you've been working in partnership with James Eads on construction of the ironclads and
that your recommendations were instrumental in having
the project approved by the War Department and President
Lincoln. For your service to the nation during this crisis, I
am to commend you."

"I thank you, sir, but I hardly did more than any
American would do," Hayes hedged, inexplicably nervous
at the compliment. "Besides, James Eads was the one who
got the project under way."

"Nevertheless, your nation is grateful, and in more
peaceful times your actions would be suitably recognized.
But instead of rewarding you, it is my duty to ask you to
undertake another mission for the sake of the Union."

Hayes waited, making no comment. What was it Pincheon
wanted him to do?

"As you must know, the ironclads were designed spe-
cifically to capture the forts the Confederates have built to
guard the Mississippi River system, and it is vital to the
war effort that these waterways are opened to Union vessels. To that end General Grant is about to embark on a
campaign meant to claim areas of the Mississippi basin
and surrounding territory for the Union."

"Yes, sir, I am aware of that," Hayes put in. It was not
difficult to anticipate the thrust of the spring offensive, and
Hayes wondered if Travis had been scouting in Tennessee
in preparation for the upcoming maneuvers.

"What I'm asking you to do, Banister, is to go along
with the troops and evaluate the use of the ironclads in

actual battle situations. Normally, a civilian engineer would not be allowed to accompany a fighting force like this one, but you are to be an exception. We need to know if the ironclads are working up to their full capacity and if there are mechanical or tactical changes that could enhance their efficiency. We want to know if Grant is using their firepower to the best advantage on land and if Admiral Foote is deploying them successfully on the water."

"But why are you asking me to make such a report? Surely your own military people are better able to make those judgments than I. And besides, it is James Eads who should be asked to go since the construction of the ironclads is largely his doing."

"Don't you want to go, Banister?" Pincheon taunted, his cold eyes raking over the other man. "Do you feel you've done enough to serve your country?"

A dull red flush rose under Hayes's skin at the other man's tone. "Are you asking me if I'm a coward, Pincheon?"

"I'd never have accused you of it a few years ago when you were risking your neck to run slaves north. That was far more dangerous than what I'm asking you to do now, but some men just don't like the sound of battle."

Hayes was plainly angry, but held his temper in check. "I chose to serve my country in this crisis where I thought I could do the most good: building warships. When my usefulness runs out at the shipyards, I will sign on to fight somewhere else."

Pincheon nodded cannily, as if the questions had been some kind of a test. "I simply want an opinion of how the ironclads operate under battle conditions from someone who knows their capabilities. You're a younger and fitter man than James Eads, and I've heard he's not well."

It was true. James had worn himself out with worry over the deadlines for completion of the ships and because the government had not come through with the money it had promised him. James was in no condition to undertake a military campaign, but Hayes knew Eads would be disappointed at being denied a chance to see his ironclads in action.

"What do you want me to do?" Hayes finally asked.

The hand that stroked his silky moustache hid Pincheon's victorious smile. "I would like you to go down to the area around Forts Henry and Donelson before the battle to scout any obstacles the ironclads might encounter. You might be able to spot things a man without your background would overlook. Travis will accompany you, and when you're finished, you will join Admiral Foote to accompany the flotilla into battle."

"Is that all?" Hayes asked sarcastically.

"What you'll be doing is vitally important," Pincheon continued, watching Banister through narrowed eyes, "vital to the security of this campaign and to the future of the warships you helped design. Your cooperation will be appreciated by President Lincoln, the war department, and myself."

Pincheon's were heady words, but there was a pragmatic side to Banister's nature that demanded the particulars of this operation. "How soon do we need to leave? And how will we get behind Confederate lines?" Hayes demanded.

"Grant will be mobilizing in Cairo any day now, so the sooner you and Travis can get on your way, the better. As for the other, Travis has had a great deal of practice with just this kind of maneuver, and I commend you to his care."

Hayes frowned. Essentially, he and Nathan Travis would be spies, moving behind enemy lines like two wraiths, caught up in deception and intrigue. Hayes did not welcome such a role. He had always preferred to tackle problems head-on, not through guile and cunning. Besides, he needed time in St. Louis to resolve things with Leigh before he went off to risk his life for the Union. He didn't like the secrecy of the assignment, the urgency, or the odds. Still, he was being compelled to accept it in spite of his misgivings.

"I can't leave sooner than the middle of next week," he negotiated.

Pincheon frowned but nodded, both agreeing with Hayes's request for time and dismissing him. The interview was over, and Hayes could not help but be overwhelmed by the changes the past hour had made in his life.

"By the way, Banister," Pincheon added as the younger man rose to go, "the letters you sent Travis about the troop movements in Tennessee gave him the warning he needed to get out of there before things got too tight. But how did you know about General Buell's maneuvers ahead of time? And who sent your letters through the lines?"

Hayes grinned, pleased that the "Christmas messages" he had sent through contacts from his days with the underground railroad had reached and alerted Travis to the presence of Yankee patrols and the uproar they would cause. "I keep my ears open at Eads's office and at the social gatherings I attend; from the things our officers let slip, it's not hard to guess what's going to happen." It was the truth, though any loyal Northerner might wish it otherwise.

"You'd make a damned good spy, you know," Pincheon offered, his eyes narrowed consideringly. "If it's that easy to glean information, I'll have to send General Halleck a note asking him to talk to his officers about commenting too freely on Union maneuvers. But how did you get the letters to Travis so quickly?"

Again Hayes grinned. "A young lady I know sent them for me. It seems there are quite a lot of letters smuggled out of St. Louis to the Confederacy."

Pincheon's frown deepened. "I'll have to do something about that as well, I suppose. These Rebel women can be damn clever."

Banister chuckled, thinking about Leigh's reluctance in posting the messages for him. If she'd had any idea what the letters to his relatives had really said, she would never have sent them. But the messages to his "Uncle Nate" had been carefully coded to seem like nothing more than inquiries about his family's health and welfare. Banister smiled again, and his host rose to see him to the door.

"Let me wish you good luck, Banister," Pincheon offered. "What you'll be doing for us is important and dangerous work. You deserve credit for undertaking it so willingly."

Willingly? If this had been willingness, Hayes wondered what reticence would be like, or outright refusal. Aloud he acknowledged the other man's words. "I know that, sir.

And in spite of what I said, I intend to serve my country faithfully.''

Outside, Travis was waiting, sitting in a straight-backed chair at the end of the hall. In the split second when his coal-black eyes met Pincheon's, Hayes felt communication flash between them. "He's one of us now," the intelligence officer said softly.

And just as softly came Travis's reply: "I'll take good care of him, then. Don't you worry."

Within moments, Hayes and Travis were outside on the street, headed toward a nearby tavern. Once settled at a table in one corner with two glasses and a bottle of whiskey between them, they discussed their imminent departure for the Tennessee backcountry.

"I've some loose ends to tie up," Hayes insisted stubbornly when Travis pressed him for a speedy departure. "Some things I can't just go off and leave." As he spoke, Leigh's face rose up before him, and he blinked the image away.

Travis considered him for a long moment, then frowned. "Well, since you're going to need some time in St. Louis, I think I'll pay a visit to someone in Cairo."

Travis had given no hint that he was going to see a woman, but instinctively Hayes knew who it was. "Delia Dobbins?" he asked softly.

Travis poured himself a whiskey and took a long swallow before he answered. "I never thought I'd find another woman . . ."

Nathan's voice trailed off, but there was no need to say more. Hayes knew how Travis felt: awed, reluctant, a little frightened by the feelings growing inside him. A bittersweet smile of understanding twisted his mouth.

January 20, 1862—St. Louis, Missouri

"Oh no!" Leigh muttered as she pushed open the hospital's main door and saw Hayes Banister in his usual place under the street lamp. After that last afternoon on the *Barbara Dean*, Leigh had hoped never to set eyes on the man again, but Hayes was waiting, just as he had been every day for the past week. During the leave she had been granted to recover from the shock of Lucas's death, Hayes's presence outside the hospital had been the cause of much speculation. Now she would be forced to face him for the first time since that awful afternoon under the scrutiny of dozens of eyes.

He had obviously seen her in the doorway, and it was too late to retreat. Perhaps it was better to face him and get things settled once and for all, Leigh reflected, resigned to her fate. There was nothing to do but descend the steps and inform him of the course she had decided to follow.

In the past days of solitude, Leigh had come to realize that avoiding Hayes and denying any feelings she might have for him was the only suitable penance for having betrayed Lucas's love. It was neither fair nor right to spurn a man who had done nothing more than what she asked, a man who had offered her passion in the name of solace, a man who had proved himself her friend time and again. But only the vow to turn away from Hayes would appease her nagging conscience. She had known for a long time that she eventually would be forced to admit to and then deny any feelings she might harbor for Hayes Banister. Now that time seemed at hand.

Hayes's expression was grave as he approached the bottom of the steps, his eyes searching her face as if seeking some clue to how he would be received. "It's good to see you, Leigh," he greeted her. "I've been very concerned about you."

"I've been as well as can be expected, under the circumstances," she told him softly. Her words conveyed meanings no others could hear.

He was quiet for a moment as he studied her, the intensity of his pale blue gaze like an inquisition. Leigh steeled herself to accept his scrutiny, wondering if he would notice the dark smudges beneath her eyes and guess at their cause. Would he suspect that she had lain awake night after night remembering both the past she had shared with Lucas and those intimate hours in Hayes's cabin on the *Barbara Dean*? Was it possible he could know about the strange, bittersweet longing that filled her at the memory of his hands and mouth upon her body or her particular horror at the response she had given him? Could he even guess at her pain in resolving to turn aside his friendship for the sake of what was now nothing more than a broken promise and the memory of love?

"I've rented a carriage," he said, breaking into the awkward silence as he gestured to the vehicle at the curb. "I was hoping you would allow me to see you home."

"It is kind of you to offer, but I—"

"Leigh, please, I really think it would be wise for us to talk."

Hers had been a token protest, and she was resigned to this conversation as inevitable. But the steel beneath his polite words underlined a determination she had not expected to find in him. With a mute nod of assent, Leigh allowed herself to be handed into the closed carriage.

Once the cab had begun to roll, Hayes faced her squarely. "Leigh," he began with unaccustomed gravity, "Leigh, I want you to marry me."

The statement, without warning or preamble, stunned Leigh, and it took her a moment to respond. She had not expected Hayes to offer her the protection of his name after what had passed between them. It had been something quite different from the seduction that usually elicited such a proposal, and the noble sentiments that must have prompted it made it so much more difficult to do what she must.

"Is this sudden offer an attempt to do the honorable thing for a woman whose virtue you've sullied?" she burst out when she caught her breath. "Well, I assure you, Hayes, it's not necessary. You're hardly responsible for what we did the other day on the riverboat, and I am quite willing to admit I threw myself at your head."

"I don't want you to admit anything," Hayes stated flatly. "I want you to marry me."

His obdurate tone stirred some contrary part of her nature, making her refusal sharper than she'd intended. "I can't. No, I won't. I don't want to see you ever again, Hayes, much less marry you."

He was obviously prepared to be patient. "Be sensible, Leigh," he urged her. "There are consequence to what we did—"

"Yes, Hayes, I'm well aware of that."

"Then since you are, there can be no question about what we must do. After what happened, you could be pregnant, and I am willing to take the responsibility if you are."

There was nothing romantic about this proposal, and somehow that stung. Lucas had played the gallant the afternoon he had asked Leigh to marry him, bringing her flowers, taking her hand in his and dropping dramatically to one knee as he spoke of his love and asked her to be his wife. Hayes's words were cold and businesslike, a bargain being struck between them. It was as if he were offering a trade of her virginity for the protection of his name.

"That's very generous," she conceded, "and your concern for my welfare does you credit, but I assure you, Hayes, there is no need to marry me."

"Are you certain?"

It was clear what he was asking, and her cheeks flamed brilliant red. As a nurse she was well aware of how a woman knew she was carrying a child, but having a discussion about her own bodily functions filled her with embarrassment. "Not positive, no," she answered, her voice tremulous.

"Well, then, I think it's obvious what we must do."

He was not going to make this easy for her, and she steeled herself to continue, strangely piqued that there should be no tenderness in what he was proposing. He was not offering her emotional ties, nor was he asking for love in return. Instead he was taking the blame and accepting the consequences for something that was her fault alone. Somehow that realization devastated her, and Leigh looked past him out the window, with the ache of unshed tears in her throat.

Marriage should not be a punishment for past mistakes, but a pledge to the future that would bring love and joy to both parties. It should be a melding of two wills and lives. But then, she asked herself tiredly, how could there ever be joy in a union between her and Hayes now? It would be a union based in ill-considered passion, a union begun in the ashes of another love. Lucas would always be between them, just as her feelings for Hayes would forever have stood between her and Lucas Hale. Startled by the unwelcome admission, Leigh forced the thought away.

She had never set much store by marriage anyway. Knowing it was not just tender feelings that had brought her own parents together, she had never been able to believe in the rosy dreams of love that most girls cherished. Yet Leigh had been willing to chance marriage with Lucas. Even as she considered the paradox within her own nature, she understood the reason she had accepted his suit. It was because Lucas had been safe, familiar, and secure; because she had known him all her life and trusted him implicitly. And now that Lucas was dead, she would never again know that kind of certainty, that kind of security with any other man. Only with Lucas had there been any chance of contentment.

Surely a marriage between people as diverse as Hayes and she could not succeed. It was madness to consider it. What had brought them together was her need for comfort and the transient physical bond that had turned desire into fleeting delight. How could anything so ephemeral promise a future, something that would grow and endure? Didn't she know firsthand the consequences of a marriage based in lust? Hayes was a fine man, a man of strength and conviction, as his proposal of marriage attested. And because he was such a man, he deserved a woman far better than she. Surely a union between them could only end in unhappiness and in an intimate disaster she could neither cause nor bear.

Besides, the voice of guilt whispered, to marry Hayes now would be the final betrayal of all the love and loyalty she had felt for Lucas Hale. Leigh could not live with that shame.

With a sigh she turned her attention to extricating herself from Hayes's unsettling proposition, casting around for a suitable argument, and then seizing the offensive when one occurred to her.

"Hayes, am I the first woman you've taken to your bed?" she asked pointedly, breaking the silence that had been billowing between them.

It was Hayes's turn to color up. "I don't see what that

has to do with what we've been discussing," he sputtered, startled and confused by her question.

"I'm not your first woman, then?"

"Leigh!"

"Am I?" she persisted.

"What in God's name—"

"Since I'm not and since you're not married already, then I think it's safe to assume that an encounter like the one we had the other day doesn't necessarily result in the birth of a baby."

She paused as a new thought struck her, and before she could consider the impropriety of what she was about to ask, it was out of her mouth. "Or do you have a passel of by-blows out there somewhere?"

Hayes's face darkened ominously, but Leigh was too preoccupied to consider what his reaction might mean.

"I may be naïve, Hayes," she continued undeterred, "but I know that the chances of conceiving a baby the single time we—we did that are fairly remote. And frankly, I'm not willing to spend the rest of my life married to a man I do not love on the chance that one encounter has got me with child."

Forcing the thought of Monica and her son from his mind, Hayes considered the woman before him. She was a paradox: uninitiated in the ways of love, she had not known that her first time with a man would hurt and change the essence of her body forever. Yet now she was citing an understanding of the workings of nature with a certainty that could only come from an impersonal understanding of medicine. She had been trained to cure the human body as a mechanic is trained to repair a machine, without the intimate knowledge that gave depth to what she knew. Still, he could not fault her logic, and that made him angrier still.

"Since it's unlikely I'm going to have your baby, Hayes," Leigh continued, pressing her advantage, "I think I must refuse your noble offer."

"I didn't offer to marry you to be noble," he snapped furiously.

Her eyes opened wide at his declaration. "Why did you offer to marry me, then?"

"I want to marry you—I want to marry you—Oh, hell!"

He couldn't tell her that he was asking her to be his wife because he loved her, because he wanted her with him always. He couldn't tell her that now, not after she had loudly proclaimed that she felt no love for him in return. His pride would not let him go that far in declaring himself, so he turned aside the question with one of his own.

"After the other day on the *Barbara Dean* you are no longer a virgin. How will you explain that to whatever man eventually wins your hand?"

Leigh had not thought beyond the ramifications of his proposal, but after a moment she answered defiantly. "I will tell them Lucas was the one to make me a woman. We were betrothed. That way it won't make an enormous scandal."

Suddenly fury burned through Hayes at the thought of some other man claiming this woman's sweet, alabaster body for his own, having the right to call her his when Hayes could not. He loved Leigh. He wanted Leigh for a hundred reasons he could not voice, but she would not let him take her to wed. Her responsiveness the other afternoon had been no dream, nor had he imagined the way their bodies had fit together. What existed between them was rare and precious, something that came only once in a lifetime. But Leigh was refusing to acknowledge its importance, its uniqueness. For reasons he could only guess, she was denying everything that had grown up between them since that first day at Camp Jackson, everything that was tender and beautiful. There had been something uniting them then, and there was something uniting them now. Why couldn't Leigh admit to it?

Leigh sensed the trend of Hayes's thoughts and the depth of his frustration. At another time, in another situation, she might have been able to give him the answer he sought, but as things stood, it was impossible for her to accept his proposal. She owed Lucas her loyalty now that he was dead because she had not given it unstintingly when he was alive. She owed his memory and her own guilt this sacrifice.

And what was even more basic, she owed Hayes freedom from a marriage based on an afternoon's mistake.

The carriage rolled to a stop at the gate to the Pennington town house with nothing resolved between them. Hayes had not received the answer he wanted, and Leigh had not convinced him that she intended never to see him again. For an instant they sat speechless, watching the confusion in each other's eyes. Then both began talking at once.

"Promise me, Leigh, if you find you are going to have my child, you will accept my offer of marriage."

"Hayes, I think it would be unwise, in the light of what happened the other afternoon, to continue to spend time together."

There was a moment of silence as each took in what the other had said before Banister spoke.

"Surely you don't mean that, Leigh. Making love can't have changed everything."

Leigh stared down at her hands as if the creases in her leather gloves were unique and engrossing. Making love he had called it. Was that what they had done? Were the feelings she'd harbored for him in those minutes of closeness been love? Was love what he had felt for her? Or had they been drawn together in order to satisfy his physical desire and her need for comfort? Well, whatever it had been, love, passion, solace, it was now over. Her conscience, her loyalty to Lucas Hale, and her concern for Hayes demanded it. During these last few minutes in his company she had to make Hayes understand that whatever had once been between them was over.

"Leigh?" Hayes's light touch on her coat sleeve made her newly aware of him beside her.

"I do mean it, Hayes. What happened the other afternoon did change everything. I don't want to see you again. I don't want to find you waiting for me when I leave the hospital; I don't want to dance with you if we meet at parties. All I've ever wanted was your friendship. I was wrong to turn to you when I found out about Lucas's death, and I've never regretted anything as much as I do that. But it changed things between us, changed them irrevocably. There's no going back, Hayes. I'm sorry."

Hayes reached for her, but she had already opened the carriage door and was scrambling down the steps to the ground. A moment later she was gone, leaving her last words echoing in the silence: "There's no going back, Hayes. I'm sorry."

As Hayes sat alone in the chilly carriage, there was a moment when he was overwhelmed by all he'd had and lost, appalled by what he'd thrown away. Then the hard, indomitable part of his personality asserted itself, and his face took on a dark, determined set. He loved Leigh; he wanted Leigh. In these last lonely days he had come to accept his need for her. And though he didn't know how or when, he was going to win her back.

For now there were other things to claim his time and energies, things beyond his personal concerns. But when he returned from the expedition to Forts Donelson and Henry, once his duty to his country was fulfilled, he would find a way to win Leigh's love. There would be time then to build the future with her he had just begun to plan. He would make Leigh his wife one day because he loved her, because they belonged together, because he could not bear to live without that dream.

9 ❧

Pulling the rough woolen blanket closer against the cold that penetrated the flapping canvas tent, Hayes Banister tried to will himself to sleep. His body ached with the fatigue of these last days, but his mind was alive with images and experiences from his first glimpse of battle. He lay, as so many did this night, shivering in the frigid February weather but thankful to be alive.

As Pincheon had ordered, Hayes and Nathan Travis had scouted the area between the Cumberland and Tennessee rivers where Forts Henry and Donelson lay guarding the Confederate left. During the last days of January the two men had taken a steamboat up the Ohio from Cairo and then moved on horseback through the triangular piece of land between the rivers. It was an unappealing, swampy area: a tangle of trees and vines, scored by interconnecting waterways, and steep-sided gullies that were sticky and awash with mud. Even with the pale winter sun filtering through the tall grasses and the birds singing, there was a desolation about the place, a grim emptiness that played on Banister's nerves.

The forts they had been sent to investigate had been thrown up the preceding year to protect the meandering river system that sliced deep into the heart of the South. The Rebels had seen the rivers offered an invasion route that could divide the fledgling Confederacy and sever the vital flow of supplies from west to east. Of even greater importance was that Henry and Donelson guarded the supply depot at Nashville and the Memphis and Charleston Railroad that passed just south of the forts through Corinth, Mississippi. It was an area the Rebels could not afford to lose and a sector the Northern troops must take in order to begin an offensive that could win the war for their side. It was a piece of ground worth dying for, a piece of real estate that would be bought and paid for with the lives of both Yankee and Confederate soldiers.

As ordered, Hayes and Travis had joined the river flotilla on February second just north of where Panther Creek spilled into the swollen Tennessee River. For four days the ironclads had lain in readiness, riding low in the water, awaiting a chance to prove their abilities while the infantry and cavalry were ferried down from Cairo for the combined land and water attack. Finally, on the sixth, orders to begin the bombardment of Fort Henry arrived.

The low-lying fortifications, manned by inexperienced recruits and armed with only a few powerful field pieces, fell to the ironclad fleet's artillery even before General Grant and his men arrived overland. For the Navy and Hayes, as builder of the ironclads, it was both victory and vindication. The strange-looking gunboats had proved their worth.

During the battle the *Essex* had taken most of the enemy fire and retired to Cairo for repairs while the rest of the fleet steamed back up the Tennessee to the Ohio River, then down the Cumberland to Fort Donelson. Meanwhile, in preparation for the forthcoming battle, Grant marched his men across the slender neck of land that separated the forts.

Fort Donelson was not as vulnerable as Fort Henry had been. Built on higher ground, garrisoned by a stronger force of men and longer guns, it was sure to offer stiff resistance.

While Grant maneuvered his men to form a semicircle beyond the fort and its entrenchments, the naval bombardment began. Employing the tactic that had worked so well before, the ships pulled closer and closer to the shore batteries. But in doing so, the ironclads came under heavy attack. The more powerful guns within Fort Donelson and the higher angle of fire quickly took their toll on the armored ships.

From the pilothouse of the flagship *St. Louis*, where Hayes and Nathan Travis had observed the battle, they could see the hammering the other ships were taking and feel the bombardment of their own. Smoke and the acrid smell of burning powder filled the air and all but obscured the bank only two hundred yards away. There was the sound of shouted orders from the gun deck below and the thunder of their own pieces answering the deadly challenge from the fort. Flashes of flame sparked through the smoky gloom as new shells left their guns, and the decks rolled with both the recoil of the weapons and the rain of deadly Confederate fire. Plumes of water flared up around them as Confederate shots fell short of the ships, and there was the constant thudding of explosions as other bombs found their marks or imbedded themselves in the ship's heavy iron plating.

Then, with a flare of light and noise, one side of the pilothouse burst with the force of an incoming shell, sending glowing metal and splinters of wood flying everywhere. Total confusion reigned as men were thrown to and fro by the force of the concussion and the ship bucked beneath them like an unbroken colt. Hayes had been catapulted across the room as the explosion detonated, and for a few seconds he lay stunned and confused by the intensity of the blast. As his head began to clear, he had looked up to see the pilot melting slowly to the deck, a jagged splinter of wood protruding from the center of his chest. There was blood everywhere, slippery and dark against the walls and floor, staining the clothes of those who had escaped the worst of the explosion as well as the men who lay wounded and dying. Admiral Foote, the ranking naval officer, had been injured, and as the ironclad heeled sluggishly against the current, a gaping hole in the side of the cabin and its steering gone, Hayes had moved to where the officer lay. Doughty and gruff even in what must have been excruciating pain, he was every inch a commander and was determined to see to his men and the battle before he sought attention for himself. In the explosion the wheel had been blown away, and the *St. Louis* began to slide slowly downstream, disabled and out of control.

In the course of the battle, the other ironclads suffered similar fates, and the ships withdrew to Cairo for repairs while Hayes and Travis stayed with Grant's forces to observe the land battle that ensued. For two days the Yankee and Confederate troops fought at both ends of the Union line: the Confederates determined to keep the route to the south open for escape toward Nashville and the Federal troops equally determined to tighten the deadly noose around the fort.

Hayes and Nathan Travis had been little more than observers of the military drama being played out on the swampy stretch of land between two of the South's major rivers. They had witnessed the charge up the slope to the outermost bastions of the fort and heard the wounded crying for help afterward as they were burned to death where they lay when the grass ignited from cannon fire. They had ridden with Grant on the second morning of the battle to the westernmost edge of the Union line and heard him exhort his men to recapture positions lost just after dawn. They were in the farmhouse General Grant had made his headquarters when General Bruckner's note demanding terms of surrender was received. In the end, several of the ranking Confederate officers did manage to slip off into the night, but Grant's demand for the unconditional surrender of Fort Donelson gained him a reputation as a stern officer and set the tone for future battles he would fight throughout the war.

Now Hayes lay reliving the horrors and triumphs of the last days, while outside his tent he could hear the barren trees creaking in the wind and the muted voices of those who had been no more able to sleep than he. Banister had spent his day trying to offer what aid he could to the overworked orderlies, helping to carry the injured from where they had fallen during the two days of bitter fighting to the inadequate, ill-equipped hospitals that had sprung up behind the lines. The weather had turned cold and wet the first night of the campaign, and the swampy ground where the wounded lay had hardened around them, encasing them in ice and their own frozen blood. Today had been filled with things that angered and appalled Hayes, and those, as well as the incidents on the ironclads and during the fighting, had combined to rob him of his rest.

Groaning, he hauled himself to his feet, giving up the attempt to sleep in favor of searching out a pot of coffee and some companionship to dull the edge of his memories. Travis had gone off into the swamps shortly after noon, and Hayes doubted that he would see the other man until his scouting was done.

As Hayes left the confines of the tent and the snoring officer beside him, he noticed a glimmer of light moving across one of the fields where the battle had taken place. As he watched the eerie glow, tracking slow and close to the ground, he was reminded of the stories he had heard of scavengers who prowled the scene of a battle under the cover of darkness to loot the bodies of the dead. The grisly thought preyed on his mind until he gave up any attempt at finding a fire and a pot of coffee and went to investigate.

The earth was hard as macadam beneath his booted feet as he moved across the rutted field, and he set a course to intercept the light, noting how it fluttered and disappeared into the dips and gullies that scored the uneven terrain. He moved quietly and with deliberate stealth until he topped a slight rise and came upon the intruder.

"Halt! Who goes there?" he called out.

To his surprise it was a woman who turned to face him: a tall, gray-haired woman wrapped in nothing more than a worn woolen shawl to protect her from the penetrating cold.

"Who are you, and what are you doing on the battlefield at this hour of the night?" Hayes demanded.

As she raised her lantern higher, he could see the concern and pain written in her features, and he knew instinctively that she had come to help and not to plunder.

"I came to search the fields myself," she told him in a rough, gravely voice. "I know the stretcher bearers are not always as careful as they might be in seeking out the wounded, especially as exhausted as they are after these last two days. I couldn't sleep for fear that there might be a few, poor, living boys remaining out here with the frozen dead.''

Hayes was moved by her simple declaration and offered her his help. Together they crossed the roughened battlefield as the wind tore at their clothing and rattled the brush that grew along the sides of the gullies. They stopped to raise the lantern beside corpse after corpse to check for signs of life: for warmth among the stone-cold bodies, for the thready beat of life in a soldier's chest. It was nightmarish work, but no worse than the battle the day before had been. The bodies of the slain lay where they had fallen in stiff, twisted poses, frozen into the earth, some covered with a dusting of snow. Some had lain unattended for two days in favor of the living, and would eventually be collected in wagons and prepared for burial.

It seemed to Hayes as if they had been crossing and recrossing the windswept field for hours when they came to one wiry corporal whose chest rose and fell with shallow breathing. The shawled woman knelt beside him and spoke low, trying to force a bit of the tea she had brought between his pale, cracked lips. After a few minutes of care he moaned slightly and opened his eyes. ''Mother,'' he whispered.

As color began to return to the corporal's ashen cheeks, Hayes felt as if he were watching a miracle unfold. This woman, with her determination and compassion, was breathing life back into a man who was all but dead. Unexpectedly Hayes's throat closed up.

''I'll go for a wagon to transport him back to the hospital tents,'' he offered and, without waiting for affirmation, strode off into the darkness. It was some time later when he returned to where he had left the woman, and beside her the man was stirring, shivering with the cold after being chopped out of his icy prison, but very much alive. Making him as comfortable as possible on the floor of the dray Hayes had commandeered, they continued their search, finding more than half a dozen of the living trapped by the ice or under long-dead comrades.

By the time the sun had crested the trees to the east to herald the start of a new day, the men had been delivered to one of the makeshift hospitals to await their turn with the few nurses available or one of the even fewer field surgeons. While the last of the men were being taken into the hospital tent, Hayes stood beside the tall, rough-hewn woman. As they had searched the battlefield for those who lived, Hayes worked with calm dispatch, but his mind had not fully accepted the desperately important work they did. Now, as that realization washed over him, Hayes was filled with thoughts of Leigh and the mission she had undertaken at the outset of the war. If she had been here, it would have been her beside this woman offering what comfort she could, undaunted by the cold, the horror, or by the weariness she saw in this woman's face.

As he watched this compassionate stranger, a new understanding of the woman he loved blossomed within him. It was an understanding filled with equal parts pride and fear. Leigh knew what it was she had to do, and she would fulfill her duty with a determination that would not stop short of exhaustion. Hayes suddenly realized, as he had not before, how desperately important the course Leigh had chosen to follow really was. He could not help fearing for the hardships and heartbreak she would see in her chosen calling or the dangers she would face. But now he saw the strength and courage it took to follow her convictions.

"Who are you?" Hayes whispered as the woman turned toward the tent and the never-ending demands for help and succor. "Why are you here?"

The woman faced him with a smile on her narrow, determined mouth. "I'm here because I'm needed," she answered. "And most of the men just call me 'Mother.'"

February 21, 1862—En route to St. Louis, Missouri

Hayes Banister leaned against the balustrade on the promenade deck of the *Ben Franklin* and stared out across the river. On the far bank the fields were beginning to turn from lifeless winter brown to a promising shade of green. Spring was coming to the Mississippi Valley, but this year, instead of life and bounty, it would mean death and destruction. Still, the river itself seemed unchanged, either by the war or the passage of time, and, to a man who had once made his living plying its unpredictable course, that offered a strange kind of comfort. The Mississippi was enduring, its ceaseless flow the one constant in the changing world. In the past few days he had seen too many of man's endeavors go awry not to appreciate clear evidence of nature's superiority.

Hayes drew a long breath as he took his pipe and tobacco from the pocket of his jacket and stared moodily out across the water. From its familiar swirls and eddies, from its mysterious green-brown depths came thoughts of days gone by. They were days best put behind him, but in spite of his best intentions, the memories engulfed him. It had been on early spring days like this one when the trees were just beginning to leaf and the wild flowers to blossom, when the sky was this same spectral shade of blue and the wind was warm and fresh, that he and Monica would meet at his cabin in the woods outside Vicksburg to revel in the earth's reawakening. More than once they had made love on the ground like two wild things: with the loamy smell of soil in their nostrils; the heat of the sun on their bare limbs; and the soft, new grass crushed beneath their straining bodies. Those were strong, poignant memories, painful yet bittersweet. And though Hayes knew he no longer loved Monica, he could not deny that she was with him still, an inextricable part of his past.

As the sun-washed breeze brushed his cheek like a remembered caress, Hayes wondered what this year would bring to Monica and her son. Were she and Charles still in Vicksburg? Would they stay on if the fighting moved closer? Were they sheltered and getting enough to eat? How was the war affecting the women and children in the South? Monica's husband was too old for soldiering, so he must be there to see to the welfare of his family, at least. Hayes was thankful for that. But what would happen to them as the war moved farther and farther downriver? Was there anywhere they could flee to remain untouched by battle? Dear God, if only there were some way to be sure they were safe! For a long time Hayes stood staring sightlessly into the water, lost in thought.

At last he stretched, filled his pipe from the pouch of tobacco, and struck a match, shielding the flame with his hands until the bowl glowed orange. From the stern of the steamboat came the rhythmic rush of the paddles churning through the water, and Hayes could hear the hum of the boilers on the deck below. He had been extremely lucky to get passage on the *Ben Franklin,* he reflected. It was only the fact that he had made himself useful to the contingent from the Western Sanitary Commission that enabled him to travel from Fort Donelson to St. Louis with this boatload of wounded. The troop transport, loaned to the Commission by General Grant's chief surgeon, was filled to the gunnels with men on their way to the city's hospitals, and though it was totally unsuited for their care, the wounded had been brought aboard by the score. The Commission had sent a load of sanitary stores to Fort Donelson shortly after the fighting began, and the men who had brought them had stayed on to offer their help at the hospitals. It had quickly become apparent that there were too many wounded for the facilities the Army had provided, and both the supplies and the volunteers from St. Louis were welcome. The worst was now over: the dead buried, the more than seven hundred prisoners of war dispatched to Camp Douglas near Chicago, and the wounded on their way north to various hospitals along the river. But the days after the battle had been a damned grim time, a time that would haunt him all the days of his life.

Hayes was just finished his pipe when two men came out of the salon to stand by the rail. They were deep in conversation, and their words drifted across the deck to where Hayes stood.

"I think it's an inspired idea, Mr. Yeatman," one man was saying, "to convert a riverboat to a floating hospital."

"Yes, it is, isn't it?" Yeatman agreed, sounding very pleased. "I can't imagine why it didn't occur to us before." Hayes knew the speaker was James Yeatman, president of the Western Sanitary Commission, Dorothea Dix's representative in certifying nursing volunteers, and a citizen well-known throughout St. Louis for his good deeds.

"We could outfit the ship," he was saying, "with beds, a dispensary, and a large galley for preparing food. A ship like that could have a permanent staff to look after the injured and carry extra supplies as well. It's a brilliant idea, and we must put it into action immediately.''

Hayes turned to face the man, a plan forming in his mind, one that would aid both their cause and his own. "Please, gentlemen, forgive me for eavesdropping, but I think designing and building a hospital ship is a fine goal, one I'd be delighted to help you achieve.''

"It's Mr. Banister, isn't it?'' Yeatman acknowledged him. "You've been working with James Eads on building those splendid ironclads. Do you know Mr. Forman?''

Hayes nodded in greeting and continued. "I couldn't help but overhear that you were discussing the conversion of a riverboat to a floating hospital, and I thought that as a naval engineer I might be able to help.''

"The hospital ship does seem to be a likely idea,'' Yeatman said enthusiastically "don't you think? The railroad cars we converted last summer have proved to be quite effective.''

"Indeed I do,'' Hayes agreed, "but the idea was suggested to me some months ago by a young lady working in one of the St. Louis hospitals. Will you permit me to bring the plans I drew then to the Sanitary Commission offices? Perhaps they will offer some suggestions you have not yet considered, or you could advise me how to alter the drawings to make them more feasible. Either way, I'm offering my services, if you want them.''

"That's very generous of you, Mr. Banister,'' Forman broke in. "We'd welcome your advice.''

"There's one thing I'd like to suggest,'' Hayes continued casually, though a dimple crept into one cheek. "You might talk to some of the Sanitary Commission nurses before you put your plans into motion. Women familiar with the problems of caring for the injured might well be able to make practical suggestions we men would overlook.''

Yeatman considered the younger man for a long moment. "That idea does have merit, Mr. Banister. Do you have someone particular in mind?''

Hayes's eyes twinkled, and a self-satisfied smile curled his generous mouth. "Well,'' he began with counterfeit reluctance, "Leigh Pennington first gave me the idea for a hospital ship, so it only seems right that she should be consulted."

"Very well, Mr. Banister, Miss Pennington will be among the nurses we include on our committee. I know Dr. Hodgen thinks highly of her, and she has proved herself very competent in her care of the men at City General Hospital."

Banister's smile became a grin, and he felt more lighthearted than he had since the night Leigh had staunchly refused to marry him. "Good, Mr. Yeatman, good. But will you do me the favor of not mentioning my name when you ask her?"

"Of course, Banister, if you say so," Yeatman agreed, though he eyed the younger man curiously.

"I do, Mr. Yeatman. Yes, indeed, I do."

10 ⌒

February 26, 1862—St. Louis, Missouri

Automatically elevating the hem of her gown the prescribed, ladylike two inches to keep the flowing black fabric out of the mud, Leigh Pennington crossed the busy St. Louis levee. The sun had finally broken through the overcast after a day of gloom, and the sketchy gray clouds that hung just above the horizon were tipped by the intensity of the slanting, yellow-gold light. As she teetered over the uneven cobblestones toward the line of riverboats that nuzzled along the waterfront, James Yeatman came striding toward her.

"Good heavens, Leigh," the trim, middle-aged man admonished, "you should have waited at the edge of the road for someone to come and help you."

"I'm quite used to doing for myself these days," she answered as she looped her hand gratefully through his elbow, "though it's nice to have someone to lean on now and then. Is that the *City of Louisiana*?"

In the scant two weeks since Forts Donelson and Henry had fallen to Grant's combined land and river forces, nearly ten thousand wounded men had been brought to northern hospitals, transported on troop ships that had neither staff, supplies, nor facilities to see to their needs. Now the Western Sanitary Commission was making arrangements to charter and refurbish the *City of Louisiana* as a hospital ship for removal of the wounded from battles that would be fought to reclaim the Mississippi Valley for the Union.

The boat that lay before them at the edge of the river was a handsome craft, typical of the luxury packets that had plied their trade on the river prior to the war. Painted crisp, clean white, the upper decks dripped cobwebs of gingerbread from every upright, and brilliantly colored glass sparkled in the skylights that overlooked the salon. Yet, in spite of the lacy ornamentation and its opulent details, the boat's long, graceful lines spoke of speed and maneuverability.

The *City of Louisiana* was a beautiful boat, but it had seen much less than its usual service since the war began. In its heyday the main deck would have been crowded with roustabouts, slaves, and common folk; with cargo and livestock; with huge stacks of wood or mounds of coal awaiting sacrifice to the riverboat's engines for the sake of greater speed. Above it rose the promenade deck with accommodations for more affluent passengers. Here men would have passed their time between St. Louis and Keokuk gaming and talking in the packet's saloon, while the ladies gathered farther toward the stern in the plush, carpeted sitting room decorated for their pleasure. This long central salon was generally flanked by cabins, outfitted with bunks and washstands, where passengers would retire for the night. Above that was the Texas deck, the crew's domain, where the captain, mates, and pilots had their quarters. Overseeing it all was the pilothouse, the nerve center of the ship, where life and death decisions were made a dozen times a day.

Leigh had given the concept of a hospital ship a good deal of thought since the night she had discussed it with Hayes Banister, and it was gratifying to know that the *City of Louisiana* would be transformed into the kind of vessel she had envisioned. What's more, she was surprised and delighted that she had been asked to make suggestions for refurbishing it. She had gambled her reputation and respectability for the chance to help the sick, and she interpreted this invitation as vindication for the sacrifices she had made. She had proved herself as a military nurse, and the acceptance this committee appointment represented meant far more to her than anyone knew.

As Yeatman escorted her up the gangway, they greeted the rest of the committee: Mrs. King and Mrs. Foster from the Ladies Union Aide Society, as well as Mr. Forman and Dr. Thompson from the Sanitary Commission. Leigh was the youngest person in attendance, and she was proud they had considered her ideas valuable. Not long before, she had been denied a chance to prove her skill at military nursing by the very people who were seeking out her opinion now. Her presence here was a great victory, but one she was well bred enough to celebrate in silence.

Once they were assembled, Yeatman led the way upstairs, reassuring the committee about the boat's soundness and mechanical condition as they went. On the promenade deck, they entered what had once been a well-appointed salon. It was all but empty now, except for a long table near the front windows and the few bentwood chairs gathered around it. Leaving the others by the door, Leigh walked the length of the room. The late afternoon sun streaming through the stained-glass transoms at the roofline cast rich, jewel-toned shapes across the floor, and two rows of gaudily painted doors stood like sentries guarding the staterooms beyond. Those staterooms could be pressed into service for the use of the nurses and doctors assigned to the boat, Leigh decided as she eyed them, and for isolating the more serious cases being carried north. Already in her mind's eye she could see neat rows of cots running the length of the room and efficient, well-trained nurses moving between them. Yes, the *City of Louisiana* did look promising indeed, and outfitted properly it could carry close to five hundred men.

Smiling her approval, Leigh turned back to the group that had gathered around the table, but the smile froze on her lips as she recognized the man who had joined them.

It had been well over a month since Leigh had refused Hayes Banister's marriage proposal, and in that time she had done her best to force both it and Hayes from her mind. She still believed that no good could come from an allegiance between them, an allegiance based on illicit passion and betrayal, and she had been determined to avoid him, lest he find a way to convince her otherwise.

She had not wanted to see Hayes and had deliberately denied herself his friendship. Yet when she heard he had gone into battle with the ironclads, dread had stolen through her, a dread that miraculously evaporated at the sight of him across the room.

Of course she was glad to find him well and strong, she told herself defensively, especially when she saw such horrendously wounded men in her nursing. But in spite of her silent admonitions and her wordless denials, a starburst of relief and welcome sparked within her and moved with tingling pleasure through her blood. Her eyes drank in the sight of him, noting the way the blue broadcloth coat strained taut across his shoulders as he reached to unroll one of the drawings, the way the sunshine highlighted the sinewy strength of his hands. Then he turned from the table to where she stood.

"Leigh, how good it is to see you," he greeted her, his cool, aquamarine eyes filled with satisfaction.

She studied his expression for a moment before comprehension began to dawn, and then the pride she had felt at being selected as one of the committee to plan the hospital ship gave way to a sharp twist of disappointment. It was suddenly obvious why she was here; Hayes Banister had arranged it. Her merit as a military nurse had nothing to do with her selection; she had not won anyone's respect with the good she had been able to do at the hospital. She was aboard the *City of Louisiana* only because Hayes Banister wanted her to be. With that realization, her disappointment and hurt pride became controlled, but brilliantly glowing, anger.

Seeing her reaction but at a loss to explain it, Hayes raised one hand to gesture graciously toward the table. "I hope you'll be pleased by the plans I drew for the hospital ship you suggested."

Fixing him with an icy stare, Leigh crossed the floor to stand beside him. On the table was a diagram of the promenade deck of the *City of Louisiana* with the space meticulously divided and labeled.

"This will be the surgery," Hayes pointed out, as if speaking to her alone. "I located it in the front of the salon to take advantage of the best light and ventilation. And these forward cabins will be used to prepare the wounded."

A ripple of surprise and pleasure moved through Leigh in spite of her anger. It was just as she had pictured the ship herself. Behind her she heard the other members of the committee murmuring in agreement.

"This area behind the operating room will be a large general ward with as many cots as we can conveniently fit. Some of the staterooms could be removed to provide for even more beds," Hayes continued. "The section at the rear of the salon will be turned into a dispensary, and I've indicated the location of more bathroom facilities, complete with hot and cold running water."

"What about the kitchen?" one of the women asked. "We will need to have tea and soup prepared at all times in addition to the regular meals we'll cook there."

"Then I think the kitchen area might need to be enlarged," Hayes answered thoughtfully. "If that's the case, I suggest we enclose these areas on the afterdeck."

Leigh was frankly impressed by what he proposed and was pleased that it so closely paralleled the ideas they had discussed months before. "Where will the nurses and doctors stay?" she asked.

"Since a hospital ship won't employ a full crew, I thought the Texas deck could be pressed into service for the staff. The rooms are small, but they won't be used for much more than sleeping. It might also be welcome to have the staff's accommodations somewhat removed from the ward areas."

"Where will the sanitary stores be transported, Mr. Banister?" Yeatman asked. "There will be times when the *City of Louisiana* will need to carry far more than she can use herself."

"Those supplies would be stored on the main deck, much as cargo was stored before the war. I think it's safe to say that the *City of Louisiana* can transport whatever additional supplies you need for the wounded."

For the next hour they talked, making changes in the plans, suggesting modifications, and discussing problems.

Hayes adjusted the drawings as they talked or made notes along the margins in a bold, legible hand.

Finally James Yeatman spoke. "And how long will it take you to finish the modifications we've decided on?"

Hayes was silent for a moment as he studied the drawings. "If we start tomorrow, I think I could promise you completion by mid-March. Few of the changes we've discussed are structural, so the work should go quickly."

"And the cost?" he persisted. Hayes named a figure, and Yeatman nodded. "Then we should be able to have the entire project completed for about three thousand dollars. Very well, Mr. Banister, get on with the work, and let us know as soon as we can begin to bring beds and supplies aboard. Now, if you will excuse me, I need to stop by City General Hospital before supper."

"Leigh, would you like a ride home in my carriage?" Mr. Forman asked as the group began to break up.

"I'll see to Miss Pennington," Hayes offered quickly, and Forman had turned to follow the others before Leigh had a chance to object.

"I don't want you 'seeing to Miss Pennington,' " she stated furiously as she watched the rest depart. "I didn't ever want to see you again!"

"Hush, Leigh, we have things to discuss," Hayes whispered, "and besides, when I met your father the other day in the street, he gave me permission to escort you home this evening.'

"You seem to have this entire venture very well planned," she accused angrily.

"I won't deny that I wanted to see you, and I was pleased by the way things fell together." His voice was calm and even.

"Well, I don't appreciate your ordering my life for me, Hayes Banister. I told you before I no longer welcomed your company, and I meant it! How you have the unmitigated gall to force yourself on me, to request that I be included in this project simply because—"

"Simply because these ideas were originally yours? Because you've nursed long enough to understand what's needed to make a venture like this succeed?"

"Simply because you wanted me here for your own nefarious purposes!" Leigh accused.

Hayes seemed determined to remain unruffled by her accusations and to see beyond her anger. Taking in the disillusionment in her eyes, he realized that her tension was based in something deeper than he had supposed. "What's really bothering you, Leigh?" he asked softly.

His perceptiveness unnerved Leigh, and color rose in her cheeks. "Whatever do you mean?"

"You're more upset by this than you should be. What's really the matter? Is it your parents?"

A spasm of misery twisted through Leigh. For months Hayes had been her confidant and friend, and she missed the closeness they had shared. He had been the only one who understood how the hostility in the house on Locust Street affected her. He had shared the joys and sorrows of her days at the hospital and kept her safe from Aaron Crawford's advances. For so long she had accepted his friendship and strength, offering in return companionship and laughter to banish his loneliness.

For both their sakes, she longed to resume the warm relationship that had developed between them. She needed a friend so much right now, and she knew Hayes would not have gone to such trouble to approach her if he was happy as things were. But she could not help but wonder at his reasons for seeking her out. Was he merely concerned about the ramifications of what had happened that afternoon on the *Barbara Dean,* or did he miss her as much as she did him? With all her heart she wished that her friendship with Hayes was still intact, but it was not. In the depths of her grief for Lucas, she had asked Hayes to make love to her, and that had ruined everything.

"Leigh, please tell me why you're angry?" Hayes's voice was soft, gentle, and beguiling, playing on weaknesses he knew she possessed.

With a frown of resignation, she gave him her answer, masking her regret and disappointment with difficulty. "I thought I was being asked to help with this project because of the good I've been able to do at the hospital, because someone valued my opinion as a nurse. But as it turns out, I'm only here because you wanted me to be."

Hayes nodded in understanding, and with a finger beneath her chin, turned her face to his. "You're here because you deserve to be," he told her. "Months ago you had the inspiration for a ship like this, and it only seemed right that you should see your idea come to fruition. I admit I asked that you be included in the committee, but it was because you have been a part of this from the start, not for any other reason."

Standing in the graying twilight with the last apricot rays of the setting sun playing across his features, Hayes seemed so honest and sincere. Was he telling the truth? Could she afford to believe him?

Before she could make up her mind, Leigh became intensely aware of Hayes: of the strength of his hand beneath her chin, of the clean citrus scent that was so much a part of him, of the warmth that emanated from his body in the unheated salon. He was the man who had made her a woman, and, standing only inches from him now, she remembered everything that had passed between them in the name of passion. Sensations stirred across her palms, and she clenched her fingers into fists in mute denial of her desire to touch him.

"I thought you wanted to see me home," she whispered, determined to ignore the feelings sweeping through her.

"I do"—he spoke slowly, as if he did not want this moment to pass—"but first I need the answer to one question."

It was obvious what he wanted to know. Leigh turned away to stare out across the levee, determined that he would not sense her thoughts. "Yes, what is it?"

She heard him draw a long breath before he put his question into words. "Is there any reason for you to change your mind about marrying me?"

She tried to analyze his voice, to read the feelings reflected by the inflection and timbre. There was concern and tenderness overlaid with something she could not identify. "No, I'm not going to have your child, so you won't be bound to me on that account."

Hayes drew another long breath, and she turned her

head to look up at him. His pale, blue-gray eyes were stark and impenetrable, and she was surprised by his expression. He should be relieved that he wasn't going to be forced to take her to the altar. He should be as glad as she that there was no reason to spend their lives together. Surely he hadn't wanted to marry her, had he? For an instant it seemed that another question was poised on his lips, but with a frown he quelled whatever it was he had been about to say.

They stood for an eon without speaking: Leigh with her heart beating high in her throat, totally aware of the danger of being alone with him, and Hayes seeking God knew what in her face.

Finally, Leigh forced herself to break the silence. "Isn't it time you took me home?"

Hayes shrugged and turned away. "I only need to gather up my drawings," he mumbled.

Leigh watched him roll the papers into cylinders, then slide them into narrow tubes. "The plans for the hospital ship were wonderful," she admitted softly after a minute. "They were just as I had pictured it myself."

At her words of praise, Hayes glanced up with surprise and pleasure. Light shone in his eyes and warmth softened his hard features.

"Leigh, I—" he began, but Leigh cut him short. She wanted so much more from this man than her conscience would let her accept.

"Please take me home, Hayes, just as you promised. Please take me home and let that be an end to it." With a clatter of shoes on the decking, Leigh hurried toward the door.

Hayes was too powerful, too determined, too tempting, too close to being irresistible, Leigh acknowledged as she fled the intimacy of the deserted salon. Already she had betrayed Lucas with him once, and she could not let that happen again. The night she had learned of Lucas's death she had made three vows to appease her conscience: to devote herself exclusively to the care of the wounded, to show compassion to Rebel and Yankee alike, and never again to give herself to Hayes Banister. She had made the promises in the depths of grief and guilt, knowing they were the only way to atone for what she'd done. She had betrayed Lucas with another man, betrayed his loyalty and his love, and never could she forgive herself that transgression.

But in the days since then she had discovered another reason for keeping her distance: she missed Hayes with a compelling physical ache that had nothing to do with her love for Lucas Hale. She had liked Hayes's touch and the sensations of his hands and mouth upon her body, reveled in the intense, intimate pleasure of his long-limbed form against her own. Her awareness of these new, unexpected sensations set off a whole series of doubts within her. She knew far better than most the price that could be extracted for succumbing to the lure of insidious sensation, and for both their sakes it was imperative that she maintain her distance from the man who had awakened her desire.

Leigh had reached the gangway when Hayes caught up to her. "Is that really the way you want it?" he demanded, hauling her roughly to a stop. "Do you really want me out of your life for good?" In the dusk his face seemed stern and remote, but once again there was something piercing and unfathomable in the depths of his eyes. "Don't you ever want to see me again?"

Leigh stared at him a moment, realizing what an affirmative answer might mean. It meant that she was ending a friendship that had offered her warmth and security, denying a bond that had been between them from the start. It meant that she was turning from a man who had taught her all she knew of passion. As difficult as it was, in her heart Leigh knew what she must say.

"Please find me a carriage, Hayes." Her voice was soft and low. "And then let's say good-bye."

March 26, 1862—Near Corinth, Mississippi

Hayes Banister lay in the gully at the edge of the road, sighting down the barrel of his pistol at the four Confederate cavalrymen talking with Nathan Travis. Even from the distance their butternut uniforms looked torn and faded, and he could see the boots they wore were Union, not Confederate, Army issue.

Travis, dressed in farmer's garb, gestured down the road, and by his tone Banister could tell he was asking questions. From where he was concealed in the underbrush, Hayes could hear the men's voices but not their words, and with difficulty stifled the urge to move a little closer so he could make out what the Rebs had to say. Still, he dared not succumb to curiosity and make his presence known. Nathan's only safeguard in approaching the Confederate patrol was that Banister lay hidden, ready to come to his aid if need be.

He had not wanted to be a part of this scouting mission, Hayes reflected as he watched the men before him, but Albert Pincheon had insisted. For reasons Banister did not fully understand, the other man had been delighted by the reports he and Travis had made on the battles at Forts Henry and Donelson, and Pincheon had been adamant that they scout the next phase of the campaign, the move on Corinth, Mississippi. The town of Corinth was vitally important to both armies in that the Memphis and Charleston Railroad passed directly through it, linking the eastern and western parts of the Confederacy. In order that the flow of supplies and fresh men from the agricultural West continue, it was vital for the Southerners to retain control of the railroad. Conversely, the Federal forces would gain a great advantage if that flow could be disrupted.

The hand clamped tight around the butt of his pistol grew clammy as Hayes waited for Nathan Travis to conclude his conversation. Would they learn anything of value from these rough, unkempt Southerners? To his mind, it was courting danger to expose yourself to the enemy, but Hayes had learned to trust the other man's judgment, and Travis had welcomed the chance to approach them.

As Banister watched, the Confederates reached for the slender, dark cigars Travis had taken from his pocket. Pausing in the conversation to strike a match and light his own smoke, Travis cupped his hands around the flame and was offering it to the leader of the patrol when a deer broke cover directly behind where Hayes lay concealed in the underbrush. All the Confederates' heads snapped up at the sound, their cigars still clamped between their teeth. The tangle of brambles at the roadside that had seemed to offer such good camouflage a moment before was suddenly useless as cover, and Hayes lay exposed and vulnerable before the Rebels' narrowed eyes. For a moment the troopers seemed frozen, then their hands flashed toward their guns as what had seemed like a friendly conversation suddenly became a confrontation.

As the leader trained his rifle on the spot where Hayes lay, Travis pulled the pistol from his belt and fired. The Confederate's weapon discharged as he fell from his horse, sending a minie ball whizzing past where Banister lay. Almost without volition the gun in Hayes's hand answered the challenge, catching the man to the leader's left full in the chest. The horses were spooked by the sound of the erupting fire, and it was a moment before either of the remaining Rebels could get off a shot. One of them sighted on Travis at point-blank range while the other man's ball embedded itself in the ground just beyond Hayes's elbow. As the troopers adjusted their aim, Hayes burst from the underbrush, firing as he ran. The first shot felled one of the two men, and though the other fired at him, Hayes's marksmanship was better. A moment later the last Rebel crashed to the ground to lie motionless between his horse's feet.

Hayes froze where he stood, tensed and alert for any sign of movement, his smoking gun hot in hand. A sulfurous cloud of spent powder hovered over the woodland clearing, the late-afternoon sunlight trapped in the drifting, smoky haze. Reacting slowly, Banister moved to where Travis lay.

"Damn it, Hayes, check to be sure those Rebs are dead before you see to me!" Nathan said fiercely between clenched teeth, clutching at his shoulder. "Don't you have any sense at all?"

If the men were only wounded, they might well be very dangerous, but Hayes was not used to thinking in terms of survival. Slowly he approached the leader of the patrol. The man was where he had fallen, with Nathan's bullet through his chest. Moving to examine the three men he had shot himself was difficult but necessary. The first still hung in the saddle, though he was clearly dead. The second lay sprawled in the bloodstained dust, his head half blown away. Hayes swallowed hard and approached the remaining man. He lay on his side, and Hayes pulled gingerly at his shoulder.

The last Confederate rolled onto his back, and as he did, his hand came up filled with a cocked pistol that he coolly leveled at Banister. For an instant a century long, Hayes watched the hatred and pain in the other man's face, seeing his desire to avenge the death of his comrades. This trooper was hardly more than a boy, yet his murderous intensity was ancient and deadly. His finger tightened around the trigger, and Hayes's chest contracted in anticipation of the bullet tearing through it. But though the Rebel pulled his trigger, the gun did not fire, and it was Hayes's shot instead that echoed in the clearing.

As the sound faded, so did the light in the young man's eyes: surprise giving way to confusion, then to a penetrating introspection that slowly dimmed to nothingness. As Hayes watched the Confederate's passage from life to death, the realization of his own part in the process washed over him in a debilitating tide. The sunlit clearing spun dizzily around him, and he fought an almost overwhelming urge to be sick.

It was Nathan Travis's need for care and the danger they were facing that forced Hayes into action. Using techniques he had learned after the battle at Fort Donelson, he bandaged Nathan's wound. The ball had passed completely through his shoulder, and Hayes hurried Travis onto his horse as soon as the bleeding was under control.

With the skirmish in the clearing, their welfare had suddenly become Hayes's responsibility, and he did not welcome the new role he was expected to play. Travis had a natural instinct for survival that Hayes did not, but he used the things the other man had taught him to set a course back toward the Union lines. They had finished their work for Pincheon, and there was little more required to them but to turn their information over to their contact on General Grant's staff.

Their mission had been successful, and Hayes was cer-

tain that their information would do a great deal to augment Grant's intelligence. There were indeed Confederates
gathering at Corinth: an army of nearly forty thousand men
under Albert Sidney Johnston. With him were Beauregard,
the hero of Fort Sumter and Bull Run, Generals Braxton
Bragg, Leonidas Polk, William Hardee, and their massed
armies. The Confederates were preparing to defend with
all their strength the vital railway that ran through the sleepy
Southern town. But would they fortify Corinth and wait
for the inevitable Federal attack, or would they launch an
offensive of their own before Carlos Buell's army from
Nashville could rendezvous with Grant? Already the Union
forces were threatening Corinth, bivouacked in the woods
only twenty-two miles away. Might it not be better for the
men under the Confederate command to take advantage of
Grant's limited strength and attack before Buell arrived?

They were questions Hayes was not prepared to answer.
He was no military tactician, nor was he cut out to be a
spy, regardless of what Pincheon thought. He was an
engineer, more at home with a steamship's plans and
construction than the offensives in a war. And with a
single-minded desperation he longed for the familiarity and
safety of his office in St. Louis.

For most of the afternoon Nathan Travis was weak but
lucid, clinging to his horse with singular tenacity, but by
nightfall a fever had come upon him. As they moved
stealthily through the dark, he muttered incoherently, his
eyes glassy and vacant. Though Hayes knew Travis needed
rest, he pressed on, wanting to put as many miles between
them and the Confederates as possible before they were
forced to stop.

As Hayes picked their way through the forest and across
roughened farmer's fields, he let himself think for the first
time about what had happened in the clearing. His perceptions of the incident were astonishingly clear: the shock of
being under fire, the moment of paralyzing fear, and then
the spark of ruthless anger running through him, urging
him to action. Caught up in those fierce, uncontrolled
emotions he had killed three men. He had taken human
life! With what realization, nausea clawed at his throat,

but he stubbornly fought it down. He accepted the spontaneity of the deed, the need to kill or be killed, but he also sought to understand the scope and effect of his mindless actions. Hayes considered himself a supremely rational man, yet it had taken no conscious thought or consideration to deprive another man of life. He had done it swiftly, casually, callously, and he was appalled by what he'd done. It was as if someone else had pulled the trigger, some ruthless, violent stranger had aimed and fired his gun. The act had been sudden, cold-blooded, irrevocable, and Hayes was stunned that danger could have unleashed this unsuspected facet of his personality.

Yet, at the same time, he was discovering a raw, unquenchable will to survive stirring inside him. It was a will that made him feel strong, resilient, and vitally alive. It negated all his feelings of horror or responsibility. His actions this afternoon had freed him from any doubts about his courage, but they had also bound him with the understanding of the terrible power for life or death he held within his hands.

Travis began to murmur vague requests for water, and Hayes realized that he must stop to see to Nathan's needs. Food and a chance to rest would do them both good, he reasoned, so Hayes followed the sound of rippling water through the forest and made camp beside a stream. He dared not light a fire for fear that there were enemy nearby, but he took a bit of the johnnycake they had made at breakfast and forced Travis to eat, washing the coarse bread down with water. Before rolling the other man in both their blankets, he checked the wound for further bleeding and sponged Nathan's burning face and chest. By tomorrow they would reach the Union lines, and Travis would get the kind of medical attention Hayes could not provide, but for now he had made the other man comfortable.

Nathan drifted into an uneasy sleep, and Hayes propped himself up against a tree to watch over him. In the loneliness of the seemingly endless night, when the man beside him muttered in delirium and his own thoughts were hardly less confused, Hayes's mind was filled with visions of Leigh: Leigh with holly woven through her mahogany hair, dancing in his arms; Leigh teasing and laughing as they stood together waiting for the horsecar; Leigh flushed and willing beneath him the single time he had made love to her. During the past month, he had missed Leigh desperately, but she had cut herself off from him completely by refusing involvement in the hospital-ship project.

In the cold, wet, lonely night, Hayes readily acknowledged his need for her. He wanted her beside him always, and he once more searched his mind for a way to make her his wife. Somehow just the sight of her and the sound of her voice had the power to soothe him. And, dear God, how desperately he wanted and needed to be soothed!

He could not tell her what had happened today. She would understand neither the events that led him to take a life, nor his feelings about what had happened. But Leigh did have the power to give him comfort and succor; Leigh alone could offer rest to his weary soul. In the darkness, the tension of the past days overwhelmed Hayes, and in the somnolent world of wishes granted Leigh came to comfort him.

April 4, 1862—St. Louis, Missouri

Althea Pennington stabbed her needle into the rough cotton fabric, letting the shirt she was sewing absorb the brunt of her frustrations. She was known for her ability with a needle, for her intricate embroidery and the delicate tatted lace that spilled from her busy fingers like strings of gossamer snowflakes. She wasn't at her best on such mundane things, but hundreds of these wretched muslin shirts were needed for the sick and wounded in the hospitals and convalescent camps that surrounded the city. At least it was a chance to be useful, she rationalized as she adjusted her thimble, though she was at a loss to explain why she was doing anything at all to support a war she could not condone. She hated every aspect of this conflict and resented the changes it had wrought in her life.

She supposed she resented the change in her marriage most: that Horace no longer had time or patience for her, that during the few precious hours he was in St. Louis he was busy with political meetings or preoccupied with business concerns. She also despised the part he had elected to play in the war. It was bad enough that he believed in Lincoln and in preserving the Union, but to actually involve himself in procuring supplies for an army that was moving deeper and deeper into the heart of her homeland was truly intolerable. Nor was she pleased that his job entailed prolonged visits to central Missouri, where hostilities between the North and South raged unresolved. Conditions in the city were bad enough without venturing into the lawless no-man's-land that the western counties had become. His was a foolish and dangerous occupation, in addition to being one of which she heartily disapproved.

Of course, animosity was rife within the city, too. Northern and Southern supporters no longer spoke when they passed in the streets, and the town was filled to overflowing with refugees from the West. The influx of Federal supporters driven from their homes by Rebel marauders had grown so large that General Halleck had ordered a levy paid by the most vocal Confederate families to help support the homeless. Of course, the people involved had refused to pay such an unfair tax, so their household goods were confiscated and sold at public auction to pay what they owed. Because of Horace's support of the Union, the Penningtons had not been affected, but the tax and confiscation had given Althea and her husband one more thing to argue about when they were together.

How things had come to this, Althea could not say, and the estrangement from Horace made her sick at heart. Their marriage had always been a volatile one, but before, the differences had been fleeting: loudly argued, then swiftly forgotten. This time, it was well over a year since they had spoken a civil word to each other or shared a bed. It was no wonder that when Horace was home, hostility hung in the air with the silent menace of an approaching storm. Sighing, Althea set her sewing aside. She still loved her husband deeply, but it had been a very long time since he had made her happy. And she was beginning to realize that her discontent ran far deeper than the war.

Listlessly she rose and took a turn around the parlor,

pausing at the window to look up and down the street. The
house was quiet at this hour in the afternoon with Horace
downtown seeing to his business, Leigh away on a trip
with Dr. Phillips for the Sanitary Commission, and the
servants going on about their business at the other end of
the house. It was quiet and far too conducive to reflecting
on things that Althea preferred to ignore. Still dark, oppressive thoughts assailed her.

She was worried about Leigh. Her daughter had changed
dramatically since the tragic news of Lucas Hale's death
had reached them, and she was working far too hard at the
hospital. Leigh had even begun to put in some time at the
Western Sanitary Commission's busy offices. Though Althea could not help but envy her sense of accomplishment,
there was no respite from the duty that seemed to drive
her. Leigh was submerging her grief over Lucas in the
grueling hours she worked. But in spite of her feelings for
her fiancé, this was no way for a beautiful girl of twenty-
three to behave.

Althea would not have been so concerned about her
daughter if Leigh had at least taken an interest in the
parties and galas that were being given to raise money for
both Union and Confederate causes. Though both Althea
and Aaron Crawford had tried to convince her to attend,
Leigh would not stir. It was as if she were trying to cut
herself off from anything that would take her into public
life, anything that would bring her into contact with eligi-
ble men. She had even refused to become involved with
the Sanitary Commission's efforts to outfit a hospital ship,
though any other time Leigh would have been wild to
work on such a venture. Althea could not imagine what
ailed her daughter. Was Leigh condemned to be a spinster
because of Lucas's death? Other women were widows and
then brides again in shockingly short times. Why wouldn't
Leigh even entertain the thought of seeing men beyond her
work at the hospital? Even a marriage like the one Althea
was enduring with Horace was better than being alone.

Frowning, she drifted back to her chair and reluctantly
picked up her sewing. She only needed three more of these
miserable shirts to complete the even dozen she had prom-

ised to have ready by Saturday. But, good heavens, how
she hated the job!

It was late afternoon when Althea heard someone come
to the front door. She listened carefully to the voices in the
corridor, thankful for the diversion. Through the heavy
double panels that separated the parlor from the hallway,
she could just barely discern the deepness of a man's
voice, and she wondered who it was. Moments later a
maid appeared to appease Althea's curiosity. Putting down
her needle, she glanced at the calling card on the silver
card tray. In beautifully embellished script was a name she
had not heard for several months. "Mr. Hayes Banister."

There had been a falling out between this man and her
daughter, but Leigh stubbornly refused to discuss it. Now
Mr. Banister had shown up here late in the afternoon,
obviously hoping to find Leigh at home. It was all very
interesting, and suddenly Althea hoped that Hayes Banister
had indeed come looking for her daughter.

Once, Althea had harbored the hope that the friendship
between the two would blossom into something deeper.
There was an air about Banister that spoke of both strength
and tenderness; qualities any man who married her daughter should possess in infinite quantities. Hayes had hinted
at his deeper feelings for Leigh at the disastrous party
they'd attended just after Christmas, but since then Leigh
had hardly mentioned his name. Now Althea was certain
that whatever had caused the estrangement between them
was her daughter's doing and not Hayes Banister's.

If he had braved coming to the house like this, had
made an appearance after so many months' absence, he
must care a great deal more for Leigh than Althea had
suspected. She would see the man at least, she conceded.
Without giving away any of her daughter's secrets, she
would listen to what Banister had to say.

Thoughtfully she turned the card between her fingers.
"Show Mr. Banister in, Lucy," she instructed, wondering
what excuse he would make to explain his call.

A moment later Hayes Banister's masculine vitality filled
the room, and Althea smiled a greeting, pleased to see him
on more than her daughter's behalf.

"How good it is of you to stop by, Mr. Banister. You've been away from our door far too long."

There was unusually high color along Hayes's cheekbones and an expression on his face that was a combination of determination and chagrin.

"It's good to see you too, Mrs. Pennington," he answered, as his flush deepened. "I've come to see about my hat."

11 ❧

April 6, 1862—St. Louis, Missouri

Hayes Banister had just finished shaving in preparation for a leisurely Sunday breakfast at the Planters' House Hotel when a message from the president of the Western Sanitary Commission arrived aboard the *Barbara Dean*:

Dear Hayes,
General Halleck has received word that a battle has been joined with General Albert Sidney Johnston's Confederate troops north of Corinth, Mississippi, at Pittsburg Landing. We are outfitting several steamboats as hospital ships and would welcome your help.
Yours truly,
James Yeatman

The news of the battle was unexpected, and since Hayes was certain that General Grant had not considered a Confederate attack on his positions a possibility, the Rebels must have taken him by surprise. Hastily, Hayes wiped the remaining lather from his face and pulled on a shirt, wondering when they would receive more news. The battle was bound to be a confrontation of some magnitude, he reasoned, simply because of the size of the armies involved. Between them Johnston and Grant must be able to put close to eighty thousand troops into the field. As he hastily tied the knot in his cravat, Hayes thought about the

inauspicious landing and the surrounding woodland that at
this minute must be echoing with the sounds of shot and
shell. Had Sherman at the landing and Grant farther upstream at Savannah, Tennessee, had the foresight to prepare for a Confederate advance? Less than a fortnight
before, the Union generals had been unwilling to even
consider the possibility of attack and had refused to heed
the warnings that both he and Nathan Travis had voiced.
Surely they had seen evidence of Confederate troop movements on their positions in the days since he had left
Tennessee for Cairo and St. Louis, and had prepared
themselves to hold their lines. Dear God, he hoped they'd
had that much foresight, at least.

Twenty minutes later, Hayes was fully dressed and striding purposefully toward the far end of the St. Louis levee,
where Western Sanitary Commission volunteers had already begun to gather. They were milling around on the
cobblestones listening to Yeatman's directions while a couple of heavy delivery drays loaded with hospital stores
were pulling up beside the two large riverboats lolling in
the current.

It was a few minutes before Yeatman had finished or-
ganizing the others, and Hayes waited impatiently, his
mind full of questions. "James, what can I do?" he asked
in greeting when Yeatman was finished.

"Hayes, I'm so glad you could come. We've made
arrangements to use the *Continental* and the *Crescent
City*"—he nodded toward the steamboats tied up at the
edge of the river—"to transport our medical people and
supplies to Pittsburg Landing. The *Imperial* is going to
meet us there as soon as she can. What we need is to turn
these boats into floating hospitals and get them under way
as quickly as possible."

Hayes took the measure of the two ships that lay along
the levee, pleased by what he saw. "What is the word
from the battle? Will the casualties be heavy?"

Yeatman frowned. "News is sketchy at best, but it
looks like things are pretty bad. The Confederates attacked
just after dawn while Grant's troops were still at breakfast.
It seems they weren't expected."

Hayes refrained from commenting on the situation on

the Tennessee River and nodded instead. "What about the *City of Louisiana*?"

"She's been at Pittsburg Landing already with a load of supplies."

"That's fortunate, at least. Will she stay there or return?"

"She went to deliver stores and pick up men with pneumonia and chronic problems. She should be well on her way back with them by now. Besides, we'll need her to help transport supplies and the volunteer nurses we're mustering," Yeatman explained.

Hayes tried unsuccessfully to bite back his next question, already more than sure of the answer. "Is Leigh Pennington one of those volunteers?"

"Leigh's already at Pittsburg Landing," Yeatman told him distractedly, watching some men maneuver another wagon down the steeply sloped levee.

"What?" A jolt of fear went through Hayes at Yeatman's answer. What the hell was Leigh doing down at Pittsburg Landing?

"She went with the *City of Louisiana* a day or two ago," Yeatman continued. "Since she asked to be removed from the hospital-ship committee, she's been working with Dr. Phillips on the dispersal of Sanitary Commission supplies. The two of them went to Tennessee to find out if our methods are working successfully."

Hayes ground out a curse between his teeth. So Leigh had been on her way to Pittsburg Landing the afternoon he had visited with her mother. Why hadn't Althea Pennington told him where she was instead of letting him sit there for the best part of an hour, hoping to get a glimpse of her elusive daughter? What possessed Leigh to go to Pittsburg Landing in the first place? He could only hope that she was safe on the *City of Louisiana* instead of tending to the wounded somewhere under fire. With difficulty Hayes turned his thoughts on the problems at hand.

"While the boats are being loaded, would you like me to check to make sure they're mechanically sound?"

"That would be wonderful," Yeatman agreed enthusiastically. "We want to leave as soon as possible."

"James," Hayes tossed over his shoulder as he moved

toward one of the riverboats. "I'm going with you when you leave, if that's all right."

"Fine, Hayes, fine," Yeatman agreed, headed in the opposite direction. "I have a feeling we'll need all the help we can get."

April 6, 1862—Pittsburg Landing, Tennessee

Wounded men lay in uneven rows on the floor of the Federal troop transport ship *Emerald,* their pleas for water filling the air. It was midafternoon, and the battle that had begun at dawn with a Confederate charge on Union positions was going badly. It was evident by the torrent of wounded that swept across the gangplank, the spent shot that had begun to patter on the deck like summer rain, and the growing number of deserters gathered in a bleating mass at the foot of the river bluff. Panic was in the air, a panic that only the turning tide of battle could dispel. It could be heard in the increasing intensity of the firing, smelled in the haze of gunpowder that rose above the trees, measured by the need to station an armed Medical Corps captain on the gangplank to turn away all but the most seriously injured men.

Leigh Pennington paused in the center of the troop ship's main salon long enough to wipe the sweat from her brow before going back to dippering drinks for the soldiers awaiting medical attention. Gunshot wounds brought on a consuming thirst, and it was all that Leigh could do to keep up with the escalating need for water. The men should be washed, their wounds bandaged and tended, but already the number of people caring for the injured was totally inadequate for the many in need.

From the men's talk, Leigh had begun to piece together an understanding of what had happened earlier in the day. The first confrontation had come up near the Shiloh Meeting House, where General Sherman's troops were just cooking Sunday breakfast. Leaving their skillets on the fire, they had snatched up their arms and marched into battle when the scope of the Rebel attack became evident. It had been a futile, sketchy defense, filled with moments of great valor against overwhelming odds, but ground had been lost and with it many lives.

The women in the camp, wives and mothers come to visit their husbands and sons bivouacked in southern Tennessee, told Leigh another part of the story when they came seeking shelter on the troop ships. They told of hasty good-byes to loved ones, spoke in fear of the artillery roaring overhead and the hail of bullets falling all around them, and wept with fear for the man they loved.

As the morning progressed, Leigh had heard that some of the Union forces had turned and run, spreading panic through the ranks, while Sherman's and Prentiss's men had held their line until overpowered by attackers. Wounded who had come in just after noon spoke of a narrow sunken road where the federal forces had re-formed to make their stand against wave upon wave of Confederate charges.

Fields to the south and east of the landing were said to be carpeted with the dead and wounded of both armies, lying untended with bullets buzzing overhead. Leigh had already nursed men with numerous wounds, some from the deadly rifle barrages, others from exchanges of grapeshot or from the fierce hand-to-hand fighting taking place along the northern perimeter of the field. Her heart reached out to the wounded still on the battlefield, but there was nothing she could do to ease their suffering until the men on the ship were bandaged, washed, and fed.

Behind a screen of army blankets at one end of the room, several doctors operated, removing bullets and amputating limbs under the most primitive conditions. The air in the salon was heavy with the smell of chloroform that wafted from beyond the curtains, of blood and urine, of unwashed bodies and despair. Around Leigh rose the clamor of a hundred voices raised in pain, in prayer, or in groans so primitive that their sound belied a human source. Yet the scene before her filled Leigh not with horror but with boundless compassion, and her heart went out to those in need.

Moving with her bucket and dipper in hand, she bent beside a pale young man with a full set of ginger-colored whiskers. "See to my brother, will you, miss?" he pleaded, gesturing to the man to his left. "He's been lying quiet for so long I'm afraid he's slipped away."

Leigh moved to look down at the corporal sprawled beside him. He was the essence of the other man, gaunt and solemn, with the same thick, unruly brows. He was breathing evenly and deeply, and his skin was cool to the touch.

"I think he's going to be fine," she said, turning back to his brother. But her words of reassurance came too late. In those few seconds, the first man's chest wound had taken his life.

News from the battlefield got no better as the day progressed. Suppertime came and went with the word that Wallace's troops had fallen back from the sunken road and that Prentiss's command had been captured by Confederates. The cannon barrages were closer now, and the rumor that Grant was deploying his men not half a mile from the river ran through the boat like a shudder.

Leigh had no time to ponder what this might mean to the wounded on the transports. She was the only woman on board the *Emerald* who had any nurse's training and knew what needed to be done. She put some of the women who had come seeking shelter to work making tea and farina from the Sanitary Commission supplies, while others washed and removed the soldiers' bloodstained clothes. Meanwhile Leigh cleansed and bandaged the less serious wounds, dusting a little powdered morphine into the open flesh to relieve the pain.

In the confusion on the *Emerald*, Leigh was hardly aware that the wooden-clad gunboats the *Tyler* and the *Lexington* had begun to bombard the Confederate positions farther downriver, and it was some time before she noticed the shells tearing through the darkening sky overhead. The flow of wounded slowed at nightfall, and when Leigh stepped out on deck for a breath of air just after midnight, it had begun to rain. In spite of the thunder echoing the sound of cannons, the lightning forking through the smoky sky, and the hissing deluge that pelted the ravaged earth, some of the transports had begun to ferry Buell's reinforcements across the river by the light of torch baskets set on either side of the steamers' bows. Watching the fire's

golden flames dancing on the inky water and the red-
orange glow reflected in hundreds of somber faces, Leigh
stood for a moment in the pouring rain. Did the arrival of
General Buell's troops mean that there would be a continu-
ation of the battle in the morning? How many more wounded
would she see tomorrow than she had seen today?

Shortly after 4:00 A.M. the *Emerald* left its mooring,
bound for the hospitals set up near Grant's headquarters
nine miles downriver at Savannah, Tennessee. As the boat
ran through the dark on its mission of mercy, it was with
the knowledge of all on board that they must return before
daybreak to be ready for more casualties. It was an overwhelming thought to those who had worked tirelessly through
the day, but in spite of her fatigue, Leigh was pleased to
have found among the people gathered to help with the
wounded two old friends: Delia Dobbins and Mother
Bickerdyke.

"Lord, child, it's good to see you!" Mother Bickerdyke
had greeted her with a crushing hug. "I thought you were
safe and happy in your fancy St. Louis hospital."

"Oh, Leigh, I've missed you so!" Delia had welcomed
her with the same enthusiasm, but there was little time to
talk during the flurry of seeing to the wounded, and it was
not long before the *Emerald* was getting under way.

"When the battle's over, promise you'll come to Savannah and work with us!" Delia had shouted as the boat
pulled out.

"I'll try!" Leigh had called back, waving at her friend
through the rain.

Though Grant's troops carried the second day of the
battle, it was far worse than the first for the women on the
Emerald. Reinforced by the arrival of Buell's fresh troops,
the Yankees took the offensive and attacked the exhausted
Southern army. Though the Confederates fought bravely,
they were driven back the way they had come. With the
Federal advance over the ground that had been lost the
day before, the litter bearer gained access to the wounded
who had lain between the lines all night.

Many in both armies had not survived the rain and cold,
and their corpses lay huddled close as comrades and
enemies had sought warmth together. The living were little

better off. Lying in the mud or half-buried beneath other men, they had called weakly all night long, their voices pitifully frail against the roar of the thunder and cannons.

When these men arrived aboard the *Emerald* their needs were far different from the men who had come the day before. They were parched with thirst from the hours of neglect and the raging fevers that had already begun to consume them, thoroughly chilled and soaked to the skin from lying unprotected in the rain. The women had to set about seeing to these needs before wounds could be tended or medicines administered.

Day turned into night and then to day again before Leigh had a chance to rest. There had been too many who needed her skill, too many who deserved her comfort for her to take time for even her most simple needs. And when she awoke after a few hours' rest, the demand for care, compassion, and comfort was every bit as overwhelming as before.

April 9, 1862—Pittsburg Landing, Tennessee

Nothing in Hayes Banister's experience prepared him for the things he witnessed in the days following the battle at Shiloh Church. When the *Crescent City* pulled into Pittsburg Landing nearly thirty-six hours after the last shots had been fired, the scene laid out before them was one of devastation and despair. Midway up the hill lay endless rows of wounded, some tended and neatly bandaged, but many still as they were when they had been brought from the battlefield. The ground around the landing was rutted with the wheels of countless wagons, scarred and cratered by the explosion of far-reaching shells; the grass on the slope above it was stained a reddish-brown to mark where the wounded had lain. There were horses and mules wandering at will along the lapping water of the Tennessee, boxes of supplies crushed into the sucking yellow mud or lying half-submerged at the edge of the river. A terrible desolation lay across the scene, fueled by the heavy silence in the air and the all-pervasive smell of death.

Almost as soon as the hospital ship tied up beside the landing, the wounded were gathered to be brought aboard. Some hobbled across the gangplank of their own volition, others came leaning heavily on their comrades, but most of the men had to be carried, too ill or too severely wounded to manage on their own. They came missing arms and legs, with bandages masking their ruined faces, with fingers and feet shot away, with raging fevers that robbed them of their vitality and will. They were men who had seen the worst humanity had to offer and were marked by it, men who were fighting with fearful tenacity to live or willing themselves to die.

Even his experiences at Fort Donelson had not prepared Hayes for the severity of the wounds or for the enormous number of injured. There were battalions whose numbers were decreased by half, brigades without men to command them. The scope of the destruction was devastating, the need for mercy overwhelming. Hayes worked tirelessly throughout the day and long into the night setting up bunks on the open deck to augment those in the salon, loading wounded from among the thousands who waited, but when the hospital ship left for St. Louis at nine o'clock the following morning with its load of nearly five hundred casualties, Hayes elected to remain behind. There were still living men lying untended at the field hospitals, dead to be prepared for burial, and his personal quest for the woman he loved and had not found. There had been no time to ask after Leigh Pennington, and he could not leave Shiloh until he saw her and assured himself of her safety.

Walking for the first time in the direction of the battle with a group of litter carriers in search of more wounded, Hayes was stunned by the intensity of the fighting that had taken place. Trees were denuded of their leaves and branches by the fierceness of the fire; a farm pond was tinted rusty red by the blood of the wounded men who had crawled there to drink. In the peach orchard near where the old meeting house stood, the flying bullets had cut the delicate blossoms to shreds, covering the ground and the bodies beneath them with a pale pink dusting of petals. Before the rutted road where Prentiss's men made their stand, bodies lay so thickly that a man could walk from the Union to the Confederate line without once stepping on the scarred and bloodstained earth.

There was a profound stillness in the air, broken only by the sound of soldiers going about the gruesome business of gathering up the corpses or those, like himself, who were seeking living men among the dead. The latter lay in rows to await burial, and beside them were grisly piles of severed limbs awaiting similar disposition. On the far side of the field greasy gray smoke rose into the sky, and as Hayes moved closer, he could see the carcasses of the horses that had fallen being disposed of in the only way possible. On the perimeters of the field trench graves were being dug: some for the Union soldiers who had fallen and separate ones for the Confederate dead so that enemies would not lie together through eternity as they had on the field of battle.

As the day passed and he went from hospital to hospital moving patients, he searched fruitlessly for the woman he was desperate to find. The tents and ramshackle buildings pressed into service to house the wounded were so inadequate that Hayes could not comprehend how the men were being cared for at all. Many lay outdoors without even a blanket to cover them, and it was obvious that if any of these casualties were to survive, they must be taken north as quickly as possible.

The end of the day brought him to a hospital near the river where a large number of Confederates lay among the Union wounded. As Hayes moved through the tents searching in vain for any sign of Leigh, he heard a reedy voice calling out his name.

Pausing beside a man covered with a deep gray film of sweat and gunpowder, Hayes recognized a face whose lines and angles were very like his own. It was his cousin, Justin Dean. The insignia on the sleeves of his cousin's jacket identified him as a lieutenant in the Confederate artillery, just as the blood on the breast of his gray wool coat confirmed his wound as one that would not heal.

"My God, Justin," Hayes whispered, kneeling down beside the man who had been his playmate and childhood friend. "What on earth has brought you here?"

"The Confederate army, Cousin Hayes," the other man drawled as he reached to take Hayes's hand. Justin's voice was pale and filmy, and his fingers against Hayes's palm were hot and dry.

"I didn't know that any of the Deans had signed up to fight for the Confederacy."

Justin nodded wearily. "Robert and William are fighting, too. Though they tell me William's with the cavalry, and that isn't quite the same."

"But why, Justin? Neither you nor your brothers owned any slaves."

"We went to war because Tennessee seceded. How could we not support the state we Deans had helped to found?"

There was no answer Hayes could give, but he settled down beside his cousin's pallet determined to make him comfortable. "What do you need, Justin? What can I do for you while I'm here?"

"You're not with the army, are you, Hayes?" Justin asked, as if reluctant to accept help from an enemy.

"No, I'm with the Sanitary Commission."

"Then I'd like some water, if you please. I've been thirsty for so long, and there's not a soul to fetch a drink for a man who marched with Sidney Johnston."

Within minutes Hayes was back with water, and as he bent above his cousin, Hayes saw the waxy pallor of his skin and the feverish glow bright in his eyes. Dear God, how long had Justin been lying here without proper medical attention? How long had he been lying here alone, waiting to die?

As if sensing Hayes's thoughts, Justin spoke again, his voice low and resigned. "There's nothing anyone can do for me, Hayes, nothing to be done at all. The doctors might better expend their efforts on someone they have a chance of saving. But I'd be happy if you'd sit with me a while."

"Of course I'll stay," Hayes answered. "I'll stay with you as long as you like." The promise seemed to soothe his cousin, and Justin drifted off to sleep.

As day faded into night, Justin's fever rose, and though he tossed restlessly on the bed of straw, he was, for the most part, lucid. They talked as Hayes worked over the other man, sponging his fevered body with water, loosening the constricting clothes that bound him. They spoke of childish pranks they'd played on other members of the family; of the skinny, pigtailed urchin, Sarah, who had dogged them at their play and who Justin, just a year before, had taken for his wife. Once they had been the best of friends, but the miles and the years had separated them.

As the hours passed, Justin's voice faded to a whisper, and it was Hayes who spoke and remembered. How much the other man heard or understood, Hayes was never sure. But while Justin's fever burned away two score years of life, their friendship was rekindled. When Justin died just after dawn, Hayes ached with the loss, not only of a man he cared for, but also for an irretrievable part of his past.

Reluctantly he took the things from Justin's pockets: a daguerreotype of Sarah and his baby, a sewing kit, a tin of matches, and some crumpled Confederate bills. Before he carried his cousin's body outside to see it buried, Hayes took the signet ring Justin always wore and placed it on his own little finger. One day Justin's son would treasure the remembrance of his father, and Hayes would keep the ring safe until the day he could take it to his cousin's widow.

Exhaustion and sorrow dragged at Hayes as he made his way back toward Pittsburg Landing. For all his searching the hospitals at Shiloh, he had found misery, not solace, responsibility, not relief. Nor had he found any sign of Leigh. Had she returned to St. Louis on one of the hospital ships? Could he be sure she was safe? Saddened by Justin's death, devastated and disillusioned by all he'd seen, Hayes wanted to find Leigh and simply hold her close. A ruthless desperation was building in his blood, a rhythmic, pulsing need to see and be with Leigh. He was instinctively seeking an island of sweetness, calm, and serenity in the raging sea of war.

A troop ship was leaving for Grant's headquarters at Savannah when he reached the dock, and without even knowing why, Hayes went aboard. Things at the hospital there were better organized than at Shiloh. The tents were lined up in an orderly formation, and he moved in the direction of the largest one, determined to continue his search.

"Pardon me," Hayes began wearily, approaching an area where several nurses were cooking over open fires. "I was hoping to locate—"

At that moment the tallest woman looked up from the pot of soup she was stirring. "I know you, don't I?" she interrupted almost harshly. "Weren't you the man that helped me find the wounded the night after Fort Donelson fell?"

It took Hayes's numbed brain a moment to realize that the shawl-shrouded figure on the battlefield and the woman standing before him were one and the same.

"Mother Bickerdyke?" someone broke in before he could respond. "Where do you want these crates of shirts and bandages?"

"Mother Bickerdyke?" Hayes echoed. "Is that who you are?"

Mary Ann Bickerdyke motioned the man with a wagonload of boxes to the rear of the tent before answering. "I'm Mother Bickerdyke, I reckon. What can I do for you?"

Somehow Hayes had never made the connection between the woman in search of "her boys" at Fort Donelson months before and the almost legendary figure Leigh had spoken of so often when she returned from Cairo. In the light of that discovery, Hayes was almost afraid to voice his question, for if Leigh was not here with this woman she respected, the woman Leigh credited with turning her into a military nurse, he would not find her anywhere.

"Please, Mother Bickerdyke," he asked almost reluctantly, "is Leigh Pennington here with you?"

The woman studied the tall man before she gave her answer, wondering at the lines of exhaustion in his face and the haunted expression in his red-rimmed eyes. "She's around the back of the tent catching up on a bit of sleep."

Hayes wavered for a moment with relief and fatigue. "I won't wake her, I promise you. I just need to see her for a minute to be sure—to be sure she's safe."

"You look as if you could use a bit of sleep yourself,"

Mother Bickerdyke called after him as Hayes stumbled away.

The area behind the hospital tent was piled head-high with supplies and medicines, and it was a few minutes before Hayes could penetrate the maze of boxes to find Leigh, sound asleep in their very midst. Curled up on two crates of blankets pressed into service for her bed, with a battered, lumpy carpetbag serving as a pillow and her green wool cloak tucked around her for warmth, she looked cozy and comfortable. Her hair was bound in a long heavy braid that curved across her shoulder like a wide, red road flowing over verdant hills, and her hand lay beneath her cheek in a pose that was both childlike and seductive.

For a long time Hayes stood staring, overwhelmed by relief that she was safe, smothered by feelings of love and exasperation. He was furious at the worry she'd caused him, euphoric at finding her safe. He wanted desperately to hug her tight and feel the contours of her body mold to his, but he knew he would not disturb her. From the shadows that lay beneath the rusty fan of lashes and the translucent pallor of her skin, he could see how tired she was.

Slowly he slid to the ground at the foot of her bed, and of their own volition his fingers closed around the hem of her cloak, tightening over the warm, soft wool as if it were the essence of the woman herself. He was exhausted, worn beyond weariness by the efforts of the last days, the things he had experienced and seen. There was a need for comfort in him that had begun the terrible afternoon he had taken human life and had grown the morning he learned Leigh was here at Shiloh instead of safe at home. It had swelled to almost unimaginable proportions during his night with Justin, watching someone he loved die. Now it beat within his veins, insistent and compelling.

Even in sleep Leigh seemed to sense his need, and though he had been careful not to disturb her, Leigh's eyes fluttered open. "Hayes?" she murmured, a frown of confusion between her graceful brows. "Hayes, what are you doing here?"

He was breathing hard with the force of emotions, trembling, but not with cold. Before he could answer, she recognized his pain and instinctively sought to assuage it. Without another word she sat up and drew Hayes to her, offering him the closeness he craved.

His head came to rest heavily against her shoulder, his face turned into the warm, smooth haven of her throat. Leigh was at last beside him, and that alone brought relief.

He felt her hands move over him soothingly, stroking his back, his arms and hair. Her sweet, orange and spice scent wove through his senses, pleasant and familiar, bringing a comfort of its own. Her arms cradled him close, tenderly enfolding him, and she rocked him gently while she crooned a litany of senseless endearments against his ear.

His arms came around her too, crushing her close, and with greedy desperation he drank in all she had to give. To him her serenity was an anodyne for war: a cure for disillusionment, a remedy for loss, a tonic for weariness, a balm for his tired spirit. Beside Leigh Pennington, soothed and petted in her arms, Hayes found contentment: contentment based in the love he felt for this woman, contentment based in her compassion and gentle strength.

Gradually the strain of worry and grief overwhelmed Hayes, and Leigh eased him down on the boxes where she had made her bed. And though he tried to protest, she made him lie still, holding his hand and stroking his brow until he slept. For a very long time Leigh sat silently watching over him.

April 14, 1862—Savannah, Tennessee

"You look lovely, Delia, simply lovely," Leigh assured the girl who primped before a scrap of looking glass in the small canvas tent behind the hospital. "I've never seen a more beautiful bride."

"Oh, Leigh, do you really think so?" Delia patted her hair nervously. "I had always hoped that when I married it would be in a proper church with colored-glass windows and an organ playing. And there I'd be, dressed in a gown of silk and lace."

Leigh nodded with understanding. That was the kind of

wedding every girl dreamed of, but Delia was giving up those dreams to marry Nathan Travis in a glade in the woods. Delia's gown was only the dark, drab nurse's garb she wore every day, but the wild flowers twined in her silvery hair and the expression in her eyes transformed her into something very special. "With or without all that, Delia, you are beautiful. You simply have to look at Nathan, and you glow."

It was true. Since Nathan Travis had arrived in the camp two days before, Delia had been glowing, and so for that matter had Travis. The love he felt for Delia softened the severity of his imposing features and brought a light to his eyes. Love made his angular face almost handsome and mellowed his taciturn manner. It was an amazing transformation, one Leigh would not have believed if she had not seen it with her own eyes.

When Delia stepped away from the mirror, Leigh took a moment to see to her own attire, straightening the white lace collar at her throat and smoothing the skirt of her own dark gown. Delia had insisted that she pin flowers in her hair to match the bouquet she would carry as maid of honor, and the delicate pale pink blossoms tucked behind her ear were the perfect foil for the heavy mahogany-red braid wound around her head.

From somewhere in the distance came the wheeze of an ancient violin, the signal that the bridal procession was beginning. Leigh took a long moment to hug Delia and whisper wishes for her happiness before they went to join the wedding party forming up outside the tent.

Nathan Travis was waiting when Delia flung back the flap, and the expression on his face was that of a man enchanted by his bride. For a moment Leigh studied him, wondering what it was that had brought this quiet, serious man and her ebullient friend together. Surely there was no similarity of personality or outlook to bind them, nor had they had much time to become acquainted. Yet they were daring to marry in a time of grave uncertainty. There was danger from the war on every side: from bullets flying in the midst of a fight to the fevers that ran through the military camps, claiming soldier and nurse alike. What Delia and Nathan Travis shared might be snuffed out in an instant; yet with an optimism that touched Leigh's heart, they were embarking on a lifelong journey together. Leigh's gaze lingered on the tall, wiry groom, noticing how the white sling on his wounded arm contrasted sharply with his somber broadcloth suit. Did Nathan's mysterious injury have anything to do with Delia's sudden decision to marry him? Had Delia decided to savor what happiness she could in spite of what tomorrow might bring? Were the feelings Delia and Nathan shared enough to guarantee their happiness? Would Leigh herself have had the courage to marry Lucas before he went away to war if he had asked her?

Delia and Nathan's was clearly a marriage based in love, and in spite of her own skepticism about the state of matrimony, Leigh wished only the best for her friend and the man she had chosen for a husband.

With a smile that seemed to shine from the depths of her soul, Delia stepped forward to place her hand on Nathan's arm, and behind him Hayes Banister advanced to offer his arm to Leigh. Hayes's unexplained appearance at the hospital nearly a week before still troubled Leigh. What business did Hayes have here in the aftermath of battle? And if he had come to Shiloh with the hospital ships, why was he staying on preparing the wounded for transport when the more likely place for him to be was with the ships ferrying the casualties north? Leigh could not bring herself to ask him those questions, and Hayes had not volunteered any answers. She only knew that his presence was a threat to her peace of mind.

Now he stood before her waiting, one elbow cocked in her direction, a challenging light in his eyes. As she drew nearer, awareness of Hayes rushed over her like a breaking wave: his warmth intruding on her senses, the essence of his body invading the air she breathed, the force of his personality overwhelming her. He delighted, unsettled, and terrified her. Fighting the urge to flee, she stepped up beside him and primly placed her hand in the crook of his arm.

They made their way down a slight rise and through a canopy of old trees to a wooded glade where a parson waited. Gathered there beneath the old bowed elms, amid the clusters of wild flowers that bloomed beneath them, were other nurses and as many of the patients as could safely make the journey down the path to the clearing in the woods.

As one of the wounded soldiers scraped out the last notes of a hymn on his violin, they took their places, waiting for the minister to intone the old familiar words of celebration and welcome: "Dearly beloved, we are gathered here . . ."

From beneath her lowered lashes, Leigh watched Nathan and Delia. Never, she admitted reluctantly, had she loved Lucas as these two loved each other: fiercely, unstintingly, without any regard for the future. She had agreed to marry Lucas because she had been secure in the life they had planned, content in the role she would play as his wife. Yet Nathan and Delia had something more, something Leigh viewed with a strange kind of envy.

Leigh gradually became aware of Mother Bickerdyke's penetrating stare upon her and glanced around to smile at her. But as she met the older woman's eyes, they shifted to where Hayes Banister was standing. In spite of Leigh's best resolves to ignore his presence, her own gaze rose to follow Mother Bickerdyke's to the tall, brown-haired man who stood straight and proud just beyond the bridegroom. It was impossible to gauge Hayes's expression, but the line between his brows and the narrowing of his mouth gave the hint that he was troubled. Then, abruptly, he raised his eyes to lock with Leigh's, his blue-gray gaze holding her captive, delving deeply into the well of her secret feelings. Leigh tried to look away, but she was mesmerized, caught in the multifaceted pools of clear aquamarine.

The phrases of the wedding ceremony eddied around her: ancient, sacred vows of love and commitment. The words took on a new meaning as she stared across the clearing at Hayes Banister, until they lay like a bond of truth between them. They became tender, gentle words with a power of their own for comfort and forgiveness; special, healing words with the strength to banish anger and guilt. Tears crept down Leigh's face as she listened, watching Hayes intently, and she sensed that he was as touched and shaken by the vows as she. Then the benediction rang out through the clearing, and Leigh was able to look away at last.

The wedding celebration filled the rest of the day, and the wounded as well as the nurses and doctors welcomed the opportunity to celebrate the happy occasion after so much sadness and death. Somewhere someone had commandeered a pig, and it had been left roasting on a spit all the night before. Dried fruit from the sanitary stores had been stewed for the occasion, and there were pickles, fresh bread, and even a bit of wedding cake Mother Bickerdyke had made. Some of the men had found a crate of whiskey that had been earmarked for medicinal purposes, and it was certain that by nightfall none of those dosing themselves freely would be feeling any pain. One of the less seriously wounded men played the harmonica, and he blended his talents with the fiddler who had played earlier in the day. There was music for dancing, and even Mother Bickerdyke took a turn with the groom and then each of the Army doctors, putting aside her animosity toward the surgeons until another day.

Leigh danced as often as any of the nurses, but Hayes did not come near her until Nathan and Delia had gone to bed. They were to spend their wedding night in the Cherry Mansion, where General Grant had made his headquarters until the day before.

"Leigh," Hayes asked softly, coming to her from the shadows, "will you dance this dance with me?"

"If you like," she replied, strangely uneasy at the thought of being held close in his arms.

The song the musicians played was a sad, lilting melody that added a strange poignancy to their dance. For a time they moved in silence, their hands clasped gingerly, their feet stepping carefully in time, but gradually they were caught up in the music and began to move as one. Leigh closed her eyes and let the man beside her guide her, remembering the other times when she and Hayes had danced. How sure and strong his hands were upon her body, how gently and yet masterfully he led her through a turn. They might have been in the most fashionable ballroom, clothed in the most sumptuous fashions, instead of here in this wilderness clearing, caught up in the savagery of war. For a few minutes she let herself forget all that had happened between them, all that had set them apart. They were nothing more than a man and a woman: he tender and compassionate and she so much in need of his strength. She did not even resist when he led her from the circle of other dancers, down the path to the clearing in the woods. It seemed so right to be here with Hayes, so good to be alone with him at last.

From far away they heard the sound of singing, and they paused to listen to the voices ringing through the night. "It's the men serenading our newlyweds," Leigh told him with a smile. "They wanted to hold a traditional charivari, but I threatened them with all sorts of terrible things if they did. Delia and Nathan only have a few days together, and I won't see their time spoiled by some back country mischief. Still, the singing sounds kind of nice, don't you think?"

Leigh saw Hayes nod in mute reply. He was standing so close to her Leigh could feel his warm breath stir her hair; she could sense his attraction for her as strongly as a magnet pulls at steel. Still she fought the almost overwhelming urge to rest her head against his chest and put her arms around him.

"Leigh," Hayes began, his voice holding a note of something she could never remember hearing in it before, "Leigh, we can't let this go on. It's tearing both of us apart."

She knew instantly what he meant and briefly considered denying his words, but she knew it was fruitless to begin an argument she would eventually have to concede. What he said was true; these last months of estrangement had been trying and difficult for them both. She missed his diverting presence, his humor and his understanding. And it seemed he had missed her as well. Yet could they possibly go back to the time when they had been nothing more than friends, a time before she had begged him to make love to her?

She drew a long sigh, listening to the night sounds around her: the chirping of the peepers, the fluttering rustle of the wind through the leaves. A soft, loamy breeze brought the smells of earth and growing things to her

nostrils, mixed with the faint citrus scent of Hayes's co-
logne. The darkness was all encompassing, tangible, peaceful, and her feeling of surcease included the pleasure of
Hayes's presence beside her. He was comfort, contentment, and security. But he was also excitement and desire
that could run through her blood like wind-driven flame.
And she well knew the terrible price such uncontrollable
desire could extract.

Could she share one part of her life with Hayes, Leigh
wondered, and totally deny another? Would Hayes let her
forget the passion that had flared between them so they
could return to the satisfying friendship they had once
shared? What was it that Hayes wanted? And did she have
the strength and will to deny what he might ask in return
for the comfort she so desperately craved?

"Leigh?" Hayes's voice was softer still, tinged with
compassion and concern. "Leigh, can you deny that there
has been a bond between us from the very start? Can you
deny that there are things between us now that you've
never felt before?"

It was a question she did not want to answer, but
something in his tone made it impossible to lie. "No, Hayes,
I can't deny it." Her words were a bridge between them,
but it was a bridge she did not have the courage to cross.

She heard Hayes's slowly indrawn breath and sensed the
conflict it masked. His next words were a long time coming, and when he finally spoke, the question was not what
she had expected. "Leigh," he asked almost in a whisper,
"is it so difficult to return to what we once had?"

"Is that what you want, Hayes, to return to the time
before Lucas died?"

Hayes was silent for a long moment. "It's not what I
want; it's not what I had hoped for, but if that's all you
can give me, I'll have to be satisfied."

Leigh turned her face to him in the dimness of the forest
glade, wishing she could read the intent in his eyes. "It's
all I'll ever have to offer you, Hayes," she told him. "It's
all I'll ever be willing to give."

Hayes nodded, and she thought she could detect a smile
on his lips. "I think that's enough," he said softly, "enough
for now."

12 ⟡

May 23, 1862—St. Louis, Missouri

"Did you or did you not send letters through the Confederate lines at Hayes Banister's request?"

Major Aaron Crawford stood glaring down at Leigh in the confines of Dr. Hodgen's office at City General Hospital, demanding answers Leigh did not want to give. Ever since that blustery afternoon months before when Hayes had thrust a handful of messages at her to send south, Leigh had known they would bring trouble. She had tried to refuse him then just as she tried to refuse the same request less than a week ago when Hayes had approached her with another letter. Nor had she met with more success resisting him this time than she had the first.

Raising her chin, Leigh faced her inquisitor, determined to learn the reason for Aaron Crawford's interrogation. "Isn't sending letters to Confederates against the law?" she asked innocently.

"Do you expect me to believe that the law against communication with the Rebels is never broken?" he countered, eyeing her.

"Though it is against regulations to send messages south, I understand there are a great number of people who continue to do just that," she argued. "And what can you expect in a city like St. Louis with such divided loyalties?"

Crawford frowned. He knew what Leigh said was true. Illegal mail service to the Confederacy had been flourishing ever since the opening days of the war. Now, even in the lush, full-blown spring of 1862, the Union had found no way to combat it. Smuggling mail south was the kind of resistance it was impossible to curtail because as soon as one courier was discovered and arrested, another sprang up to take his place, Southern men and women proud to flaunt the Yankee rule.

Crawford prowled across the tiny room. "Have you sent letters south, Leigh?" he asked.

Leigh's mouth narrowed. She knew it was a Federal offense to correspond with the enemy and considered her answer carefully. Surely Crawford would not be here this afternoon unless he had proof that she had been sending mail south, unless one of her letters to Brandon Hale had gone astray. "Yes," she finally admitted, "I have sent letters through the lines, and so have at least half the other families in the city." She did not tell Aaron Crawford that smuggling messages out of St. Louis was getting more difficult and dangerous every day. Since the spring offensive had begun, the Yankees were much more careful about security.

"And is Hayes Banister included in the number involved in that pursuit?"

Leigh shrugged negligently. "Why don't you ask Hayes that question, Aaron, instead of wasting time I might better be spending with my patients?"

Aaron Crawford settled himself on the edge of the desk, frowning down at Leigh. She was a thoroughly irritating woman, he thought as he watched her. Irritating, yes, but as desirable as a woman could be. Even in a severe dark dress and prim white apron, even with her lush red-brown hair confined in a black chenille snood, she was exquisite. And so very much like her lovely mother.

Briefly, thoughts of Althea flitted through Crawford's mind. Althea was still a breathtaking woman with a rich, mature beauty that few would ever attain. And, he noted with a swell of satisfaction, in these past few weeks her resistance to his advances had been dwindling. It had been clear from the moment he met her that Althea was married to a man who had ceased to make her happy, and because of that she was vulnerable, prey to his particular kind of charm. Lonely women, women abandoned by their men for the sake of business or other pursuits, were tremendously flattered by the attentions of an attractive, virile male. They were hungry for compliments, starved for the semblance of romance, and he knew just what it was they craved. Married women like Althea Pennington, women who could hide their liaisons with him in the guise of visits to their seamstress or drives in the country, made charming and generous conquests, and Crawford was looking forward to enjoying Althea's favors in the not-too-distant future.

But it had only been since he had met Althea Pennington and then her lovely daughter that a new depth had been added to his lust. He had thought Leigh would fall into his hands like ripe fruit after the death of her Confederate fiancé. Instead it was Althea whose resistance was weakening, Althea who would be the first of the two to succumb. It was not what he had expected, but she was half of what he craved. And once he had seduced the mother, he would find a way to conquer the daughter as well.

Aaron Crawford sighed imperceptibly and put his thoughts away. He was not here today to satisfy his carnal desires. He was looking for proof that Hayes Banister was a Confederate spy. And how gratifying it would be to accuse the man when he found evidence of his duplicity.

Judging from the packets of Confederate mail the Federal Army had managed to intercept, most of the letters sent South were innocuous. They related greetings, family news, the prevailing weather, and because of their mundane contents were no treat to read. But occasionally something would catch his eye and make Crawford wonder at the writer's intent. Hayes Banister's letter to a woman named Sarah Dean in southwestern Tennessee had been one of these.

Crawford's interest was aroused at first by the writer's position in St. Louis. As an aide to James Eads, Banister would be an ideal position to glean military information. Surely Eads had advance notice on deployment of the ironclads in order to make spare parts available and keep the vessels in working order. Doubtless other tactical information was made known to Eads and his associates as well. Until Crawford had begun to delve into Banister's activities and background, his connection to the Confederates had seemed unlikely. But as Crawford followed his hunches, questioning first Eads and now Leigh Pennington, his suspicions about Banister grew.

Again the Yankee major turned his attention to the self-possessed young woman before him. How much did Leigh Pennington know about Banister's activities?

"Leigh," Crawford began, "I know Hayes Banister is sending messages south, and I want to know why."

"It's possible he is concerned for friends and family in the Confederacy just as many of us are," she suggested.

"No, I think his reasons are deeper and more sinister than that," Crawford drawled.

Leigh's head came up sharply, clearly grasping his unspoken charge of treason in spite of his casual manner. "Are you saying Hayes Banister is a Rebel spy?" she demanded when her first wave of astonishment had passed.

"The man does have connections to the Confederacy through his family and from his years as a riverboat pilot. And he has never made any attempt to sign up to fight for the Union."

Leigh's eyes sparked at the allusion to Hayes's cowardice, and her rebuttal was swift and cutting. "Don't you think that the work Hayes has been doing at the shipyards is at least as important as providing cannon fodder?"

Crawford made note of the girl's willingness to defend Banister before he continued. "Then too there is his association with a man named Nathan Travis who bought up large numbers of Negro slaves in the years before the war. Banister has been seen in Travis's company on several occasions since the fighting began."

Aaron paused, watching Leigh for signs of response, catching the flicker of recognition when he mentioned Travis's name.

"Furthermore, I have reason to believe that both Travis and Banister have traveled unopposed behind Confederate lines."

Though Leigh fought to keep her face impassive, Crawford's words filled her with confusion and nameless dread. She had heard rumors of Hayes's mysterious trips to Forts Donelson and Henry and to the area near Shiloh in the weeks before the battle. Why had Hayes left the busy shipyard to travel into what was then Southern-held territory? And what was Hayes's relationship to Nathan Travis? The friendship between them had been evident that first afternoon in Cairo; now Leigh wondered if there was a special reason for their closeness. But then that implied her best friend's husband was a spy, and Leigh could no more accept that conclusion than the one that Hayes was working to further the Rebel cause.

Travis had spent several days in Savannah after the battle at Shiloh and did seem to know more about the area than a casual visitor might, but he had come to the makeshift hospital to marry Delia, not for clandestine reasons of his own. Yet for a man who was newly a groom, he and Hayes had spent an inordinate amount of time together, sitting up late by the light of a lantern, talking in voices that no one else could hear. Then too there was Travis's wound. When she asked him how he'd been hurt, he had given her a slow, wry grin and muttered something about having spent time with the "wrong companions." Had she imagined the conspiratorial glance that had passed between the two men when he'd given his reply? Could Aaron Crawford be right in his accusations? Was Delia's new husband a Confederate spy? And was Hayes Banister his accomplice?

"Aaron, this is madness," Leigh protested, trying to mask her doubts. "Hayes is the last person in the world I would suspect of disloyalty to the Federal cause!"

"Then prove it, Leigh. Tell me about the messages you sent south for him."

Leigh struggled with her conscience for a moment, weighing personal loyalty against the truth. "I sent no messages south for Hayes," she finally said.

"Leigh, be sensible," Crawford cajoled. "We found letters to your mother's family and to Brandon Hale in the same pouch as the letter Banister had sent to Sarah Dean."

"That doesn't prove a thing."

"Not by itself, no." Crawford paused. "But the courier confessed that you brought Banister's letter to her only a few days before, along with half a dozen others."

"The courier could be mistaken," Leigh volunteered, "or lying to save herself."

"I think not."

Then a new idea struck Crawford, born of Leigh's denial. Was it possible that Leigh Pennington herself was involved in smuggling information south? Leigh was from a family with strong Confederate ties, and she had never declared herself for one side or the other in this conflict. What were the woman's politics; just where did her loyalties lie? And how would she respond to an accusation of treason?

"Could you be keeping Hayes Banister's secrets because you're both involved in the same deception?"

Crawford had expected some reaction, but not the angry intensity that flared in Leigh's eyes when her stunned surprise had dropped away. "That's absurd!" she snapped.

"Is it? I think you know far more about Banister and Nathan Travis than you are letting on, and perhaps the reason is that you are in collusion with them to undermine the Union."

Leigh said nothing, but swiftly began to realize both the savage ruthlessness of her inquisitor and her own untenable position.

"Leigh, tell me what you know about Hayes Banister and Nathan Travis."

There could be no doubt that it was unwise to give Major Crawford the information he was seeking, but under his unrelenting eyes, Leigh felt deceived and hopelessly vulnerable. What was it Hayes had done, and why was she protecting him?

"Leigh." Crawford leaned forward from his perch on the edge of the desk until his face was inches from her own. "Leigh, this needn't get unpleasant. Tell me what I want to know."

She could see the malicious set of his lips beneath the sweep of his hussar's moustache, smell the faint, sickly scent of his hair oil in the tiny, stifling room. His threat was implied, but as real as the horror of nightmares in the dark, as real as her own fear of betrayal and impermanence. Yet Leigh stubbornly refused to yield.

His hands closed hard upon her arms as Crawford dragged

her out of her chair. "Leigh, I want you to tell me everything you know about Nathan Travis and Hayes Banister."

His fingers were embedded in her shoulders, like the talons of a hawk sunk deep in its prey. With equal parts of pain and anger stirring her blood, Leigh shook her head.

Crawford's eyes darkened as he recognized her defiance, and he caught her wrists in one hand, twisting them behind her. Leigh fought helplessly against his hold, but could not break away. With deliberate menace Crawford drew her closer, until she lay along his length, her breasts pressed close to his broad chest, her skirts tangled with his legs.

"Tell me what I want to know, Leigh," he murmured against her mouth. "Tell me about Banister's letters."

As he spoke, his free hand caught in her hair, his fingers clenching in the open grid of the snood, catching the heavy strands beneath and holding her helplessly immobile. With almost playful malice, he lowered his head and brushed her lips with his.

"Let me go, Aaron," she hissed, struggling within his grasp. "I won't tell you anything, no matter how you mistreat me."

Abruptly Crawford loosened his hold and shoved her toward her chair. "Since when are a man's attentions mistreatment?" he demanded, furious and red-faced. "There's no reason why you should refuse me either the information I am seeking or the simple pleasure of a kiss."

Truculently her chin came up, and she held her ground. "When a man forces his attentions on any woman, as you've tried to do on me, it is a violation of both her body and will. Nor can I tell you things I know nothing about."

Silence fell in the small, stuffy office as the major glared at the woman before him. It was this fiery spirit, tempered with icy resolve, that made Leigh Pennington so tempting to possess. Still, he knew he should not confuse his role as seducer with the one he had come here to play. He was the provost marshal of St. Louis, seeking to apprehend a clever Confederate spy, and this woman knew more about his activities than she was prepared to admit.

Perhaps it was time to play on more basic loyalties than those Leigh felt for the other man.

"I still need information about Banister's letter, Leigh, and about any other messages you might have sent south on his behalf," he continued, returning to his probe. "As you must know, there are far more unpleasant ways for me to convince you to talk about Banister than the ones I have employed thus far.

"I could have you thrown into the Gratiot Street Prison for corresponding with the enemy or on suspicion of being a spy," he suggested, then paused, searching her face for any sign of reaction. "And perhaps for company, I could have your mother join you. As I said, we found letters from Althea in the sack of mail we intercepted. And in the midst of a war as desperate as this, we must carefully guard our secrets."

"Mother's only written to her family in Louisiana!" Leigh cried passionately, breaking her self-imposed silence.

Crawford's voice was soft and chilling in response. "I only know that those who break the law are subject to their punishment."

Leigh raised her eyes to the glacial gray of his and found no mercy in their depths. "She doesn't know anything about Union secrets or sending messages south. I took the letters to the courier. Please, Aaron, leave my mother out of it! This is between you and me."

"Is it?" Crawford taunted. "I already have quite enough evidence to have you both arrested."

Crawford was smugly silent as he watched Leigh, knowing that he had found her weakness. For too long, she and her father had conspired to shield Althea Pennington from any unpleasantness, to see that nothing interfered with the genteel life of leisure Althea loved. And as he watched the woman before him, Crawford knew it was for her mother and not herself that Leigh was most afraid.

"I doubt that Althea would like the prison any more than you," he pointed out. "It's a place whose horrors are legend: the filth, the food, the vermin."

"What makes you think that you can get away with imprisoning us?" she challenged in a desperate effort to resist him. "My father has friends in high places, and his loyalty to the Union cause is unimpeachable."

"And for all his influence, Leigh, there are just as many who know of your mother's support of the Confederacy, including General Halleck himself."

Color drained from Leigh's face. What Aaron said was true. Halleck had reason to remember his humiliation at Althea Pennington's hands and might welcome a chance for revenge.

"I'll do it, Leigh," he persisted. "I'll sign the order this afternoon. Can't you simply tell me what messages you sent south for Hayes Banister?"

The need to protect Hayes rose in her again, warring with the threat to her mother's safety. Doubtless Hayes could withstand the rigors of the Gratiot Street Prison better than either Althea or Leigh herself, but if he was arrested as a spy, he would be in far graver danger than they. While it was only a matter of time before their innocence was proved, Hayes might well face a trial for treason, a trial that could lead him to the gallows.

Whatever Hayes was involved in, whatever he had done, Leigh knew she must protect him. She could not talk about the letter to Sarah Dean or the others Hayes had given her just before Christmas. She could not tell Crawford that all of them had been sent to Nathan Travis at a series of addresses in western Tennessee. That would come too close to proving the major's suspicions, and no matter what the forfeit, Leigh would not betray Hayes's secrets.

"The need for these constant threats is quite tedious, Leigh. Please tell me what I want to know so I won't be forced to bully you." Crawford's voice broke into her thoughts, and as he spoke, he reached to take one of her hands in his. Hers was a capable, work-roughened hand: slender, but not fragile; feminine, but with underlying strength. "Please, Leigh, be sensible," he murmured as he exerted subtle pressure in the center of her palm that sent a thread of unexpected pain chasing up her arm.

Leigh shook her head, and raised stunned, accusing eyes to his as the grip on her fingers tightened. She had withstood his advances, his threats, and now Crawford was trying a new tactic to force her compliance. It seemed impossible that such a simple thing could cause her so much pain. Leigh drew a ragged breath and shook her head. "I don't know anything about messages Hayes Banister sent south. Please, Aaron, let go. You're hurting me."

"Don't you know anything about them, Leigh? I neither want to hurt you nor send you off to prison, but I will have the truth."

A blur of pain was beginning to overwhelm Leigh, and she dimly realized that she must convince Aaron that somehow he had succeeded in forcing her to tell him everything she knew. Crawford obviously had intercepted Hayes's letter to Sarah Dean, she reasoned foggily, so it seemed safe to acknowledge taking it to the courier. If she could make him believe that the single message he had intercepted was the only one she had sent for Banister, perhaps she could save both Hayes and her mother without volunteering more information. The pain in her hand and arm was gradually increasing, making Leigh light-headed and bringing tears to her eyes.

"I hate you!" she whispered breathlessly, as wetness spilled down her cheeks. Yet she hesitated one last moment before she gave him the answer he was seeking. "All right, Aaron, I admit that I sent a letter south for Hayes."

"Tell me about it," he demanded, loosening his hold a little.

"It was addressed to a woman named Sarah Dean; she is his cousin's wife, I think. He wrote to tell her that he had been with her husband at Shiloh when he died."

"When did you mail it and how?"

"I took it to a woman who lives on Washington, just west of Eleventh Street, last Tuesday or Wednesday." Leigh said. "I had written to Brandon Hale, and my mother had letters ready to send to her family. I took those there as well."

The information was accurate, as Crawford was well aware. "What other messages have you sent south on Banister's behalf?"

"None, I swear it!"

His hold tightened again, and a sheet of sweeping agony moved up her arm. Leigh twisted helplessly in her chair, but his grip was unrelenting. "Tell me the rest of it, Leigh!" he threatened.

"Oh, God! Aaron, please. There's nothing more to tell! Hayes and I had a falling-out just after the new year, and I hardly spoke a word to him between then and when we made up at the hospital after Shiloh."

Aaron knew that Leigh and Banister had been at odds, and it was more than possible that Leigh was telling the truth at last. Satisfied for the moment, Crawford released her, and Leigh crumpled back against her chair, cupping her wounded palm.

"Oddly enough, Leigh, I do believe you, at least for now. With what I already know about Banister's activities, I think I can convince my superiors of the need for further investigations. But, Leigh"—Crawford gathered up his hat and gauntlets and moved to stand by the door—"no more letters south, not your own, and certainly not for Banister. Do you understand?"

Leigh nodded mutely.

"Good," he added as he took his leave, "and by all means, Leigh, give my best to your charming mother."

Leigh sat for a moment glaring after him, loathing the major with a dark, ferocious hatred that was foreign to her nature. How her mother could bear the man's company was beyond Leigh's comprehension, and she intended to tell Althea just how Aaron Crawford had treated her. But more important, she needed to talk to Hayes Banister and find out what he was doing and where his allegiance lay. They were to go for a drive in the morning, and it seemed the perfect opportunity to determine if Hayes was indeed what Aaron Crawford accused him of being: a Confederate spy.

May 23, 1862—Alton, Illinois

"No, Pincheon, I'm through with you and your missions!" Hayes Banister reiterated as he took a turn around the small hotel room. Its shades were drawn to provide the other man with either the privacy or the perpetual gloom he seemed to crave, and the air hung thick as a blanket in the confined space. "The ships I'm building with James Eads are quite enough to keep me occupied, and I don't need your plots and intrigues for further diversion."

The smaller man sat back in his chair silently, letting Banister's aggravation run its course.

"The mission to Corinth was more than enough to satisfy any craving I might have had for adventure," he continued, "and I'm not planning to stir from St. Louis again for anything short of a Confederate invasion!"

The suggestion of a smile played beneath the heavy fringe of Pincheon's moustache, and he stroked the pointed beard below. "Let's hope you have no reason to leave then, Banister. But then neither can you claim to have had any part in preventing such a dire eventuality," he observed mildly.

Hayes threw himself into a chair across from the one Pincheon occupied and glared at him. The flicker of amusement that had been briefly evident on the older man's face was replaced by a quizzical expression, calm and unemotional in spite of Banister's refusal.

"I am sorry you feel you can no longer help us, Hayes," Pincheon continued. "There are several situations where your expertise could be very useful. But I do understand your reluctance; you've taken more than your share of risks."

Hayes felt the sarcasm in Pincheon's tone and tried to ignore its sting. "You're not going to convince me to get involved in this, no matter how hard you try. I was a fool to even respond to your note; I should have stayed away."

Pincheon allowed Hayes a moment of complacency, a moment of false victory before he continued his attack. "Would it matter if I told you there were lives at stake, lives your cooperation could save?"

"Surely there are others you could send," Hayes suggested.

"Others? Oh, yes, there are others, but not with the contacts you have along the river, not with your knowledge of the terrain."

A weighty silence filled the room, and Hayes did his best to ignore it. There were so many risking so much, so many who would not return to their homes and families as a result of the war, that it seemed wrong to refuse Pincheon's request. Yet he had already gone on two missions for this man, Hayes argued silently, and was devoting himself single-mindedly to the Union. He had built gunboats and hospital ships, and there was so much more he could do to further the Federal cause as a naval engineer than as a spy.

Why was Pincheon pursuing him, then? Surely his experiences before the war with the Underground Railroad were not so extraordinary as to make him indispensable to this man. And how was it that Pincheon could make him feel guilty, selfish, and cowardly, in spite of all he had accomplished? He was not a selfish man, Hayes told himself, not a less than patriotic man, but he wanted to fight this war in his own way. He wanted to use his brain and skill to help the Union prevail. Why couldn't Pincheon understand that?

Still, he had agreed to meet with the Western coordinator of the Union intelligence service, in spite of his determination to refuse whatever assignment Pincheon offered him, in spite of the realization that to come here was courting disaster. Was it the promise of adventure or the crushing weight of duty that had brought him to Alton this afternoon? Pincheon was not a charismatic figure, yet Hayes had been unable to resist his summons. He had come in spite of the conviction that he did not want to be a part of any more of Pincheon's schemes.

Banister hated the loss of life his last mission had caused, was haunted by the memory of the Confederate he'd shot and then watched die. The thousands he had seen lying dead and wounded on the fields at Shiloh had filled him with anger, especially since the information he and Travis had risked their lives to obtain had been ignored. That alone should have convinced him of the futility of what Pincheon was asking him to do. Why couldn't he simply put the man and his assignments out of his mind? What could he say to convince Pincheon that he no longer wanted to be part of the network of agents the man employed?

Banister had been so preoccupied by his own thoughts,

he was hardly aware of the older man standing over him, preparing to see him to the door.

"I thought our business was concluded, Banister," Pincheon prodded, "unless, of course, you've decided to change your mind."

Hayes unfolded his long-limbed body from the chair and spoke with deliberate finality. "No, Pincheon, I want no part of the things you're planning."

Pincheon paused with his hand on the doorknob. "Well, it is a shame about Travis, anyway."

Hayes hesitated, well aware of the bait Albert Pincheon was dangling before him. In spite of the jump in his pulse, he nibbled at it warily.

"Nathan Travis?" Hayes asked casually. Damn the man! Why hadn't he said straight out that Nathan was in danger? "What does Travis have to do with this?"

"As you said yourself, my operations don't concern you anymore, Banister. Why don't you just be on your way?"

Hayes stood before the door with his hat in his hands, sensing that the other man was angling, preparing to set the hook. He could not walk away from this assignment if Travis was in danger, and Pincheon knew it. Still, Hayes resisted, fighting the inevitable capitulation as long as he could. He put his hat on his head as if to go and offered his hand to Pincheon.

"We'll find someone to go after Travis," Pincheon continued. "Of course, it's a shame about his missus if Nathan shouldn't make it back. She's a pretty little thing, I understand. They've been married just a little more than a month now."

Hayes knew exactly how long Delia and Nathan had been married. The question leaped to his lips in spite of his desire to bite it back. "When had you expected Travis to report in?"

Pincheon cocked his head to one side, shooting Hayes a sidelong glance. "The end of last week. He was just supposed to move on down toward Memphis and poke around a little."

"I do know a few people around Memphis from my years on the river," Hayes ventured as if unaware of the contest of wills they were waging.

Pincheon said nothing, giving the line plenty of play.

"If Nathan were in trouble, I can think of a few places he might go."

The other man reeled Hayes in with silent skill.

"I suppose I could go down that way and make some inquiries."

The expression in Pincheon's eyes was smug and self-satisfied, but when he spoke, his voice was conversational. "That might be very helpful," he conceded.

Hayes was caught hook, line, and sinker. "I suppose I should be on my way to Memphis as soon as possible, then," he conceded.

The bearded man nodded, and Hayes cursed the bonds of duty and friendship that made involvement in Pincheon's scheme inevitable. "Yes. It seems wise."

"Is tomorrow soon enough?" Hayes asked.

Pincheon glanced across the room at the warm amber light filtering around the edges of the window shade. "Soon enough, I reckon."

Gravely Hayes nodded and turned to go, and for a second he had the odd sensation that he had made a pact with the devil—and come up short.

May 24, 1862—St. Louis, Missouri

From where Leigh stood on the levee, half-concealed by a pile of crates and barrels, she could see that there were neither goods nor passengers on the *Barbara Dean*'s decks. Wherever the steamboat was going, it was obvious it was making the trip without concern for either appearances or profit.

Since her interview the day before with Aaron Crawford, Leigh had been waiting impatiently for her chance to talk to Hayes. When the message arrived this morning canceling their outing and saying Hayes had been called away, Leigh had dashed to the waterfront with confrontation on her mind. Why determining Banister's loyalty was so important to her, Leigh could not say. She only knew that resolving the question of Hayes's allegiance was vital to her peace of mind. Perhaps it was that she resented being a pawn in someone else's game, Leigh reflected as she stood watching the *Barbara Dean*'s crew preparing to leave port, or because Hayes had not trusted her with the truth about himself when she had offered him so much. Clearly he was something more than James Eads's associate, and the fact that both Delia and Nathan Travis seemed to know Hayes's secrets when she did not hurt and infuriated her.

As she stole a few feet closer to the riverboat, Leigh's mind teemed with unanswered questions. Why was Hayes leaving so suddenly, and where was he headed? Was he fleeing St. Louis in fear of his life? Could he be a Confederate spy, a man on a sinister mission for an alien government, as Crawford claimed? Or was there a perfectly good explanation for this trip and everything else he had said and done? Whatever the answers, Leigh knew only that she had to learn the truth.

She could hear the laboring of the boat's engines as the *Barbara Dean* was readied for departure. Soon the crew would be casting off, and unless she acted immediately, Leigh might never learn whether Aaron Crawford's accusations were fact or fancy. She had only seconds to decide. Without pausing to question either her motives or the consequences of boarding the steamer, she scampered up the gangplank. Ducking beneath the slope of the stairs, Leigh paused to catch her breath, thankful that no one had seen her. But if she was to remain aboard the *Barbara Dean* long enough to discover Hayes's destination, she would need to find a place to hide. From the look of things, the passenger cabins on the promenade deck were unoccupied, and they seemed a likely spot to pass some time. Tucking her parasol under her arm and gathering her flowing skirts around her, Leigh ran up the stairs.

The first stateroom she looked into was filled to the rafters with crates and boxes, as were the two just beyond it. Her palms were slippery as she twisted the ornate knob on the fourth door, and she started at the sound of footfalls on the deck above her head.

"Cast off, men. Let's get under way," a familiar voice ordered.

Aware that she was plainly visible on the open deck and driven by evidence of Hayes's nearness, Leigh desperately

nudged the cabin door with her shoulder. It resisted her
assault at first, then swung wide, and she stumbled into the
stateroom. Closing the wooden panel behind her, she stood
wedged in the narrow space, surveying her surroundings.
This cabin was filled with chairs: delicate gilded chairs
with jewel-toned seats, stacked like acrobats, one on top of
the other. Nor was this one of the more opulent cabins
she'd ever seen. It was small and the furnishings simple.
Two austere single berths were built against one wall, and
a washstand with a ewer, basin, and chamber pot stood at
the foot of the beds. Yet there was more space in this
stateroom than in any of the others she had tried.

Frowning, Leigh considered her options. Should she
continue her search for another place to hide and run the
risk of being seen, or make herself comfortable here? If
she meant to discover the secrets Hayes was keeping, she
must remain undetected, and while this cabin had its draw-
backs, Leigh could be sure she was safe. With her decision
made, she locked the door to insure her privacy, took one
of the gilded chairs from the pile beside the bunks, put
aside her reticule and parasol, and sat down.

From outside came the voices of the deckhands calling
their good-byes to the people on the landing, and she could
sense the riverboat pulling out, then being caught by the
rushing river current. By the way it moved with the Mississippi's flow and by the sound of the engines, Leigh
surmised that they were moving downstream to the south.
But were they headed for Cairo or even New Madrid, or
was Hayes on his way to places even farther downriver,
places behind Confederate lines? Leigh wished she could
step out onto the deck and watch the city fade away behind
them, but she knew she could not. To reveal herself too
soon was a mistake she refused to make. Determinedly,
Leigh settled down to wait.

As the day progressed, the temperature in the tiny stateroom soared. By noon, she had taken off her gloves and
was using her flat-brimmed straw hat for a fan. By midafternoon when the sun came around farther to the west, the
heat became unbearable. In desperation she eyed the narrow transom above the door and dragged her chair closer
to investigate. Standing on the seat, she could just barely

reach the catch at the bottom of the glass, and once she had released it, Leigh used the handle of her parasol to push the window wide. Welcoming the gush of air the open transom afforded, Leigh stood for several minutes enjoying the fresh spring breeze.

It soon became evident that the upper bunk afforded the coolest place to sit, but Leigh knew she could not climb up there dressed as she was. Setting aside the parasol, she lifted her skirt to release the tapes of her wide hoops, and eased them silently to the floor. Once the springy cage was collapsed and stored against the wall, Leigh looked down at her dress. She had selected a lovely new gown of turquoise lawn for her ride in the country with Hayes, but the sweeping, ruffled skirt and the gathered sleeves were not at all suited to these accommodations. Quickly she slipped the buttons from their holes, drew the dress over her head, and spread its delicate, lacy folds across one of the chairs. In the name of practicality, her heavy petticoats quickly followed it, and at last she stood in the crowded stateroom clad only in her corset, pantaloons, and chemise. This costume, while less modest than what she had been wearing, was practical for her enforced mode of travel and considerably cooler than full dress had been. Silently, Leigh hoisted herself to the upper bunk and stretched out on the mattress, enjoying the flow of air that drifted across her body.

From her perch, she could see the gentle undulations of the riverbank, thick and velvety with newly leafed trees. Occasionally tiny river towns moved past. That they relied on the Mississippi for survival was evident in the way the buildings huddled at the edge of the water and by the amount of activity along the levee. Goods were gathered in piles awaiting shipment, and wood and coal tenders were strung out along the edge of the river ready to provide fuel for the steamboats that passed upstream and downstream in an endless cavalcade. Leigh could imagine the excitement when one of the boats pulled in, the people who would pour from the houses and stores at the sound of the whistles that signaled a landing. St. Louis was a city tied to the Mississippi by its history and its economic life, but not with the same overwhelming dependency that these smaller towns must be. As grim as the last year of war had been for the city of St. Louis, Leigh could imagine the effect the diminished river trade must have had on them.

She could also see people along the bank outside the towns, boys with their fishing lines cast hopefully into the murky water, and men working in the rich brown fields. It was a time when crops were beginning to sprout, a time when weeds must be dug and cultivating done. Sometimes she noted a red flag tied to the end of a dock to signal a passing steamboat to stop for cargo or passengers. But the *Barbara Dean* ignored the summons and moved steadily south on a course of her own.

Fine houses were visible along the riverbank, too, mansions nestled like jewels between the trees. Some of them stood back from the water, elegant and proud, with tall pillars and ornate pediments, glistening crisp and white against their verdant surroundings. Some of the houses stood narrow and grand, conceding much to the Federalist styles of the fashionable east, and nothing to the hot, sultry summers along the Mississippi. Others were built to withstand the heat, crouched low in the old French style, with wide, cool verandas and broad hipped roofs. Leigh knew that riverboat pilots took their bearings from the mansions on the banks as they plied the winding river, so that the homes along its course had come to serve a purpose their builders had not intended.

Leigh spent hours watching the river towns and the lovely old mansions move past her in an endless parade, but finally she fell into a doze, awakening only when the deep red of the setting sun blazed through the transom window. Smells from the galley were drifting up to her, and hunger argued eloquently for making her presence known. Still, Leigh might never learn Hayes' destination if she let him know she was here, and her curiosity was by far stronger than her need for food.

As she lay trying to ignore the smell of baking cornbread and roasting meat, Leigh began to realize what a hare-brained scheme she had undertaken. It was more than worthy of her days with Lucas and Bran and was the kind of stunt that would have gotten their bottoms warmed. In her hurry to leave the house this morning, she had not told anyone where she was going, and as the supper hour approached, she knew her mother would be worried. If only Horace or Althea thought to question her father's driver, they would at least know she was safe. As she lay trying to ignore the murmurs of complaint from her empty stomach, Leigh began to realize the full scope of what she'd done. With her good sense overwhelmed by curiosity, she had impulsively climbed aboard a steamboat without any idea of its destination, put herself at the mercy of a man who might well be a Confederate spy, and freely courted scandal. There was no telling how long they would be away from St. Louis or whether they would ever return. Nor did she dare think what this could do to her reputation if word of her escapade got out.

Leigh cursed her own stupidity, her sudden vulnerability, and her impetuousness, but somehow she was not sorry she had come. Hayes Banister was caught up in something clandestine and sinister, and she could not rest until she found out what it was.

Nightfall came, and once all was quiet, Leigh dressed and tiptoed along the deck to the rain barrel, desperate for a drink after her long, hot day in the cabin. After she had assuaged her thirst and filled the washstand ewer with water for the next day, Leigh bathed as best she could and stood lurking in the shadows as the night breeze whispered softly against her skin and the moonlight danced across the water.

Leigh was awakened early the next morning by the sound of a key turning in the stateroom's lock. Instinctively she shrank back against the wall as the door began to open, and though she was hidden from her unexpected visitor's view by the height and depth of the upper bunk, she realized what he must be seeing down below. Last night she had undressed in the dark, leaving clothes draped across the chairs. Her dress and petticoats were spread wide like flower blossoms opened to the sun; her stockings and garters were pooled over the tops of her shoes; her bonnet, parasol, lace-trimmed pantalettes, and even her stiff corset were set out for an unobstructed view. Then, with her heart beating high against her throat, Leigh became suddenly aware of the state of her undress, of how revealing her delicate batiste chemise would be if she came face-to-face with her visitor. But before Leigh could think of what to do, she heard Hayes's voice just outside.

"What's going on in there, Wilson?"

"There are women's clothes strewn all over the cabin, sir," came the baffled answer.

"Women's clothes?" Hayes demanded.

"Yes, sir. I noticed the transom was open and went inside to close it. That's when I saw the petticoats and things draped everywhere. But there's no sign of the lady herself."

"Well, where the hell could she be?"

Leigh pressed tighter to the wall as Hayes brushed through the doorway.

The other man had not been able to see her huddled at the back of the top bunk, but Hayes's greater height gave him a glimpse of one rounded hip and a creamy shoulder visible over the edge of the bed. Cursing volubly, he hoisted himself up to get a better look at their feminine stowaway.

For an instant he stood staring, stunned by what he saw. Then the white heat of his gaze moved over Leigh: from the bare feet and calves to the flare of her hips, over the natural slimness of her waist to where her breasts billowed above the neckline of her chemise.

Leigh steeled herself for the moment when his eyes would meet hers, but she was not prepared for the rage she saw in their gray-blue depths or the scorching vulgarity he hurled at her.

"Go get the dressing gown from my cabin," he snapped at the man hovering below, "and don't be gone all day!"

After he left, Hayes turned back to Leigh. "You damn fool woman!" he exploded. "What in God's green earth are you doing on my ship?"

Leigh squirmed under his hostile glare and tried to think of an appropriate answer. This wasn't the way she had planned to confront Hayes: half-dressed, half-asleep, and cowering.

"Here you are, sir," the crewman said, returning, having taken seriously Hayes's admonition to hurry.

"Go out and close the door," he ordered. "I'll be out in a minute myself."

In silence he extended the blue silk dressing gown to Leigh, and when she took it, he left the stateroom, slamming the door behind him.

Leigh clambered down from the upper bunk, wishing she had time to dress and see to her hair, but she was sure Hayes would not wait that long for explanations. Sighing, she swept the oversize dressing gown around her and stepped out onto the deck. Most of the crew had gathered to get a glimspe of their stowaway, but, without a word to either the men or to Leigh, Hayes caught her arm and dragged her up the stairs to his cabin.

The moment they were inside, he turned to face her, more angry than she had ever seen him. "All right, Leigh, you owe me an explanation. What in hell are you doing aboard the *Barbara Dean*?"

When Leigh had pictured this confrontation with Hayes, she had imagined herself as the one in control, the one who had discovered all his secrets and then revealed herself to him. Unfortunately, that was not the case this morning. Hayes had found her out long before she had learned anything of value, and he was making it clear that she was an unwelcome intrusion, an impediment to whatever he was going south to do. That realization further unsettled Leigh, but no more than the open hostility she saw in his eyes.

In the year since Hayes had rescued her from the mob at Camp Jackson, Leigh thought she had come to know him well. She had seen the light of laughter shining in his face when something pleased or amused him, had heard the concern and sympathy in his voice when she had been in need of comfort, had shared the anger and grief he felt when his cousin had been killed at Shiloh. But she had glimpsed the side of his personality he was displaying this morning only once before: the night he had been willing to challenge Aaron Crawford for her virtue.

That man, that stranger filled with barely leashed anger, was stalking her now, moving in ever-tightening circles like a big cat scenting his prey. His pale blue eyes were narrowed until only the pupils showed, dark and sharp as needles probing her expression. His fury was a palpable thing, and she was aware of a tensile hardness in him, a dangerous, intimidating ruthlessness that he had never before turned on her.

With difficulty she suppressed a shiver of fear. What did she know about Hayes Banister after all? she asked herself. Could he be a Confederate spy? Was he something more than the kind and tender man he had always seemed? The *Barbara Dean* had been moving steadily southward, and all at once their destination became crucially important to her. Where was Hayes going? What would happen when he got there? And what would he do with her?

Hayes came to stand before her, his feet braced slightly apart, the angry set of his body mere inches from her own. The heat of him radiated against her thighs and belly, setting off a thudding in her chest. Awareness of his size and bulk, the breadth and strength of his shoulders overwhelmed her. Yet in spite of his intimidating presence, or perhaps because of it, Leigh found herself standing taller, facing him defiantly.

She had never let any man bully her, not her father, not the military doctors who held nurses in such low esteem, not Aaron Crawford, and she would not let Hayes Banister bully her now. But how could she explain her reasons for being on the *Barbara Dean* without telling Hayes everything Aaron Crawford suspected, the things she had begun to believe?

"Why are you aboard the *Barbara Dean*?" He thrust the question at her a second time, his voice dangerous and low.

"When I got your message yesterday, I came down to the riverfront," Leigh answered with a studied insouciance she was far from feeling, "and boarded the riverboat on impulse to find out where you were going."

"And have you figured that out?"

"No," she answered carefully. "I know we're headed south."

"South. Yes, we are headed south."

"As far as Island Number 10?" Leigh managed to say, seeking the truth in his eyes. Island Number 10 was the southernmost Yankee position along the Mississippi. To be traveling farther south than that would prove her suspicions correct.

For an instant Hayes hesitated, his eyebrows lifting slightly. "Even farther south than that."

Leigh drew a breath, dizzy with the implications of his statement. What was it Hayes was telling her? That she was in danger because she had come with him? That he was indeed a Confederate spy?

"But why?" she asked in a whisper.

"It seems to me you must have some theories of your own if you were curious enough to stow away," he observed.

There was a subtle change in him, Leigh noticed, as if his anger had been tampered down, subdued. It was still there, evident in the tension at the corners of his mouth and in the smoldering depths of his eyes, but it was overlaid with a carefully leashed watchfulness that made her even more wary than before.

This would be the moment to tell him about Aaron Crawford's accusations, explain how she had needed, beyond all reason, to know if they were true. But she could not tell him. She was too angry with the way he was treating her, too appalled by what he must be, too confused by the emotions sweeping through her to put her answer into words.

"Well, it hardly matters what you think, though your presence here is"—he weighed and measured the word—"inconvenient, since by tomorrow night I am not going to be aboard to be your host."

Leigh's head snapped up at the admission. "Where—where are you going?"

"The question you should be pondering, Leigh, is where *you* are going to be staying while I'm gone."

"And where is that? I'm sure you've already decided the answer." There was bitterness in her tone and disillusionment in her eyes, but she stubbornly held her ground.

Something like respect flickered across his features before he turned toward the door. "That should be very obvious, Leigh. You're staying here until I return, locked right in this cabin."

"I will not stay here! You can't lock me in!"

"Oh, yes, Leigh, I can and I will. If you were foolish enough to stow away, you can hardly expect any say in how you'll be treated. It's quite comfortable in here, really. There is a bed and a desk and things to read, and I'll see that meals are brought to you." He paused for a moment. "Have you had anything to eat since we left St. Louis?"

"No, just water from the rain barrel."

Hayes sighed and shook his head. "I'll send someone by with breakfast, then."

"Hayes, wait!"

"No, Leigh. I have a great many things to do before tomorrow night, and your presence is hardly conducive to getting them accomplished. I'm not sure how long I'll be away, but when I return, Leigh, there will be a score to settle between us." With that threat hanging in the air, he left, closing and locking the door behind him.

Leigh rushed across the room to test the strength of the solid wooden panel with her shoulder. "Hayes Banister, don't you dare lock me in! I want this settled between us here and now! Come back here this minute! Hayes, please come back. Hayes. Hayes? Hayes!"

13 ~

May 30, 1862—Off Randolf, Tennessee

Silence. Soft, soothing silence, broken only by the rushing sound of the river's passage and the faint wheezy creak of the ropes that shackled the *Barbara Dean* to the forested bank. There were guards posted on the deck, sitting hidden by the night, their pipes smoldering and their eyes alert for any movement in the trees or on the surface of the river. But to Hayes Banister they were invisible. He was almost too tired to see, too exhausted and disheartened to think of any more than the expanse of bed that awaited him and the delicious oblivion of slumber.

His body ached with weariness, and his mind was numbed with failure, knowing full well what his inability to find Nathan Travis might mean. The web of agents who had helped smuggle runaway slaves north before the war was the basis for Travis's scouting operations, and though Hayes had visited the people they'd known and the places they'd frequented during their years with the Underground Railroad, he had found no sign of the other man. Either Pincheon's information was wrong, or Travis had stumbled into danger. The latter was a grim thought, and Hayes refused to dwell on it. Nathan Travis was a man with an incomparable instinct for survival, and now he had the most important reason in the world for coming home safe: a woman who loved him.

As Hayes approached his own cabin, he turned his thoughts to the woman locked inside. He was glad for the late hour so he need not face her questions and accusations. A confrontation was inevitable between them, but he did not want it tonight, not with his wits dulled by weariness, not while he was distracted by concern for Travis. With stealth tempering his movements, he turned the key in the lock and slipped inside his stateroom. In the faint light that filtered through the transom, he could see that there were subtle changes in the cabin since he had left it five days before: a book lying open on the seat of the chair and more piled up by the bed, a half-finished puzzle laid out on the desk, and a feminine scent in the air. The copper tub sat at one end of the room as if Leigh had recently used it, and the thought of being clean again held a powerful appeal.

With stiff movements Hayes stripped off his sweat-stained clothes and poured water into the basin. Standing naked in the moonlight, he lathered his face and chest, then splashed away the soap, bent to wash his legs and feet, rubbing the wet cloth slowly upward. Water beaded on his shoulders, then trickled down his spine, tracked a pathway along his legs to pool on the floor around him. While he shaved away the five-day growth of whiskers by the light of the summery moon, the breeze from the open window dried, refreshed, and renewed him.

Barefooted, he approached his bed and the woman sleeping there. She was beautiful in the half-light, a woman of strength, character, and will. And though her face was placid in slumber, Hayes well knew the fire within her. He was not looking forward to answering her questions and recriminations in the morning and was glad for these reflective moments when he could simply drink in her loveliness.

Smiling, he noticed Leigh had commandeered one of his shirts as a nightdress, and where the oversize garment gaped away, even her ample, long-limbed body seemed delicate and fragile. Hayes teased the covers lower until the curves of her breasts were exposed, until the hazy halos of her nipples were visible through the soft, loosely woven fabric.

She lay half on her side, sleeping peacefully, but her tousled hair and the sheets tumbled in disarray gave evidence of long, fitful hours before she slept. What had made her so restless? Hayes wondered. What had robbed her of her sleep? Had he been in her thoughts these last few days as much as she had been in his?

It was already impossibly late, not the time to ponder such questions. And though Hayes knew he should not linger at her bedside, he did not want to go. How delightful it would be to share his own wide bunk with Leigh, he found himself thinking, to wake and find her snuggled in his arms. What a pleasure it would be to share her warmth, stretched out close beside her.

The thought was as intriguing as the woman herself, and the urge to act on it grew. He was seeking companionship, not intimacy, he argued with himself, sleep, not seduction. He was too tired to do anything more than hold her, anyway. What harm could it do if they shared a bed one night in the midst of the war? Who could it possibly hurt if he didn't try to make love to her? But even as he raised the covers and settled gingerly on the edge of the mattress, Hayes knew he was making neither a wise nor rational choice.

In the grainy, moonlit darkness, he was very aware of Leigh: of the strands of russet hair that slithered across the pillows to tease and tickle his skin; of the tendrils of her warm, sleepy scent that crept up from the sheets to enfold him. The purloined shirt had ridden high, and as he tried to wriggle closer, he met bared flesh from hip to knee and was seared by the heat of her skin. His reaction was sharp and instantaneous, and he lay as if turned to stone, waiting for her to stir. Yet he heard nothing but the rhythmic flow of her breathing, felt only the boneless weight of her limbs, and saw the thick, dark fluff of lashes lying motionless on her cheeks.

He moved carefully after that: one hand, one arm, one foot, easing deeper, seeking purchase toward the center of the bed. Shifting slowly against the pillows, he fit his body to the shape of Leigh's until their shoulders were aligned, until his legs followed the contours of hers. Through it all, Leigh lay still, lost in the void of sleep, defenseless and unaware. Finally satisfied, Hayes nestled into the mattress and slowly let out his breath. He was wholly content as he

lay there, Leigh's body entwined with his own. Smiling
into the darkness, he let his eyelids close.

Exhaustion drifted over him, and his thoughts were
floating free when Leigh murmured something under her
breath and turned toward him in her sleep. The soft, slight
shift of her weight brought one hip across his loins, and
Hayes came awake abruptly with a flare of unexpected
desire. He was instantly, vividly aware of Leigh's cheek
against his arm, of her hand curled limply across his waist,
and of her thigh between his legs. Heat from that intimate
contact radiated through him in giddy waves, and it did not
matter that moments before he had only wanted to hold her
close. Breathing deeply, Hayes tried to regain control, to
turn his mind from thoughts of Leigh. But with her sprawled
against his body, with her flesh yielding against his own, it
was impossible to think of anything but his growing need
to make love to her. He remembered the taste of her mouth
and skin, recalled the thrill in her artless caress. Hayes
willed himself to leave the bed, but it was already far too
late.

From the moment he had found Leigh stowed away,
half-dressed and half-asleep in one of the empty cabins, he
had known this moment was inevitable. He wanted her too
much, had denied himself too long to ever let her go. For
months he had hated his ever-present desire and her continued coldness, his weakness and her strength. But this
time his weakness would prevail. And when weakness
meant the triumph of love over loneliness, of pleasure over
pain, how could weakness be wrong?

Slowly he lowered his mouth to the curve of her cheek
and brushed it with a kiss. She was passive with sleep,
limp and accepting as she might not otherwise be, and a
ripple of guilt stirred through him for taking more than she
might want to give. Yet beneath her borrowed shirt his
hand crept unerringly upward, encountering first the rise of
her hip, and the swoop of her waist beyond. It skimmed
the high-arched crest of her ribs to the swell of her
supple breasts. Almost reverently Hayes molded his hand
to the shape of her, the fullness conforming to the curve of
his fingers, the nipple ripe against his palm. With the

certainty that this was meant to be, Hayes began to stroke her gently.

Leigh stirred beneath his touch to turn her head away, and as it fell back against his arm, her throat was bared to tempt him. Like a man caught in the slow, sweet magic of a moonlit dream, Hayes bent to kiss her skin, to savor the exotic, subtle spice of her throat, her cheek, her mouth.

Leigh lay full against him now, the weight of her thigh against his loins where his body was hard with need, the contour of her breast shaped to his hand as his touch grew bolder still. His blood swirled sluggishly through his veins as he lost himself in her: the subtle velvet nap of her ivory skin, the rough raw silk of her hair, the lick of her breath across his throat, and the span of her hips against him. His limbs felt hollow and weightless, melted and waxen, as if their bodies had already begun to flow together.

Deliberately he deepened his kiss, no longer content to play the phantom seducer. It was time to awaken Leigh to the intimacy of this night and the rapture that loving could bring. It was time she came to know the full measure of desire and the extent of intransigent ecstasy. When she had come to him before, she had been a lost child seeking comfort, an untutored virgin neither knowing nor understanding the price extracted from those who sought solace in pleasure. She had learned those painful lessons well, and now it was time to teach her the rest, the sum of what loving could mean. His lips moved slowly over her in a rackingly gentle caress, then deepened with burning persistence until her mouth began to cling to his.

Leigh rose from the mires of sleep to a hardly less dreamlike world where a strong, dark man bent above her, raining kisses on her face. Then his mouth was covering hers, his lips a brand, his tongue a dart of heat probing the uncharted depths of her.

"Hayes!" she whispered breathlessly in recognition. "Oh, Hayes."

Her voice was sultry and low as she whispered the word, and with a smile of satisfaction he claimed the sound of his name from her lips. He took the name, her breath, her thoughts and made them his own. Took them, and claimed them, and owned them all, before she had a chance to deny him.

Turning gently, Hayes pressed her back against the pillows, kissing her fiercely and long, and with the flush of awakened passion, Leigh began to kiss him back.

It did not matter that once he had hurt her, nor that she had pledged loyalty to Lucas Hale. She could not hold back for sanity's sake or for what surrender might mean. In this moment, with this man, the rest of the world fell away. There was nothing but sweeping desire and the need to hold him close. A shudder of something wanton and primitive swam through her blood, and for now, for tonight, without regrets, Leigh gave herself to Hayes.

Hayes instantly felt the change in her, from acceptance to welcome, from confusion to joy in his caress. Without guile, without remorse, without conscious thought, he renewed his demands on her.

His fingers splayed across her back, stroked down along her spine, spanned the curve of her narrow waist, then slid lower to cup her hips. Wrenching the buttons from the holes of her shirt to bare the inner slopes of her breasts, he pressed his lips to the valley between with a murmur of pure satisfaction.

"Leigh," he whispered against her, his voice silky soft and low, "there's so much I want to teach you, so much for you to learn. Please, Leigh, let me make love to you; let me show you what passion's about."

Leigh closed her eyes for a moment, as seduced by his words as by his touch, as caught in the web of his promises as in the one he had spun of delight. Beneath the cover of the open shirt, his hands claimed and held her breasts, his thumbs circling her satin-smooth nipples, his palms filled with her milky-pale flesh. Then his tongue was tracing hot, impatient patterns from her throat to her loins, lacy, intricate patterns that left her shaken and aching with need. Sensation flowed through her body, in lightning-swift strokes of delight, leaving smoldering trails of desire in response to his kisses and touch.

Valiantly, she tried to quiet the jarring of her heart and think what surrender might mean. But her thoughts were mired in pleasure, and her body craved to know more. She wanted to learn the things Hayes could teach her, to seek passion in his arms, to explore the wonders of loving with a man who could show her the way.

Her willingness remained unspoken, but Hayes taught her with kisses and touches and breathless words the scope and the meaning of bliss. She learned how a man's hands could move on a woman's body, gentle and strong and sure; about the pain and pleasure a woman could feel, clothed in the guise of delight; about a world of wants and needs that she had never known; about giving the gift of tenderness and receiving unstinting returns. Then his mouth moved lower still, nudging her legs apart, and pressed to her wondrous budding core, Hayes taught her the end to it all.

Like an arrow streaking into the sky, she was flying fast and free—higher, stronger, swifter, farther than she had ever flown before. Fear raced along her nerves before reality fell away, and then there was only Hayes holding her as she blossomed with exultant joy. The world seemed to expand before her as she surged higher than before, stretching, pushing, seeking, reaching for something elusive and pure. Rapture welled over her suddenly: like sunlight beyond the clouds, like stardust in her veins, like the fantasies of love she had held in her heart made real. And for a shining, silvered moment she hung lost in boundless ecstasy.

Hayes rode the waves of sensation with her, sought her joy as if it were his own, showed her the reaches of passion, helped her define and achieve delight. And when the storm was over, he held her tenderly, celebrating her fulfillment as something they had shared. Her initiation into the rites of love had been as fulfilling to him the guide as to her the novice, and at that moment he wanted nothing more than to claim her as his forever.

They lay entwined together, a rope of tangled limbs, stroking, sleeping, touching, kissing in the light of the setting moon. By that slow, cool, mellowing glow, Leigh raised her head to look at Hayes. He was, as she had always known him to be, a strong and beautiful man: generous, selfless, and gentle. But there was more to Hayes tonight, and she was seeing him anew. His was an arresting face, the features vivid and almost harsh: a broad, intelligent brow; a narrow-bridged nose; a hard, square jaw; and a mouth that for all its determination was sensuously curved and vulnerable.

Then, drawn by forces she did not understand, she marked the long, deep, masculine dimples with her thumbs, cradled his jaw in the curve of her cupped palms. But even as she touched him, the need for greater contact grew, and her hands slid lower still to explore the column of his throat and the half-moon hollow at its base. She liked the suppleness of his warm, smooth flesh beneath her fingers and continued to explore him gently.

Moving with lazy grace, Leigh curled back on her heels and traced the contours of his body with the thoroughness of one gone blind. Her hands lingered on his shoulders; rode the swell of his rock-hard arms; explored the smooth, bronzed planes of his powerful chest, delineated in wondrous symmetry. Her palms moved downward across the arch of his stomach and spanned the bridge of his hips before they swept down the sinuous cable of muscles in his powerful thighs and calves.

Even as her hands moved over him, Leigh knew she should not allow herself the luxury of exploring him so freely, yet there was a delicious, secret thrill in touching his perfect physique. She reveled in the masculine regularity of his form, in his power and latent strength. And it was impossible, after all the ruined men she'd seen and comforted, not to celebrate Hayes's wholeness as he lay rugged and hard before her. She wanted to remember him just as he was, rangy and virile and strong, learning him with touch as well as sight, so that when the war claimed its price from others, she could know how they once must have been.

As her hands lingered on his skin, a slow, sweet hunger was budding in her loins, a growing, seeping, aching need that only Hayes could satisfy. It moved beneath her skin, a subtle, undeniable glow, creeping through her body like dawn across the sky.

Hayes sensed the growing ardor in her touch and saw it in her eyes, but it was tempered with some desperate, private sadness he sought to understand and rectify.

"Leigh?" Her name was an endearment, rumbling deep within his chest. It was a question, an invitation, a demand that Leigh could not ignore.

Slowly she raised her eyes to his and was caught in their glittering depths. Their cold, clear shade of blue was warmed tonight, silvered by the moon, and they held Leigh helplessly mesmerized so she could not turn away. Stretching back along his length, she answered his query with a kiss, letting the flavor of his mouth seep slowly into hers.

That single kiss grew tenfold, then ten times ten times ten. They crowded to the corners of the mouth and eyes, fell carelessly on chins and hair, spun in skeins of delight along their bodies, and pooled upon their skin. Those kisses were feather soft and light, were slick and wet and warm; they clotted with growing passionate need, subsided then swelled again.

Their bodies tangled as they kissed, and still kissing became one. They turned and twisted tenderly, each seeking for the other a wondrous gift only they could give. Hayes's body probed the depths of hers, and Leigh's offered a welcoming sheath: a warm, sweet haven of tenderness where a man could find release. Clinging, kissing, arching, pressing, the fervor of their passion grew, and together they sought the moment when their hearts would beat as one.

Then it was upon them, the flicker of rapture, the rush of delight, the moment of ultimate truth. It came with wanton abandon, racing like an errant wind, giving a dazzling fulfillment that neither had ever known. A spangle of sensation moved along their limbs as they clung with breathless need, their bodies melding closer as they succumbed to mindless ecstasy. With a trail of shivers it dwindled at last, waning in a gentle caress, leaving them spent and broken, but sated and renewed.

The sound of the deckhands stirring in the murky dawn brought Hayes awake at last, and he found Leigh, soft and limp as a wilted flower, curling close beside him. In the veiled half-light of approaching day, he watched her as she slept, realizing the scope of his devotion, the extent of his need for her. He had loved this woman before and had wanted her for his own, but never with this sweeping intensity, this primitive desire that filled his soul with longing. He drew her body closer still, with a vow to make Leigh forever his, to claim the woman of his dreams for love, for life, for all eternity.

May 31, 1862—New Madrid, Missouri

It was the change in the incessant, dunning rhythm of the riverboat's engines that woke Leigh, and she was immediately aware of the slight lag in the boat's forward movement that meant they were approaching a landing. A moment later, she heard the hails of the crew on the decks below, an answering clamor of voices from the shore. Then came a soft, slight nudge as the *Barbara Dean* nuzzled against the riverbank. Where were they? Leigh wondered. She scrambled to her knees to peer out the window high above the bunk and abruptly realized the state of her undress.

Color flooded her cheeks, and her curiosity about their whereabouts swiftly abated as she unwillingly recalled how she had come to be lying naked in Hayes Banister's bunk. Appalled by what had transpired the night before, confused by what she felt, Leigh curled up in the center of the mattress and drew the covers over her head. Her memories of the hours between midnight and dawn were mercilessly clear, and the icy hands she pressed to her cheeks did nothing to extinguish the flush that swept through her.

She had come to consciousness slowly, sensing first an enveloping warmth, then a soft, recurring touch. As she twisted to escape it, the gentle stroke had become goading, intrusive, demanding. Then she had realized that a virile, dark-haired man was bending above her: a man with lips that moved like velvet on her skin, a man with a taunting power in his caress. Her mouth already bore the taste of his kisses, and her flesh was tingling from contact with his. The magic that was Hayes had already begun to engulf her. Yet there had been a brief moment of crystalline sanity when Leigh could have turned away.

Instead her arms had made a circuit of his neck, and her mouth had opened under his. As they kissed, a strange compulsion had seeped through her veins, a need that she found hard to comprehend. She had wanted to explore the mysteries of her own sensations, reaffirm the vague, half-remembered wonder of the other times they had been together. When Hayes had offered to teach her what passion meant, Leigh had been desperate to learn whatever secrets he was willing to share. She had trusted Hayes with her curious, strangely pliant body, and he had, once again, done nothing more than what she asked: he had made slow, exquisite love to her.

Last night she had sought that delight as fiercely as he, and today she wished she could deny it.

Hayes had brought her devastating, unexpected pleasure; he had helped her to understand and fulfill her woman's needs. She was both gratified and confused by the exultant pleasure in her own response. But however wondrous the realm of self-discovery, however compelling the need to experience delight, last night had been a mistake, and Leigh knew she could never succumb to Hayes's charms again.

Her reticence went beyond the guilt she felt at betraying Lucas Hale to the basic beliefs she had adhered to all her life. Her mother had raised Leigh to be a lady, and no lady engaged in the behavior Leigh had enjoyed last night, nor would a lady entertain the thoughts that threaded through her brain this morning. She had stepped quite a distance over the line between propriety and licentiousness, and if she was not to lose everything, she would need to mend her ways.

Mercifully Hayes was not here now, but she knew that within minutes, or hours at best, she would have to confront him. And what could she say when he stood before her? Dear God, what would she say?

Last night Leigh had been uninhibited and wildly responsive. Would Hayes expect the same behavior by the light of day? Could he possibly expect to find her waiting for his return in wanton anticipation, sprawled naked and eager across his bed?

It had been a mistake to have allowed him carnal knowledge of her that first time when she had been so desperately in need of comfort. But it was worse to have accepted his caresses again. Surely whatever respect he had for her was gone now, destroyed by her irresponsible willingness, her unbridled desire.

Once he'd been honorable enough to offer her marriage, but he would not offer it now. Nor did she want him to. She did not want to be bound to a man she did not love simply because she had succumbed to the tyranny of her errant senses. Nor could she ever enter into a marriage where passion was the only bond. She had long been a witness to the consequence of such a union and was terrified of building her life on something as fleeting as desire. The thing she must make clear to Hayes when she saw him again was their need to avoid each other or at least to avoid situations where their own weaknesses might overwhelm them.

The first thing she must do was to explain her new resolve to Hayes, she decided. And surely he would be more receptive to her arguments if she greeted him in somewhat less dishabille than she was in now. That entailed washing, dressing, and preparing herself to confront Hayes Banister when he returned. Resolutely, Leigh got up.

Hayes did not return to the *Barbara Dean* until the late afternoon, and by then Leigh had rehearsed all she planned to say to him. It was the rush of response at the sight of him that surprised her, almost as much as the warmth she saw shining in his pale blue eyes. For a long moment they stood staring, Hayes with his hand clenched on the door-knob and Leigh with her book lying open in her lap.

"Good afternoon, Leigh," he finally said. "I'm sorry I was gone so long. It took more time than I expected to find what I was looking for here in New Madrid."

"New Madrid? Is that where we are?"

He nodded and closed the door behind him, then gingerly approached her chair. "I had something I had to take care of, something I needed to do before I saw you again."

Inexplicable uneasiness stirred through Leigh at the admission, and she raised her eyes to his. "Oh?" she barely managed to answer.

"I wanted to find a parson and make arrangements for our wedding this evening."

For an instant Leigh stared at him without comprehension as cold shock swept down her arms. "Our wedding?"

Hayes nodded, his eyes intent on her expression. "Yes, Leigh. After last night it seemed the only decent thing to do."

Once again he was offering her marriage for the sake of honor, but was it his honor or her honor he meant to appease?

Hayes cleared his throat twice before he continued. "I've made arrangements for a ceremony at the pastor's house this evening, then we can come back and have a wedding supper in the salon if you like."

All at once Leigh was on her feet, the bonds of shock and restraint abruptly loosening, leaving her free to voice her refusal. Leigh sensed that this time it would take more than polite words and bland evasions to put Hayes off, and she searched for an effective arsenal of excuses to repulse him.

Her natural anger and indignation seemed an effective first defense. "How dare you go ahead and make such plans without consulting me! How could you—"

"I'm sorry, Leigh, but I thought it was necessary to settle things as quickly as possible. We're only going to be in New Madrid overnight. It seemed wise for us to be married before we reached St. Louis, but if you would rather wait—"

Leigh shook her head vehemently. "No, no! You don't understand. I'm not going to marry you."

Hayes came a step nearer. "Leigh, don't be unreasonable. Of course we're going to be married. Surely you can see it's necessary after what happened last night. I want to give you the protection of my name before it happens again."

"It's not going to happen again!"

"Oh yes it will." His words were irrefutable.

"I won't let it happen again."

"I wasn't aware that you were capable of such steely self-control," Hayes observed dryly, studying her with narrowed eyes.

Color rose in her cheeks.

"I think you enjoyed what happened last night every bit as much as I did," he continued conversationally. "You see, I know you found your own resolution and experienced pleasure more than once."

Her flush brightened, and she tried to look away. "I did not," she snapped, but without enough conviction to give credence to the lie.

"Do I need to undertake a demonstration to remind you how your body responds to mine?" His voice held a melting, persuasive quality that was more dangerous than threats.

Leigh shook her head. She would not be able to argue her cause effectively with her mind blunted by the passion Hayes could arouse in her. She would not have the strength to oppose him once he had taken her in his arms. That acknowledgment effectively negated one part of her argument and left her terrified of her own susceptibility. Hadn't her very life been a part of the disastrous aftermath of consuming passion gone wrong? Hadn't her parents' arguments always filled her with fear and guilt because of it? She would not let Hayes convince her to repeat her parents' mistake.

"I won't marry you," she repeated stubbornly, buying time to marshal her forces against him.

A frown gathered at the corners of his mouth and marred the smooth plane of his brow. "Why are you fighting this, Leigh, when you know as well as I do that marrying me is the only way you'll ever be able to hold your head up in polite society? Surely you have been reported missing by now, and only the story that we impulsively eloped will appease the gossips in St. Louis. Even that will cause a stir, but—"

"I don't give a damn about polite society, and I refuse

to bow to a few dowagers' dictates for the sake of a little gossip!"

"Don't be so hasty, Leigh," he advised. "Have you really stopped to think what this might mean? Even if nothing had happened between us, your reputation would be ruined. By the time we reach St. Louis, you will have been gone for more than a week in the company of a man who is not your husband. There would be speculation right and left about what went on between us."

"And the gossips would be right in their suspicions, wouldn't they?" she snapped.

Hayes regarded her evenly, retreating into that taciturn part of his nature that made it impossible to tell what he was thinking.

"Leigh, stop and consider for a moment what you'll be throwing away if you refuse me."

"I've already considered what I'll be throwing away if I accept you. I'll be throwing away my freedom, my self-respect—"

"You'll also be throwing away your chance to work as a nurse."

Leigh paled. "What do you mean?"

Hayes came closer to lean against the edge of the bed. "At the beginning of this war nursing was considered an unladylike occupation, as you well know; it was a job that only the lowliest kind of woman did. But in these last months all that has changed. The women who nurse are now from the highest strata of society, and there's not a town in the North without a group of society do-gooders organized to care for the men who have been wounded. It has become a woman's Christian duty to care for these men, and where genteel women used to gather for tea and gossip, they now roll bandages and pack parcels to send to the front. These women live for their aid societies and their stints at nursing the wounded."

"And it's a good thing too," Leigh countered, "since the Army Medical Department has proven itself incapable of providing for the men in its care. We women have banded together in this crisis for the good of all."

"That's true, Leigh, but you miss my point. Those

proper ladies are not about to allow a 'fallen woman' in their midst, much less give her access to the poor, susceptible boys who are lying sick and injured. Think of the taint they might pick up.''

His words hurt; and what was worse, they were probably true. ''If I'm a fallen woman, Hayes Banister, it's your fault!'' Leigh cried in frustration.

Hayes was silent for a moment, willingly accepting the blame. His feelings for Leigh, though basically honorable, were the cause of her current problem, but also the key to resolving it.

''Leigh,'' he said gently. ''Leigh, we both know you're hardly a fallen woman, but after traveling with me for a week, that's the way those proper ladies will see you. And they will no more allow you into their society than into their hospitals, no matter how good a nurse you are.''

''They haven't got that much power!''

Hayes nodded. ''Oh, yes they do.''

Leigh stared down at her hands clasped tightly around her lacy handkerchief.

''And, Leigh,'' Hayes went on, pressing his advantage, ''what if a child is the result of what happened last night? Would you condemn him or her to be a bastard, an outcast, because of your stiff-necked pride?''

Still Leigh said nothing.

''Leigh, sweetheart.'' The endearment slipped out before he had a chance to bite it back. ''Leigh, why are you fighting this so when you know as well as I do that marriage is the only sensible way to handle this situation?''

When she raised her eyes to his, they were welling with tears, and he could read raw fear in their smoky, sprucegreen depths. For an instant the emotion startled him, then anger and hurt were burning in his chest. Didn't Leigh realize that he would never do anything to hurt her? Didn't she know how much he cared?

''I won't have a marriage like my parents','' she cried, her voice quivering with anguish. ''I won't live my life in a constant state of war.''

Hayes swallowed hard before he spoke. "I've never been married so I don't pretend to know all the answers, but I don't think you should confuse tranquility in a marriage with peace. Tranquility can be boredom or indifference. Sometimes people fight to show how much they love each other. It's only when fighting becomes the only way to express love that those people are in trouble."

Were her parents' arguments based in love? Leigh wondered. Frankly, she doubted it. How could two people in love say the terrible, hurtful things to each other that she had heard her father and mother say? They had been forced together by mutual passion and her untimely conception, but over the years that passion had turned to hostility and bitterness. Now there was nothing left between them except the discord of two wasted lives.

Leigh would not let that happen to her and Hayes. Their need for each other might have been strong last night, but she could not believe that it would last. Surely it would fade in time to be replaced by the same emptiness she saw in her parents' eyes. She would not condemn herself to that kind of future, nor would she condemn Hayes. He was too good a man to be saddled with her for the rest of his life because their desire had burned out of control. She would not marry him; she could not marry him! It would be courting intimate disaster to pledge herself to be his wife. She had proof that passion was not enough to make a marriage work, and Hayes had never offered her anything more than desire.

Sudden perversity put words into her mouth. "Do you love me, Hayes? Do you expect me to believe that all our disagreements have sprung from that emotion? For all our dalliances, you've never once told me that you care. And in truth, the emotions I harbor for you could hardly be called love, either."

Hayes recognized that there was a certain twisted truth in what she said. Their arguments were often the result of the strong feelings he had for her, the tightly held emotions she would not allow him to express. And he suspected, or hoped at least, that the very thing that made her fight him most fiercely was the love she was trying to deny. Either way, pride forbade him an answer, though he wished with all his heart that he could simply declare himself and take her in his arms. But, even as he longed for the simplicity of that solution, he knew he must try to win this argument by logic and emotion, not by passion or force of will.

"You were willing to marry Lucas Hale," he observed. "You were even looking forward to the wedding. Weren't you afraid that marriage would be like the one your parents have?"

"Lucas was different," Leigh conceded. There had been a time when she wished Lucas was capable of exciting her as Hayes seemed able to do, but now she was glad he had not. Passion was a trap for the unwary, and her fantasies of life with Lucas had been curiously devoid of desire. "Lucas was special," she continued, "and he knew me to my bones. Lucas and I never fought, not even when we were children. Lucas was someone I could trust."

"You have fairly stringent requirements for the candidates to be your husband," Hayes observed, trying to mask his hurt with a sardonic reply.

"I suppose that's why I'll never marry."

"Oh? Never marry? It's not just me, then?" he continued as an eyebrow tipped upward while the corresponding corner of his mouth turned tellingly down.

"Hayes, please don't make this more difficult than it is."

He could see the desperate expression in her eyes, but his patience was wearing thin. He knew what had to be done and how determined Leigh was to oppose it. But there came a time when logic and appeals to the emotions had to be set aside in favor of common sense. Hayes straightened and faced her.

"This is not difficult at all, Leigh. Tonight at seven-thirty, you and I are going to be married. The minister is expecting us, and Nathan Travis will be there, too. He came aboard just after dawn, and I've asked him to stand up with us."

Leigh surged suddenly to her feet, and Hayes came to stand beside her. "Haven't you heard a word I've said?"

she demanded fiercely, staring up into his face. "I've told you in the clearest words I know that I will not ever marry you!"

"Oh, yes you will, Leigh. You just think over your options: bearing a baby out of wedlock, giving up the nursing you seem to hold so dear. You'll marry me tonight, Leigh; you haven't any choice."

It was not the way he wanted to leave her, with a threat on his lips and defiance in her eyes, but it seemed the only way to make her understand. With great deliberation he reached across to gently caress her cheek, trying to soften the words they had said to each other. "Don't worry, Leigh, in time we'll come to love each other. I promise you."

With a single motion she jerked away. "Not enough, Hayes, we'll never love each other enough!"

He stood for a moment as a wave of helpless fury moved over him, then turned on his heel and stalked to the door. "Prepare yourself for a wedding, Leigh, for whether we love each other or not, there will be one before this day is over."

*   *   *

Dearly beloved, we are gathered together in the sight of God, and in the face of this company, to join together this Man and this Woman in holy Matrimony; which is an honorable estate, instituted by God. Therefore it is not by any to be entered into unadvisedly or lightly; but reverently, discreetly, advisedly, soberly, and in the fear of God.

Leigh took the minister's charge to heart as she stood beside the tall, dark-haired man who was to be her husband. Why she had agreed to this wedding was more than she could understand. This was not to be a reverent, well-advised, or sober union. It was meant to do nothing more than sanctify a night of illicit pleasure. Surely Hayes must realize that as well as she.

Into this holy estate these two persons present come
to be joined. If any man can show just cause, why
they may not be lawfully joined together, let him
speak now or forever hold his peace.

In the moment of silence that followed the minister's
words, Hayes felt a frisson of fear creep up his spine as
thoughts of Lucas Hale intruded. The man was more a
rival in death than he had ever been in life, and it seemed
almost as if Hayes were waiting for Lucas's dark specter to
rise up and answer. Leigh was what Hayes wanted more
than life, and he was almost afraid to believe that the
wedding he had wanted for months was actually coming to
pass. Until Leigh had stood before him on the foredeck,
dressed and ready for the ceremony, Hayes had not been
sure she would agree. But she had come to him, her
bearing straight and resolute, her hands clasped tightly
before her, and told him she was ready. Now as he stood
listening to the minister's words, there was a sense of
relief in knowing they would be bound together at last.

I require and charge you both, that if either of you
know any impediment, why you should not be lawfully joined together, you do now confess it.

Leigh drew a long breath, aching to speak. There were a
hundred reasons why she should not marry this man,
starting and ending with the fact that she didn't love him.
She was here tonight because of the victory of pleasure
over common sense, because of the triumph of expediency
over integrity. If she was not bound by the conventions
that ruled her world, she would refuse to marry Hayes. If
she did not care about going back to nursing the wounded
men who needed her, if it did not matter about the shame
she would cast on the parents she loved, she would cry out
that she was being forced into this union against her will.
She could feel the intensity of Hayes's blue-gray eyes
upon her, threatening, cajoling, willing her to silence. She

could also feel the almost equal press of the angry words against her throat, the seething need to speak, to escape the charade of a marriage that Hayes had planned for them.

But in spite of it all, Leigh kept silent. She knew the price she would pay if she spoke, and she judged it higher than if she held her peace. She would still have the things that meant the most to her: her parents' love, the respect of her community, the nursing that sustained her. To maintain all those, she had only to forfeit her body and her self-respect, to condemn them both to a marriage that was a mockery of all a marriage should be.

Hayes, wilt thou have this Woman to thy wedded wife, to live together after God's holy ordinance in the holy estate of Matrimony? Wilt thou love her, comfort her, honor her, and keep her in sickness and in health; and, forsaking all others, keep thee only unto her, so long as you both shall live?

A wave of emotion moved through Hayes as his eyes sought the face of the woman by his side. She was beautiful in the candlelight: her cheeks warmed by feathery strokes of dusty rose; her eyes deep, mysterious turquoise, her coronet of heavy braids regal and mahogany-dark atop her head.

Would he have this woman, this fine, strong woman of fire and passion as his wedded wife as long as they both would live?

"Yes, I will."

Leigh, wilt thou have this Man to thy wedded husband, to live together in God's holy ordinance in the holy estate of Matrimony? Wilt thou love him, comfort him, honor him, and keep him in sickness and in health; and, forsaking all others, keep thee only unto him, so long as you both shall live?

It was too much to promise, too much to ask. Too much, far too much to demand when she was so afraid.

"Leigh?" the pastor prodded.

"Yes, I will."

Her pause had made something inside Hayes go weak and weightless, and he was singed by quick remorse. Was he forcing Leigh into a marriage she could not abide? Everything he was doing was for her sake because he loved her, but was he asking more than she could give? Only time would tell.

Who giveth this Woman to be married to this Man?

"I do," Nathan Travis answered, disentangling the fingers that had been clutching desperately at his arm and giving them a paternal pat.

As he did, Leigh raised her gaze to his, finding both comfort and disillusionment in his solemn presence. This was not the way her wedding was supposed to be; it should have been her father in Nathan's place and her mother discreetly sniffing from the row behind them. There should have been a high-arched church above her instead of this single, stuffy room; there should have been a gown of white satin appointed with rows of lace instead of the wilted turquoise dress she had put on in St. Louis that morning more than a week before. But the single and most poignant lack was of the tall, golden-haired groom she had always imagined would be beside her when she spoke her vows. Instead of the man who had filled her childhood fantasies, the man who had known and loved her all her life, there was a stranger, a man who was forcing this wedding upon her. To hide the searing rise of tears, Leigh bowed her head.

The minister took Leigh's trembling fingers from Travis, then placed them in the hand of the man who stood still and sober by her side. They lay cold and lax upon his palm for an instant, and then Hayes's grip closed tight around them, binding her close.

Repeat after me, Mr. Banister. "I, Hayes, take thee, Leigh . . ."

"I, Hayes, take thee, Leigh, to be my wedded Wife, to have and to hold from this day forward,"
Forever, Leigh. This binds us forever.
"For better for worse."
No matter what happens, I'll always love you.
"For richer for poorer."
What man would not be rich, indeed, with a woman like you to share his life?
"In sickness and in health."
Through war and pestilence, through happiness and joy. Through the good times and the bad.
"To love and to cherish."
And care for and comfort. Oh, Leigh, I want nothing more than this: to be with you every day, to share your sorrow and your delight, and have you share mine.
" 'Til death do us part."
I'll love you all my days, Leigh, until my last breath.
"According to God's holy ordinance; and thereto I pledge thee my troth."

Now, Miss Pennington, you must give him your answer. "I, Leigh, take thee, Hayes . . ."

"I, Leigh, take thee, Hayes, to be my wedded Husband."
Unwillingly, under duress, filled with the fear that we can never find happiness together.
"To have and to hold from this day forward."
Such a long time. Oh, Hayes, how can I pledge myself to you forever?
"For better for worse."
What can be worse than this moment, when I agree to spend my life with you, a man I want but do not love?
"For richer for poorer."
This is a mistake, horrible and now irrevocable.
"In sickness and in health."

Oh, yes, Hayes, I'll care for you because now you are
my responsibility, but I would have been there anyway, a
friend whenever you needed me.

"To love and to cherish."

Oh, Hayes, don't you realize that this can never work,
that this marriage could spoil everything we've felt for
each other?

" 'Til death us do part."

You may well be condemning us to a lifetime of misery
and pain. For misplaced honor you're wedding a woman
who can never make you happy.

"According to God's holy ordinance; and thereto I give
thee my troth."

It's done now. For better or worse we are one.

It's done now. For the rest of our lives we are one.

May I have the ring.

A wave of panic moved through Hayes at the minister's
softly spoken words. The ring. In his preoccupation to
have this ceremony accomplished, in his determination to
make Leigh agree to it, he had not bought a ring. Confusion and regret touched his soul. He should have found a
way to get at least a simple gold band as a sign of his
commitment. Though where he would have found a ring in
a town this size, he did not know. How could he have
come to the ceremony without something so basic, something so binding?

Distractedly he looked down at his own hands. There,
on the little finger was the only ring he had ever worn. It
was Justin's ring, the ring he had taken from his cousin's
lifeless body on the battlefield at Shiloh. He had meant to
send it to Justin's widow, Sarah, and his son one day.
Surely neither Justin nor Sarah would mind if it was used
to pledge Hayes's love to the only woman he would ever
want. It would only be for a little while, just until he had
time to buy Leigh a wedding band of her own. Surely they
would understand.

Slowly he drew the gold signet ring from his finger and
held it clasped tightly in his palm as memories of the man

who had worn it filled his mind. He could remember the childish pranks they had played together, the pleasurable hours they had spent in the tree house they had built in one of the huge elms at the back of the Dean property, the closeness they had felt as friends as well as cousins. Justin was dead now, but he would always live in Hayes's mind: a boy whose warmth and generosity had bound them together, a man whose loyalty and convictions had cost him his life.

Slowly he offered the gold ring to the minister, who spoke a few quiet words over it, then handed it back to Hayes.

Place the ring on Leigh's finger and repeat after me. "With this ring . . ."

"With this ring, I thee wed: In the name of the Father, and of the Son, and of the Holy Ghost. Amen."

Leigh's fingers curled around the metal, accepting it, holding it in place. The vitality of Hayes's warmth touched her through the ring, branding her as his. Was this what she wanted, to be bound to a man she only thought she knew? Could they find some small measure of happiness in their marriage, or were they condemned to live together for the rest of their days for the sake of propriety and their uncontrolled passions? With confusion, doubt, and hope in her eyes, she turned to look at Hayes. There was a sober intensity to him in the half-light, a tenderness and determination that Leigh had never seen. And even as she listened to the minister's closing words, she wondered what life with Hayes would be like during all the years to come.

Then the minister's voice cut across her thoughts as the words of benediction rang through the silent room.

Bless, O Lord, this ring, that he who gives it and she who wears it may abide in thy peace, and continue in thy favor, unto their life's end. Amen.

Forasmuch as Hayes and Leigh have consented together in holy wedlock, have witnessed the same before God and this company, have given and pledged their troth, each to the other, and have declared the same by giving and receiving a Ring and by the joining of hands; I pronounce that they are Man and Wife. And those whom God has joined together, let no man divide.

14 ⌖

From her vantage point on the Texas deck of the *Barbara Dean,* Leigh could see her mother waving a joyous greeting as the riverboat pulled in. Beside her Horace Pennington stood, his stern pose a counterpoint to Althea's animation. At the sight of him, the knot of apprehension in Leigh's middle snarled tighter, making her wish that Hayes had not insisted on wiring them news of the wedding. Leigh could not fault his good intentions in wanting to spare her parents' worry and explain her absence from the city, but she dreaded the forthcoming confrontation. Surely it would have been better to meet her parents for the first time in the privacy of their town house rather than here on the public landing.

There would be no problem with her mother, Leigh knew. She would be glad to have her daughter's future settled at last, and Althea had always approved of Hayes Banister. It was her father's reaction that concerned Leigh. Would he accept the story she and Hayes had decided to tell, or would he see through it and reject the marriage her new husband had forced upon her. In a way, Leigh almost hoped her father would object. But then, there was no point in that. Her union with Hayes was a fact; her future with him was sealed. Loosening her grip on her twisted handkerchief, Leigh raised one hand to wave back.

"Did you expect your parents to come down to meet

us?" Banister asked as he came to stand beside her at the rail.

Her overwrought emotions put acid in her tone. "How should I know what they might do?" she hissed.

Hayes looked down at her in surprise before comprehension began to dawn. "What's the matter, Leigh? Are you afraid to face your parents?"

Instead of acknowledging the question, she stared out across the landing, but her silence told Hayes all he wanted to know. "It's going to be all right, Leigh. They'll accept what's happened."

As always, she was startled by his perceptiveness and by the depth of his concern. Perhaps her parents would willingly accept their marriage. The greater question was, could she?

Leigh drew a long breath. Hayes had been the soul of consideration these last days and deserved more than the rough side of her tongue. During the trip from New Madrid, he had been kind and solicitous, and she had decided to try to make the best of their enforced marriage. But her dread of the coming confrontation and her fears about the future had made her forget her resolves.

"I'm sorry, Hayes," she apologized with true contrition. "I guess I am worried about facing my parents for the first time, and especially about how Father will react. He's just unpredictable enough to call you out rather than shake your hand and welcome you as his son-in-law."

"He'll welcome me as a son-in-law. Don't worry," Hayes promised her. "Now just smile and wave to your parents, Mrs. Banister. They've come to welcome us home."

There was a good deal of confusion on the levee as the riverboat tied up. The waterfront seemed busier and more crowded than it had been since the war had begun, and Leigh was glad to see so many working, even if they were loading supplies for the Union armies fighting their way south. There were a large number of troops on the levee, too: men awaiting transport to distant battlefields to fight and die for the Federal cause. How many of these men would she see in the coming weeks? she wondered. How many of them would be returned battered and broken, sent to St. Louis to die or be healed? The futility of the war weighed Leigh down.

While she waited for Hayes to finish his business on the steamboat, Leigh bid good-bye to Nathan Travis. He had accompanied them from New Madrid, and was heading farther north before he would return to his wife in Cairo.

"You take good care of yourself, Nathan," she admonished him, "and give my love to Delia when you see her."

"I'll do that, Leigh. I surely will. Just wait until I tell her you and Hayes are married. Delia will jump for joy."

Travis must have read the change in Leigh's demeanor and bent a little closer. "I know you didn't get off to the best beginning with Hayes, but give him a chance. He's a good man, Leigh, and he cares for you very deeply. Trust him, and you won't be sorry."

Leigh started to protest, but before she could utter a word, Travis was turning away, heading toward the gangway with his long, measured stride.

How could Nathan understand the way things were between her and Hayes? Leigh reflected as she watched him go. From the beginning he and Delia had been made for each other. Delia had known Nathan was the man she wanted to marry that first afternoon. And watching them together on their wedding day had been like staring into the sun.

She and Hayes were not bound together as Delia and Nathan were. There were too many things standing between them to ever achieve the kind of happiness the other couple seemed to share. Nathan didn't know about Lucas, about her betrayal of his memory in Hayes's arms, or about the danger of being so caught up in passion that good sense lost its sway. It would be to her eternal regret that she and her husband did not love each other the way Nathan and Delia did. For now she and Hayes were eternally bound together, whatever the future might bring.

A wave of devastating sadness moved through Leigh at the thought, and she stubbornly subdued it. In a few moments she would face her parents and begin to live a lie. From this moment on she must work to convince them, and the rest of St. Louis as well, that she and Hayes had been so desperate to be together that they had eloped rather than bear the wait it would take to plan a proper wedding. It was a ruse that would take all the theatrical ability she could muster, but it was necessary to everything she held dear.

"Leigh?" Her husband's voice sounded behind her. "Are you ready to go?"

With difficulty Leigh accepted the casual intimacy of his touch and raised her eyes to his. "Yes, Hayes, I am."

They had crossed the forward gangway and were making their way up the levee toward the Penningtons' open carriage when Aaron Crawford suddenly stepped between them and their goal. In the past days as she had tried to grapple with her new role as wife and lover, Leigh had hardly given Aaron Crawford's suspicions a thought. They had been her reason for boarding the *Barbara Dean,* but she had put them out of her mind the night Hayes had made love to her. And in the days since her marriage, she had not been anxious to complicate their new relationship with things that had not seemed to matter. But now with her husband's accuser standing officiously before them, a jeering smile upon his mouth and a detachment of men at his back, Leigh wished with all her heart that she had warned Hayes about Crawford's suspicions. Her fingers tightened on Hayes's arm as if to telegraph her concern, but even her knowledge of the major's suspicions did not prepare her for his next words.

"Hayes Banister," Major Crawford announced clearly, his voice ringing across the levee, "by the power vested in me as provost marshal of St. Louis, I arrest you as a Confederate spy."

Silence descended on the busy levee for one long moment, then the buzz of voices rose louder than before.

"What?" Leigh heard Hayes say. "Crawford, what the hell is the meaning of this?"

"What's going on here, Major Crawford?" Horace Pennington blustered as he pushed his way through the curious crowd that had begun to gather. "What business do you have with my new son-in-law?"

The news of a marriage between Hayes Banister and Leigh Pennington seemed not to faze the Union major.

"I've come to arrest Mr. Banister on a charge of treason," he said with a sneer. "We have information that this man has been trafficking with Rebel agents and traveling freely behind enemy lines."

A second murmur of surprise moved through the crowd that was echoed by her father's exclamation.

"I can't imagine how you came to these ridiculous conclusions," Hayes said, "but I hardly think this is the time or the place to discuss them. Shall we go somewhere and straighten this out?"

"At last, Banister, we agree on something. And since you are under arrest, I suggest we continue our discussion at army headquarters."

Hayes's face hardened. "Very well, Crawford. The sooner we get to the bottom of this, the better. But I warn you, there are going to be some serious repercussions to my arrest."

"We shall see about that, Banister. We shall see. Corporal Cody, shackle the prisoner's hands."

"Now see here, Crawford—" Horace Pennington began, but Leigh cut him short.

"No, Aaron. Please!" she cried, as a soldier stepped from the ranks to clasp heavy iron manacles around Hayes's wrists. "What I sent south was only a letter to his cousin's wife. Please, Aaron, I told you it was nothing more."

Leigh was too concerned with convincing Crawford of Hayes's innocence to see the sequence of surprise, disillusionment, and reproach that sprang to her husband's eyes, but Crawford noticed it and instantly surmised the cause. Leigh Pennington might well have impulsively married Banister, but she had not told him all her secrets. And that fact alone, he reflected, could make the forthcoming interrogation very interesting, indeed.

"Yes, and I appreciate your help, Leigh, though as Banister's wife, you must realize you can no longer give evidence against him. But never fear, I found several collaborating witnesses, even someone to verify the letters he had you send south just before Christmas."

Leigh fell silent, filled with fear. How could Aaron have found out about the Christmas letters? She had been careful to keep her peace about those. Their destination and the

identity of their recipient would cast even greater suspicion
on Hayes than the other things Crawford had discovered.
Of course, the courier would have known, Leigh realized,
and she might well have reason to sell the knowledge in
return for favors. Was that where Crawford had gotten his
information?

She cast a sidelong glance at her husband, read the
accusation in his eyes, and knew immediately what he was
thinking. Hayes was convinced that she had betrayed him,
informed to Crawford about his clandestine activities and
the messages he had sent. In that instant, she longed to
shout a denial, but she could not. There were too many
inquisitive ears listening, too many who would learn too
much if she spoke out.

She should have warned Hayes about Aaron Crawford's
suspicions, but in the last days she had been first too
angry, and then too preoccupied with their changing relationship to chance telling Hayes something that had no
bearing on the adjustments they were making as man and
wife.

While Leigh was trying to grapple with this turn of
events, Crawford led Hayes to a wagon and had him
loaded roughly inside.

"Where are you taking him, Crawford?" Horace
Pennington demanded. "What will you do with him now?"

For a moment Crawford hesitated. He had more than
enough evidence to hold Banister on a charge of treason,
and nothing Pennington's high-placed friends could do
would free him.

"We'll be interrogating him for a while at headquarters," he replied with another leering grin. "Then he'll go
to the Gratiot Street Jail to await trial."

"Now, see here, Crawford . . ." Pennington began.

While Aaron and her father argued, Leigh moved to
where Hayes sat on the floor of the wagon. "Hayes, I'll
do what I can to get you out of this," she promised. "I
swear I will."

His cold, blue-gray eyes moved over her, and she was
singed by the contempt in his gaze.

"Will you?" her husband asked caustically, dismissing
her words as a lie. "It seems you've done more than

enough for me already, Leigh. I'm probably far better off on my own.''

Before she could respond, Crawford had clambered onto the wagon seat and the vehicle had begun to roll. There was no time for denials and explanations, and Leigh stood watching it go. When Hayes and Crawford's troopers had disappeared down Wharf Street, her father led Leigh to their carriage, where Althea was anxiously awaiting explanations.

''A fine son-in-law you've given me,'' Horace admonished his daughter once they had told Althea what had happened. ''A son-in-law and a Confederate spy all rolled up in one.''

''Leave her alone, Horace,'' Althea snapped in Leigh's defense. ''She's hardly to be blamed for something Mr. Banister did.''

Ignoring his wife, as had recently become his habit, Pennington continued. ''I don't suppose you know whether he really did what Crawford claims.''

''No,'' Leigh admitted, twisting her lace handkerchief in her lap. ''I really don't know if Hayes is a Rebel spy or not.''

''Oh, Leigh, how awful for you!'' her mother sympathized.

Leigh was silent for a moment as tears gathered in her eyes. She might not have told her husband about Aaron's accusations, but Hayes had hardly been forthcoming about his own activities, either. She still hadn't discovered where he'd been or what he'd done when he left the riverboat. She didn't know anything at all about her husband's clandestine activities, except that Nathan Travis was somehow involved.

Abruptly Leigh's head came up, and she clutched her father's arm. ''Father, you must help me find a man named Nathan Travis!'' she began. ''He came north with us on the *Barbara Dean* and can't have gone too far. Oh, please, Father, tell Jed to turn the buggy around. Nathan will know what to do to help Hayes, if only we can find him.''

Horace considered Leigh's words and the hope shining in her eyes. ''What kind of a man is this Travis. Where is he likely to be?''

Leigh obediently told her father everything she knew about Nathan.

"Then, from what you say, Travis might as likely be a Confederate spy as the man you've taken as a husband," Horace pointed out. "What you may be doing, instead of helping Hayes, is giving this other man a warning, a chance to get out of town before he is apprehended."

"Nathan wouldn't desert Hayes!" Leigh protested. "He'll help him. I know he will!"

"But will he help him by explaining this situation or by breaking him out of the Gratiot Street Prison?" Horace mumbled under his breath.

It was a question that bore consideration, but Leigh ignored it, intent on finding a way to get her husband out of a situation her secrecy had caused. "Will you help me find him, Father?" Leigh asked.

"Oh, yes, Leigh, I'll help you find him. If he's still in St. Louis, we'll locate him. But don't get your hopes up. Men of this sort are very good at hiding, especially when they have a reason for not wanting to be found."

But even her father's words and the truth they undoubtedly represented did not dim Leigh's faith in Nathan Travis. If they could find Nathan, if they could explain the danger Hayes was in, Nathan would help. One way or the other, he would see that Hayes Banister did not hang as a Confederate spy.

Hayes was taken to the impressive building that General Halleck and the members of his staff were using as headquarters. There, shut up in a small, stuffy second-story room, Crawford and several other officers began interrogating him by turns, firing volleys of questions at him, obviously hoping that he would break his silence and tell them what they wanted to know. But for all their demands, for as many questions as they asked, for as many answers as they surmised, Hayes said nothing.

"All right, Banister, if you won't admit to sending letters through the lines with information for the Confederates," Crawford said with exaggerated patience, "explain, if you will, why you were in the area around Forts Henry and Donelson in the days before Grant's campaign.''

Hayes took a deep breath and stared blankly over Crawford's shoulder, just as he had been doing for the better part of four hours. Whatever else he felt for the man, he had to concede that the major was good at his job. He had managed to unearth more about Hayes's life than close friends and family knew. Crawford had discovered why he had elected to become a river pilot rather than joining the Banister Shipyards, found evidence of his love affair with Monica Bennett, and even questioned, as Hayes himself had, the paternity of her child.

The major had thoroughly investigated Hayes's friendship with Nathan Travis. He even knew how Hayes had come to be associated with James Eads and the ironclads. Nor had Crawford overlooked his mother's Dean relations, who owed allegiance to the Confederacy, and the friends he'd had at Princeton who came from established Southern families. But what Crawford had missed, and what Hayes was sworn to conceal, was his connection with the Underground Railroad and the trips he and Nathan had made on Albert Pincheon's behalf.

Actually, Crawford made a fairly convincing case against him, Hayes was forced to admit. If he did not know better, he might well believe that this Banister fellow was operating as a Rebel spy. What that might mean in the long run, if Crawford brought his case to trial, worried Hayes more than a little. When he had taken on his first assignment for Pincheon, he had known and accepted the risk he was running of being caught and tried as a spy. The final irony was that it was the Federal government, not the Confederacy, that was accusing him of treason.

But even as the barrage of Crawford's questions assaulted him, Hayes's mind was filled with thoughts of Leigh. From the moment on the landing when she had admitted her involvement in this affair, there had been a persistent sick feeling deep inside him, a sense of disappointment and a fear of betrayal that he could not dismiss. Her revelations seemed to be the larger part of Crawford's case against him. But what was the reason for Leigh's defection? Why had she turned against him, and what did she hope to gain by telling Crawford about the letters she had posted for him? He had trusted Leigh, and she had played him false. How could a man so misjudge the woman he had made his wife?

Had she voluntarily told Crawford about the messages he had sent south, as the major implied? Her own words seemed to convict her of the act. But why had she told the major about the letters? What had made her turn him in? And had she revealed the facts voluntarily, or had Crawford found some way to coerce her?

Nightmarish visions of the scene that night in the library, when he had found Crawford forcing himself on Leigh, flickered through Hayes's head. If that bastard had laid hands on Leigh trying to make her tell him about the messages she had sent south, he would—

Irritation rose in him. He had always been very good at self-deception when it came to Leigh Pennington, Hayes chided himself. Hadn't he been able to convince himself, from that first afternoon at Camp Jackson, that there was something rare and wonderful between them? Wasn't he the fool who thought it would be enough to be with her as a friend? Hadn't he gone ahead and fallen in love with her when she had made it plain that she did not love him in return? Hayes silently cursed his own vulnerability. He should have known better than to give his heart to Leigh. His years with Monica should have taught him something about trusting women, but they had not.

"Banister! Damn it, Banister," Crawford threatened, breaking into Hayes's thoughts. "I want answers to these questions. Eads said he trusted you. Did you use your connections in his office to gain access to confidential papers? Was that where you got information to pass to your associates in the south?"

Crawford had this figured so neatly, Hayes reflected. Everything was tied up with a bow. It would be a pleasure to disprove his theories, wonderfully satisfying to see his ultimate humiliation. But that would have to wait; he didn't have the authority to tell this mere Army major what he had been doing. For now, there was nothing to do but bide his time until word reached Pincheon that the overanxious provost marshal in St. Louis had exposed one of his operations. A smile lurked at the corners of Banister's mouth. Crawford would be saluting privates when the truth came out.

But Hayes's momentary pleasure abruptly vanished when he considered how Crawford had come to these conclusions. Leigh must have told him everything he wanted to know.

He should have suspected something was amiss when she had appeared aboard the *Barbara Dean*. She had as much as admitted that she thought he was a Rebel spy headed downriver to pass on information. Leigh would not have come to that conclusion on her own; it was not in her nature to be suspicious. That should have made him realize someone was aware of the game he had been playing. But he had been too angry that she had followed him, too concerned for her safety during the days the boat had been lying just north of Memphis waiting for him to return, to even consider why she had stowed away.

Beyond that was the thing that had haunted him from the moment Crawford had approached them on the levee. It had drummed in his blood and echoed in his brain as the major and his cronies had asked their endless, pointless questions. Sitting in the tiny, stifling room as the heat of a June afternoon beat through the shutters, Hayes dwelled on a single question of his own: How could Leigh have failed to warn him, her own husband, the man who loved her more than life, that Crawford suspected he was an agent for the Confederacy?

Leigh and her father had been looking for Nathan Travis since midafternoon, scouring the waterfront and checking with all the shippers who had boats going upriver that day. There had been two headed up the Missouri, another destined for Keokuk and a fourth on its way to Alton and Rock Island, Illinois. It would have helped if Leigh had been sure where Nathan was going, but all he had said was "north." Still, for all their searching, there had been no sign of the man.

Shadows were swiftly fading into full dark, and lights had begun to come on in the windows of the taverns and bawdy houses that lined the narrow streets above the landing, when Leigh was forced to admit defeat. She was disappointed and disheartened, but there seemed nowhere else to look for the elusive Nathan Travis. She had been so sure they would find him; that once they had, he would be able to help Hayes elude Major Crawford's charges. But her hope was swiftly dimming with the fading light.

Though she had confirmed that the two men were working together in whatever Hayes had been arrested for, Horace had been more than willing to help his new son-in-law out of his difficulties with the provost marshal. But as the hour grew late, he had lost his enthusiasm, and finally even Leigh was forced to concede that their search seemed fruitless.

"I suppose, Father, there is no point in continuing this further tonight. All the shippers know we are looking for Mr. Travis, and we can't even be sure that he will be traveling north by water. It's just that I was so sure Nathan could do something to help Hayes, to explain away all that's happening."

Horace patted his daughter's hand consolingly. "It's all right, Leigh. Things will look brighter in the morning. We can come out and look again, and perhaps your Mr. Travis will hear from another source what has happened to Hayes."

Leigh nodded glumly. She did not put much store in that kind of coincidence, but there was nothing more she could do now. They were both tired and disillusioned and needed to rest and recoup their forces. "Would you mind, Father, if we went past Army headquarters on our way home to ask after Hayes?" she queried softly. "I'd feel a good deal better if I knew where he was spending the night."

"They may still be questioning him, Leigh, and you won't be able to see him."

Leigh acknowledged his words. "I know that. It's just that I'll worry a lot less if I know for sure how he is faring."

"Very well, dear," he agreed and gave the order to the driver.

They had just turned onto Market Street when Leigh spotted a lone figure striding along in the shadows. From the distance she could not make out the man's features or his clothes, but there was something about the way he moved, the tightly coiled power in his walk, that made her certain of his identity.

"Pull over, just there!" she cried, directing the driver, and jumped out of the carriage as soon as it had rolled to a stop. "Nathan? Nathan Travis, is that you?" she called out, praying the man was the one she was seeking.

The dark figure hesitated until he had identified the speaker, then came over to where she stood. "Leigh, what are you doing here?"

"Oh, Nathan, we've been looking for you everywhere! Where have you been all day?"

"I thought while I was in St. Louis I'd buy some things for Delia. But what's the matter, Leigh? Why have you been trying to find me?"

The tone of his voice reassured her, and taking his arm she pulled him toward the carriage. "Oh, Nathan, it's Hayes!" Quickly Leigh sketched the story of what had happened on the levee, about Hayes's arrest and the danger he was in. Leigh could see Travis's expression harden as he listened, and when she was finished, he nodded.

"I'll need to send a telegram and get an answer back before we can approach the authorities," he explained as Horace gave the driver instructions to the telegraph office. "But once that comes, Hayes will be a free man again." His words calmed Leigh, and she sank back into the carriage seat, more than willing to let Nathan take charge of what was to come.

The cable was sent just after ten o'clock, and then the long hours of waiting began. Leigh spent them pacing the length and breadth of the telegraph office, jumping with anticipation whenever the line began to clatter. Her father and Nathan Travis sat trying to make themselves comfortable on the straight-backed wooden benches, shifting and stretching more often with every passing hour. She did not ask who Nathan was wiring in Washington, nor did she speculate on what a cable to the nation's capital might mean. She just felt immensely better that he had sent his message for help there rather than anywhere else. It proved that Hayes was indeed more than he had seemed, but it also indicated that he was in no danger of being found guilty as a Confederate spy.

The answer came in just after three o'clock, a brief curt cable, signed with a single name. What Hayes's involvement was with a man like Albert Pincheon neither Leigh nor Horace asked, but both were pleased that such an influential person had answered Nathan's summons.

They set off for Army headquarters at a gallop, and when they pulled up in front of the building a few minutes later, the first floor was all but deserted, though a few lights burned through the shutters on the upper floors. The sleepy sentry on duty was reluctant to answer their questions, but eventually they convinced him that they did indeed need to talk to Major Crawford. Finally, the soldier disappeared up the stairs, and hardly more than a minute later Crawford came down, looking irritable, worn, and disheveled.

"What the devil is this all about?" he demanded. "Don't you realize the time?"

Without a word, Nathan Travis handed him Pincheon's telegram.

Crawford read it twice before acknowledging the words. "What does he mean: 'Banister has been involved in matters of secrecy for the government.' I need more information than that before I can turn my prisoner loose."

"I'm sorry, Major, that's all I'm authorized to tell you," Travis apologized, without seeming one bit sorry.

"I need to know specifics if I am to let Mr. Banister go," the Yankee major blustered. "I'm not even sure if this telegram is genuine."

Nathan shrugged. "You can check with the clerk over at the telegraph office or send to Washington for verification if you wish. But I'd be damned careful if I were you. Albert Pincheon is not a man to cross, and right now I'd say he probably isn't too pleased with you for exposing one of his operations."

The drawled threats seemed to have the desired effect, and with a mumbled curse Crawford stamped up the stairs again.

While the major was gone, Travis gave Leigh a reassuring hug, shook Horace's hand, and took his leave, saying something about catching a steamboat heading out just before dawn.

It was some time later that Crawford brought Hayes downstairs. He looked tired and disheveled too, but not much more than the major did. When she saw him, Leigh's first impulse was to run to him and throw her arms around him in relief that their ordeal was over and he was safe. But there was something cold and forbidding in his blue-gray eyes that froze her where she stood.

"You watch yourself, Banister," Crawford warned as the three of them turned to go. "Your friends in high places may have saved you this once, but I'm still not convinced you are as blameless and pure of heart as you claim. I'll be watching, Banister, and waiting for any mistake."

"And I assure you, Major Crawford, that you will be waiting in vain." Hayes's parting words were accompanied by a low bow that spoke of utter contempt rather than of courtesy.

The ride from Army headquarters back to the landing was accomplished in total silence, as if the passengers in the carriage preferred not to disturb the murky, predawn stillness. Even Horace's questions were forgotten, and Leigh could not bring herself to ask for explanations about his hours in Crawford's custody or what Hayes had been doing on Albert Pincheon's behalf. The only intrusions on the quiet were the sounds of the horses' hooves on the cobbled streets, and of Hayes's and Leigh's footfalls on the stairtreads as they made their way to their cabin on the *Barbara Dean*. Leigh had decided that Hayes did not mean to say anything about his arrest and his connections to the Federal government until they were both calmer and rested. But once they were inside the stateroom, with the door closed to shut out the world, Hayes hurled his coat across the room and turned cold eyes on her.

Before he said a word, Leigh read the reproach in his face. But though she knew what he thought she'd done, nothing prepared her for his anger or the words that slashed through the quiet cabin.

"Is there no loyalty in you, Leigh?" he asked furiously. "Don't I matter to you at all?"

Leigh tried to stammer a denial, but it caught in her throat behind the knot of unshed tears. As she watched the glaring accusation in his eyes, she realized how frightened she had been for his safety. It had been a fear she had not acknowledged until now, but all at once she wanted nothing more than to cling to him, to simply hold him close. But with the tone of his outburst, with the stinging accusation that lay between them, she knew she could neither voice her fear nor seek comfort in his arms.

She knew she had done everything in her power to see him released from Crawford's custody, but Hayes did not seem to recognize her efforts on his behalf. Instead he was filled with disillusionment based on the major's lies, on the misleading conversation on the levee, on the irrevocable fact that she had not warned him of Aaron Crawford's suspicions. Nor was he giving her time to explain. A strange mixture of dread and disappointment roiled within her as she watched him pace the width of the cabin.

Then relentlessly he turned on her, his words, for all their softness, biting as deeply as the sharpest lash. "You may be the most beautiful woman I've ever known," he said angrily, "the one whose body I crave above all others, but tonight I learned a lesson no man should ever have to learn. I learned that our marriage is a travesty. That for all the hope I'd had for our life together, I cannot trust my wife!"

15 ❧

September 9, 1862—St. Louis, Missouri

"It's so wonderful of you and your mother to let me come and stay for a few days while Nathan and Hayes are away on business, Leigh." Delia chattered happily as she poked at the dish of peaches set before her on the elegantly laid breakfast table. "It's marvelous to sleep in a real feather bed and enjoy food that isn't left over from the things we feed the men."

Leigh smiled across the table at her friend. "I'm glad you could come, Delia. I think being away from our hospitals for a few days will do us both a world of good."

"I couldn't agree more," Althea interjected. Already her friend's presence seemed to be raising Leigh's spirits, and after the tense, strained months in the town house, Althea was ready to embrace anyone who could bring a little laughter and gaiety into the gloom.

It was odd, Althea reflected. She had expected that Leigh's marriage to Hayes Banister would be a good thing for her daughter. Hayes was a fine man, and it was clear that he cared deeply for Leigh. But instead of the relaxed, settled air she had expected to see in the younger woman, there was a subtle, growing discontent.

Perhaps it had been a mistake to ask Leigh and Hayes to move in with her, Althea fretted, but since Horace was gone so much, it was a relief to have someone in the house. Besides, Leigh needed someplace more to come home to than a single cabin on a steamboat. But living in close proximity, it was easy for Althea to see that the first days of her daughter's marriage were not going well. Leigh and her husband did not fight, at least not the way she and Horace did. Their battles were waged with silence and a few harsh, well-chosen words. It was hard to believe that two people who had seemed to be at odds from the very beginning of their married life had eloped to be together. Althea sighed. She had hoped for so much more for Leigh when it came to marriage, but her daughter seemed every bit as bitter and disillusioned as Althea was herself.

Felicity Hale's words broke in Althea's dreary thoughts. "And what is it you two young ladies plan to do today?" she asked. It had become Felicity's habit to take meals with the Pennington household to save her servants trouble.

"I think we're headed down toward Verandah Row," Leigh answered.

"Yes," Delia agreed enthusiastically. "I have a long list of things to buy for women working in the hospital at Cairo. I wouldn't be a bit surprised if, when I go back on the steamer, I'll have another whole trunk of purchases to take aboard."

"Well, Leigh, perhaps while you're out you could get me some more yarn so I can finish those socks for the troops."

"Of course, Felicity, I'd be glad to," she assured the older woman, then turned to the servant who had come to stand by her chair.

"Yes, Matty, what is it?"

"Miss Leigh, there's a man here with a message for you," the maid reported.

"Who is he? Do you know him?"

"It's Mr. Brandon's man, Miss, the one they call Plato."

"Oh, no!" Felicity cried, paling. "Oh, no! Oh, no! They've not killed Brandon, too!"

Leigh rose and hurried into the hall where the grizzled black man who had gone off to war with Lucas and Bran stood waiting. Taking one of his gnarled hands, Leigh led him back into the dining room where the other women waited. "What's the news, Plato? Is Bran all right?"

"He's been wounded, Miss Leigh, and needs someone to bring him home."

"Wounded, oh dear!" Felicity gasped with a hand clutched over her heart.

"Delia, will you help Felicity with her smelling salts?" Leigh suggested, and Delia moved to do as she was bid before Leigh continued her conversation with the man at her side.

"How badly is Bran wounded?"

"He lost a leg, Miss Leigh, about a month and a half ago. He wouldn't let them take it the night he was shot, but then the fever come upon him and he didn't have no choice."

Leigh heard her mother moan softly, and her own face was grim. "Where is he now, Plato?"

"He was wounded down in Arkansas, and when he was able, we headed home. Some people going to Kansas City agreed to take us that far, and Mr. Bran said we could find a way to St. Louis once we got there. But Mr. Bran took sick again just outside Nevada, Missouri."

"And he sent you here to me?"

"Yes, Miss Leigh. I left him with a widow woman at the edge of town. He said you'd come to get him, that you'd know what to do."

Leigh could well imagine the shape Bran was in. She had seen too many like him in these past months. When he was wounded, he had undoubtedly tried to deny the need for an amputation as so many brave men did, but the putrification that set in when treatment was delayed had doubtless been a greater threat to his life than losing a leg might have been. If his recurrent fever was related to the amputation, rather than to some other cause, Bran might well be dead before she could reach him in Nevada. Still, she knew she had to try.

"Very well, Plato. You look as if you could use hot food and some sleep. While you're resting, I'll make arrangements for us to leave for Nevada in the morning."

"Leigh, you can't seriously be planning to go all the way across the state to get Bran yourself!" her mother gasped. "That whole area near the Kansas border is a virtual no-man's-land overrun with bands of guerrillas from both the north and south!"

Leigh's decision had been made the moment she heard of Brandon's plight, and she didn't welcome her mother's interference. "Who else is there to go? I can't ignore Bran's needs."

"But, Leigh, it's bound to be dangerous for a woman to go out there alone."

"I fully intend to go with her, Mrs. Pennington." Delia Travis spoke up unexpectedly, her cool, steady gaze locking with the older woman's.

"Two women alone will hardly make it any better," Althea protested. "Can't you wait until either Hayes or your father returns to accompany you?"

"And what if Bran is dead by then? What if I could have done my part to save him but waited here instead?" Leigh's deep-green eyes flashed with the strength of her convictions, and Althea fell silent, knowing further protests were futile.

"Matty, take Plato to the kitchen, feed him, and give him a place to sleep," Leigh continued, impatient to begin preparations for the trip to Nevada. "Mother, have the cook take the supplies we will need for a two-week stay from the household stores. Delia and I will have some things to prepare, as well."

Leigh came around the table to the frail little woman who had raised Lucas and Bran. "Now, Felicity," she said softly, taking the elderly woman's hands. "don't you worry. I'll bring Bran home as soon as I can, and together we'll nurse him back to health."

They started out the next morning just after sunrise, with Plato riding beside the well-sprung wagon Leigh had rented from a livery stable. Though taking the railroad as far as Rolla would have been faster, Leigh and Delia had decided a well-equipped wagon might better suit their purpose. The previous evening they had moved a rope bed with a thick, soft mattress into the back of the Conestoga, then carefully packed away supplies, camping equipment, and a chest of bandages and medicines. Brandon might be too ill to be moved, or he might be able to tolerate only a few hours of travel a day. This way they could stop and make camp whenever they deemed it necessary.

Once they had left the city behind, the rolling Missouri countryside spread out before them. There were prosperous farms with grain standing in the fields awaiting harvest, and rows of rustling corn ready to be picked. Sheep and cows dotted the hillsides, and sturdy farmhouses were nestled into groves of ancient trees. It presented a pleasant bucolic scene, but Leigh knew that as they traveled west, farms like these would become scarce, for in the last months the Union army and the guerrillas had bled the western counties of Missouri dry. The houses and crops of Yankee sympathizers had been burned and their livestock driven off or slaughtered by the roving bands of bushwhackers who claimed allegiance to the Confederate cause. But, in truth, the Union troops sent to capture the guerrillas were little better than the Rebels, taking the same revenge on Southern families suspected of harboring the fugitives.

After his travels into the western counties of Missouri for the Quartermaster Corps, Horace Pennington had told tales of rape and murder done more for the sake of plunder and mayhem than for any patriotic ideal. Leigh had not made the decision to go into the disputed area lightly, but with Bran's life in the balance, she felt she had no choice. Still, she had tried to prepare herself for trouble as best she could. Beside her on the high seat of the wagon, half-hidden by her flowing skirts, was a new rifle, and a pistol in its holster hung from the frame of the canopy behind her. If only they were lucky enough to stay clear of the bands of marauders led by Lane, Jemison, and the notorious Quantrill who rode roughshod through these counties, Leigh would be fervently thankful.

Beside her, Delia seemed not to share Leigh's concerns and chatted happily. Perhaps it was this indomitable facet of Delia's character that drew Nathan Travis to her, Leigh reflected, slowing the horses as they approached a particularly rough stretch of road. Travis seemed by nature such a quiet, sober man that Delia's good spirits and perpetual optimism must somehow complement and lighten his somber moods. Whatever it was that bound them, it was evident that theirs was a happy marriage. Nathan's tenderness when he touched Delia and the way he bowed his head to catch her words spoke eloquently of his feelings for his wife. When Leigh watched them together, she felt the same despairing jealousy that had filled her the day they were married at Savannah months before. From the first, everything about Delia and Nathan had shown their contentment, and her wistfulness was even sharper now when she realized how far she and her own husband were from that ideal.

The marriage Leigh had been so apprehensive about on her wedding day had turned out to be every bit as difficult as she had feared. She and Hayes didn't fight, and for that Leigh was profoundly thankful, but neither did they seem to be in any way connected. Hayes was still working long hours at the shipyards, and sometimes stayed away all night with the excuse of some particularly pressing project. Leigh was busy too, for when the wounded from a battle arrived, she stayed at the hospital as long as she was needed.

But even when they were together, something was missing, something that had been an integral part of their relationship in the past. When once they had shared their lives, there was now isolation. Where once there had been satisfying conversations, there were now uncomfortable silences. And somehow in those silences an undefined antagonism was clear.

At first Leigh had thought that when Hayes learned how she had sought out Nathan Travis to see to his release from the provost marshal, things would be resolved between them. But in spite of her actions, Hayes seemed determined to maintain his distance. To him Leigh's reticence in revealing Crawford's accusations had been betrayal, and he was not a man who easily forgave breaches of either friendship or loyalty.

Even the physical side of their relationship had been altered in some subtle way. Hayes still wanted Leigh and was capable of turning her mindless with desire. But since they had returned to St. Louis, since Aaron Crawford had arrested Hayes as a Confederate spy, something elemental was missing even when their bodies clung together.

Leigh sighed and tried to turn her thoughts to other matters, but vague, half-remembered images of Hayes remained. In her mind's eye she could see him hunched over pages of calculations he had brought home from the shipyards, his dark hair burnished and his hard look of concentration softened by the glow of the lamp on the desk beside him. She could recall the lazy, drawling sound of his voice when she had come home one sultry afternoon to find Hayes and her father enjoying ice-cold juleps in the shade on the side porch. There was even a secret pleasure in observing Hayes's morning routine: in smelling the citrus tang of the shaving soap he slathered over his face, in listening to the rasp of the straight razor as it moved along his throat, in watching the frown gather between his brows as he trimmed the edges of the long, full sideburns that swept across his cheeks. But her delight in those small intimacies was not enough to make up for the rest. And Leigh despaired for their future, for all the years they would remain together.

Their marriage was all she had feared it would be, and Leigh clearly understood the reasons for her own unhappiness. What she could neither comprehend nor accept was the keen sense of disappointment that assailed her day after day, and the envy of Delia and Travis she had experienced before was now tinged with a bitter sense of failure she could neither dismiss nor deny.

They crossed the state quickly, getting on the trail before sunup and making camp in the evening twilight, fighting the heat and dust of the steamy days of the lingering Missouri summer. By the end of the week when they reached the little town near the Missouri-Kansas border, exhaustion ran through their veins, thick and heavy as lead. But at the sight of Brandon sitting on the porch of the Widow Garland's cottage, pale and thin but obviously improving, Leigh's fatigue and doubt fell away. Hauling the wagon to a stop, she hardly took time to set the brake before she was scrambling to the ground. She crossed the yard at a run and threw herself into Brandon's arms. Clinging together, they wept for all that had happened since they last had been together and for the wondrous joy of being reunited.

September 15, 1862—St. Louis, Missouri

"I hope no one saw me coming here," Althea Pennington whispered, brushing past Aaron Crawford into the suite of rooms he kept in the National Hotel.

"There's really no danger of that, my dear, as long as you used the servant's stairs," he assured her, closing the door.

"I did pass one of the stewards," she told him fretfully.

Aaron came up behind her and closed his hands around her arms. "You mustn't worry, Althea. The staff here is really very discreet."

Althea took a step away. "I'm sorry, Aaron, if I'm being foolish. This is the first time I've ever done anything like this, and I'm very nervous."

"Of course you are. And your concern is understandable."

Althea turned to Aaron, seeking reassurance. "No one will find out about this, will they? I don't want anything we do to hurt either Horace or Leigh."

Crawford stroked his hand from her shoulder to waist and pulled Althea into his arms. "Only the two of us will know, never anyone else. Now, my dearest, would you like a glass of sherry to calm you before we begin?"

The auburn-haired woman hesitated for a moment before refusing the drink and saw the gleam of victory in Crawford's dark eyes.

"Then, if you'll have no refreshment, kiss me, Althea," he ordered, lowering his mouth to hers. "Kiss me and put everything else out of your mind."

Althea tried to do as Aaron asked as his lips drew demandingly on her own. This was what she wanted, she told herself stubbornly, to find reassurance and satisfaction once again in a man's arms. It had been so long since Horace had kissed her, much less made her feel protected and treasured as a woman longed to be. She needed to see the light of appreciation in a man's eyes; craved the meaningless little gifts of flowers and candy brought as tokens of affection; ached for the pretty words that only a gallant would know.

Once her husband had given her those things as a matter of course. For years his favors had made up for the sudden flares of temper that erupted between them, and their disagreements had been softened by his whispered words of love. But somehow that fine balance between passion and antagonism had been lost, and Althea's self-confidence with it. If there was any chance that those days could be recaptured, Althea would not be here with Aaron Crawford. But with wrenching disappointment, she recognized that they were gone forever. Closing her eyes more tightly, she tried to blot out the memories of the way things had once been with the only man she ever loved, the man she had run away to marry.

Determinedly, she turned to Crawford in a flurry of counterfeit desire, seeking forgetfulness and respite for her unsatisfied physical hungers. Her lips opened willingly beneath the onslaught of his kiss as her hands caught in his thick, silver-dusted hair. This was the way to reassurance and satisfaction, Althea reasoned. This was the way to bury passions past.

Still kissing her with fervent desire, Aaron swung an arm beneath her knees and carried her through the double doors to the adjacent bedchamber.

"Althea, my dear, I never thought you would be so eager," he said breathlessly, "but your abandon adds to my delight."

Standing her before him, Aaron began to remove Althea's clothes: taking the reticule from her clenched hands, draping her heavily embroidered shawl across a chair, stripping the gloves from fingers, carefully laying her mauve silk bonnet aside. Then he turned her from him and began to work the row of fasteners on the back of her gown.

Althea stood motionless as his fingers moved over the tiny covered buttons. She could feel the brush of his knuckle against her nape, the cool air of the bedchamber on her back as the bodice began to part. She knew this should have been a moment of great excitement and desire, but instead tremors of guilt were shuddering along her nerves.

This *was* what she wanted, she insisted silently. This act

would still the restless craving in her blood, this act would end the months of disappointment and frustration. But even as Aaron brushed feather-light kisses against her bared flesh, she felt little of the wild anticipation she had known when her husband had made love to her.

Oh, Horace, she cried soundlessly. Oh, Horace, how is it that I have come to this? Tears burned against her down-cast lids when she thought of the man who was her husband. For all of the years of her marriage, he had been what mattered most, and even now Horace was the one who claimed her heart. But if that was true, why was she here in an opulent hotel room with a man she was not sure she wanted and clearly did not love.

Through her turmoil, Althea became aware that more of the tiny buttons were being slipped from their holes, and that the stiff fabric of her bodice had begun to gape away from the curves of her breasts. In a matter of moments the protection of the high-necked garment would be gone, and with it the last chance to change her mind about bedding Aaron Crawford. Did she want to go through with this assignation? Could she live with herself if she did?

A sob rose in her throat, and the tears that had been threatening began to spill down her cheeks. What she had come here to do was clearly impossible, and if she was to escape the consequences of her actions, she must leave this hotel room immediately.

Crossing her arms on her chest to hold the top of her gown in place, Althea stepped away and turned to face her would-be lover. "I can't do this, Aaron," she murmured softly and could not seem to meet his eyes. "I'm sorry, more sorry than you know."

Doubtless there were things she could say to soften her refusal. She could tell Aaron that she still found him attractive, that later she would undoubtedly regret these moments of reticence. If there was any correct or fashionable way to end an affair, Althea did not know it, and though she searched her mind for appropriate phrases, there were none to explain her sudden reversal. But no matter what she said or what he replied in return, she knew she could not allow Aaron Crawford to make love to her. As she looked up into his face at last, she was embarrassed, confused and then suddenly afraid of the menacing anger in Aaron's hard, gray eyes.

Swiftly she refastened the only buttons she could reach, the highest ones of the neckline of her gown, and swept the shawl around her shoulders.

"So you really are going," Crawford snarled as he watched her. "I suppose I shouldn't be surprised. None of you Southern women have the stomach to submit to a real man, a man who will treat you as a woman is meant to be treated. You want to be fawned over, pampered. Well, Althea, if you chose to leave it's your loss, your cowardice that will rob you of a woman's greatest pleasure."

Heat rose in Althea's cheeks at Major Crawford's words, and somehow beneath his hostile glare, she managed to gather up her hat, gloves and reticule. Going back the way she had come, Althea slipped down the servant's stairs with guilt and confusion dogging her footsteps. It was only when she was inside the hired cab that she dared to draw a breath.

But in spite of her decision to leave Aaron Crawford, in spite of her last-minute retreat, the ride home alone in the hired carriage was a foretaste of what hell must be. Guilt at what she had nearly done swept over her in waves, and the motives for the liaison that had been blissfully obscure on her way to the National Hotel were suddenly defined in horrendous clarity for Althea to contemplate.

She had wanted to hurt Horace by taking a lover, to pay him back for all the times he had ignored her or been too busy or too angry to see to her feminine needs. She acknowledged that a woman craved a man's attentions to assure her of his love, but taking a man like Aaron Crawford to her bed was hardly a fitting revenge for Horace's simple sins of omission. Horace had never deliberately hurt her, and even the things he shouted in anger never deserved such a betrayal.

As much as she had tried to deny what Aaron Crawford was, Althea knew, and her shame was worse for knowing. She had been smugly judgmental of the lonely women who it was said had succumbed to the major's charms, and she was filled with disgust at how close she had come to being another of his conquests.

Both Horace and Leigh had warned her about Aaron, but somehow their words had added to his devilish glamour rather than detracting from it. She had stubbornly flaunted his friendship in her husband and her daughter's faces, seeking to seize the independence they had been so unwilling to grant. The terrible irony was that perhaps today she had unwittingly proved them right in their judgment of her. She had been weak and pliable, self-centered and shallow, unable to discern wheat from chaff.

Althea sighed bleakly and looked out the window of the hired carriage, caught in a flood of remorse. Her entire life was in disarray: her husband would go to any lengths to avoid her, her daughter was far more capable that she. And now she had come very close to breaking the most sacred vow she had ever made, the vow to cleave to her husband alone. Guilt hung like a stone in her chest, and she was desperate to find a way to atone for what she had done. Because of their estrangement, she could no longer make things right with Horace, but she was desperate to find a way to rebuild her self-respect. Something like Leigh's good works with the wounded soldiers might absolve her of the sins of indulgence and vanity she had committed; something she could do to make the lives of others a little less grim might help her find peace. But what, Althea wondered as she crept home through the streets of St. Louis, what was there that a woman born to a life of ease could do to help in a time of such desperate need?

When she arrived at the townhouse, Althea was too preoccupied by her own concerns to notice Nathan Travis waiting in the parlor, and she had thought she was alone until her son-in-law came thundering down the stairs.

"What the devil is going on here, Althea?" Hayes demanded. "The servants say Leigh and Delia have gone off somewhere to rescue Brandon Hale? Who's with them? Where have they gone?"

"Oh, Hayes, how glad I am you've returned!" Althea fluttered. "I tried to tell them not to go, that it was too dangerous an undertaking for two women alone."

"Damn it, Althea! Will you tell me what's going on?" Hayes was furious at what he had discovered thus far, and when Mr. Travis came into the hallway, he seemed tense and enervated, too.

Briefly Althea related the incident that had taken place almost a week before, and the two men's faces became grimmer as the tale unfolded.

"Nevada, Missouri? Are you certain, Althea, that is where they were going?" Hayes questioned her carefully.

"That's over near the Kansas border, where all that bushwhacker trouble has been." Travis was every bit as concerned as Hayes and showing it.

"Yes, I'm certain that's what they said," Althea assured them. "Plato, Brandon's man, was to guide them across the state."

"Good Lord!" Travis exclaimed. "There are two headstrong women, a slave and a sick man out there in the roughest, most lawless, no-man's-land there is anywhere in this war!"

"Althea," Hayes instructed, his decision already made, "I want you to instruct the cook to pack a couple of saddlebags with food for the trip and have someone saddle the two fastest horses in the stable."

"Are you going after them, Hayes? Now? Tonight? Before dinner?" Althea asked anxiously as Travis muttered something about gathering his gear.

"Althea," Hayes explained with great deliberation, obviously holding his temper in check with difficulty, "there may be lives at stake. Now go and do as I say."

As Althea scurried toward the kitchen to do her son-in-law's bidding, she heard him muttering a furious litany as he pounded up the stairs.

"God damn! God damn! God damn independent women!"

September 19, 1862—Near Wheatland, Missouri

Leigh settled Bran as comfortably as she could, spreading a blanket on the ground and bracing a pillow against one of the wagon wheels so that he could watch while the rest of them made camp. Already Delia had gathered enough kindling to start a small fire, and Plato was busy seeing to the horses. Leigh herself was turning away to see to her own duties when Brandon caught the hem of her skirt and pulled her to a stop.

"Sit with me a minute before you get on with your chores," he coaxed her, employing one of his boyish smiles to win his way. "We've hardly had a moment alone since you arrived in Nevada, and your company is one of the things I've missed most about being away."

Leigh had missed Bran too, and it was true that they had not had a chance for more than the most inane conversation in the three days since she, Delia, and Plato had arrived at the Widow Garland's door to take him home. Leigh looked down at him consideringly, trying to discern if he would be better left to rest.

The pale, spare man before her did not seem to show the weariness she felt, but neither did he bear much resemblance to the robust boy Leigh had grown up with, nor the strong young soldier who had marched gallantly off to war. He was too thin, too worn, too fragile for a man of twenty-four years. Either his illness or the hardships he had endured in Sterling Price's army had sharpened his youthful features and destroyed his vitality and strength. But, in spite of the shocking change in him, he was still essentially Bran, with light and life in his hazel eyes and mischief in his smile.

To her way of thinking, he might well have benefited from another week of rest before setting out across the state, but he had been adamant about leaving Nevada as soon as they possibly could. Since the stump of his amputated leg was healing well at last and Bran was free of fever, Leigh had relented. Traveling relatively short distances and stopping early in the afternoon seemed not to tax Brandon too severely, but Leigh knew he was still weak and she worried that he might tire himself out long before they reached St. Louis.

"Leigh, please. Surely you can spare me a few minutes," Bran cajoled. "I think there are some things we need to discuss."

Leigh was aware that it was often easier to do as Bran asked rather than waste time and energy opposing him. "It was only you I was thinking of," she admonished, dropping down on the blanket beside him in defeat. "I was afraid you might be worn out from all the traveling."

"How hard do you think it is lying in that feather bed from dawn till sunset?" he challenged. "Besides, I wouldn't have asked you to sit with me if I was too tired to talk. There aren't things you need to be doing, are there?"

"Well, I suppose I could change the dressing on your leg," she conceded gruffly, "so as not to waste the time completely."

While Brandon waited, Leigh brought out the box of bandages and medicines she and Delia had gathered for the trip. There were several types of dressings packed in the sturdy wooden container along with alum and silver nitrate to inhibit bleeding; morphine, a bit of opium, and chloroform for pain; carbolic acid and alcohol to clean wounds; as well as calomel, quinine, digitalis, and some sodium hydrochlorate to treat gangrene. Luckily, Brandon seemed to have no sign of that, Leigh thought as she began to loosen the bandage around his thigh.

"I'm glad we're having this chance to talk," Brandon commented casually, "because I was beginning to think, Leigh, that there were things you didn't want me to know."

Leigh felt an uncomfortable warmth rise in her cheeks, and she bent closer to her work.

"Delia says you're married, that you have been married for several months." When she gave him no answer, Bran continued undeterred. "Didn't you plan to tell me, Leigh? How long did you plan to keep me in the dark?"

His voice was even and calm, but every word he spoke seemed to Leigh an accusation.

"Why didn't you write me that you were married? Or tell me about your husband the other night when Delia was talking about hers?"

Leigh drew an unsteady breath. She didn't want to discuss her marriage to Hayes with Brandon Hale, didn't want to acknowledge how soon after the news of his brother's death she had sought shelter in another man's arms.

But she also knew Brandon well enough to realize that until his curiosity was appeased, he would not let the subject drop. He would pursue the truth with single-minded purpose until he had learned it all. That certainty came from years of sharing her secrets, whether she had wanted Bran to know them or not. He had a way of wheedling things out of her no matter how hard she had tried to resist, a certain way of asking the right questions so that she could never refuse him an answer. He had always known the places where she hid her treasures, the presents she had bought or made for everyone at Christmas, when she changed from a girl into a woman, and even who had given her her first kiss. She had told him her fears and her dreams, confided her torments and her joys. She had shared everything with Bran when they were growing up, and he had shared as much of himself with her. It seemed useless to think of deceiving him about all that had happened with Hayes, though for both their sakes there were things Bran could not know.

"How much did Delia tell you?" Her voice was low and resigned.

"She said only that you were married at the end of May and told me the man's name, since you had not seen fit to do so."

Bran sounded hurt by her omission, and though she had kept her peace to protect him, she had not meant to shut him out.

"It was a marriage of convenience, Bran," she explained begrudgingly, "a marriage of convenience, nothing more. Hayes had compromised my reputation and was gentleman enough to offer me the protection of his name rather than have me face a scandal."

Bran gave a long, hard look. "Aren't you happy in your marriage, Leigh? Is that why you refuse to discuss it?"

"Bran, please!"

"Or is it that you're ashamed of marrying this fellow Banister? What kind of a man is he, anyway?"

Leigh's hands faltered momentarily, and the ends of the bandage she was tying slipped from beneath her fingers.

"Is there something wrong with Banister?" he demanded. "Isn't he worthy of you?"

"It's not Hayes I'm ashamed of, Bran," Leigh confessed and hung her head. "The one I'm ashamed of is me. Aren't you appalled at how quickly I married, at how disloyal to Lucas's memory I've been?''

He hesitated for a moment, stung by surprise, then put a finger beneath her chin and raised her face to his. There were tenderness and exasperation mingled in his expression. ''Oh, Leigh, don't be a goose! Lucas has been dead for over a year, and your life has continued, just as it should. You loved Lucas, and you made him happy. But he's gone, and even he would not want you to waste precious time mourning him. You've taken the first step toward making a new life for yourself, and I'm glad.''

Unexpected tears rose in Leigh's eyes. She had not realized how deeply she felt her guilt or how relieved she was to be absolved. ''Are you glad, Bran? I was so afraid you would hate me because I had married Hayes.''

He pulled her into his arms and held her close. ''No, Leigh, it's as things should be. Be happy with your new husband. It's the way Lucas would have wanted it.''

It felt good to be held and comforted by Bran again after all the months they had been apart, and Leigh realized anew how much she had missed him. They sat comfortably together with her cheek pillowed on his chest, with his arm slung around her shoulders, and it was Leigh, not Bran, who drifted off to sleep.

The sun had sunk much lower in the sky when Bran awakened her. ''There are riders coming,'' he said, nodding toward the hazy cloud of dust that hung on the darkening horizon.

Leigh sat up and looked in the direction he indicated. ''Who do you think they are?''

Bran shrugged. ''It could be Union troopers, that or bushwhackers. It doesn't bode well for us either way.''

''Do you suppose they'll turn off before they get this far?''

''I don't know. You'd better warn the others.''

Leigh quickly packed up the medicines and put them in the wagon. Delia and Plato had seen the dust too, and preparations for the evening meal slowed as they watched the cloud grow larger and more menacing. Then the distant roar of hooves reached them, growing steadily louder as the band of men approached. None were wearing Yankee blue, and that left one possibility even more desperate than the other. Leigh prayed that the riders would turn aside, but the band seemed drawn, either by the glow of the blazing campfire or to the stream that pooled just beyond the trees.

With a neighing of horses and the eddying of dust, a group of about forty men pulled up less than a hundred feet from the wagon. They wore no recognizable uniform, though there were military touches to their clothes: sashes that hung from shoulders, striped trousers, and bits of braid. But from where Leigh stood, she could see that they were armed as if for battle, with rifles slung across their saddles and pistols buckled low on their hips.

As she watched, the leader dismounted from his horse and limped slowly in their direction. Then, in spite of her own drumming fear and the grasp Brandon held on the hem of her skirt, Leigh moved beyond the circle of firelight to meet him.

"Good evening, ma'am," the rough-looking man greeted her, taking his hat in hand. "We saw your fire and thought we might come by to see who was camping here by the stream."

The man was fair-haired and slender, only slightly taller than Leigh was herself, but there was something in his pale, heavy-lidded eyes that spoke of deceit and some vague menace. He would make, at worst, a formidable enemy and, at best, a treacherous friend, she decided in that first moment. Then, with every intention of making him the latter, Leigh extended her hand in a semblance of welcome.

"Good evening, sir. I'm Leigh Banister. We're on our way back to St. Louis with my neighbor who has been wounded."

The man continued to study her with those strange, shaded eyes, taking in the curves of her lush body and the proud angle of her head. Then he turned to where Bran sat. "What army were you with, sir, and who was your commander?"

Bran hesitated, and Leigh wondered, as she knew he must, what answer the man expected. Both Union and Confederate guerrillas were roaming Missouri's border areas, killing and robbing all those not in sympathy with their cause. Bran's reply might well decide their fate.

Predictably, he chose to tell the truth. "I've been with Sterling Price," he answered, "since the first days of the war."

The leader limped closer and held out his hand. "My men and I were with Price at Pea Ridge. Did you lose that leg there?"

"No, later," Bran told him, "in a skirmish not even deserving of a name. I'm Lieutenant Brandon Hale, Confederate States of America, at your service."

"Captain William Quantrill," the other man replied.

At the name a shiver of fear and revulsion shot through Leigh. This man's vile deeds were legend to the refugees who had made their way to St. Louis in fear of their lives. He and his band of cutthroats had left a wide swath of destruction across western Missouri: of men killed, women raped, livestock slaughtered, goods confiscated, and houses burned. If the rumors about the man were true, he was the devil incarnate, vicious, wicked, and cruel, and his men were no better. But standing over Bran, conversing about the war, he seemed no different from any other man Leigh had ever known.

"We'd be pleased to camp here by the stream tonight, if you folks wouldn't mind," Quantrill was saying. "And it would be a real treat to take advantage of a woman's cooking, if you ladies would agree."

They all knew they had no choice but to accede to Quantrill's wishes, and while the rest of the men dismounted and set up a camp of their own, Leigh and Delia began to prepare a meal from the things that were brought to their fire. The guerrillas had a surprising array of stores, from game shot during the day to whole hams and slabs of beef that had been liberated from someone's smokehouse. There were vegetables too, potatoes and yams and ears of corn already soaked and ready to be roasted.

While the women worked, half a dozen fires blossomed in the growing dark, and when pickets were set up to encircle the encampment, Leigh could not help but wonder if they were more secure for the guerrillas' vigilance or in even graver danger. It seemed a point useless to ponder, and she diligently went on about her chores.

"I was wondering, ma'am," Quantrill began, approaching her again, "if you would mind taking a look at my leg. Lieutenant Hale says you're a fine nurse, and there are several of us in need of care."

"I would be more than happy to see to your needs, Captain Quantrill," she replied. "Just let me get my kit of medicines."

Quantrill's leg wound was healing well, but clearly benefited from a good cleansing and a fresh bandage. Once she was done with him, other men wandered over for sympathy and care. From their conversation Leigh gathered they had been wounded in battles that had taken place several weeks before at Independence and Lone Jack. The fighting had been fierce, and Leigh listened to their accounts of the incidents, horrified by their tactics. These men seemed to fight without any regard for the gentlemanly rules of war, fiercely, with only survival in mind. They fought "under the black flag" they said, without giving quarter or expecting any. The stories of their exploits sickened Leigh, and she tried to concentrate on tending their wounds and not on their boastful words.

While Leigh had been caring for the men in need, Delia had been working to prepare the meal to feed close to fifty people. It was no larger a group than they cooked for at the field hospitals, and when Leigh returned to help, they made remarkable progress.

Just as they were slicing ham to be fried, in addition to the beans and potatoes that were already cooking over the fire, gunshots erupted from beyond the eastern perimeter of the camp. Instantly, men were on their feet ready for action, with rifles and pistols clutched in their hands. But the disturbance was short-lived, and the guerrillas had settled down again when one of the sentries came into the camp prodding two prisoners with his gun.

Leigh glanced up as the picket approached where Quantrill was sitting with Bran, and she suddenly went tingly and light-headed with shock. Beside her she heard Delia's gasp of alarm and reached across to still the girl's instinctive movement. There, beneath the cold, steely bore of the sentry's repeating rifle, stood her husband and Nathan Travis.

They had been disarmed and stood totally vulnerable before the guerrilla leader. What Hayes and Nathan were doing here, Leigh did not know, but from her vantage point near the fire she could see the difference in the two men's demeanor. Travis was coiled tight but at ease, with his features carefully masked. Hayes stood tensed and waiting too, but there was a simmering belligerence in his pose, a reckless challenge about him that Leigh had never seen in her husband before.

Don't do anything foolish, Hayes, Leigh willed him, wishing she could shout the warning across the clearing.

Slowly Quantrill came to his feet to face the two prisoners and their guard. "Who are these fellows, Kit?" he demanded. "Are they scouts for the Union patrols?"

"I don't rightly know," came the answer, "but they were surely sneaking around the camp as if they were a couple of Yankee spies."

"What were you doing?" Quantrill addressed the men before him. "What is it you want here?"

Neither of the prisoners answered, unwilling to endanger Leigh and her party.

"I said," the guerrilla leader repeated in a threatening tone, "what is it you are doing here if you are not Union spies?"

Again there was no reply.

Quantrill came a few steps closer to where Banister and Travis stood. "What is your purpose for prowling around our camp in the dark?" he demanded again. Then, without warning, he struck Hayes a backhand blow that sent him staggering.

Incandescent fury lit in his eyes, and only Travis's rough, restraining hand spared Quantrill from Hayes's retaliation.

Quantrill took in both Banister's movement and the tightening at the corners of Travis's mouth, and knew instinctively that they would get no information from these men by normal means.

"Kill him!" Quantrill ordered coldly, indicating the tall, brown-haired man who seethed with silent rage. One of the men raised a gun to obey his leader's command, pointing it at Hayes.

Quantrill's transformation from rational man to cold-blooded killer momentarily stunned Leigh, and then she was across the clearing, throwing herself protectively between her husband and the guerrilla with the rifle. "No! No! Don't hurt him! Please!"

For an instant Quantrill studied the man and woman before him. "Who is this man to you?" he demanded of Leigh. "Why are you begging for his life?"

"He—he's my husband."

There was a parchment-brittle silence around the fire as the Confederate raider considered Leigh's words. If what the woman said was true, there was no need to fear Yankee patrols, and that in itself was a relief. And, he supposed, a man could be forgiven for coming to take home a wayward wife. But there might well be an advantage to this turn of events that he had not foreseen.

One hand came up to rub his stubbly jaw as his eyes drifted over the woman who stood before him, coming to rest at last on the curve of her lips. From the moment they had ridden into the camp, he had been attracted by her beauty, but because she was under the protection of a defender of the cause, he had been reluctant to approach her. But now, as the wife of a man who had been spying on the camp, she was fair game. And in this hunt he was the man with an advantage.

"I would like to spare him for you, ma'am," Quantrill drawled, his eyes sliding over Leigh once more, "since you've been nice enough to tend our wounded and cook our dinner. But to tell you the truth, there's not much reason unless you are willing to give me some incentive to make me change my mind."

It was plain to everyone within earshot what it was that Quantrill wanted, and a few men drifted closer to see the matter resolved. Leigh could feel Hayes's eyes boring into her back, sense Bran's frustration and Delia's horror at what she was being asked to do. But she tried not to think about anything more than what it would take to save her husband's life.

A slow, feral smile lit Quantrill's face as he went on. "I

think I might be in need of the tender ministrations of a pretty woman," he suggested. "It's been a long time since I've been treated by a woman with such a soft and supple body or with hair that shines in the firelight like a thousand tiny sparks."

The tension spun out like a skein of fraying rope, as both the guerrilla and Hayes waited for Leigh's answer.

"You've named your price for sparing my husband, Captain Quantrill," she said finally, standing steady and unbowed. "And for his safety I will pay you what you ask."

"No, Leigh—" Hayes protested, reaching out to catch her arm. But before he could do more, one of the guards brought the butt of his rifle down against his skull. Hayes gave a single moan as his knees gave way, crumpled to the ground, and lay still.

Leigh was instantly beside him, assessing his condition with discerning hands. When she was certain Hayes would recover from the blow, she turned fiercely to address Quantrill. "He will be unharmed, *unharmed*," she insisted, "or there will be no bargain between us."

Something approaching respect shone in the guerrilla leader's eyes, and he nodded slowly. "As you wish, madam. My men will not hurt him further."

"Have I your word, sir, your word as a Southern officer?"

"Yes, my word," Quantrill hesitantly agreed.

Leigh nodded in turn, acknowledging the bond between them. "Very well. Are your needs pressing, or can you wait until after dinner?"

"I think after dinner is time enough, my dear. Until then I shall await your pleasure."

Without another word Quantrill made his way toward one of the distant campfires, leaving his men to bind and bring the prisoners.

When Leigh once again joined Delia by the fire the younger woman's voice was raw with fear. "Do you think Nathan and Hayes will really be safe? Will Quantrill let them leave with us in the morning?"

They were questions Leigh did not care to ponder, and she shrugged away Delia's concern. "They'll be fine, I promise you," she assured her friend. "Just leave their future to me."

Then came words of understanding to express a conflict only another woman could feel. "Oh, Leigh," Delia whispered softly, "how will you give yourself to such a man?"

Leigh drew a long, steady breath, watching as their two husbands were bound and led away, considering the circumstances she had been forced to accept. She understood why the two men had felt compelled to come after them, but in the end their arrival had made matters worse instead of better. Quantrill's ruthlessness was known far and wide, but she felt certain they would have weathered it without disaster if there had been no opposition. And though she did not voice her concern to Delia, she was not sure any of them were safe after what had happened. The guerrilla was unpredictable and dangerous, and somehow the tenuous balance had been upset by their husbands' arrival and what had followed. All their futures hinged on what she did, and Leigh knew only that she had to act to insure everyone's safety.

Wearily she came to her feet. "I don't know how I will face what's to come, Delia. But somehow I must, somehow I will." Squaring her shoulders, Leigh moved to get more supplies from the wagon.

For the next hour, they cooked for the men, boiling yams with a little bourbon, frying thick slices of smoked ham. They baked biscuits over the fire, and from a cache Leigh had guarded she brought a pound of rich, dark coffee and made a pot for the raiders to enjoy.

"Good grub, ma'am."

"Best meal I've et in weeks."

"This is as good as my ma's cooking."

The comments greeted Leigh as she made her way to where Hayes and Nathan were being held.

"You don't mind if I've brought a little something for the prisoners, do you?" she asked the guard as she approached. "I imagine they have been on the trail all day too and must be as hungry as you and your men are."

The man shrugged. "As long as you don't ask me to untie them, they can have their victuals."

"With their hands bound the way they are, I think they can both manage a spoon."

"I tell you what, ma'am," the guard offered. "I'll let you sit right here and help them, if'n you give me one of them cups of coffee."

Leigh smiled at the man and extended one of the plates, offering the cup that sat at the edge. "That's kind of you, sir, and when I go back, I'll get you a refill if you'd like."

Leigh set the dishes before her husband and Nathan Travis and helped each one to grasp a piece of silverware. It was not the easiest way to eat, but they fell upon the food with relish.

"You needn't be so pleasant to them," Hayes muttered between bites of ham. "You treat these men as if they were something more than outlaws."

"If you'd treated them a damn sight better or left well enough alone, we might not have come to this!" she muttered back in the same scathing undertone.

Hayes scowled and reached for his cup of coffee, but with a lightning-swift movement that seemed almost accidental, Leigh upset it, spilling the contents on the ground. Hayes had opened his mouth to comment on her unaccustomed clumsiness, when he saw a flash of warning in her eyes. Travis seemed to have caught the furtive glance that passed between them too and nodded almost imperceptibly in return. Leigh waited until the two men had finished their dinner, then took a look at the lump on Hayes's head.

"Does that hurt?" she murmured sympathetically, touching the place with a cool, wet cloth.

"Yes, damn it, it does!" he snapped loudly for the sentry's benefit, then whispered desperate and low. "Leigh, don't go to Quantrill. Travis and I will find a way out of this somehow. I don't want you to—"

The guard's gruff voice interrupted. "You 'bout finished there, ma'am? I'm more than ready for that second cup of coffee."

There was no time to discuss the things Leigh had promised to do to save their lives. "I have no choice now, Hayes," she whispered as she rose to go. "It's far too late to change my mind."

Without another word she gathered up the dishes and took them back to the campfire.

While Delia helped Brandon back to his bed in the wagon, Leigh prepared herself for her night with Quantrill. Her hands were steady as she washed the sweat and dirt from her body and coiled her hair high on her head. A strange kind of anticipation flowed through her veins as she donned a pretty yellow gown. She felt exhilarated and tense, ready for imminent action. She alone bore responsibility for all of their fates, and the course she had chosen was set.

When Leigh was finally ready, she poured a fresh cup of coffee and carried it across the compound toward Quantrill and his men. As she passed the spot where the prisoners lay, she felt Hayes's blazing gaze upon her. She sensed his agitation, the frustration of knowing where she was going. And though he would eventually understand why she had agreed to the guerrilla's demands, she could do nothing to reassure him now.

"I was just about to send someone to see what was keeping you." Quantrill greeted her with a leering grin, coming to his feet.

Leigh stood her ground before him, her gaze intent upon his face. "I wanted to tidy up a bit before I came."

It was obvious that he had taken time to see to his appearance as well.

Encouraged, she offered him the cup she was carrying. "Your men seemed to so enjoy the coffee, I thought you might like a second cup yourself, Captain Quantrill."

"That's kind of you," he acknowledged, taking a long draught of the brew. "We don't get real coffee often enough, not with the war cutting off the river trade from New Orleans."

With difficulty Leigh stifled the urge to twist away when Quantrill took her arm. "I've had my men prepare a tent for us, over there beyond the trees," he told her. "You haven't changed your mind about our bargain, have you, Leigh?"

"I wouldn't be here, Captain Quantrill," she replied precisely, "except to spare my husband's life."

A frown came and went at her answer, but he acknowledged her words at last. "That is what we agreed."

As he spoke, his hand came to rest on Leigh's waist, and he pulled her close against his side. When his mouth sought the gentle curve of her throat, Leigh fought down a wave of revulsion. Her reason for being here was clear, she told her cringing senses. Without what she had agreed to do, both Hayes and Nathan might be dead. Quantrill's lips were hot, and his hold was far from gentle as his hands moved restlessly over her. He stopped on the sloping path that led to the stream and nuzzled along her throat, tasting the flesh bared above the neckline of her gown, then moving ever lower.

"Lord, but you're soft, woman," he groaned, "as soft and as sweet as a field of clover."

Then Quantrill abruptly raised his head and dragged her down the path behind him. His men had indeed prepared a place for them: a good-sized canvas tent with a fire blazing brightly before it. He led her to the interior but did not lower the flap.

"Undress for me, pretty lady," he commanded and sank down on the pile of blankets, his smoldering eyes devouring her.

For a heartbeat, Leigh's courage threatened to desert her, but she reluctantly obeyed, knowing she had no choice. Her fingers slipped from one button to the next, and inexorably the opening between the panels of her bodice widened to reveal the corset and chemise she wore beneath. Quantrill's gaze focused on the growing display of Leigh's lush charms, and with a hoarse, muttered growl he exhorted her to hurry. The bottom of the placket was reached, and Leigh was forced to bare first one softly rounded shoulder and then the other as the fabric slipped to her waist.

"Now your skirt and petticoats," he said, breathing raggedly. "Lower them one by one."

Leigh silently complied, aware of the man's glazed expression and the terrible necessity of doing exactly what he asked. The full skirts and petticoats dropped in a pool about her feet, and at last she stood attired only in stays, pantalets and chemise, waiting to learn his pleasure.

"Go on! Go on!" he urged, lying back as he sipped his coffee. "Go on, my lovely mistress. How I long to see you naked and spend myself between your thighs!"

The lust was plain in his pale eyes, and Leigh steeled herself to comply, slipping the fasteners of her stays and dropping her pantalets.

Standing by the fire in her chemise, Leigh's silhouette was plain to the man who lay sprawled on the rumpled blankets. He saw the high, full breasts swaying gently with her movements; the slender waist and flaring hips that seemed designed to tease and please a man; the long, shapely legs with her sweetness tucked between them. Her limbs were outlined by the firelight, the wavering, golden aura from the flames reflected on her skin.

"Let down your hair," he ordered hoarsely, his pale eyes glazed with lust.

Searing hatred and wild frustration filled Leigh at what Quantrill was forcing her to do, and she tried not to think beyond this moment to what must inevitably follow. Slowly, she raised her hands to her hair and did as he asked: slipping the pins from the knot on the top of her head, then shaking the rippling mass free.

Quantrill drew a ragged breath and came up on his knees to pull her close, slipping his hands inside the chemise to trace her thighs and hips. Filling his palms with her buttocks, clenching his fingers into her flesh, he pressed his face into the curve of her belly before toppling her down beside him.

"Lovely, lovely," he said with a groan and spread himself above her. Grinding Leigh deep into the nest of blankets until she was branded with his need, Quantrill claimed her as his possession, for this night at least. When her thin chemise barred his way, it was quickly wrenched aside, and he feasted on her body like a wolf upon its prey.

Up until that moment Leigh had been in control of her reactions. She had steeled herself to allow Quantrill to look and touch at will, telling herself that she must do what he asked or forfeit her husband's life. But with the baring of her flesh and the evidence of his burning need, Leigh knew she could stand no more and fought wildly to be free. Twisting, she loosened one hand and swung it at her tormentor's face, hitting just above his cheekbone with sudden, surprising force.

The guerrilla leader reared back, and Leigh tried to squirm away, but Quantrill recovered quickly and forced her back against the blankets.

"Have you forgotten our bargain, Mrs. Banister?" he asked, pinning her beneath him. "Have you changed your mind about keeping it? Unless you want to be a widow, you will do exactly as I say."

Still, Leigh seethed beneath him, struggling with all her strength. But against his wiry, whipcord body, she was weak, ineffective, and helpless. At last she lay panting beneath him, staring up into his pale, cold eyes. But instead of the deliverance she had hoped to find, there was nothing in them but his lust.

He chuckled softly and bent his head, rasping his cheek against her chest, callously abrading her sensitive skin as punishment for her resistance. She tried her best to shrink away, but there was nowhere she could go. She was trapped against the blankets as he lowered his mouth to her breasts.

"Yield to me," he murmured against her, "yield to me, Leigh, yield to me now, and your husband will still go free. Come to me tonight, see to my pleasure, and he will live to see the light of day."

Defeat and resignation brought lethargy to her limbs, and with a soft, sobbing breath of surrender Leigh acknowledged her defeat.

Quantrill sighed deeply and rested his head in the crook of her shoulder. "Better, better," he whispered. "So much better now. Let me take you, pretty lady. I've never wanted any woman more."

Leigh tensed and lay waiting for his penetration, resigned to giving this villain all she had hoped to withhold. And with a sense of welling despair, she knew her plans to escape Quantrill had failed.

His hand fumbled with his trousers, and he muttered a slurred curse against her skin. Then without warning, he sagged heavily against her.

It took a moment for Leigh to realize that the escape she

had hoped for was at hand. The drugs she had put in the coffee had finally taken effect. Now she was pinned to the ground by Quantrill's inert body when before she had been held by his strength, flattened beneath his weight but not a victim of his desire.

Relief seeped through her though she lay crushed and fighting for breath, praying that the rest of the encampment had succumbed to the drugs in the coffee as well. Pushing with legs, arms, and shoulders, she struggled to free herself from the man who lay as limp and inert as a ton of wet sand above her. He was heavier than she had guessed, and her muscles trembled with the effort to move him.

Then there was the sound of footsteps coming down the path, and she froze where she lay. Her breath caught in her throat, and her heart pounded in her ears as she waited, desperate to know if this newcomer was deliverance or disaster.

"Leigh! Leigh?" a voice finally called out softly. "Leigh, is Quantrill asleep?"

"Nathan," she whispered in relief. "Nathan, yes, but I'm trapped underneath him. Can you set me free?"

A moment later Quantrill's weight was rolled away, and Leigh scrambled to find her clothes. Nathan Travis gallantly turned his back to her as she pulled the gown over her nakedness and gathered the front together.

"Is Hayes all right?" she asked as she fumbled with the fasteners, her fingers clumsy in their haste. "Why—why didn't he come to get me instead of sending you?"

"Oh, Leigh!" She heard the rush of Nathan's laughter as he bent to gather up her things. "He was more than willing to rescue you, but I wouldn't let him come. He surely would have killed Quantrill, and that would have been even more foolhardy and dangerous than what you've done already."

September 22, 1862—Near Jefferson City, Missouri

In the cool, gray dawn, Leigh awoke to find
Hayes pressed against her, as if he had been seeking her
warmth and softness in the dark. A sleepy smile curved
her lips as she nestled closer; then with a jolt of alarm she
remembered the danger they were in and the need for
constant vigilance. Raising her head, Leigh quickly sur-
veyed the campsite. All seemed as it should be, and after
lying alert for several minutes, she willed herself to relax.
Perhaps Quantrill and his men had given up the chase, and
they were safe after all.

Sighing, Leigh settled back against her pillow. With the
threat of the guerrillas' retaliation dogging them, they had
traveled all the day before and most of the previous night,
stopping only to rest the horses. But at sunset Hayes and
Travis had deemed it necessary to make camp and picked a
readily defensible spot in a copse of trees near the outlet of
a woodland spring. Because of the persistent danger, the
two men had agreed to stand guard, and while the rest
went to bed, Hayes and Nathan took turns watching over
them.

But now Hayes lay beside her beneath the wagon, deeply
asleep. Slowly she turned her head to watch him, seeing
the leashed power in the line of his body and enjoying the
protective way one arm lay across her waist. She had
always felt secure when Hayes was close at hand, and this
morning was no exception. But in the last thirty-six hours
she had found that there was far more to Hayes Banister
than comfort and security. As Leigh lay awake in the
early-morning twilight, she contemplated the stranger she
had discovered in the guise of her husband. The dangers
they had faced and the difficulties they had overcome in
escaping from Quantrill had showed her a new side to
Hayes, one that both confused and intrigued her.

To Leigh, he had always been a supremely rational
man, in control of his life, his job, and his emotions. Yet
two nights ago Hayes had been filled with a stony belliger-

ence and a brightly burning fury that she was stunned to
find in the man she thought she knew. Hayes had been
more than willing to face down Quantrill for her sake and
might have done murder if Travis had let him come to
rescue her. That fierce, primitive facet of Hayes's nature
seemed strangely out of character for the man who had
taken her for his wife.

Perhaps it was seeing him away from the cool, impersonal life they lived in St. Louis that enabled her to focus
on things that had seemed hidden from her before. Leigh
realized that Hayes was strong, not dictatorial; courageous,
not just determined; primitive and passionate when he had
always seemed so rational and controlled. There were
depths to him, reservoirs of emotion he had not let her see.
Or perhaps she had been too caught up in setting barriers
between them to notice that this was a man from whom
she needed no protection. For reasons of her own, for fears
and guilt that ran deep, she had refused to acknowledge
the strength of Hayes's emotions. It seemed possible that
he had suppressed them too, and she was only beginning
to surmise his reasons for remaining aloof.

The solitude of early morning was a time best given to
introspection, and as Leigh lay watching the first pale
streaks of apricot peep from beyond the horizon, she realized that she must admit, at least to herself, what Hayes
had come to mean to her. In the split second when Quantrill
had ordered Hayes killed, Leigh had come face-to-face
with her feelings for her husband. There had been no time
to consider the intensity and passion of her response in her
need to spare his life. But afterward the strength of it had
rung like an echo through her being, its persistence forcing
her to acknowledge the truth: that she cared for Hayes far
more than she had realized.

As she watched his face, soft and vacant in slumber, she
found new emotions welling in her heart. Her gaze caressed his hard, beard-stubbled jaw, the inconsistently gentle curve of his mouth, and the flare of dark lashes against
his sunburned cheeks. She had always recognized how
compelling his features were in their harsh, determined
way, but she was only now becoming aware of the tenderness and vulnerability that lay within him.

The new thoughts and feelings stirring in Leigh were
having an odd effect, and she knew if she stayed beside
Hayes much longer, she would do what she had never
before done in their married life: she would kiss him
awake and ask him to make love to her.

The thought sent Leigh's mind reeling, and she knew
that she might better get on about the business of a new
day than expose the subtle, uncomfortable changes her
new understanding of Hayes elicited. Carefully she slid
from beneath his arm and squirmed toward the edge of the
blanket. Even in sleep, Hayes seemed to register her defection, and a faint frown came and went between his
brows. Still, he slept on, and Leigh was anxious to escape
his unsettling presence.

It seemed to have been days and days since she'd had
time to herself or even a chance to bathe. Coming noiselessly to her feet beside the wagon, she decided to go
down to the spring before the rest of the camp was stirring.
With stealthy movements she crept into the wagon, seeking soap, towel, and some fresh clothes to put on after her
bath.

Though she had not made any sound, as she turned to
go she saw that Bran was watching her.

"Are you all right?" she whispered, bending close beside him.

Bran nodded. "And are you?"

"Yes, of course. Why wouldn't I be?"

"You had a close call with Quantrill the other night,
and traveling the way we have can't have been easy for
you." His consideration touched her, but she did not
welcome his concern.

"I'm fine, Bran. You need not worry."

"And how is Hayes?"

"Hayes?" Leigh was baffled by the question.

"He's a fine man, Leigh," he continued, "and he loves
you so."

"Loves me?"

Since they were conversing in whispers, Bran must
have missed her tone of incredulity.

"It was so evident the other night," he went on. "When
Travis went to get you from Quantrill, Hayes was beside

himself with worry. And the expression in his eyes when he saw that you were safe was almost painful to behold.''

Brandon's words brought color to Leigh's cheeks and served to complicate her already confused thoughts.

"Bran, hush. You'll wake the others," she admonished him in a whisper. "And I will have my bath before the rest are up. I'll warrant you could do with a bit more sleep, too.''

Leigh left the wagon as silently as she had entered and sneaked one last look at Hayes before she headed for the stream. He was sleeping soundly with one hand stretched out as if he were searching for her in the empty space beside him.

On the slope down to the spring, she came upon Travis leaning back against a tree with the long rifle braced across his knees. "Good morning," she called out softly as she approached him. "Is everything quiet?''

Nathan nodded. "Going to have a bath?" he queried, noting the towels and fresh clothes she was carrying in her arms.

"I suppose that spring will be as cold as ice even at this time of year," she answered, "but a quick dunking will do at least a bit to get me clean.''

Swinging around a curve in the path took her out of Nathan's sight, and Leigh reveled in the freshness of the morning breeze and the sound of the chirping birds in the treetops. Even before the spring came into view, she could hear the gurgling water and smell the dampness of the forest glade. Moving behind a screen of bushes, she quickly found a place to undress.

The shallow natural pool that had formed in the rock just below where the spring came to earth was brilliant azure blue, and as Leigh waded in, ripples trembled across the shimmering surface, disturbing the reflections of the late-summer sky. With teeth chattering and gooseflesh blossoming all over her body, Leigh immersed herself in the frigid, hip-deep water, but once the initial chill had passed, she began to enjoy the invigorating cold. Movement seemed to warm her, and she busied herself washing first her hair and then the rest of her body. The longer she stayed in the pool, the less the temperature bothered her, and when she was clean, she lay back against the shallower rim of her natural tub and let herself drift with the spring's gentle downhill flow.

It was going to be a glorious day. High above, the sky blazed deep lapis blue and was brushed with pale, soft wisps of clouds. The uppermost branches of the trees that wove a delicate, open pattern above her were catching the intensity of the sun, its low-angled rays gilding the rustling leaves with apricot and amber. But if the sun was up, Leigh knew the others back at camp would be rising too, and she needed to get on with her chores. It was a wonder that no one had come to disturb her solitude.

With silvery droplets streaming from her hair, breasts, and flanks, Leigh rose from the pool and turned back to where she had left her clothes.

"I wondered how long you would be able to stand the cold," a familiar voice said, "but then I didn't want to bother you, a wood nymph at her bath."

Leigh's head snapped up at Hayes's teasing words, and she saw her husband standing at the foot of the path with a bucket in his hand. "What are you doing here?" she snapped through chattering teeth, though his reasons for being at the stream were patently obvious.

"I'm just keeping watch," he told her, grinning as if he were thoroughly pleased by what he was watching.

Guessing the trend of his thoughts, Leigh sank back into the water. "So you were just keeping watch over me as I bathed?" she asked with evident skepticism. "How wonderfully gallant."

Hayes came to stand at the edge of the pool, and Leigh could tell by his expression that the water did little to obscure his view of her. "I watched over you last night as you slept, so why shouldn't I keep watch over you as you bathe?"

In spite of the pool's temperature, a flush rose to darken Leigh's skin. It gave her an odd, strangely intimate feeling to know that he had watched her the previous night much as she had watched him this morning.

"How cold is that water, anyway?" he went on. "I've been thinking about taking a bath myself."

Leigh nibbled thoughtfully at her bottom lip before she

issued her invitation. "Why don't you come and join me? The pool is big enough for two."

If Leigh had expected reticence on Hayes's part, she was destined to be disappointed. Without pausing to consider that he had been sent to get water for breakfast, Hayes quickly stripped off his clothes and splashed into the pool to join her.

She laughed when he drew a shuddering breath in response to the temperature of the spring water, and she wriggled over to make room for him beside her. "Duck down, and after a minute it won't seem so bad," she advised, trying to hide her grin. His response to the cold was much as hers had been, and she ran her fingers over his skin as if to smooth away the goosebumps.

"Jesus, woman!" he exclaimed. "Your blood must be turned to ice by now."

"Hardly," she replied and realized it was true, for there was a strange new warmth coursing through her, a warmth only Hayes's nearness could have caused. Reaching across where he lay shivering in the shallows, Leigh took the cake of soap from the rock where she had left it.

"Dunk your head," she instructed, "and I'll help you wash your hair." Though Hayes scowled at her, he did as she asked, huffing again at the chill of the water as he broke the surface. Rubbing the bar of soap between her hands, Leigh worked up a foamy lather and began to rub it in. Her fingers wove through the thick thatch of walnut brown, working the soap into a cap of trailing bubbles, massaging his scalp with slow, languorous strokes.

"You're going to make me smell like a maiden aunt," he complained, sniffing at the scented soap.

"You could have brought some soap of your own," she countered, smoothing her thumbs along the froth at his temples, "but no matter what I use, you'll smell like you."

That statement seemed to intrigue Hayes. "And how do I smell?"

Fresh color flared in Leigh's cheeks. "Oh, I don't know," she stammered. "Clean, mostly clean, sometimes with a touch of tobacco and a kind of citrus scent."

Somehow this was becoming a very unsettling conversation, and Leigh was at a loss to explain her discomfort.

"Now rinse," she ordered gruffly and waited for him to comply.

With water streaming down across his neck and shoulders, it seemed only natural for her to continue with his bath. Taking up the soap again, she made more lather and smoothed the foam across his shoulders, then slowly down his arms.

"You have a redhead's scent," he said rather abruptly, picking up the dangling thread of their conversation. "That first afternoon at Camp Jackson, before I even saw your face, I remember thinking how good you smelled—like sunlight and spice."

"Oh?" Leigh's hands were poised against his breastbone, and she was unreasonably aware of the thudding of his heart.

There were drops of water clinging to his lashes and shimmering in the thickness of his hair. More slid toward his jaw and gathered in deep valleys that bracketed his smile. Driven by a compulsion she could find no way to deny, Leigh leaned ever so slightly forward and caught one of the shining droplets with her tongue. The roughness of his whiskers rasped against the tip, a prickly, abrasive texture that sent shudders chasing down her spine. As she gathered the drop into her mouth, she became unwillingly aware of the taste of Hayes, of the heat and vitality of his skin, of her newly discovered feelings for this man.

The drop rolled slowly down her throat, and she moved to catch another, lapping gently upward toward his nose and then out across his cheek. He went utterly still beside her, as if reveling in the sensation, and beneath her trembling palms she could feel his heart beat double time. Questioningly she raised her head, and they froze staring, each lost in the glow of the other's eyes. Then Hayes's mouth came down to claim hers in a kiss sweet and ripe with longing.

At the simple touching of lips, a restless, red-hot tide began to flow between them, and Leigh's tongue seemed drawn to trace the softening contours of his mouth. There was no resistance to her tentative, delicate probe, and she pressed deeper to explore the warm, moist cavity beyond.

She savored the texture of his tongue, the fresh subtlety of mint, and knew that he had chewed some of the leaves that grew along the trail to the spring just as she had done. She laved the interior of his mouth, touched the smoothness of his teeth, drawing ever closer within the circle of his arms.

He seemed willing yet restrained, eager but somehow wary. The contradictions she sensed within him were fuel to her tumultuous emotions, and though she ached to bind him closer, caution held her back. Things between them were suddenly different than they had ever been before, and she needed time to consider whether he or she had changed.

Pulling away in confusion, she slid the bar of soap along his ribs, then moved lower in a tentative caress. Hayes stirred restlessly beneath her hands, a high flush rising in his cheeks, but he made no claims upon her. Somehow he seemed to understand and accept her reticence, though Leigh herself could not.

Still, it pleased her to touch and hold him, to show instead of tell him of the changing scope of her emotions. Her fingers trailed along his body, gently, provocatively, leaving ruddy color beneath his skin. She well knew the effect her nearness was having on him, recognized how much he must be holding back to remain impassive beneath her hands. Surely he knew that he could demand and claim so much more from her than what she had already given. Yet he seemed willing to wait, willing to give her time to come to terms with what she wanted. Then, as if in reward for his fortitude and patience, her fingers drifted to his thighs and the swollen shaft that rose between them.

For Leigh the touching and fondling of his manhood was an intensely ardent act, and Hayes accepted the intimacy with joy singing in his veins. Her unaccustomed willingness, her tenderness, the emotions in her eyes loosed feelings he had long held guarded. They welled through him, washing away all the restrictions he had made himself obey, freeing him to express his true feelings for his wife at last. Leigh might not be able to say the words, but he saw the love in her eyes, and he could no longer deny the scope of his emotions.

His breathing shuddered as she sought to please him, his

back arching and his eyelids fluttering closed as he succumbed to a potent mixture of pleasure and anticipation. Hayes's head fell back against the rim of the pool in a pose of total abandon and trust. He was making himself completely vulnerable to her, and Leigh was seduced by his lack of reserve. He was giving her a responsibility she both welcomed and craved, but it was a responsibility she was not at all sure she had earned.

Yet the strong brown column of his throat lay bared before her. The sculptured line of his jaw and the sinewy yoke of his shoulders tempted her to touch and explore. She was drawn to press her mouth to his smooth, cool skin; to the half-moon hollow at the base of his throat; to the fluff of dark hair that sprang beneath it. On her lips and tongue was the taste of Hayes, the vital, stirring essence of the man she loved.

In a blur of welling desire, she felt Hayes's hands creep over her, caressing and arousing her until Leigh moaned aloud. For both of them the sense of place and time slipped away, and their world was complete with nothing more than this. They drifted in a realm of perfect passion, sensing needs and assuaging them, abandoning self and finding self renewed. Each mirrored the wants and desires of the other until they were joined together in a perfect whole.

Hayes was trembling with emotion, and she was trembling, too. He was murmuring words of love, and she was taking them to her heart. He was arching with the need to possess her more fully, and she was opening to give him all. There were no barriers between them now, and Leigh knew that for the first time in their married life they were truly one.

Then they were lost to coherent thought, his hips rising up beneath her to thrust deeper than before, her body taking gladly and giving pleasure in return. Her hands rose to encircle his throat, feeling his pulse beat wildly against her palms. His fingers locked around her hips to guide her movements, bringing them both closer and closer to the edge. She lifted; he arched. He thrust; she withdrew, twisting and gasping with furious need.

Fulminating desire masked his face with lines of tension: fierce, primitive, basic, impossible to control. His eyes were closed, his lips parted, and his breathing came in gasps. She could feel his approaching crisis and held him closer than before, wanting to take his essence deep, so deep inside her. Then the strain in his face was washed away, blurred with blazing joy and incandescent ecstasy.

The scalding heat of him rose within her, moving with painful, exquisite languor to fill her very core. And as she arched against him in reply, she felt her nerves catch fire one by one. The flame spread slowly, radiating from her loins, building in intensity as it swept along her spine and down her arms. It enveloped all of her in sweet sensation and left in her veins a lambent, helpless glow, a warm sense of satisfaction and debilitating bliss.

When it was over, they sank together against the edge of the pool, spent and limp, content and happy. The ripples on the surface of the water ebbed away to leave it calm and mirror-smooth around them.

Leigh lay pillowed on his chest, and Hayes held her close. He stroked her hair and kissed her temple; she nestled against him, lost and secure in wonder.

"I love you, Leigh," Hayes murmured gently. "I'll love you until the day I die."

His words drifted through the lazy fog of contentment that engulfed her and found a place deep in her heart. She felt strong with that knowledge locked inside her, valiant and brave and sure at last. And she knew that what had been missing from their marriage these past months had been nothing more or less than the admission of their love.

"Hayes," she murmured, her tone slurred and soft with tenderness. "Hayes," she whispered, her eyes blazing with emotion. "Hayes, my darling Hayes. I love you. I love you, too."

16 ∿

Happiness. How long she had been wishing
for that intangible commodity, how diligently she had
searched, and how elusive it had once seemed. But in the
end, finding happiness and accepting the serenity only
complete contentment could bring had been as simple as
falling in love with her own husband.

Leigh marveled at the change in the life she and Hayes
shared. That change had been wrought in the terror of
Quantrill's threat on Banister's life, in the tense hours on
the trail as they fled the guerrillas, and in the icy spring-
fed pool where she and her husband had bared their feelings for each other for the first time. Now their newfound
happiness was echoed a thousandfold in the simple intimacies of daily life. It was evident to Leigh in being kissed
awake every morning; in being met outside the hospital, as
long ago had been their custom; in being touched and
caressed by a man who held nothing back.

Leigh did her best to make Hayes aware of the change
in her feelings, though for her the expressions were more
difficult, less spontaneous. It was the difference in their
two personalities, the difference in the way they had been
raised, that made the show of affection come less readily
to Leigh. But Hayes seemed so grateful for her attentions,
so delighted by the simplest gestures that Leigh practiced
less and less restraint.

With the approach of winter weather the offensives in the West dwindled, and with them the demands on both Hayes's and Leigh's time. Because fewer ships were being built, his duties at the shipyard were lighter. At the hospital the number of patients had dropped to manageable levels as some were furloughed home or discharged from the Army, as others were sent to the convalescent hospitals that had sprung up around the city, or succumbed to their wounds. This lull in the war effort gave Hayes and Leigh time to travel into the country on the crisp, gold and blue days of autumn: to picnic at Glencoe and magnificent Castlewood overlooking the Meramec River, to drive the pleasant winding road that followed the Mississippi north. They attended plays at the Varieties Theater and fundraisers for the various aid societies that were active in the city that winter. And there were long, lazy afternoons when they would retire for a "nap" but would drift to sleep only when other, more pressing needs were satisfied.

It was not at all what Leigh had thought married life would be. It was far better.

One quiet evening in late November, Leigh looked up from the sock she had been knitting. As Dr. Phillips had prophesied in the opening days of the war, her knitting had improved, and she was proud of having mastered a skill that had vexed her in her youth. Across the sitting room Hayes was reading the *Missouri Republican* as he smoked a last pipeful of tobacco before bed. With the filmy gray smoke wreathing his head, his carpet-slippered feet propped up on a footstool, and the crumpled paper bowed between his hands, he seemed the very image of domesticity. And somehow that pleased Leigh immensely.

"Hayes?" she began, almost reluctant to disturb the serenity of the scene before her. "How has Mother seemed to you these last few weeks?"

Hayes lowered his newspaper to look at his wife. "Why do you ask?"

"Well, she's been different somehow since we came back from Nevada with Bran. I can't put my finger on it exactly. She seems vague, preoccupied."

"That started before we got back," Hayes observed thoughtfully. "When Nathan and I returned from down south and found you and Delia gone, I could hardly get her to settle down long enough to tell me where you'd gone. Though I suppose the change in her could be tied in to your father's absence. He's hardly been home at all since the end of August.''

''I don't know why that should make a difference. They fight the entire time they're together.'' The shudder that ran through Leigh at the thought of her parents' arguing was not lost on her husband.

''His presence does make a difference, though,'' he went on, ''at least to your mother.''

Leigh let the knitting sink to her lap. ''How do you mean?''

''It's obvious that your mother craves your father's attention, and she's not particular about the kind of attention she gets from him.''

It took a moment for the meaning of his words to sink in. ''Do you mean she baits him to make him notice her?'' Leigh was incredulous.

Hayes nodded. ''I'll warrant there was a time in their marriage when she got all the attention she needed in much more pleasant ways, but as your father got busier with business and politics, he had less and less time for Althea. Since then she's found some very effective ways to make him pay for slighting her.''

''But, Hayes, they've fought for as long as I can remember,'' Leigh protested.

''Yes, but from what you've told me, they always used to make up.''

Leigh pondered her husband's words. Was Althea so desperate for Horace's attentions that she would prefer anger and discord to being ignored? Had her mother found a frightening, destructive way to make her husband pay for turning from her? Was the reason for the volatile relationship between her parents based in something other than the marriage of convenience forced upon them by Leigh's conception? To her it was a revolutionary thought, one that deserved to be considered at length.

''If you're right about why she's baiting him, Mother is behaving like a spoiled child!''

Hayes weighed his words before answering. ''And since

both you and Horace treat her as a child, why shouldn't she behave like one?" he asked softly.

Leigh's forthright nature battled with the need to deny the truth in her husband's quiet accusation. She and Horace had always sheltered her mother, saving her from any unpleasantness. Althea wasn't emotionally equipped to deal with life's realities, and what they conspired to do was meant to protect her. Surely they hadn't been wrong to see that Althea lived the kind of life she had been raised to lead?

Hayes's question broke into Leigh's thoughts. "Why did you ask me about your mother? Has something happened to concern you?"

"I noticed a difference in her when we got back from Nevada, but I was too busy taking care of Bran to think much about it. Since then she's seemed"—Leigh groped for the word—"restless, impatient, almost angry. But it's as if she has turned those emotions inward. Instead of lashing out at Father or me as she might have done in the past, she broods. Mother has never been one for brooding. And she said the most extraordinary thing to me today."

Leigh could feel her husband's gaze on her, bright with interest and concern, warm with love and understanding. "What did she say?"

"She told me she was going with a group of other women to the Confederate prisons in the city to see to the care of the men being held there."

"Don't you want her to go?"

"Good Lord, no! She's not strong enough to do something like that. Do you know what things are like in those jails?"

"No worse than the prison camps in the South, I suppose."

"I've heard horrible tales of the sickness and the lack of sanitation, of the inedible food and the vermin." Leigh shuddered again.

"It sounds as if those men need whatever help they can get," Hayes offered mildly.

"They do! But my mother isn't able—"

"I think your mother is capable of far more than you

give her credit for, Leigh," he interjected. "Althea has finally made a decision about her part in the war effort, and I give her credit for taking on such a difficult and unpopular task."

"But, Hayes, I can't let her do this. I don't think she is fit for hospital work, much less caring for prisoners. And Father will be livid when he finds out."

"Look at it this way, Leigh," Hayes advised. "She didn't try to hinder you when you wanted to work in the hospitals at the beginning of the war, and I'm sure you remember that there were those who didn't think you would be able to stand the rigors of military nursing. Give Althea a chance to prove herself. If the prisons are too much for her, she will find some other way to help."

Hayes set his newspaper aside and crossed the room to where his wife sat. Gently he smoothed away the worry line that had formed between her brows, then bent to kiss the spot.

"I love you, Hayes," she whispered.

"You could say that a hundred times a day, and I would never get tired of hearing it," he whispered back as he pulled Leigh to her feet and guided her toward their bedroom.

On the following Thursday afternoon, Althea Pennington returned from her first visit to the Gratiot Street Prison. Leigh met her in the foyer filled with questions, but Althea, white to the lips, brushed past her and ran directly to her room, where she was violently ill in the chamber pot. Later Leigh sat at her mother's bedside, holding a cool cloth to her head as tears slid down across Althea's temples and into her hair.

"I hope this makes you realize, Mother, what a mistake it was to volunteer to visit the Confederate prisons," Leigh admonished her. "You must write a note tomorrow and tell Mrs. Washburn that you are no longer able to work with her and her committee."

Althea's soft brown eyes seemed immense in her pale face. "I will do nothing of the kind, Leigh," her mother answered in a voice that was low but remarkably steady. "Today only proved that what we few Confederate women are trying to do is vitally important to those miserable wretches in jail. We are all the hope they have, and I intend to be with those women on Tuesday when they visit another of those—those snake pits.''

Leigh had argued with her mother, but Althea had been adamant about her visits to the Confederate prisoners. In the weeks to come, Althea continued to go to the jails and returned home each time to be sick and retire to her bed.

Christmas came and went with a quiet celebration with Felicity and Bran and gifts and messages from Hayes's family asking the two of them to visit. But with Horace still away with the Quartermaster Corps, Leigh could not bring herself to leave her mother.

Delia and Nathan came to stay for a few days late in January, and because things at the shipyard were slow, Hayes traveled back to Cairo with them, then on to where the ironclads were stationed along the river north of Vicksburg. Since autumn Union troops had been concentrating their efforts on either capturing or bypassing the commanding city on the bluffs, for with the fall of that Confederate stronghold and the fortifications at Port Hudson would come Union control of the Mississippi valley, uniting Farragut's fleet and Bank's troops from New Orleans with Porter's flotilla and Grant's army from the north. Meanwhile, in the eastern theater of the war, command of the Army was swapped between equally ineffective generals as if it were a prize in some children's game.

One evening while Hayes was away, Leigh went up to her mother's bedroom to see if she was recovering from a particularly trying day of visiting the prisons. An untouched dinner tray sat at the bedside, and as Althea lay back against a bank of pillows, she seemed particularly pale and worn.

"Mother, I wish you would reconsider what you have been doing these past months," Leigh chided her. "You're wearing yourself out with these visits. I haven't insisted that you stop going to the prisons before this because I thought you would eventually be able to steel yourself against the things you see, but each time you come home more shaken than the last.''

Althea's eyelids dropped in acknowledgment of her daughter's words. "But how do you do that, Leigh? How do you steel yourself against the things you see? Those poor men need so much more than we can give them, and their gratitude for even simple kindnesses is a difficult thing to bear. You work with sick and wounded men every day, Leigh. You have seen the same kind of things that upset me so. How are you able to go on?"

"You learn to harden your heart."

"Not harden your heart, surely," Althea protested.

Leigh paused, considering her answer more carefully. She did not want to delve too deeply into the defenses she had erected to enable her to accept the things she saw. Even for her the line between pity and duty was finely drawn. To think too much about how she did what was necessary might destroy the fragile balance, the tenuous grip she held on her emotions. She had done what she must to survive, but her mother, seeking to find her own way to accept the horrors of war, deserved a truthful answer.

"No, you don't harden your heart exactly," she admitted. "For every death I've witnessed, for every young man I've seen maimed, I've grieved. But I've never let that grief interfere with what the other men need. Those who are struggling to survive are the ones I think about, not the ones who have gone beyond my ability to help."

Althea saw the fire flare in her daughter's eyes and understood both the difficulty of the admission and the strength of her determination.

"But why do so many men die," she asked fretfully, "not in battle, but later, in the prisons and even in the best hospitals?"

Men did die the way her mother said, many more after they had received treatment than before. They burned up with fevers no one could name, were wasted by dysentery and virulent coughs that echoed through the wards at night. Their flesh putrefied and stank until the poison circulating in their blood claimed their lives. Since the first days of the war, much had been learned about treating wounded men, and Leigh had developed a few ideas of her own about the importance of cleanliness, good food, and rest. But whatever medical advances had been made by having a chance to test new ideas and theories, they had not learned enough. Dear God, not nearly enough!

"Why do they die, Leigh?" her mother repeated.

"I don't know," Leigh replied, an odd inflection in her voice. "It's not as if I were a doctor."

By noon the next day, Althea had become one of the casualties of the war. When Leigh arrived home from the hospital, her mother was delirious and unable to keep anything down. Hayes's return at the end of the week found Althea no better. By then Leigh was worn to a vacant-eyed wraith by the constant demands of being at her mother's bedside. After that they took turns sitting with Althea, but the older woman hovered near death for days before showing any signs of improvement.

The night Althea took a turn for the better, Hayes carried Leigh to their room in spite of her ineffective resistance and mewed protests. She had been sleeping in snatches on the fainting couch at the foot of her mother's bed since Althea had fallen ill, and he was determined that Leigh would see to her own needs now that the older woman was out of danger. Buttoning the neck of her nightgown, Hayes kissed Leigh quickly, then tucked her beneath the covers, murmuring admonitions and assurances. That it had taken less than a minute for her eyes to close proved how close to exhaustion she had been, and it was only after three days of enforced rest and the unstinting attentions of a doting husband that Leigh was allowed into her mother's room again.

"Leigh," Althea murmured when Leigh reappeared in the sickroom, "when I'm well enough I want to go home, home to Louisiana."

"Mother, you don't mean that," Leigh had whispered soothingly, stroking her mother's hair. "You've been ill, and you'll see things differently when you get your strength back."

"No, Leigh, promise me. I'm tired of living here, away from my own people."

Leigh heard the pain in her mother's tone and could surmise the cause. She had wired her father several times during Althea's illness, but Horace had been unable to come to see his wife. Though Leigh understood the demands made on men by a country at war, she found it difficult to forgive her father for not being with Althea when she needed him.

Horace Pennington's visit in March and his demands that his wife remain in St. Louis for the duration of the war made no impression on Althea. Nor did her determination to return to the Mattingly plantation wane during her long, slow convalescence. Finally, Leigh discussed the problem of her mother's future with Hayes.

"Do you think we should side with Father and prevent her from going south?" she asked as she and her husband lay curled together in bed.

He was silent as he considered his answer. "I think once she's strong enough, she may undertake the journey on her own. And that will have two results."

"Which are?"

"That you will never be sure she has arrived at your uncle's plantation, and that you will be estranged from her forever."

"You sound as if you want her to go," Leigh accused.

"I want what's best for both of you. She needs to get away, to prove herself, to think." His voice was gentle. "Because the area around New Orleans is occupied by Union troops, we can be relatively sure that she'll be safe and getting enough to eat. She won't like living under Yankee rule, but it won't be much different than being here in St. Louis. And you, Leigh, need to stop protecting her."

Leigh considered his argument, recognizing the truth in what he said. Still, the projected change in her life threatened Leigh.

"You needn't be afraid for Althea," Hayes continued softly, "or for yourself."

As always her husband's perceptiveness startled Leigh, and she turned her face into the curve of his throat, nestling close.

"Can we take her south?" she asked after a time.

"As far as Tuscumbia Bend above Vicksburg, at least. She'll have to travel overland for a ways unless Vicksburg falls."

"That hardly seems likely, does it?"

"No." Hayes's voice had a deep, troubled timbre.

"Perhaps one of my uncles can come to meet us and escort Mother to the plantation. I'll write tomorrow to see what arrangements we can make. And she'll need a pass to get through the lines."

Hayes nodded. "Are you planning to ask Major Crawford for one?" he teased, his momentary seriousness past.

"Good grief, no! I'll never ask that man for another thing as long as I live!" Leigh declared, then giggled at her own venom.

He hugged her close and brushed a kiss across her temple. "I'll take care of getting the pass, if you like."

"I surely would!" she whispered back, turning to offer him a kiss as his reward. "And thank you, Hayes."

"It's all right, love. You know I'd do anything in the world to make you happy."

April 14, 1863—Near Vicksburg, Mississippi

Leigh set the tea service down on the table beside the bed in one of the more luxurious cabins on the promenade deck of the *Barbara Dean* and poured a cupful of the strong brew for her mother. Dressed in a becoming ice-blue morning gown, the woman propped up on a bank of pillows did not seem like one who was recovering from a life-threatening illness. Color bloomed bright in her cheeks, and her eyes sparkled with the excitement of the trip she was undertaking. She was thinner than she had been, and she did seem to tire more easily, but even Leigh was forced to admit that Althea was well enough to make the trip to Louisiana.

"Leigh, dear, I don't know why you insist on treating me like an invalid when I am perfectly willing to take tea in the sitting room," the older woman admonished her daughter.

"It's pointless to tax your strength unduly, Mother," Leigh countered. "Besides, here we can catch the breeze off the river and enjoy the scenery." The warm, wet spring had brought the greenery out in lush profusion, and the redbuds and dogwood provided splashes of frivolity along the forested banks of the Mississippi.

Althea took the cup of tea and sipped it appreciatively. "Oh, Leigh, I am going to miss you," she said unexpectedly.

All the conversations they'd had about Althea's trip to Louisiana had begun and ended with Leigh fruitlessly arguing to change her mother's mind and the older woman remaining steadfast in her determination to leave St. Louis. There had been no appeals to play on the emotions, no personal declarations to color their discussions, not until now. To admit any semblance of regret would have weakened Althea's argument, and it had never been Leigh's way to reveal her feelings. But now with the move all but a fact, Althea seemed to be determined to say what needed to be said.

Leigh's eyes clouded with tears at her mother's admission. "Oh, Mother, if only you'd stay," she began.

"You know I can't do that," Althea replied, concern for her daughter plain in her face.

"But why? Though we've talked about this for months, I don't think I've ever understood why you feel you must go."

Althea drew a long breath. For the first time she could sense Leigh's willingness to listen, to try to understand what was driving Althea from the city that had been her home for twenty-five years and the man who was her husband.

"I am leaving," Althea began, "because I can't live with your father, because being together is destroying us both, because loving Horace is no longer enough."

"You do love Father, then," Leigh murmured half to herself. "I have always wondered if you did."

"Of course I love him!" Althea was both shocked by her daughter's words and adamant in her declaration. "How could you doubt it? I've loved him since the first time I laid eyes on him."

Smiling at the memory, she set her teacup aside. "It was in a shop in New Orleans, a very fashionable millinery shop. I was trying on a particularly lovely hat, one with a rose-colored ostrich feather curling around the brim and wide pink velvet ribbons. As I turned from the mirror, I found your father watching me. 'Even the brightest plumage is no match for your beauty, madam,' he said, then turned away before I could reply or even learn his name.''

Althea laughed softly. ''He must have found out who I was, though, because two nights later, he managed an invitation to dinner at my father's house. He was so handsome then, your father, so tall and strong. Before the evening was over, I knew he was the only man I would ever want to marry. But my family opposed the match. He was not from our social set; he owned no vast tracts of land. He simply wasn't good enough for a Mattingly. So your father and I conspired to run away.''

There was confusion in Leigh's eyes, and she drew a long, unsteady breath before she asked the question that had haunted her half her life, knowing this might be her only chance to get an honest answer. ''You mean you didn't marry Father because of me, because you were expecting a baby?''

Althea seemed surprised by Leigh's assumption. ''No, of course not! The fact that I was great with child when we returned from Europe forced my family to accept our marriage, but we would have married anyway, one way or the other.''

Leigh was silent for a long moment, dizzy with the implications of her mother's words. Horace and Althea had married for reasons of their own, not because they had been forced into a life together by the strictures of Victorian society. They had married because they loved each other, not because of her.

Gladness raged through Leigh, and deep inside her the brutal, aching tension she had carried with her always was miraculously relieved. The difficulties in her parents' marriage had sprung from causes other than her untimely birth: causes based in differences between them, causes that had nothing to do with Leigh. It was a stunning revelation. After all the years of guilt, of fear, of accepting the responsibility for her parents' problems, she could finally stop blaming herself.

There was a lightness in Leigh at the realization, a

lightness that she had never known. She had made a wondrous discovery that left her alive and free to follow her own convictions and the dictates of her heart. Though she could not share her feelings with her mother, Leigh knew she could count on Hayes to listen and understand.

Althea's words broke into her careening thoughts. "Hadn't you ever heard the story of our elopement before?"

Leigh nodded. "Grandfather told me, but I always assumed that the reason for your hasty marriage was me, because you were pregnant."

The older woman shook her head solemnly. "No, Leigh, no. We married for love."

"But then why have you always fought? Why were you both so unhappy?"

Althea retrieved her teacup and took a bracing sip. "Many of those hours I lay abed during my illness were spent thinking about Horace and me. I realize now that our problems began as soon as we came to St. Louis. My family impressed upon your father that I was delicate and needed protecting, that they were entrusting him with some great treasure when they agreed to acknowledge our marriage. But my family did me no favor in convincing Horace of that. He treated me like a porcelain doll, and you were no more than ten or eleven when you began to do the same."

Leigh opened her mouth to protest, but Althea continued. "You must understand, Leigh, that I had been raised to run a plantation, to live a life built on the strength of a woman's endeavor. I grew up with the belief that a woman found satisfaction in doing for her man and family: that her value lay more in her talents than in her beauty. But your father was content with only that, and for a while I was, too. Then all at once you were tagging after your grandfather everywhere he went, and Horace was more and more involved in his business and politics. There were no more babies to take your place, and my life became an empty round of musicals and needlework. It wasn't enough."

Leigh's brows were drawn together in concentration as she listened, trying to understand her mother's words, her mother's pain.

"Horace and I have always argued, but in the hours I

had alone while he was busy with his politics and business, I found differences between us I had never noticed before. The rift between North and South was the most glaring, and I let it drive us apart.''

"Oh, Mother, I'm sorry."

Althea gave Leigh a wan smile and covered her daughter's hand with her own. "When you get back to St. Louis, I want you to help Horace. He isn't ready to listen to my reasons for returning to Louisiana, but in time he will be. And when that time comes, I want you to try to make him understand."

There was a terrible constriction in her throat that made Leigh's promise all but inaudible. "I will, Mother. I will."

Two days later Leigh, Hayes, Althea, and Althea's maid Julia left the *Barbara Dean* on the west bank of the Mississippi north of Vicksburg. With the papers Hayes had been able to secure in St. Louis, they passed through the lines to meet one of Althea's elderly uncles who had agreed to escort her to the family plantation.

When the moment of parting finally came, Althea murmured a quick good-bye to Hayes and kissed his cheek, then went to where her daughter stood.

"Take care of yourself, Leigh," Althea whispered as they clung together. "And take care of your father, too."

"I will."

"And be good to Hayes. He loves you so."

Leigh's voice was thick, and tears gathered on her lashes. "I love him, too."

"But remember, Leigh, sometimes loving a man is not enough. A husband and wife must learn to trust and respect each other. A woman's place is beside her husband, beside him to help carry his burdens, beside him so she can share her own. That is a hard lesson to learn: one neither your father nor I ever mastered. Depend on Hayes and love him, but be aware that there are times when he will need your compassion and understanding, too."

"I'll try, Mother."

"Oh, Leigh, you are so dear to me!" Althea whispered, giving her daughter one last hug.

Then resolutely the older woman turned away from her daughter, away from the comfortable existence she had known in St. Louis. Althea was searching for something in the fading echoes of a life she had once led, and Leigh hoped desperately that she would find what she was seeking. Her mother did not want to return to days gone by, but instead needed to pick up the misplaced threads of her past so she could create a place for herself in the future.

Whether Horace Pennington was a part of that future, Leigh did not know. But for both their sakes—for Althea who was discovering her strength, and for Horace, who, Leigh suspected, would soon discover his weaknesses— she hoped there was a time when they would be reunited.

April 16, 1863

Once they arrived back aboard the *Barbara Dean*, Hayes took Leigh directly to their cabin. It was not difficult to see how the parting from her mother had upset her, and he spent the rest of the day comforting his wife. He offered her consolation; dried her tears; listened to her reminiscences of happier days; made slow, exquisite love to her; then held her as she slept, curled trustingly against him.

It was long after sunset when Leigh awoke, feeling refreshed and renewed. As she washed and dressed, her thoughts were soft and diffused, filled with appreciation for the gentle, sensitive man who was her husband. His sympathy and understanding had helped her through one of the most difficult days of her life, and the tenderness she felt for Hayes was tempered with love and gratitude.

When she came out on deck, she realized for the first time that they were headed downstream toward Vicksburg instead of upstream toward home. Her mind was alive with questions about their destination as she searched the river-boat for Hayes, finding him at last at the front of the promenade deck staring out into the deepening twilight. There was a tension in his stance that Leigh did not understand, and the air of introspection that surrounded him was deep and forbidding. Still, Leigh approached

him, needing answers to her questions, needing to express
her thanks for what he had done this afternoon, needing
the reassuring essence that was her husband.

"Hayes," she said softly and saw a slight tremor of
surprise run through his body, as if his thoughts had been
deep and far away. "Hayes, darling, are you all right?"

He gave her an evasive smile. "Yes, of course."

Somehow it did not seem the time to express the things
that she was feeling, and Leigh asked a question instead of
approaching him on other matters. "Where are we going?"

"We're headed for Vicksburg. I received word less than
an hour ago that the ironclads are going to attempt to run
past the shore batteries tonight, to take supplies down
below the city in order to open another avenue of attack on
the town. I want to see if they make it."

Leigh knew that Vicksburg was the key Confederate
position on the Mississippi and that the city must be
overpowered before the Union could hope to reclaim control of the vital waterway. The city of five thousand on the
eastern bank of the river commanded one of the sharp,
narrow, hairpin turns that were common to the Mississippi's course, and with the two-hundred-foot-high bluffs
studded with field pieces and manned by Pemberton's
crack Confederate troops, it was in a nearly impregnable
position. That was evidenced by the fact that neither Farragut, Ellet and their gunboats, nor Grant with his nearly
twenty-four thousand troops, had been able to rout the defenders since May of the previous year. They had tried a river
blockade and shelling; direct attacks from the east and
south; circumventing the city through rivers, bayous, and
canals. They even tried diverting the Mississippi itself to
cut Vicksburg off from the river, but without success.
None of the Union plans had worked, and General Grant
was getting desperate.

"Do you think they'll succeed in running past the city?"
she asked, peering out into the watery blackness that lay
before them.

"Porter is a fine commander, and they've chosen to run
the batteries in the dark of the moon." Hayes's tone was
speculative.

"Will the Confederates be expecting them?" Leigh wondered aloud.

"I don't know. Surely the Rebels are prepared for the fleet to try something like this, but I think Porter may take them by surprise."

They were approaching an area just above Vicksburg, screened from the city by the heavily forested banks of the DeSoto Peninsula, where a flotilla was gathering. There were ironclads and transport steamers riding the current of the swirling black water, barges and mortar boats lying in wait. As they drew closer, Leigh could see that the deck of each boat was piled high with bales of cotton, wet hay, or sacks of grain to serve as protection from the incoming fire they expected once the flotilla got underway. Lashed to the starboard side of each transport were more barges filled with supplies that would sustain the army in the ensuing weeks of the campaign. Except for a single lantern on the stern of each ship, all was in darkness, and as the *Barbara Dean* jockeyed for a position along the eastern bank where boats not making the run were gathered, the muted churning of her paddle wheel seemed loud in the night.

The waiting seemed interminable even to Leigh on the deck of the steamboat, and she wondered at the thoughts of the hundreds of men who were about to risk their lives running the batteries of the heavily fortified Western city. At ten o'clock the signal to proceed was given, and Admiral Porter's flagship, the *Benton*, began to pull out, followed at two-hundred-yard intervals by the other ships. A strange, tentative silence hung over the river as the dark, hulking shapes of the boats fell in line, and Leigh found herself trembling in anticipation. Beside her Hayes waited, as tense and enervated as she. But his eyes seemed to linger on the town rising high above the river rather than on the boats skulking past the terraces of batteries.

For a time it seemed as if the ships would slide past the fortifications without incident, but all at once a warning beacon flared up on the levee, and a moment later the night shuddered with the sound of cannon. With their discovery the *Benton*'s guns boomed in answer, and the batteries on the hillside erupted with shot and shell. All along the Vicksburg levee buildings were torched to provide better light for the gunners, and Confederates on the Louisiana bank set fire to a train depot at DeSoto to provide further illumination. The inferno on the western bank cast the slowly moving ships in silhouette, and their looming dark shapes sent shadows dancing over the rippling yellow-gold water. The night became day as the other ironclads joined in the battle and rockets tore through the sky to illuminate the heavens with a hellish light.

The river opposite Vicksburg was perilous even during the day, and in the heat of battle several of the ships were caught by the treacherous eddies. They swirled helplessly in full view of the Confederate gunners, and one exploded in a burst of flame as the defenders found the range. Yet the flotilla continued downriver, passing beneath the comets that burst in the air above them, giving the reply of their own guns until one by one the Union ships moved through the several miles-long gauntlet and beyond the Confederates' range. Flares rose into the sky to mark each boat's safe passage, and after nearly two hours of incessant pounding, the Vicksburg batteries fell silent. Darkness and the drifting clouds of spent powder enveloped the town and the river, until the only sound that echoed through the murk was the endless rush of the water.

"They made it," Leigh whispered, her voice forced and low as if she had been holding her breath since the start of the battle.

"Yes, they made it," Hayes confirmed from the darkness beside her. She could hear him taking his pipe from his pocket, smell the faint, sweet scent of tobacco as he tamped down the bowl, and see the sulfurous flare of a match.

"What does it mean?" she asked as a plume of smoke drifted past her.

"It means that Grant has committed himself to a very dangerous course. It means that once his troops march across the peninsula and are ferried to the east bank of the river, they will be completely cut off from the north and fresh supplies." There was pessimism in his tone. "No ship will be able to run the batteries against the river's current, and the men below Vicksburg will be completely on their own. Grant and his troops will have to do a great deal of fighting in the next weeks to offset that disadvantage.''

"Do you think they will succeed?"

"I don't think they have any choice if they mean to survive."

"And do you think Vicksburg will surrender?"

"Not without one hell of a fight. Not unless they are surrounded."

"You mean there might be a siege?"

Hayes was silent for a long time. "It might come to a siege," he confirmed. There was something in his voice Leigh did not understand, something like fear or regret. She turned to examine his expression more carefully, but a hail from the murky darkness below diverted her attention.

"Ahoy, *Barbara Dean*. Request permission to come aboard."

"Nathan!" Leigh called out as a skiff nuzzled alongside the riverboat. "Nathan Travis, what a time of night to come calling!"

"Does that mean I'm invited aboard or not?"

"Yes, of course. Come aboard," Hayes called back.

A few moments later Nathan joined them on the promenade deck. There was excitement blazing in his dark eyes, and his face was vivid with enthusiasm. "They did it. Porter ran past the batteries and lost only one ship," he announced proudly. "What courage that took, what daring. I wish I had been with them."

"I'm surprised you weren't," Hayes noted softly.

"Oh, I'll be joining the troups marching across the peninsula to Bruinsburg in a couple of days," he told them. "But I could hardly turn down an invitation from General Grant to spend the evening drinking champagne on his headquarters ship, could I?"

"Is Grant pleased with what happened, then?" the other man asked. "He's taking a pretty big gamble, sending his boats downriver."

"It's all part of a brilliant plan," Travis enthused.

"Is it now," Leigh murmured, wondering if Nathan's animation was a result of the champagne, the evening's excitement, or his enthusiasm for the forthcoming fight. She was glad Hayes was no longer risking his neck scouting for the Union as Travis was. "Well, I wish him very good luck with what he's attempting, but I believe I'm too tired tonight to hear more about his plans. If you gentlemen will excuse me, I think I'll retire."

Hayes absently brushed Leigh's cheek with a kiss, and the two men stood in silence listening to the sound of her footsteps retreating across the deck.

Travis took out one of the dark cigars he had procured from Grant's private stock earlier in the evening and lit it, studying his friend in the glow of the flame.

"Something's bothering you about all this," he observed, then cast the lighted match over the railing to hissing oblivion in the water below.

"What Grant's doing is risky," Hayes said, puffing thoughtfully on his pipe. "He could lose both his men and his ships."

"Yes, but squeezing the city between two armies is also the only way to make Pemberton surrender and open the river to Union transportation."

"He is planning to surround the city?" Hayes wasn't really looking for confirmation; he knew very well what Grant intended.

Travis nodded. "It's all but cut off from the countryside now, anyway."

Hayes looked across the water to where the lights of Vicksburg twinkled in the distance half-obscured by the drifting clouds that were the aftermath of battle. Silence hung heavily between the two men as a frown came and went on Banister's face.

"She is still there, if you were wondering," Travis offered.

Hayes's head snapped around to look at the other man. "Who?"

"Monica Bennett, your former mistress. I was in the city at the end of last week. Most of the civilians have decamped, but she and her son were still there, alone in that big house on Cherry Street."

Hayes drew a long breath. "He's my son, too," he said quietly, not questioning how Travis knew about his relationship with Monica.

"Are you sure?"

Hayes's pained expression was all the confirmation Nathan needed.

"How do you think the citizens of Vicksburg will fare in the next weeks?"

"Food and water are already in short supply, and I expect the entire city will soon be under direct fire from the mortar barges and gunboats."

It was as Hayes had feared. Emotions he thought he had laid to rest rose inside him. He remembered Monica's beauty, the bittersweet pleasure they had shared, the pain of her betrayal. But above it all was the realization that his son was in mortal danger if he remained in the city. It was that overriding fear for the boy he had never seen that haunted him, that made him consider doing something that could undermine all he held dear.

"They're alone, you say?"

"Jacob Bennett died last winter."

"Then why the hell did they stay in Vicksburg instead of going to Monica's people in Georgia?" It was a question for which Travis had no answer, nor did Hayes expect one. The knowledge demanded a decision that Hayes did not know how to make.

By rote he packed and relit his pipe, conflicting feelings warring within him. Why did the life of a child he had never claimed and that of a woman who had once betrayed his love mean so much to him? How could he even consider going to them when it would put his life and the happiness he had finally managed to secure in jeopardy? But then, how could he turn his back on his flesh and blood when there was even a chance that he could save them? Maybe Monica was afraid to leave the city. Perhaps there was no one to take her to her parents' plantation where they would be safe. How could he live with himself if he ignored the urging of his conscience, if he refused to acknowledge any responsibility for the child he had fathered?

Hayes had stood quiet for a very long time before he spoke, and then his voice rang with misgivings and regret. "I'm going into Vicksburg tomorrow at first light to see if I can get Monica and the boy out before it's too late."

Travis did not seem the least bit surprised by Hayes's words, nor did he try to dissuade Banister. "Would you like some company?'' he offered. ''Things are pretty tight, but I think we can get in and out of the city without causing much notice.''

Hayes turned steady eyes on the tall, gaunt man beside him. ''You don't have to risk your neck because of me, Travis,'' he assured him.

''Hell,'' came the reply, soft and vibrant with the promise of adventure, ''what are friends for, anyway?''

17 ♍

April 17, 1863—Vicksburg, Mississippi

Vicksburg had changed dramatically since the last time Hayes had been there. It was still a town that melded the rough, rowdy river life with the genteel existence preferred by the merchants, planters, and businessmen. It was still a town of terraces, steep streets, and eclectic architecture. But in the ten years Hayes had been away new church spires, the Sisters of Mercy's tall, red-bricked academy, and the impressive cupolaed courthouse had altered the city's skyline. Houses had blossomed in vacant lots and seemed to have elbowed others aside to make room on the crowded side streets. But for all the improvements the years had wrought, the town appeared tattered and frayed by battle.

From the beginning days of the war Vicksburg's importance had been recognized by all concerned. Some had referred to it as the "Gibraltar of America," while to Lincoln it had been the "key" to the Mississippi that he wanted "in his pocket." Since May of the previous year it had been under attack, and the pounding the city had received from the gunboats had taken its toll. Houses and commercial buildings had been damaged by the incoming fire, and many of the dwellings stood dark and shuttered, giving evidence that the inhabitants had long since departed. The city was silent and desolate, especially in the early hours of the morning, yet there was a strange beauty to the place in the misty, pearl-gray half-light. The scent

of honeysuckle laced through the air, and spring flowers
bloomed in gardens that had been all but destroyed by
either the bombardment or the hastily slashed artillery pits
that riddled the hillsides.

Hayes and Travis found cover beside one of the out-
buildings on the Bennett property to wait for evidence that
Monica and her son were indeed in the house. It was
pointless to risk exposure without good cause, and as they
huddled behind a woodpile, Hayes found himself thinking
not of the woman he had come into the city to rescue, but
of his wife.

When he had returned to their cabin the previous night,
his decision to go into Vicksburg already made, Leigh had
been waiting for him. Curled naked in the bed where they
had first made love, she had been exquisite with her skin
glowing luminous ivory and her hair tumbled across her
breasts in artless disarray. She had drawn him down beside
her and covered his mouth with hers, silencing any of the
half-formed explanations he had intended to give her.
Instead he had eagerly taken what she offered: delicious
satisfaction and wondrous delight as unstinting proof of
her devotion.

"I love you, Hayes," Leigh had whispered later in the
rush and flow of passion. "I'll love you and want you and
trust you always."

Caught up in the blissful merging of their bodies, Hayes
had not taken time to consider his wife's words, but this
morning, waiting in the dew-soaked stillness, their significance was clear. Leigh's trust was precious and hard-won.
She had given it to only a chosen few: to her father, her
grandfather, to Lucas and Bran. And now she had offered
her trust to him. Though it was a responsibility he had
eagerly sought, Hayes felt soiled and unworthy. For in the
moment when Leigh had finally relinquished every part of
herself to his care, he had not had the courage to tell her
the truth, either about his past or about his plans for
coming to Vicksburg.

There was no reason for Leigh to know about this visit
to his former mistress if everything went as he hoped,
Hayes rationalized as he shifted uncomfortably beside the
shingled shack. All he meant to do was to find out why

Monica and their son were still in the city, then escort them to safety beyond the range of shot and shell. In spite of the fact that Hayes still harbored bittersweet memories of their days together, he had no desire to see Monica again, though the thought of meeting the boy he had fathered held a powerful appeal. He had often wondered about the child, and even if he had sought out neither Monica nor the boy, Hayes was eager to see his son at last.

Travis's nudge drew Banister's attention. "That her?" Nathan whispered.

Hayes craned his neck to see around the edge of the shack. On the side porch of the elegant Greek Revival home, two women stood. One was a black woman bent with age. On her arm was a market basket, as if she were going off to do some shopping, though it was rumored that the shelves of Vicksburg's stores were bare. The other woman was small and dark-haired, and as they conversed, Hayes recognized the gestures and stance that marked this one as the woman he was seeking.

"It's her," Hayes confirmed, his heart suddenly pounding in his ears. His reaction to Monica's presence was involuntary and totally unexpected.

As they watched the old woman make her way toward the street, the two men slipped across the yard and around the edge of the porch. "Those double doors lead into the study," Hayes murmured. "I think I'll try them first."

"Are you sure this is what you want to do?" Travis whispered, catching Banister's arm.

For a second Hayes hesitated, trying to comprehend his compelling need to see Monica and his child to safety. Still his motives were unclear. Weren't there simply some things a man must do for honor that he would not do for love?

"I'll never be at peace with myself if I don't get Monica and our son out of here," he whispered to the man beside him. "Does that make sense to you?"

Travis nodded, though his mouth was turned downward in a frown. "I'll be waiting here, if you need me."

Hayes sprang noiselessly onto the veranda and tried the latch on the first set of doors. To his relief, they swung slowly open, and he stepped from the porch into an opulently decorated study. Instinctively his gaze swept the room for signs of danger and came to rest on the diminutive figure behind the mahogany desk. It was the woman who had betrayed him.

For a full minute neither Hayes nor his former mistress stirred, as each stared intently at the other. The years had not been kind to Monica Morgan Bennett, Hayes decided. The fullness of her mouth had gone from piquant to petulant; her lush, tempting body from ripe to rotund. He was struck that he no longer found her in any way appealing, and it seemed that the flaws he had discovered in her character were plainly visible on her face.

What Monica's reaction was to him he could not guess. Her features were not altered by what she was feeling, but her golden eyes darkened until they glowed. As he approached, she came slowly to her feet. "Hayes Banister," she said softly. "Is it really you? Why have you come here now?"

Hayes stopped a foot or two short of the massive mahogany desk, watching the woman behind it. "Yes, Monica, it's me. I came to find out why in God's name you're still here in Vicksburg when there's shelling going on every day. Is that any way to care for either yourself or a child?"

Monica's eyes grew darker still. "I came back to Vicksburg because of him!" Monica spat, indicating the picture of her husband that hung above the mantel. It had obviously been painted long before Hayes had met the man, long before Jacob Bennett had taken Monica for a wife. It was a fine portrait, showing Bennett's once abundant, raven-dark hair; the finely drawn features on his long-jawed face; his slight but proud carriage.

"And I'm still here in Vicksburg because of you," she finished.

"Because of me?" Hayes's voice was incredulous.

They stood in silence for a moment before Monica explained. "Jacob died of pneumonia in late February. Charles and I returned from the accommodations we had secured at a friend's plantation on the Big Black River to see to the burial and hear the reading of the will. But there was a problem with the bequests that I had never anticipated."

"A problem?"

"Yes, my old friend," she said with a sneer, "a problem you had caused. Since Jacob accepted Charles as his son when he was born, I was sure he had made him his heir. But apparently Jacob knew about our meetings at the cabin, knew that I was expecting a child long before our affair was over. He was too proud a man to let the world know he had been a cuckold, but he was also too proud to leave his wealth to a child he did not think was his.

"Jacob left us without a penny to bless us, not a cent for Charles, not a cent for me! After all the years I spent with Jacob, catering to an old man's whims, I received nothing, not even this house. I gave that ungrateful bastard the best years of my life, my youth, my beauty. And because he was sure Charles was your son, not his, Jacob left us destitute."

A flicker of sympathy ran through Hayes's veins. He was sorry that Monica and the boy had been left without means because of him, so sorry that he would likely offer them a stipend once they were out of danger. But first he must find out the answer to the question that had haunted him since the day of their last meeting.

"Is the boy mine, then?" he asked softly. An odd assortment of emotions seemed lodged in Hayes's chest at what would doubtless be a final confirmation of the long-suspected truth.

"No! No!" Monica shrieked, angry and distraught. "That's the final irony. Charles is Jacob's son."

"Monica, listen. If Charles is my son, I will see that you have whatever money you need—" Hayes offered, stepping closer.

"Charles is not your son!" Monica shouted and, interpreting his approach as a threat, snatched an ancient dueling pistol from the top drawer of the desk. "Don't you come a step closer," she threatened, leveling the pistol at Hayes's chest. "I swore once that if you ever interfered with my plans for the future, if you ever cast any doubt on the paternity of my son, I would see you dead!"

"Monica, be sensible," he began softly, brushing aside the threat. "Within weeks or even days the city of Vicksburg is going to be under siege, cut off from food and water, under fire night and day. I came here to take you and the boy to safety before Grant's troops close in. Put the gun aside and let me help you. Once the Confederacy is defeated, you can contest the terms of your husband's will or come to me for help. For now there's nothing you can do, and it's dangerous for you to remain in the city.''

Monica raked back the hammer of the pistol as if to underline her threat. ''I don't want help from you, Hayes Banister. I want to see you dead for undermining everything I planned!''

Monica didn't mean what she was saying, Hayes reasoned quickly. She was irrational from the death of her husband, from the disappointments in the will, from the proximity of the enemy. She had found a focus for her frustration in his sudden reappearance and was giving vent to her helplessness and her overwrought emotions.

''I can take you back to that plantation on the Big Black,'' he offered softly, edging forward. ''Or I can put you on a train to your parents in Georgia, if that's what you prefer.''

Monica seemed not to have heard his words, seemed unable to comprehend the logic behind what he was saying. ''It's your fault that Jacob disinherited my son and me,'' she shouted. ''It's your fault Charles and I haven't a cent to live on, your fault Jacob thought Charles was not his son. It was only the promise of the Bennett fortune that made these past years bearable.''

''The money's hardly important when it comes to life and death. Please, Monica, let me help you. Let me take you out of Vicksburg.'' Hayes's tone was calm and soothing, low and persuasive. In a moment he would be close enough to reach across the desk and wrench the gun from her hands.

''I'll decide what's important! You have no right—''

''Mother? Is something the matter? I heard shouting.''

At the sound of a child's voice, both Hayes and Monica froze: he with one hand extended toward the gun, she with an expression of grim determination on her full-blown features. Both their heads swiveled to take in the slight boy in the doorway.

In that instant Hayes saw the child with excruciating

clarity: the thick, black hair and finely drawn features; the short, slender build, and inky dark eyes. There was nothing of either the Banisters or Deans in him, and in a flash of bitter insight, Hayes knew Monica had told the truth that afternoon almost ten years before, had told the truth again today. This child, Monica's child, the child who had haunted his thoughts for nearly a decade, was not his son.

The realization was both relief and stunning disappointment, and Hayes struggled to grasp the ramifications of this discovery. Was he free to put those years behind him? Could he live his life without the constant shadow of his past? Then his mind was flooded with thoughts of Leigh, of things he would be able to tell her, of parts of himself he would finally be able to share.

But first he had to get Monica and the boy safely out of Vicksburg. It was what he had come here for, and even if the boy in the doorway was not his son, he could do that much for them, at least. Intent on finishing this task, Hayes reached out to grab the pistol. Once she was disarmed, Hayes reasoned, Monica would crumble. As soon as he had shown her she could not oppose him, Monica would go docilely wherever he took them.

But the years had changed Monica too, and the small, dark-haired woman stood her ground. "No! No!" she screeched as Hayes's fingers closed around the barrel. "Let go, Hayes! Let go! I'll shoot; I swear I will."

There was a brief, desperate struggle as will warred with strength, as selfish hatred warred with disappointment. Then, a resounding retort filled the study, and Hayes felt the ball drive deep in his chest before the world dissolved in blackness.

"Miss Leigh! Miss Leigh, come quick!" The sharp command from somewhere on the deck below roused Leigh from the book she had been reading and brought her rushing to the rail outside her cabin.

On the water two decks down she could see a skiff bobbing by the side of the riverboat with two deckhands bent above some burden they were preparing to wrestle on board the *Barbara Dean*. There was an urgency about the men and the group that had gathered along the balustrade, and she surmised that there was someone on the skiff in need of her care. As she watched, one of the men in the boat raised his head, and Leigh recognized the deathly grim countenance as belonging to Nathan Travis.

Simultaneously, Leigh connected Hayes with Nathan's expression, and as Travis turned to look up at her, she caught sight of her husband's inert body sprawled in the bottom of the skiff. As she took in his ashen face, his lifeless form, and the mixture of blood and gunpowder that had tinted the breast of his shirt deep crimson, a spangle of cold passed along her limbs. Valiantly she fought off the wave of darkness that followed, clinging to the rail and gasping for breath as the sun and sky wheeled around her.

Then, after what might have been either an instant or an eternity, Nathan was beside her, pulling her close, offering a mooring for her careening senses. Leigh clung tight to his shoulders, hoping for comfort, silently begging for encouragement. But instead he spoke the truth, words that sent new dread coursing through her. "He's bad, Leigh, real bad," Travis murmured in her ear, "but he's not dead yet."

"How . . . ? How. . . . ?" She could not seem to form the question.

"What does it matter? I stopped the bleeding as best I could, but the ball has to come out, and you're the only one who knows how—"

Through the buzz of confusion in her head, Leigh caught the drift of what Travis wanted her to do. "I can't, Nathan. I can't!" There were tears on her cheeks, and the words were wrenched out of her on strangled sobs.

Above her Nathan's face hardened. "Damn it, Leigh! Don't go to pieces on me. Hayes needs you. You're the only one who can pull him through. I've told the men to bring him up here to the cabin—"

"No, no, not to the cabin," Leigh insisted. Even in the depths of shock, the force of her medical training began to exert itself. "Have the men take Hayes to the salon and lay him out on one of the tables where there's plenty of light and good ventilation. I will need to be able to move around him freely."

She was unsteady on her feet as Nathan went to do her bidding, but the crucial need for calm brought unexpected strength. With an effort Leigh slowed her breathing and tried to organize her errant thoughts. For Hayes she must be strong, she told herself. To insure the future they had planned, she must see her husband through this crisis. His life depended on her skill.

Stopping only long enough to get her medical kit from the cabin, Leigh went down to the salon. The crewmen had done exactly as she instructed and stood gathered around the table where the wounded man lay. They turned as she approached, their faces masks of concern for Hayes with blind faith in her skill shining in their eyes. Then her attention came to rest on her husband, lying just beyond the protective wall of bodies.

There seemed to be blood everywhere, soaking Hayes's clothes and the makeshift bandage wrapped around his chest, staining the wooden table and the floor. Gently she touched the pulse in his throat, feeling the thready beat of life beneath her fingers. His flesh was cold and clammy, she noted, and his breathing was shallow and labored. While one part of her brain took in and carefully assessed the medical information, another was horrified by his stillness and the grayish pallor of his skin.

With an assurance she did not feel, she stepped closer and began to cut away the layers of bloodstained clothing.

As Hayes's body was laid bare, Leigh could see the film of gray-black powder that had penetrated his coat and shirt and the wad of unprocessed cotton that Nathan had pressed into the wound to stop the bleeding. The jagged hole was on the left side of his chest, several inches above the arch of his ribs.

"The ball missed his liver and kidney, so we just might pull him through," she said almost to herself.

"We won't know what his chances are until we get it out, will we?" Nathan asked.

Leigh glanced up and shook her head. "No, but removing it is going to be dangerous. Once we open that wound, it's going to hemorrhage, and I don't know how much more blood Hayes can stand to lose."

Nathan acknowledged her words. "But isn't it worse to let him lie there and do nothing?"

It was an argument Leigh could neither refute nor deny.

She drew a long breath. "I'll need as many bandages as you can muster," she began softly, speaking to no one in particular, yet knowing her orders would be scrupulously obeyed. "I want all but Nathan and Frank to clear the room. And tell the pilot that he will have to hold the boat as steady as possible once I begin fishing for that ball."

While the crew jumped to do her bidding, Leigh took her grandfather's surgical instruments from the medical kit. Instinctively following the procedures he had used, Leigh placed the utensils in a kettle that was kept boiling on the wood stove in the corner of the salon. Then she scrubbed her hands and doused them with whiskey.

"He was shot at close range," she observed softly, as she returned to sponge the blood and powder from around the wound.

"With a dueling pistol," Nathan confirmed.

Leigh glanced up at the admission but asked no questions. "We'll have to watch for wadding in the wound then, too."

When the instruments and bandages were ready, Leigh administered just enough chloroform to insure that Hayes would not stir as she worked over him, then began to probe for the ball lodged somewhere in his chest.

As she worked, Leigh tried not to think about the man before her: tried to blot out the memories of the passion they had shared only hours before, tried not to hear the echo of the tender words they had whispered in the dark. She loved this man fiercely and completely. She loved his vitality, his humor, his tenderness and understanding. She wanted to spend the rest of her life at his side. No matter how serious his injury, she could not let Hayes die.

Then Leigh succeeded in forcing the thoughts away, concentrating on the task before her. With more skill than she knew she possessed, she used the techniques she had seen in operating rooms in St. Louis and in the hospital tents after Shiloh. She forced her untrained fingers to perform procedures she had only observed, to manipulate instruments she had only seen in others' hands. Once, as the *Barbara Dean* rode the wash of some larger vessel, Leigh froze, her face parchment-pale.

"I can't do this, Nathan," she whispered desperately. "I can't take out the ball."

"You must do it, Leigh," he told her. Across the table Travis glared at her, his black eyes smoldering like live coals and his expression fierce. "There is no one else who can."

But at last the ordeal was over, and Leigh dressed the wound, sprinkling it first with powdered morphine for the pain and then with a bit of alum to control the bleeding. She bound Hayes tightly to immobilize his broken ribs, then supervised the men as they carried him to his own cabin on the deck above.

With the ball removed there was little to do but wait, and as the riverboat plodded north, Hayes lay lost in unconsciousness. On the second day a fever came upon him, and Leigh was beside herself with worry. Was this a natural result of the wound beginning to heal, or was it a harbinger of some putrefaction that would take her husband's life?

As the blaze raging within him grew in intensity, it seemed to invade the peaceful world where Hayes had retreated until he tossed and mumbled senseless, half-formed phrases. Diligently Leigh bathed his burning body, cleaned his wound, changed his dressings, and forced trickles of water down his throat to offset the wasting effect of the fever.

Far away in his private hell, Hayes seemed to know Leigh was beside him. Her name was constantly on his lips: as a request, a question, a plea. The sound of her voice and the touch of her hand seemed to be all that brought him peace, and because no one else seemed able to soothe him, Leigh never left his side.

The evening before they were to make St. Louis Hayes's fever began to spiral. He stirred restlessly beneath the restraining covers, twisting and babbling a senseless litany. Even Leigh's presence could not calm him, and the cool cloths were no longer adequate to battle the inferno that was threatening to take his life. At a fuel stop one of the crewmen managed to secure some ice, and Nathan watched skeptically as Leigh packed it against her husband's burning body.

For a time nothing seemed to help, and then well after midnight Hayes's breathing seemed to ease, and his skin was damp and cooler. The fever had broken at last.

Tears seeped from between Leigh's downcast lashes as she knelt beside the bed clutching her husband's hand between both of hers. Then, slowly she became aware that Hayes's pale, heavy-lidded eyes had fluttered open, and he was watching her.

"Don't cry, Leigh," he whispered gently. "Please don't cry. I didn't mean to hurt you."

She smoothed the damp hair back from his temples, hardly able to speak for the emotion clogging her throat. "It's all right, Hayes," she croaked. "Really it is. Everything's all right as long as you're going to get well."

"I had to go into Vicksburg," he continued fitfully, though she could see how quickly his strength was waning. "I thought the boy was my son even though Monica would never admit it, and I had to be sure . . ." In spite of his best resolves to complete the explanation, Hayes's words faded into silence as sleep overwhelmed him.

Leigh rose from beside the bed, tenderly tucked the quilts around his shoulders, and stood watching her husband for a very long time. Foremost in her mind was gratitude that, as close as he had come to death, Hayes's life had somehow been spared. He was still pale and gaunt from the loss of blood and the fever, and it would be weeks before he was himself again. But Hayes was going to live, and for that she was profoundly thankful.

But even as she stood watching over him, Leigh was haunted by the words he had spoken before he slept. She had assumed that his wound had occurred on some mysterious assignment for Pincheon and the Union, but now other possibilities began to intrude. Did Hayes indeed have a son in Vicksburg? And who was this woman Monica? What was she to Hayes? Before, concern over his condition had overruled all other considerations, but now that Leigh knew her husband would live, she began to wonder about the rest. With his half-conscious apology swirling in her brain and a growing knot of apprehension in her middle, she went to find out how Hayes had been shot.

When she opened the door to the cabin on the deck below, Nathan Travis was sprawled fully dressed on the bed. But at the sound of her entrance, he came instantly awake, grim and blurry-eyed.

"He's dead?" he demanded, fully prepared to offer Leigh comfort.

"Oh, no, Nathan! He's better, much better. Hayes is going to live."

Travis sagged back against the pillows in relief. "Thank God," he murmured. "Thank God for that!"

"Yes, thank God!"

"I'm glad you came and woke me," Travis said as he rubbed his eyes. "I didn't mean to fall asleep when you might have needed me."

"It's all right, Nathan," she assured him, dropping into a chair by the side of the bunk. "You've certainly earned a few hours' rest. You've sat with Hayes nearly as much as I have these last few days."

Nathan gave her a derisive frown. "I'm glad you came to tell me he was better."

"Well, to be truthful the change in Hayes's condition is not the only reason I'm here," Leigh confessed. "I wanted to know how Hayes was wounded."

"Why?" The word had an uncooperative sound.

"Hayes was awake for a few moments, and while he was, he said something about going to Vicksburg because of his son."

Nathan sat up a little straighter, bracing his shoulders against the wall at the head of the bed. "You're sure he wasn't still delirious?"

Leigh met his eyes levelly. "I think you know as well as I do that he wasn't. The other day I didn't press you to tell me what happened because while Hayes's life was in danger it didn't matter. But now that I'm sure he will recover, I want to know the truth."

For a long moment Nathan sat watching her, seeing the determined set to her mouth and the vulnerability in her eyes. How would Leigh react when she found out why Hayes had gone to Vicksburg? Was she prepared to hear about a part of her husband's life he had never seen fit to share? Could he make Leigh see that no matter what had happened in the past, neither Monica nor Charles meant more to his friend than a debt of honor? And how would Leigh respond when she learned who had shot her husband?

"We went into the city to try to rescue some people Hayes used to know," Nathan began with obvious reluctance, swinging his long legs over the side of the bed and rising to pace the length of the narrow cabin.

"A woman named Monica?" Leigh suggested quietly, sensing that Nathan was trying to protect her, yet seeking complete disclosure instead.

"Yes, the woman's name was Monica," he confirmed, frowning. "She was Hayes's mistress years ago when he was a pilot on the river."

"And you were to rescue her son too, weren't you? Hayes's son?"

Leigh already knew too much to allow for polite evasions. Travis faced her squarely. "Hayes has never been sure if the boy is his, but he went into the city to get him and his mother to safety anyway."

There was a terrible, rigid twist to the line of Leigh's mouth that spoke more eloquently than words of the pain and confusion his revelations were causing.

"Leigh, I know how it looks, but don't you sell Hayes short," Nathan went on. "Can't you understand what a man might be willing to do for the sake of his flesh and blood? Don't you know what that kind of bond can mean?"

Leigh sat staring at her hands, clenched together in her lap. "I am well aware how precious a life can be, Nathan, and I know I'd gladly give my own for the sake of those I love."

Her hurt was a palpable thing he could sense radiating from every rigid line of her body. And while he wished to offer her comfort, he knew there was no way to change what she was feeling. "Hayes is an honorable man, Leigh, and it was honor that took him to Vicksburg, not anything else."

There was anguish in her eyes when she raised them to his face. "Not love, Nathan? Are you sure he didn't do it for love?"

"He loves you, Leigh. Hayes loves you very much."
They were stark, bare words, the unvarnished truth, but
Leigh seemed unable to believe them and accept the balm
he had meant the words to be.

"Does he love me, Nathan?" There was desperation in
her voice: a desperate need to believe warring with a
stubborn reservation that would not let her accept his
assurance of Hayes's loyalty.

Nathan didn't know what else to say to her.

Leigh's face was pale and intent as she pressed onward.
"And did he succeed?" she asked softly. "Hayes nearly
died trying to get his mistress and her son out of Vicksburg. Did he get them well beyond Grant's reach before he
was wounded?"

Leigh had demanded honesty, and Nathan couldn't find
a reason to lie to her now. "No, Leigh," he told her
solemnly, "Hayes didn't succeed. Monica shot him, shot
him down like an enemy or an intruder in her house."

"Why?" Leigh whispered when the shock of his disclosure began to ebb.

"You'll have to ask Hayes that," Nathan answered
grimly. "I had been waiting outside, and by the time I
heard the gunfire, it was already too late. Hayes had been
wounded, and all I cared about was getting him out of
there before some Reb came to investigate the noise." He
grew grimmer still, and his eyes blazed with latent anger.
"That woman didn't say a thing to me the whole time I
was trying to see to Hayes. She just stood there with the
smoking pistol in one hand, holding the child against her
with the other."

Leigh came slowly to her feet, calm and self-contained
though Travis could guess at the turmoil within her. "I
don't want to hear more, Nathan," she said weakly. "I've
already made you tell me more than was wise."

"Hayes only did what he had to do, Leigh," Travis
reiterated, reaching out to her as she moved past him
toward the door.

"I know that, Nathan," she replied. "In my head I
know why he took the risk, I even appreciate his daring.
It's just that I can't seem to make myself accept what he
did and understand his reasons."

Without another word Leigh slipped out of Nathan's cabin, seeking refuge in the night. She needed time to take in what she had learned from Nathan Travis, time to consider all the things Hayes had never shared, time to shed the tears that were swelling in her chest.

In brooding silence she climbed the stairs to the Texas deck and slipped into their stateroom to look in on her husband. He was sleeping deeply, and Leigh was glad of that on more than one account. Snatching up a shawl, she returned to the deck and leaned heavily against the balustrade, staring out across the water.

Leigh had never been a woman who gave free rein to strong emotion, but for the first time in her life, she understood the strength and scope of enmity. She was threatened by what this woman Monica had once been to her husband, jealous of the hold she had on Hayes still. He had risked his life to see Monica and her child to safety, and the loyalty he felt for them seemed to malign all he claimed to feel for Leigh. Monica, whatever her role in Hayes's life, was a threat to all Leigh held dear, and she was frightened by how close she had come to losing everything that mattered.

But even as she rejoiced in the fact that Hayes was finally out of danger, she was hurt and disappointed that her husband had never shared his secrets. At a time when Leigh was letting down her last defenses, Hayes had shut her out. He had denied her a part of himself when she was struggling to give him her all. It had never been easy for Leigh to express and share her feelings, but as difficult as it was, she had done her best to let Hayes know she loved him. It was the knowledge that he had held back, that he had kept his secrets that tore at her insides. As much as she wanted to understand her husband's motives, what he had done felt very much like betrayal.

With that realization her pain intensified and tears began to fall. They welled in her eyes and spilled down her cheeks, caught in her lashes and dripped unheeded off her chin. In the wind-washed silence of the night, Leigh sought to muffle the sound of her weeping. Yet there was wondrous liberation in expressing her grief and frustration, in giving vent to her jealousy and fear. Leigh wept freely, caught in a maelstrom of disillusionment, until all the tears were gone.

But even when she had quieted, the painful questions still remained. Why hadn't Hayes told her that he was going into Vicksburg? Hadn't he trusted her enough to share his fears and problems? Hadn't he thought her able to understand?

Perhaps there had been reasons for his silence: that the memories were painful for him or that Monica and her son were part of a past he was trying to forget. Yet the strength of their hold on her husband was very clear. Hayes had taken responsibility for their safety and fruitlessly risked his life on their behalf. Why did a man do that if not for love?

Again tears rose in Leigh's eyes, but now she fought them back. Would she have been able to accept the fact that her husband had other loyalties and responsibilities, that he'd had other loves, other lives in the past? It was not an easy thing for any woman to acknowledge, but if Hayes had given her the opportunity, she would have tried to understand.

His lapse of trust in her was the most damning thing in what she had discovered. Perhaps she could understand his loyalty, accept his past, forgive his actions. But in keeping his secrets from her, in betraying the trust she had worked so hard to give, he had altered something fundamental in their marriage, something that had made their love unique.

She still loved Hayes, would love him for all her days. Her love had its roots deep in all that had gone before: in the bond that had begun that first day at Camp Jackson; in the rich, warm days of friendship they had shared the previous winter; and even in the difficult time of their estrangement when each had ached for what was lost. Love not easily given was love not readily destroyed. Yet she wondered if love tempered by pain and disappointment could ever be as strong as love had been when it was new.

It would take time, time for Hayes to heal and regain his strength, time for Leigh to come to terms with her disillusionment. It would take weeks or months to reestablish what they had once shared. It was time that fate had decreed they take.

Leigh shivered as predawn chill wrapped itself around her, and she began to realize how long she had been standing lost in thought. Far away on the horizon she could see the slight filmy veil of gray that heralded the approach of dawn, and she knew she must prepare for the new day. Hayes's wound would need cleansing and dressing, and she had to see that there was broth, custard, and tea ready to feed him when he awoke. Hayes was going to live, and for all her misgivings about what had happened at Vicksburg, that was what mattered most. But as she turned back to the cabin where her husband slept, she no longer faced the future with the joyous wonder, the untarnished optimism she had felt only hours before.

18 ⌖

June 2, 1863—St. Louis, Missouri

Hayes stopped in the doorway of the room Leigh had occupied since their return to St. Louis nearly six weeks earlier. He frowned as his eyes swept over the worn carpetbag on the bed and the several dresses lying beside it, waiting to be packed. A cable had arrived from Mary Ann Bickerdyke only that morning telling Leigh of the shortage of trained nurses in the hospitals at Vicksburg and asking her to come. Without consulting him, without even considering his wishes, Leigh had wired back that she would be on the next transport going south.

It was hardly surprising that such a need existed, Hayes reflected as he stepped into the room, since the summer of 1863 promised to be rife with military activity. It was rumored that in the East General Robert E. Lee was preparing for a campaign, while General Rosecrans, in control of the Army of the Cumberland, was being urged by Union Secretary of War Stanton to move toward Chattanooga. Down along the Mississippi, Grant had Vicksburg under siege after a series of bloody battles and two attempts to storm the city. It was not hard to surmise that once Vicksburg fell, Grant's army would turn east to further divide the Confederacy. And like as not, any nurses at Vicksburg would be expected to accompany them.

Hayes's frown darkened as Leigh emerged from the dressing room carrying a pair of sturdy shoes and a plain cotton nightdress.

"I didn't realize you were back," Leigh greeted him. "How did things go at the doctor's?"

Hayes shrugged. "He says I'm making a miraculous recovery, that by the end of the month I'll be good as new."

Leigh set the shoes on the bed and began to fold the dresses. "You were very lucky," she observed, intent on her packing. "If that ball had hit an inch or two in any direction. . . ."

"I prefer to think my miraculous recovery had a great deal to do with the superb nursing I received," Hayes interjected, grinning in hopes of garnering a response from his wife.

"I suppose it could have made some difference," she conceded without a glance in his direction.

There had been a time only months before when Leigh would have teased him back. Then she might have bragged about her prowess as a nurse or complained about his shortcomings as a patient. It was symptomatic of the change in their relationship that Leigh would not think to do that now.

During his convalescence, his wife had been the soul of consideration, anticipating his needs and diligently seeing to his welfare. She had made sure he was clean and comfortable, tended to his wound and his diet, stayed close at hand in case he wanted her, sent Brandon Hale to entertain him when she had to be away. Leigh had read to him by the hour, brought him books, newspapers, games, and puzzles to alleviate his boredom once he was feeling better. But as solicitous as she was, as tender as her care of him had been, he was aware that his visit to Vicksburg had changed many things between them.

They had not spoken of the events surrounding his injury until one evening a week or two before when Leigh had come to his room after supper to keep him company. She had opened a checkerboard at the edge of the mattress and was preparing it for play when Hayes broached the subject.

"Leigh," he had begun, feeling more than a tinge of apprehension, "I want to explain why I went into Vicksburg to rescue Monica and her son."

Her fingers had hung poised above the checkers she

was aligning before she gave him a reply. "We needn't speak of it, Hayes," she informed him crisply. "Nathan told me what happened."

"I think I owe you more of an explanation than Nathan would have been able to give," he persisted. "Leigh, please, I know how you must feel about this, but hear me out and try to understand."

"I understand perfectly, Hayes," she had insisted. "You have a love child by a woman in Vicksburg, and you had to go into the city to see to their welfare."

He had studied his wife for a long moment, trying to gauge her feelings. She seemed calm and reasonable, but since their return to St. Louis her actions had left no doubt that there was a barrier between them, a barrier Hayes had to find a way to breach.

"Leigh," he had begun, drawing a long breath. "Leigh, I no longer love Monica Bennett; I want you to believe that. And the child in Vicksburg was not mine."

Her head had come up abruptly, her eyes wide with shock and disbelief. "He wasn't yours?"

"Ironic, isn't it? I risked everything to be sure that child was safe, and it turned out that Charles was Jacob Bennett's son, not mine."

He watched a sequence of strong emotions cross her face, but when she spoke at last, her response was not one he had anticipated. "Oh, Hayes," she whispered feelingly, "I'm so sorry."

Her sympathy was foreign and unexpected. It heartened him, yet it made him wary. She was offering him compassion as a balm for his hurt and disillusionment; she was giving far more than he had asked. But she was also treating him as if she had no stake in his revelations.

"Leigh," he tried again, "I want you to understand, I went into Vicksburg because I thought the boy was mine, not for any other reason."

"Yes, Hayes. I know that now."

Her calm voice frustrated him. "If you understand, then why do I feel as if you are holding me at arm's length? Why have things changed between us?"

For a long moment Leigh seemed to consider his words, then drew a long sigh and set the checkers aside.

"It isn't easy for me to talk about my feelings," she had begun, and Hayes recognized that there was a time when she could not have made even that simple declaration. Heartened, he had settled down to listen.

"When Nathan brought you back to the ship," Leigh continued, "nothing mattered except that you get well. But once you began to improve, I needed to know why you had gone into Vicksburg. I badgered Nathan to tell me. And afterward I felt, I don't know, threatened or jealous. It was hard for me to accept that you had ties to another woman and her child, ties so strong that you were willing to risk your life to see to their safety."

"Leigh, it was something I had to do. I couldn't be that close to the city, realize what was inevitably going to happen, and not do my best to make sure they were safe."

"Yes, I know, and I can imagine how you felt."

"But?"

Leigh hesitated. "What bothered me, even more than learning about Monica and Charles, was that you never told me about them or confided what you were going to do."

"What would you have done if I had told you?" he challenged.

She shook her head. "I'm not sure I know. I was trying so hard to share everything in my life with you that when I found that you were keeping secrets, I felt"—she groped for the word—"disillusioned—disillusioned and betrayed."

His fingers had slipped around her wrist, tightening compellingly. "I didn't mean to shut you out, and I'm willing to tell you everything now."

"It's not the same. Can't you see that?" There were tears clustered on her lashes. "I love you, Hayes," she had continued as the wetness spilled down her cheeks. "I think I always will. But trusting has never been easy for me, and it's even harder to trust you now."

Seeing her distress, he had let the subject drop, taking refuge in the assurance that time and patience could reestablish what he and Leigh had shared. Only now there was no more time, and his patience had worn thin: Leigh was going away tomorrow, and nothing was resolved between them.

He watched her put the last of her possessions into the

carpetbag, then move it to the floor. As she rose, he came to stand behind her, running his palms along her arms. "Leigh," he murmured wistfully. "Oh, sweet, sweet Leigh. What must I do to show how much I love you?"

He could feel the response his words engendered, the tremors of emotion that moved beneath her skin. She did not resist as he drew her back against his body and crossed his arms around her chest to hold her close.

"Leigh," he whispered against her ear, "I don't want for us to part like this."

With slow, deliberate movements she turned in his embrace, fitting her body to the shape of his, sliding her hands along his arms and across his shoulders, kneading his woolly lapels between her fingers.

"Nor do I," she whispered. "Nor do I."

Then, as if drawn by the warmth of his skin, her fingers traced the column of his throat and tangled in the thick brown hair at his nape.

"I do love you, Hayes," she murmured gently. "I love you with all my heart."

He felt her arch into the curve of his body and saw that the lips she raised to his were parted with anticipation. There was a roaring in his ears as he folded her closer and lowered his mouth to accept her invitation, as long denial intensified the wonder of the kiss. Tentatively each opened their mouths to the other, languishing with the sudden sweep of deep emotion. Their tongues touched, a caress as gentle as the morning mist, a caress filled with the wild, sweet poignancy of longing.

Together they sank to the bed to lie pillowed on the downy counterpane. As their hands sought the other, clothes became an impediment to the growing passion of each touch. Never breaking the tender contact, they shed their coats and shirtwaists, their pants and petticoats. Only flesh against flesh, skin against skin, would serve the intimacy that each demanded, and at last they lay bared and defenseless, unencumbered and strong. They came together in a chorus of sensation, joyous and triumphant, vital and proud. They knew now how precious each moment in life could be, how fleeting and fragile the scope of existence. And as each sought to please the other, they were filled with wondrous exultation that echoed in their veins long after the crest of loving was gone.

Footsteps on the stairs roused Hayes at last, and he rolled off the edge of the mattress to nudge the door to the bedroom closed.

As he returned, Leigh smiled at him across the rumpled sheets. "It's probably only Susan come to light the lamps," she said.

As they had lain together, the sky had grown dark, and the rain that had been threatening since early afternoon pattered through the trees outside the open window. For a long time they lay listening to the storm, the sound of the carriages and wagons moving through the wet streets, the rustle of the early summer breeze, the thud of distant thunder.

Hayes turned to kiss his wife and pull her close against his chest. "I love you, Leigh," he murmured gently. "I don't want you to go away tomorrow."

The breath of her sigh moved across his skin. "I must go. You know that as well as I do."

"But, Leigh, it's dangerous at Vicksburg. The papers say some of those hospitals are under fire all the time. Besides, you've surely had your fill of nursing with your mother, and me, and all the time you've spent working here in St. Louis."

"It's something I must do, Hayes." There was both a hint of steel and a murmur of reproach in her tone. "I always thought you knew that."

A gentle stroke moved along her arm. "I do. I just don't want to be away from you, not now, not yet. We need more time."

Leigh looked up at her husband, reading all he had left unsaid in the depths of his shadowed eyes. "I told you I understood about what happened at Vicksburg," she reassured him softly. "I understand, and I've forgiven you."

At her words, Hayes sucked in a long breath, and the quiet in the room became suddenly brittle and destructive.

"Forgiven me?" Hayes echoed at last, edging up on one elbow. "Forgiven me for what?"

Leigh seemed not to understand his reaction. "For—for going into the city to rescue your mistress and her child."

A swift spear of anger pierced Hayes as he sat staring, seeing with frightening clarity that she didn't understand at all.

"Damn it, Leigh! Perhaps I wouldn't have gone into the city if I had known Charles was another man's son, but I won't spend the rest of my life apologizing for something I'm not even sorry I did. I don't want your forgiveness. What I want is your understanding."

He was furious at her well-meaning condescension, at the lifelong reserve that made her able to understand with her head but not her heart.

"But I do understand—" she began.

"No you don't! You sit there with that sanctimonious expression on your face, considering yourself good and noble for granting me your forgiveness. You can't comprehend anything I felt when I thought my son, my flesh and blood, was in mortal danger."

"Hayes—"

"You don't understand anything: not loving, not caring. You don't know why I went to Vicksburg, and even if I spent a hundred years explaining, you could never grasp the simple truth of real emotion. God damn it, Leigh! I want a world of things from you, but forgiveness isn't one of them."

His hand tightened on her arm, and he pulled her against him, his mouth covering hers before she could respond. The kiss he pressed upon her was as rough and demanding as the first ones had been tender and gentle, but she went still beneath his attack, afraid that if she struggled, she might do him some unintentional hurt. Then there were tears on her face, despairing, helpless tears, wetting his cheeks as well as hers.

"Oh, Hayes, please, not like this," she whispered when he freed her mouth at last. "I don't want to spend the night like this. I want things settled, mended, made right between us. Please, Hayes, please! I go away tomorrow!"

He rose above her with wild, blue anger still burning in his eyes. She wanted things settled but made no effort to understand; she wanted things mended but had never learned to compromise.

And now there were other secrets he was aching to tell

her, things he could not hold back. He had not meant to shout his news in anger or use it to gain the advantage in a battle he did not want to fight. Yet the words burst from him, cutting and venomous, breathless and proud.

"And I'm leaving, too," he told her. "I'm to report on the first of July. A letter came yesterday from the Corps of Engineers in Washington. I have a commission waiting for me, and I'm anxious to go."

Her concern for him overcame her resistance and confusion. "But Hayes," Leigh protested. "You're not strong enough yet. You need more time—"

Hayes brushed her concern aside. "It's done, Leigh. I wrote to them months ago when things began to slow down at the shipyard. And Dr. Phillips says I'll be fully recovered by the beginning of next month."

"But where will you be posted? Do you think it might be at Vicksburg?"

He could hear an eagerness in her voice that touched his heart. He was no longer angry, just sad and incredibly weary.

"No, Leigh," he said softly, pulling her close, "my assignment will probably be in the East, or perhaps with the Army of the Cumberland."

"Then that means we have only tonight—"

"Yes, only tonight," Hayes acknowledged in a whisper. He silenced further protests with a kiss that blended the salt taste of tears and the promise of ecstasy, the sting of remorse and the poignancy of their love.

"Leigh, sweet Leigh." His voice had a deep and desperate timbre. "We only have tonight, my darling, so we'll have to make it last for all eternity."

June 1863—Outside Vicksburg, Mississippi

Battlefield nursing hadn't gotten any easier. That wasn't a surprise to Leigh, but she had grown used to the niceties of working in an established hospital and going home to a hot bath and a soft bed. The best accommodations Vicksburg could offer were canvas tents overrun with lizards and lumpy cots, their legs set in jars of water to keep the "critters" from crawling between the sheets. The hospitals themselves were typical of Army field hospitals anywhere in the war: underequipped, understaffed, existing in the most primitive conditions. Nor was the landscape around the beleaguered city welcoming. The terrain must have been broken and rugged at the best of times, with ravines slashing between the high, steep hills, but now with the open gashes of rifle pits and the gun emplacements scarring the rust-red earth, the land itself lay like a grisly wound exposed to the pitiless sky.

In spite of their bleak surroundings Leigh's reunion with Delia and Mother Bickerdyke was a happy one, and she found that other women who had proved themselves in battle had come to the city as well. The likes of Mrs. Livermore and Mrs. Hoge from the Chicago office of the Northwestern Sanitary Commission and Annie Wittenmyer, who had been at Shiloh, were quite different from the ladies who came to the camp to visit. These "bombastic dress-parade workers" as Annie called them, invariably arrived to see the fortifications in dainty shoes and their finest gowns. They usually decamped quickly, though, when they found that virtually every inch of the fifteen mile-long line of entrenchments Grant had strung around the city was under fire, and that a visitor might as likely be cut down by the Rebel sharpshooters as the men in the trenches.

Bombardment by both Union and Confederate forces went on twenty-four hours a day, with the only lulls in the firing coming at mealtime. Parrot guns, rifled guns, mortars, and grenades boomed and screeched in regular measure while musketry rattled to add staccato snatches to the chorus. Firing became the counterpoint to any conversation or activity, and gradually the gunshots became as familiar as the sound of peepers in a summer night. In spite of the yellow medical flags waving from the tent tops, one of the hospitals was scored a direct hit, and that only added to the death and destruction in this ravaged land.

There had been 3,400 casualties with Grant's troops when they had arrived outside Vicksburg, and the two attempts to storm the city on May 19 and 22 had added

2,500 more men to their number. With those soldiers to care for and new casualties every day, the nurses were very busy, indeed.

The summer heat had begun early in Mississippi that year, and Leigh spent much of her time when not cooking, washing, attending the surgeons, or dispensing supplies, sitting with men who burned with heat of their own. They were poor, half-delirious wretches who responded to the touch of a woman's hand and the cool water Leigh sponged over their feverish bodies with such murmurs of appreciation that she often sat up with them all night and managed to save more than a few.

One evening as she sat by one of her "causes," as Delia called them, Delia herself sought Leigh out. "I came to see why you weren't in bed," she said as she pulled a second stool up beside the man her friend was nursing. "You know, Leigh, you really should get more rest. I hate to be a scold, but you are looking rather peaked."

"I know," Leigh conceded, brushing the perspiration from her brow, "but tending these men makes such a difference. I can hardly sleep soundly when I know they need me."

"No, none of us can do that. But you aren't doing them any good by wearing yourself out. And I've noticed you aren't eating properly, either."

"It's only the heat, Delia," Leigh murmured, bending above her charge. "Nothing seems to appeal to me just now."

Delia watched her friend for a long moment. "You haven't heard from Hayes either, have you?" she asked pointedly.

A frown came and went on Leigh's face. "Not a word since I left St. Louis. I told him to send his letters through the Sanitary Commission, but now I wonder if that was wise."

"Oh, he'll write." There was a quiet assurance in the blond woman's voice. "It's just that most men aren't at their best with pen and paper. Shall I ask Nathan to look in on him the next time he's in the city?"

Leigh shook her head. "Hayes accepted that commission with the Corps of Engineers and has to report the first of July. If he decided to visit his family in Cincinnati on the way, he's probably gone already.''

Delia was quiet for a moment. "And have you tried writing to him?'' she persisted.

Leigh shook her head. "No, I've been far too busy here." It was a lame excuse, and Leigh knew it. Besides, she had said everything she wanted to say in the note she had left for Hayes in St. Louis.

"Weren't things all they should be when you left home?'' Delia pressed her.

Leigh shook her head again.

The younger woman didn't mean to pry into her friend's affairs, but Nathan had told her what happened at Vicksbrug in April, and both of them were genuinely concerned for Hayes and Leigh. "Was it that woman and her son who caused the problem?''

"They were only part of it." Leigh sighed heavily and prepared another cool cloth for her patient's brow. "Really, Delia, I'd rather not talk about what happened. Hayes and I will work this out one way or another.''

"Through letters that never come? Through letters you refuse to write? Leigh, don't you realize that every moment two people have together is precious, especially now, especially in this war? Don't let your pride get in the way of what you and Hayes feel for each other. Write him, reassure him, let him know you love him.''

Leigh recognized the truth in Delia's words and sighed helplessly. "It's already too late. By the time a letter reaches St. Louis, Hayes will be gone.''

"Then send the letter to the Department of the Mississippi. They will forward it to Hayes wherever he's been assigned. Surely he is as anxious to hear from you as you are to hear from him.''

Leigh hesitated, remembering the pain and ecstasy in the last night she had spent with her husband. "All right, Delia. I'll write him tomorrow.''

"Good," Delia declared as she came to her feet, a self-satisfied smile on her lips. "Now, won't you come along to bed?''

"I'll be there in a little while," Leigh assured her, "and thank you for your concern.''

As Delia turned away, Leigh blinked back the unexpected tears that rose in her eyes. Delia's friendship meant so much to her. Still she didn't know why things seemed to touch her so easily lately. Such ready emotion was out of character.

The voice from the bed beside her startled Leigh, and she looked down at the man she had been nursing. "Don't cry, pretty lady," he soothed her. "If you were mine, I'd write a letter every day."

Leigh did write Hayes twice in the next week, then waited patiently at mail call to hear her name. A letter did come from her mother, assuring Leigh that while life was hard in Louisiana, she was happy. Another arrived from a nurse at the hospital in St. Louis full of news and gossip. There were two hastily scrawled notes from Bran and one from her father. Nothing else came, not a word from her husband.

But life at Vicksburg was hectic, and it gave Leigh very little time to brood. The siege continued through June in the baking summer heat, and the sun beat down day after day like an unblinking golden eye. Shade was at a premium on the barren, reddish hills, and even in the depths of the hospital tents, the sun's power could be felt.

Outside the city the Union troops dug in, pressing their breastworks ever closer to the Confederate lines. Union engineers tunneled like moles in the hope of undermining the Rebels' strongest defenses, but to little real advantage. It was said that the people of Vicksburg were tunneling into the hillsides, too. Only the residents were tunneling for protection from the unrelenting fire. Rumors flew that the defenders were eating pea bread, mules and rats and had given up bathing for fear of depleting their precious supply of water. Still General Pemberton, the defender of Vicksburg, refused to surrender, and no one knew how long he could hold out.

While the sun scorched the earth and the guns boomed, scouts reported that General Joe Johnston, the Confederate Commander of the Armies of the West, was gathering troops at Jackson to attack the Union ranks from the rear. Sherman and his men were dispatched to guard Grant's lines from the eastern side, but as time passed nothing happened, and the siege continued, day after blistering day.

Union supply lines from the Yazoo River were wide open, and one night after a particularly large shipment of sanitary stores and foodstuffs had arrived, Mother Bickerdyke suggested making lemonade as a treat for the patients in the hospitals. The idea was well received, and several women gathered in one of the cook tents to prepare icy pitchers of the drink.

Leigh was among those volunteers, but as she worked cutting the lemons to be squeezed, a peculiar feeling assailed her. She had always liked the pungent, tart smell of lemons, but tonight there was something about it that went against her, making her feel tingly and light-headed. The tent where they were working seemed suddenly too close, the lantern light too glaring. There was a roaring in her ears, and her mouth went sour and wet as the queasiness she had been experiencing became debilitating nausea. Scattering fruit as she ran, Leigh rushed for the door; once outside in the thick night air, she fell to her knees and was violently ill.

Mother Bickerdyke found her sitting weakly on the grass a few minutes later, pale and shaken by what had happened. Squatting down beside Leigh, the older woman took her pulse and felt her forehead with a practiced hand. "You ain't got a fever," she observed, watching Leigh carefully. "Are you breeding?"

The younger woman's head came up sharply at the question. "No, I . . ."

"Have you been dizzy, tired, weepy? Have your monthly courses stopped?" she persisted.

"I know the signs," Leigh snapped in exasperation. "I'm a nurse, after all."

Mother Bickerdyke remained silent as Leigh drew a long breath and pushed the hair back from her face.

"I don't see how I could be pregnant," she said finally. "Hayes was injured back in April, and the only time we—we . . ."

"Was the night before you left," the older woman finished for her. "Well, that would make things about right by my count."

"But it's impossible," Leigh protested, without much conviction.

"Is it?" Mother Bickerdyke asked quietly. "Leigh, I've seen you nurse in the worst conditions, help with operations until you were asleep on your feet, clean up the most unappetizing messes without ever being sick. I don't think this is one of the fluxes, though God knows there are enough of them about. But unless you're going to have a baby, there's not a reason in the world why a bunch of lemons would do you in when all the rest never did."

Leigh was silent for a full minute, trying to digest the older woman's words. She did not want to be carrying a child, not now: not when there were so many questions in her marriage unresolved, not when Hayes was so far away. Besides, she was needed desperately here at the hospital, and she was totally committed to helping the wounded.

"Well, I won't go back to St. Louis!" she finally declared, realizing full well what pregnancy might mean. "I swear I won't! I won't get on a steamer going north even if I am going to have a child!"

It was the confirmation she had expected, and Mother Bickerdyke eyed Leigh thoughtfully, gauging the extent of her sincerity. Leigh Banister was a determined young woman at the best of times, and it seemed likely that if she wanted to stay with the nursing corps, that is exactly what she would do. Besides, the girl loved this work; she was skilled, diligent, and had a natural gift for healing. It also seemed to Mother Bickerdyke that there were things at home that Leigh was not prepared to face.

"I've never much held with the notion that a woman has to sit on a satin pillow the whole time she's expecting," the older woman finally conceded. "But if I agreed not to tell the doctors about your child, you'd have to promise to take proper care of yourself while you're here. They'll send you home as soon as you round out a little, anyway, but that should take us into fall. And who knows where any of us will be by then?"

"Oh, thank you, Mother Bickerdyke, for letting me stay," Leigh said in relief. "You must know what nursing means to me."

"I know what your nursing means to those men, and I

don't want you shortchanging them. You take care of yourself, and I'll keep your secret. But if I hear that you're not eating or sleeping or doing your job, you're going to be on a riverboat so fast it'll make your head spin," the older woman murmured gruffly. "Now, you go on to bed and sleep late tomorrow, until six at least. You hear me, Leigh?"

"Yes, ma'am."

"And, Leigh, congratulations on the baby."

July 5, 1863

The sweltering heat of midafternoon beat down on the dusty street as Leigh made her way through what had obviously been a fashionable section of Vicksburg. The remnants of grand houses stood on both sides of the road, curtained behind wrought-iron fences and hemmed by strips of ruined lawn. Here, as well as everywhere else in the town, the incessant shelling of the last forty-seven days was evident. Where the shells had scored direct hits, buildings lay collapsed in rubble, while some still stood sturdy and unscathed. A few homes had been set ablaze by incoming fire, while walls on others had been sheared away to expose the vulnerable core of domestic life in the ruined city. Everywhere Leigh had gone, she had seen crumbling architecture, bare trees, scarred earth, and gaping artillery craters.

She had entered Vicksburg early that morning to pass out the stores General Grant had ordered dispensed to the inhabitants. Though she had heard horrendous tales of life in the beleaguered city, nothing had prepared her for the hollow-eyed women and children who crowded around the wagons. Pale and gaunt from days on end without sleep or proper food, they cringed with shame at being forced to accept help from those who had defeated them. For all their days in the trenches, the soldiers were in even worse condition, and when Leigh saw the weary, haggard men, she marveled at their ability to hold off such an awesome foe.

During the surrender ceremony the day before, Leigh

and some of the other nurses had taken field glasses to the
high ground behind Union Lines. From there they had
watched the long lines of Union soldiers draw up outside
the fortifications while General Pemberton and his men
marched out of Vicksburg and stacked their arms. That
there had been no cheering from the victorious Northern
troops was a measure of the respect they felt for the city's
defenders.

Vicksburg represented a peculiar interlude in the war,
when the ordeal all had endured bound together friend and
enemy alike. Instead of imprisonment, the nearly thirty
thousand man captured with the city had been offered
parole. Though Leigh knew Grant had agreed to those
terms for practical reasons, she was glad that mercy had
triumphed, even if it was in the name of expediency.

As she walked through the ruined town, Leigh tried to
come to terms with the confrontation she was about to
initiate. Her motives in seeking out her husband's former
mistress were confusing and complex, but somehow Leigh
knew she must meet the woman who had nearly cost
Hayes his life. Her husband had risked everything for
Monica Bennett and her child. Until Leigh's doubts had
been laid to rest, until she understood the reasons for
Hayes's loyalties, there would always be a dark specter
threatening her marriage.

It had not been difficult to find someone who knew the
Bennetts, and the directions to their home had been clear
and concise. But when Leigh reached the lot where the
house should be, there was nothing left but six tall, smoke-
scarred Corinthian columns.

For a few minutes Leigh stood at the fence staring at the
remains of what must once have been a beautiful Greek
Revival mansion. Slowly she opened the gate and moved
up the path, strangely compelled to examine the destruction more closely. The trees nearest the blaze had been
singed by the heat, and the grass was tamped down by the
feet of those who had come to watch the fire. She made a
slow, silent circuit of the ruins, seeing the remnants of
years of living lying collapsed and charred in the basement. All around was the acrid, powdery smell of ash,
blackened wood, and death.

"Hey, girl," a Negress called from the lot next door. "What you prowling around there for?"

Leigh turned and walked to where she waited. "I was looking for the woman who lived in this house. I was looking for Monica Bennett."

The black woman narrowed her eyes and studied Leigh. "You found her, I reckon," she finally said.

"Found her? What do you mean?"

"She's still there somewhere, somewhere in the ashes."

It took Leigh a moment to comprehend the other woman's meaning, and a shiver of revulsion moved along her spine. "She died in the fire? Is that what you're saying?"

The Negress nodded. "When the house collapsed, you could hear her scream."

Leigh shivered again, as she imagined that tormented cry echoing above the creak of crumbling timbers. "Are you sure she's dead?" Leigh went on after a moment. "And what about her son?"

The woman knew she had a captivated listener, and slid her hands into her apron pockets before she went on. "Yes, ma'am, I'm sure. When the house caught fire from the rockets, Miss Monica took the boy into the yard. She left him there with her old mammy and went back inside to get her jewels and things. But the fire moved too fast, I guess. The place went up like tinder with no water to fight the fire."

"And Monica Bennett was trapped inside the house."

"Yes'um." The black woman nodded in confirmation.

Leigh stood stunned by what she had discovered. For whatever Monica Bennett had done to Hayes and to her, it did not warrant such an end.

"What happened to the boy, Mrs. Bennett's son?" she asked. "Where did he go?"

"I don't rightly know. He might be with friends now or in the orphan asylum. Old Mammy might have taken him somewhere herself, though I don't rightly know where that might be."

Leigh thanked the woman for her help and set off up the street deep in thought. Though Hayes had learned that Charles was not his son, he had clearly felt an obligation to insure his welfare. Now with the boy's mother dead and

Hayes not here to see to the child, the responsibility for his safety seemed to fall to Leigh. It was not an undertaking she welcomed, but it was an undertaking she was willing to accept.

Leigh spent the rest of the day making inquiries about Charles Bennett, and by noon the next day she had succeeded in locating him. His mother's mammy had taken him to the Sisters of Charity's hospital, where the two of them were sleeping on makeshift beds in one corner of the yard.

Charles Bennett, a shy child with huge black eyes, ran to the old black woman when Leigh approached. That he was clearly terrified by the turmoil in the city and the horrible way his mother had died was painfully obvious.

"I'm Leigh Banister," she told the older woman as she came nearer. "I've come to give you and the child what help I can."

The child's mammy eyed Leigh suspiciously at first and then, reading no malice in her face, spoke softly. "Do you know Mr. Hayes Banister, who came here in the spring?"

"I'm his wife," she confirmed.

The old black woman nodded. "His wife and not his widow. Well, I am pleased to hear that."

Leigh volunteered no information about Hayes or the incident months before, and Old Mammy kept silent, too. It was as if both women sensed there was nothing to be gained by bringing up the past.

"I went to the Bennett house yesterday," Leigh continued, "and when I heard about the fire, I knew that, for my husband's sake, I had to be sure the boy was safe."

"We've got no money and no home, but we're safe as can be here." There was a proud tilt to the old woman's chin, and Leigh knew she would let no harm befall the boy.

"Yes, I can see that," she agreed, "but what's to become of you? You can't live out in the open, not once winter comes." She glanced at the sea of refugees around her, knowing that they too would be needing accommodations. "Does the boy have family in the city? Is there someone who will take you in?"

The Negress shook her head. "There's only Miss Monica's family down in Georgia."

"In Georgia," Leigh repeated. "There's a whole war between you and them."

"Yes ma'am."

"But that's where you'd want to go if I could make arrangements?" Leigh offered dubiously.

The woman's dark eyes widened. "Could you do that, Mrs. Banister?"

"I suppose I could try," she agreed, wondering just how she would go about seeing to the welfare of Monica Bennett's child.

It was almost a week later when Leigh finally put Charles and his mammy on the train. Even as she gave the black woman the tickets and passes she had managed to secure, Leigh was not certain they would reach their destination. She was trusting in the fates to see the old woman and this frightened child safely through the lines, and Leigh was more than a little apprehensive as she stood on the station platform.

Through the open window, Leigh pressed a twenty-dollar gold piece into Old Mammy's hand and admonished her again to take good care of Charles. For his part, the boy only watched Leigh as he had every time she had come to see them. The huge, black eyes in his pinched face roved over her once more as the train began to roll. Leigh skipped along the platform waving, and Old Mammy waved back. Then slowly Charles Bennett raised one hand. It was the only acknowledgement of any kind he had given Leigh, and the faint, friendly gesture brought the sting of tears to her eyes.

When the train was out of sight, Leigh ambled back to the house she and Delia had been assigned after the surrender. She was glad of the effort she had made on her husband's behalf to see to Charles Bennett's welfare. There was no doubt that Hayes would approve of her actions, and she felt more at ease within her marriage than she had since learning from Nathan Travis why Hayes had gone to Vicksburg.

For the first time she was truly glad to be carrying Hayes's child, a child that would bind them forever as one. It heightened her appreciation of life in all its forms: in the child she had sent on his way to his grandparents, in the men she had fought so hard to save. It gave her hope for a future with the man she loved, a future that until that moment had seemed dark and uncertain.

Tullahoma, Tennessee
August 15, 1863

Dearest Leigh,

Those of us with General Rosecrans are preparing to move at last. Since the Army of the Cumberland has had the center of the Confederacy in its sights for some time, I don't think it will be breaching military security if I tell you that we are headed for the Tennessee River and Chattanooga beyond. With the opening of the Mississippi and the tightening block-ade of Southern ports, the only area yet to be pene-trated by Union forces is the very heart of the South. Chattanooga is the gateway to that region: a region rich in resources where most of the Rebel foundries and munition plants are located. Surely this will be one of the most significant campaigns of the war, and I consider myself fortunate to be with the Army for this crucial stage of maneuvers.

Hayes raised his pen from the page and sighed. The words he had written to Leigh seemed so impersonal and cool, not at all the sentiments a man should write to his wife on the eve of a campaign. He should pledge his love and express the feelings in his heart. But he could not bring himself to pen the words—not when so much lay unresolved between them, not when Leigh had refused to answer even one of his letters. For what must have been the hundredth time he wondered at her silence and cursed the way they had parted in St. Louis nearly two months before.

The minute he opened his eyes that warm June morning, he had known Leigh was gone. Hayes had dragged himself out of bed and across to the window, sure even before he pulled back the curtains that it was already too late to bid his wife good-bye. And, he had realized angrily as he stood staring out across the sunlit garden, this was the way Leigh wanted it: to leave without a word, without tears or explanations.

The night they had spent together had been spontaneous, filled with emotions neither one of them could deny. Leigh had given and taken pleasure freely, and they had both unabashedly murmured words of love. But this morning, Leigh had retreated. She had left without making another attempt at resolving their differences, without telling him one last time that she loved him.

Absently Hayes had begun to dress, pulling on his shirt and trousers with careless haste. But in the pocket of his jacket he found a carefully folded note wrapped in a gauzy square of lace. With clumsy fingers he had opened the paper.

Dearest Hayes,
    Please forgive me for my cowardice in not awakening you this morning. I wanted to remember our good-bye as it was said last night—with kisses and caresses, not with words. There are too many difficulties between us to try to resolve them in the few minutes we have left. We both need to think about what has happened, and perhaps it is just as well that for a time we will be apart.
    I love you, Hayes. More than anything, I want to spend my life at your side, but now there are other responsibilities calling us both, priorities far more important than our own happiness. Please be careful for my sake, and I will be careful, too. I yearn for the day when we can once more be together as man and wife. You are forever on my mind and in my heart.

Your wife,
Leigh

The words in a note or even in a good-bye could only say so much, and as Hayes read the message a second time, he felt a sting of disappointment. Yet what more was there for Leigh to say? She had told him that she loved him and promised him a future together. What more did he want from her?

The war, he realized, would have taken them apart even if everything between them was as it should be. They both had duties and responsibilities to discharge, and Leigh said she still cared. There was no doubt in his mind of her sincerity; no woman could counterfeit the feelings he had seen in her face as they had made love. Until they could be together, that memory, that unspoken pledge, would have to sustain him.

Absently he had looked down at the scrap of cloth Leigh had used to wrap the missive. The gift of a handkerchief had medieval associations: a favor from a lady to her champion, a promise of affection granted. Somehow the romantic gesture pleased him. He had always been struck by the incongruity between the frilly wisps of lace Leigh carried and the tailored clothes she wore, between the feminine bits of frippery in contrast to the strong, sensible woman he had taken for his wife. This was a fine example of her secret frivolity, a square of delicate linen with a deep fluff of Belgian lace along the edges. Even Leigh's special, spicy scent clung to the cloth. With a smile upon his lips he had tucked the square of cloth into his pocket.

Now as he sat at the edge of the campfire in the rolling hills of Tennessee, Hayes withdrew the handkerchief from the breast of his tunic and pressed it to his cheek. For weeks he had been waiting for some written word from Leigh: an answer to any of the letters he'd written, a few scrawled lines to let him know she missed him. He wanted and needed more from his wife than a promise secured by a frilly scrap of cloth. Yet the letter he had anticipated had not come, and he did not know what to think of Leigh's lengthening silence.

He glanced down at the page before him and tried to think of what more he had to say. Once they crossed the Tennessee River and turned toward Chattanooga, nearly thirty miles away, they might well be under fire. Deep inside he felt a stir of fear. Could he tell Leigh how he felt? Would she understand his uneasiness without believing him a coward?

With deliberation he penned the lines, framing sentences that expressed his concerns and uncertainties. He wrote of the country they had seen and the rugged hills that lay before them. He told her about the other men who attended Rosecrans's army as engineers and the friends he had made. This letter bore a certain similarity to the others he had written, and he ended it as he had ended the others, with a pledge of love.

Eloquently he spoke of his deepest feelings, hoping that the words would stir in Leigh the need for a like communication. Silently he sealed the letter and addressed it to the Western Sanitary Commission's offices in St. Louis. Were the nurses still at Vicksburg with Grant's army, he wondered, or had they moved on after the city fell? Had Leigh returned to St. Louis, or was she as far from home as he?

Wherever she was, whatever she was doing, he needed to hear a few words from her. It was one thing for a man to go into battle knowing that his wife and family were behind him. But Hayes had no assurance of Leigh's feelings, and it was a lonely man who posted the letter with the company clerk and went into the muggy Tennessee darkness to seek the comfort of repose.

19 &

September 23, 1863—Vicksburg, Mississippi

Leigh stood alone on the crest of Fort Hill, looking out across the earthworks and rifle pits to the city on the bluffs. Vicksburg was a town that had given its lifeblood to the war, losing its identity to a holocaust of shot and shell, sacrificing its culture in the face of the overwhelming Union victory. She had seen first-hand the destruction of Southern life that her mother had prophesied, and Leigh mourned with the people of the Confederacy for all that was being lost. Through the long, hot summer days, her emotions had become inextricably bound to the fate of the captured city, and now as she prepared to return to St. Louis, she had come seeking the solitude of this hilltop as a place to say good-bye.

As her eyes moved over the familiar scene, her melancholy grew. She saw the narrow, rutted road that ran into town, the barren, broken trees that had been shattered by the fierceness of the battle. Behind her lay Vicksburg's ruined hills, land that lay parched and exposed beneath the fiery setting sun.

How much had been destroyed in the name of slavery and union? she wondered. How much grief had been caused by the conflict of men's beliefs? Lives had been spent, resources depleted, a way of life damaged beyond repair. The price war extracted from both its victims and its victors seemed far too high for rational men to pay.

Surely anyone who viewed the scene before her could see the futility of this conflict.

Yet, miraculously, life went on. Already some of the trenches were beginning to disappear beneath a growth of vegetation as nature fought to reclaim its own, while back in town, enterprising men had begun to repair the damaged buildings. But Leigh knew the terrible division between North and South would not heal as quickly or completely as the land itself or be forgotten with the construction of a few new stores and warehouses. The rift between the factions in the nation ran deep, and it might well be decades before Americans would again call each other brother. For herself, Leigh had seen enough of war and was glad to be going home.

Her pregnancy had made that course inevitable. Though her swelling breasts and thickening waist were only now becoming evident, Leigh welcomed the prospect of returning home to await the birth of Hayes's child. There was a wondrous sense of renewal in carrying life within her body, and whatever the future brought, the baby would be her talisman against loneliness and fear.

That there had been no word of Hayes worried Leigh, especially since he had not answered the letter she had written early in July telling him she was pregnant. Was he sick or wounded or merely untouched by her news? She had been sure that once he received word of the child, he would set their differences aside and write to her. But the days had turned to weeks, and no letter had arrived.

With a sigh she turned from the familiar panorama before her to the road that led back to town. Delia's departure from Vicksburg would coincide with her own, since General Sherman's army had been ordered to Chattanooga and Mother Bickerdyke and Delia were going with them. After the Union defeat at Chickamauga, the Yankees had been driven back to Chattanooga and were now besieged by the Confederates. In the city the Federal troops were slowly being starved into submission, and if the Union Army was to survive, they must reestablish their supply lines and go on to fight again. No matter what happened far away in eastern Tennessee, Leigh knew there was always a pressing need for nurses. If it weren't for the baby she was carrying, she would be going, too.

Moving swiftly down the familiar road to town Leigh paused in the shadow of the courthouse to buy a bouquet of late-summer roses before heading back to the large, brick house she and Delia had occupied since the surrender. Since this was to be their last evening together, Leigh wanted to make it special and she knew how Delia loved to have fresh flowers on the table where they took their meals.

Coming into the entry hall, she stripped off her gloves and bonnet, then sought out a vase and took a moment to arrange the fragrant, deep pink blossoms.

"Delia?" Leigh called out when she was finished. "Delia?"

"Up here, Leigh," a soft voice answered, drawing Leigh up the steeply curving staircase to the second floor.

Pausing in the doorway, Leigh laughed at her friend's efforts to wrestle her small trunk toward the door. "Don't you know you shouldn't have more with you than what you're prepared to carry?" she admonished.

The diminutive blonde stood back with her arms akimbo. "This doesn't all belong to me!" she defended herself good-naturedly. "Some of this is Nathan's: at least two pairs of pants and a jacket, a few shirts and some boots. The last time we moved, he was here to help me, not off 'consulting in Washington.' Can you believe he just swung that trunk right up on his shoulder as if it weighed nothing at all? I have been considering calling one of the men from the yard, but it's really not so heavy, only very hard to handle."

Leigh gave an exaggerated frown. "Well, if that's all it is, I think between the two of us we can get it downstairs." Leigh bent to grab a handle, and after a moment's hesitation Delia caught the one on the opposite side of the trunk. Leigh was right. Between the two of them the trunk weighed hardly more than Leigh's carpetbag. Together they shuffled toward the steps.

"Do you want to go first, or shall I?" Leigh asked as they paused at the top.

"You go first since you're taller. I won't have to bend over so much."

As Delia said, the trunk was only cumbersome, and they made slow but steady progress down the curving stairway.

"Watch the wall," Leigh admonished as she guided her corner around the curve.

"Isn't this why they put coffin niches in the stairwell, to get big boxes like this down to the parlor?"

"This isn't nearly as big as a coffin, Delia!" Leigh said giggling.

"It certainly seems like it is to me!"

Leigh turned to make another comment and in that split second caught her heel of one of her slippers in the threadbare carpet. For an instant Leigh wavered, fighting to regain her balance, but with both hands around the handle of the trunk, there was no chance to steady herself.

"Leigh!" Delia screamed as she saw what was happening, but hampered by the trunk, she could not help.

As if time were slowly reeling out before her, Leigh felt herself falling. She twisted to catch at the stair rail, missed, and was helplessly tumbling again. She rolled twice, watching the world spin around her as her skirts tangled around her knees. Then she landed with stunning force in the center of the hall.

Delia had managed to retain a hold on the trunk to keep it from following Leigh down, but she had to struggle past it before she could reach where her friend lay.

"Leigh!" Delia demanded, bending over her. "Leigh, can you hear me?"

The concern in her friend's voice reached Leigh, though the words themselves did not. There was a buzzing in her head that sent dizziness swelling through her, and an ache centered deep inside ran weakness through her limbs. When Leigh tried to rouse herself, the hurt grew stronger until it resolved itself into a wrenching, twisting pain that tore through the center of her body. She writhed helplessly in its grip, and Leigh was vaguely aware that Delia was calling desperately for help.

Then two male servants were bending over her, lifting her gently. But with the movement Leigh's pain intensified, tearing at her vitals, and her tenuous hold on consciousness wavered and slipped away.

She never knew how long it was before she came to herself again, but after a time the blur around her resolved itself into her own room, across the hall from Delia's. One of the Army doctors was bending over her, and Delia stood at the foot of the bed, her fragile features marked with concern.

"She's going to lose that baby, and there's not a damn thing we can do about it," Leigh heard the doctor say. "She's a strong woman and will survive the concussion and her other injuries, but there's no chance for that child, no chance at all."

The sense of his words reached Leigh slowly, and she moaned, as physical and emotional pain mingled. "No," she whispered desperately. "Please don't let my baby die."

Delia was instantly beside her, catching Leigh's fingers in her tiny hand, stroking her friend's brow. "Oh, Leigh, we've been trying, trying so hard to save the baby, but there's nothing more to do."

"I want that child for Hayes's sake," Leigh pleaded, weeping. "I want it so he'll have reason to come home safely, so he'll have reason to love me again." There was a feverish desperation in Leigh, a need to fight the inevitable. There was so much more at stake than the future of her child.

"Hush, Leigh, hush," her friend pleaded. "Hayes loves you, and it's too late—"

"Delia, please," Leigh murmured, tightening her grip on the other woman's fingers. "Please, Delia, don't let this happen. I don't want to be alone again."

"You won't be alone; I promise you—"

"No, Dee, please. If we try—" The pain came again, wrenching through her body, and though Leigh fought to resist it, there was nothing she could do. It stole her strength and dulled her senses; it decimated her energy and will. She drifted away in a swirl of agony and despair as tears slid slowly down her cheeks.

"Hush, Leigh, hush. It's too late to save the baby," Delia crooned, not sure if Leigh could even understand the sense in what she was saying. "I'll stay here with you until you're better. We'll face this together, Leigh, and in time you'll mend. And when you're better, when Hayes is home again, there will be other babies."

Chattanooga, Tennessee
October 26, 1863

Dearest Leigh,

The siege here at Chattanooga continues, and food grows more and more scarce. The mountains around the city have proved nearly impenetrable to our supply wagons, and General Bragg is doing his best to starve us out. We have been existing on half rations for weeks, ever since Wheeler's raids on our supply trains proved so effective. More than three hundred wagons have been lost this month alone, leaving us without the very basics of life. It is odd what hunger can do to a man, everything from filling his dreams with groaning tables of roasts and desserts to making him see fine horseflesh as dinner on the hoof.

It's been damned cold too, and there aren't enough warm clothes or blankets. But we engineers have cooked up a little surprise for the Rebels that just might open a "cracker line" between here and the Union railhead at Bridgeport, Alabama.

Hayes could not say more to Leigh about the plan that was to be put into effect early the next morning, but he was proud of his part in it. Under the command of General "Baldy" Smith, the chief engineer of the Army of the Cumberland, Hayes and his fellows had been preparing a pontoon bridge to set into place nine miles down the Tennessee River at Brown's Ferry. If all went as they hoped, a portion of General Hazen's brigade would float downstream with the engineers to rendezvous with General Turchin's men, waiting on the eastern bank. Once the pontoon boats reached their destination, Hazen and Turchin's combined forces would fight to capture a bridgehead on the west side of the river, while the engineers bound the boats together to form the substructure for the bridge.

Normally, building bridges was not a particularly difficult or hazardous operation for engineering and pioneering corps as well trained as the ones with the Army of the Cumberland. The thing that made this undertaking so dangerous was the heavily fortified stretch of river the boats would have to navigate to reach their destination. That the pontoons would be moving with the current was a blessing, but Lookout Mountain fairly bristled with artillery, and they would have to pass directly under the Confederate guns to reach the ferry. The entire operation was an extremely well-kept secret, for if they were discovered, the flotilla might well be under fire from the moment they left Chattanooga.

Despite the dangers, the attack on Brown's Ferry was a well-considered plan, though one born of desperation. If it did not work, the possibility of the Union Army in the city holding out against Bragg and Longstreet's combined forces dwindled a little more. They had all begun this campaign with such high hopes for a speedy conclusion, but the Federal defeat at Chickamauga and now the siege at Chattanooga had again robbed the Northern forces of their momentum and a chance for victory. General Grant's arrival several days before had done a great deal for Union morale, but if the attack on Brown's Ferry was not successful, even his presence could not guarantee the Army of the Cumberland a second chance.

Hayes stared off to the southwest toward Lookout Mountain, where hundreds of Confederate campfires burned like beacons through the darkness, and then to the southeast, where hundreds more glowed bright on Missionary Ridge. Did the Union troops have any chance of escaping from the vise Bragg and his army held them in? Would the pontoon bridge open up a route of supply from the north before everyone in Chattanooga starved?

To Hayes's way of thinking, the long days laboring to turn the lumber from dismantled buildings into the pontoon boats had been time well spent, and the hours of toil had helped to take his mind off Leigh, as well. Though he had continued to write her faithfully, her silence ate at something deep inside him, and he could not help but wonder at her reasons for cutting him off. What had he done to deserve such treatment? How could she remain aloof when he had written time and time again how much he loved and missed her? It was one thing to go into danger knowing that a woman who cared was waiting for his return. But without any word from Leigh, without the reassurance he was seeking, he felt lost and strangely vulnerable.

Sighing, Hayes glanced down at the letter on his lap, wondering what more there was to say to his wife. He had complained about the cold and short rations. The way things stood between them, he could no longer write Leigh that he loved her, not when nearly five months had passed without a word. After a moment's thought he picked up the pen again and dipped it in the little traveling inkwell.

> I heard this afternoon that Mary Ann Bickerdyke and her nurses are expected to arrive with Sherman's army. This is wonderful news for the wounded from the battle at Chickamauga, since they have been desperately in need of care. But for myself, I hope you are not with her. Though my fondest wish is to see you once more, Chattanooga is a desperate place, and I hate to think of you suffering the privations the army is enduring.
>
> Since we will be up long before daybreak tomorrow, I must end my letter now. I hope this finds you well and that you will write as soon as you are able. I am impatiently awaiting your answer.
>
> > Your husband,
> > Hayes

After posting his letter, Hayes made his way back to his bedroll. It was cold in the tiny canvas tent, and pulling the blanket around him, Hayes curled up to catch what sleep he could. As he lay shivering, one hand crept inside his tunic to touch the lacy handkerchief Leigh had left him months before. His fingers moved over the soft cloth and the deeply ruffled edging, conjuring up the image of his wife. He let the flimsy handkerchief evoke memories of happier days when he and Leigh had been together, when they had been happy and deeply in love. With those thoughts in his mind and a soft smile upon his lips, he let his eyes slip closed.

It was foggy and faintly overcast when the fifty boats set out from Chattanooga at three the following morning, slipping silently from the city's waterfront in groups of five or six. They were odd craft, flat-bottomed and boxy, difficult to steer because they were the same shape fore and aft. Yet they were ideally suited to the job they were to do. Before the boats were far from shore, the river current caught them, drawing them swiftly downstream toward the treacherous hairpin curve at the base of Lookout Mountain. As they floated closer and closer to the fortifications, the men stretched out in the bottom of each boat, lying as still and silent as corpses. Only the oarsmen were allowed to raise their heads above the level of the gunnels to guide the boats along their clandestine course.

Hayes peered over the side of his own pontoon boat fighting to steer it as close as he could to the tree-fringed bank opposite the Confederate encampment. It was not an easy task, and in spite of the cold, he was clammy with perspiration. Through the shifting banks of fog, he could make out Rebel soldiers taking their ease around the campfires on the far bank and hear the songs the sentries sang to keep themselves awake. His heart beat slow and heavy as they passed beneath the eyes of the enemy, expecting at any moment to hear the pickets' cries echo across the puckered surface of the river and see the hillside blossom with smoke and flame. But finally they drifted into the downstream side of the turn, with no sign of discovery. Though they had not yet moved beyond range of the guns on Lookout Mountain, the most treacherous part of the passage was over. It was only the troops' fight for possession of the western bank and the road to the railhead at Bridgeton, and the engineers' desperately hard work of building the bridge that lay ahead of them.

When they reached Brown's Ferry the engineers discharged Hazen's troops on the western side of the river and set out to bring Turchin's men across. Though fierce resistance was being met on the far bank, the reinforced ranks of Union soldiers seemed to be progressing slowly inland, and when the last of the infantry had been transported, the engineers began to build their bridge.

Though a Rebel artillery emplacement a mile or so downstream from the ferry peppered them with fire, the pontoon bridge began to sprout from the eastern bank of the Tennessee. The nine-mile current at this point in the river made it difficult for those waiting upstream for their turn to link up with the growing span, but finally the engineers on Hayes's boat were directed to maneuver their pod into place.

As they worked to bring it into alignment with the others, shot fell to their left and right, drenching them with spray. Luckily, Hayes noted as he wrestled with one of the oars, the Confederate artillery seemed to be having a hard time getting the range. But then, just as the final connections were about to be made, the Rebels scored a direct hit at the center of Hayes's pontoon. Splinters of wood flew in all directions, and the deck bucked wildly beneath his feet as the concussion from the shell blew him backward into the river.

For Hayes there was no sense of time passing: one moment he was on the pontoon boat and the next in the freezing river water. He drifted dazed, at the mercy of the currents, and by the time his head began to clear, he was far below the bridge. He cried out to the men on the pontoon boats, but they were too far away to hear him, and the Rebel firing masked any sound he made.

Realizing there was no hope of fighting his way upstream, Hayes struck out for the eastern bank. But he had swum no more than a few strokes when the force of the current dragged him down. Light became diffused and dim as he was pulled deeper, and the sounds of voices and guns were dulled and muffled by the water. Far above him he could see the surface of the river, the lightening sky reflected through the murky, gray-brown depths. Fighting and twisting against the irresistible current, Hayes reached out for the brightness above him and the promise of life-giving air.

He had always been a strong swimmer, but his struggles were as nothing against the rampaging Tennessee. It batted him along as if he were a toy lost in a tempest, a leaf boat washed away by the force of swelling tides. He thrashed furiously against the unrelenting strength of the current, battling a phantom far stronger than he. As he struggled with the churning water, the blood drummed at his ears and temples, the air fluttered deep within his throat, aching for release. Pressure seemed to build within him until his lungs were swelled to bursting and lights flared and danced before his eyes. He felt the press of panic rising in him, a will to live throbbing fierce and strong.

But in the moment of greatest determination, he found insidious release. He was suddenly without the urge to struggle as he succumbed to forces stronger than his need for air. He lost the desire to seek the things that had seemed vital moments before: the slowly receding surface of the water, the rush of fresh air in his lungs.

Confused and broken, Hayes opened his mouth to cry out his surrender and felt the water fill his throat. Stunned, he drifted as light and shadow merged. Then darkness closed around his senses until there was no sight, no sound, no taste, no feeling. Hayes spun away into nothingness, lost and defeated by the river.

November 4, 1863—Bridgeport, Alabama

"Nathan!" Delia cried, flinging herself into her husband's arms. "Oh, Nathan, I've missed you so!"

Leigh watched with a now familiar tinge of envy as Delia and Nathan Travis stood together on the platform of the Bridgeport railroad station, hugging each other fiercely.

"I had no idea I'd be in Washington so long," she heard Nathan murmur before he kissed his wife.

Leigh knew that while Delia had not been happy about the separation, she had been just as glad to have her husband safe within the walls of the War Department rather than scouting and in danger all the time. Nathan had been called to the capital shortly after the surrender at Vicksburg and had been there until several days before. It was pure coincidence that she and Delia had been on their way to Chattanooga, too.

Hefting her carpetbag and following in the happy couple's wake, Leigh made her way to the carriage Nathan had hired for their use. After handing his wife inside, Nathan Travis greeted Leigh with a hug and a brotherly peck on the cheek.

"It's good to see you, Leigh. I hope you're feeling better."

Nathan's concern for her was evident in the set of his solemn features, and Leigh made an effort to bring some semblance of a smile to her face. "I'm fine, Nathan, just tired. Though I don't know what I'd have done without Delia this last month or so."

"I'm sorry about the baby," he said softly.

Leigh nodded. "So am I."

Not knowing what more to say, Nathan helped Leigh into the carriage, then climbed inside himself.

"I managed to rent two rooms at the hotel," he told them. "It sometimes takes several days to get passage to Chattanooga, so I thought we should be as comfortable as possible until our turn comes. Since the 'cracker line' was opened up a week or two ago, they've been shipping in supplies and reinforcements mostly."

"The siege has been lifted, then?" Leigh inquired.

"Not lifted exactly," Nathan answered, grinning, "but there's sure a big crack in the bowl the Rebels thought they had us in."

"Well, if supplies are getting through, there should be a little room for us," Delia reasoned.

"We'll manage to get you to Chattanooga somehow," Nathan reassured her, patting his wife's hand.

It was several hours later that a knock came at the door of Leigh's hotel room, and when she went to answer it, Nathan stood outside. He looked freshly bathed and barbered and more contented with himself than a cat that had lapped up all the cream.

"Come in, Nathan," Leigh offered, stepping back to let him pass.

With two long strides he was in the small room, glancing around at the décor. "These surely are tight quarters," he observed.

"Oh, they're fine really, better than we'll have at Chattanooga, I'll warrant. Where's Delia?"

"She was sleeping when I left," he said, then for no reason colored up. "We're going out to get some supper in a little while. Would you like to come along?"

For a moment Leigh considered his offer, then shook her head. "I think I'll order something in my room and turn in early."

Frowning, Nathan nodded. "Leigh, do you mind if I sit down?"

"No, of course not."

He took the single straight-backed chair, and Leigh settled herself at the edge of the bed, wondering what he wanted to say.

"Leigh," he began without preamble, "Delia is worried about you. She doesn't think you're strong enough to go back to nursing yet. It's only been a bit more than a month since you lost the baby, and—"

Leigh looked down at her hands. "I'm fine, really," she reassured him. "Delia took very good care of me while I was sick. I don't know what I would have done without her. But I want to go back to nursing; I want to feel needed again."

Nathan watched her for a long moment, seeing the sadness in her face. Once, Leigh Banister had been a beautiful, animated woman with drive and determination shining in her eyes. She had been filled with the courage of her convictions, with a vitality that usefulness brought. But she was not that woman now, and he wondered at the change in her. Was it the loss of the child and being away from the work she loved that had made her so pale and serious? Or was there more bothering her than she let on?

"Have you heard from Hayes?" Nathan queried.

Leigh's head came up sharply. "I don't know why you and Delia set such store by whether I have received a letter from my husband," she snapped, her words their own kind of confirmation.

"Have you written him about losing the baby?"

"No! Nor do I intend to!" Leigh knew her tone revealed far more than she would have liked. "He didn't care enough to write when I told him I was expecting a child, so I doubt it would make any difference if I wrote to tell him I had miscarried it."

Travis drew a long breath, his face grave. "I thought you recognized when Hayes was shot how important he really was to you."

"I knew it long before that," Leigh admitted, "but discovering his ties to Monica Bennett made things difficult between us, and Hayes hasn't written a word since I left St. Louis."

The dark-haired man sat watching her. "I can't explain his silence, Leigh," he finally said, "but there must be a reason for it. I just know that if you care for someone, you must work to make things right between you and never take love for granted. I made that mistake once in my life and vowed I would never make it with Delia."

Travis had never alluded to his life before the war, and even if Leigh had not been anxious to divert him, she would have invited his confidences. "What happened, Nathan?" she asked him softly.

Nathan hesitated, staring down at his hands. Then he began to speak, his voice husky and very low. "It was years ago in New Orleans, when I was just a young man trying to make my living on the river. I met and fell in love with a beautiful quadroon. Olivia had been raised to the only life available to a beautiful young woman of color: to be the mistress to a planter. But when we met and fell in love, she decided she preferred to be the wife of a poor man rather than the mistress of a rich one. It was not an easy life, and though we loved each other, I was gone more than I was home. We eventually had a child, and William became the delight of our life. We were very happy.

"But while I was away on the river, Olivia met one of the rich planter's sons in the French market, and he followed her home. He was not used to being denied the things he craved, especially the attentions of a woman like her. Olivia managed to lock him out of the house when he tried to force himself on her, but that night he returned with some of his friends. They were crazy drunk and broke down the door. Once they were inside, they had their way with my wife. They beat her and raped her and killed my son. And when it was over, they burned the house over her head to hide what they had done."

Leigh tried to express her sympathy, but Nathan waved her to silence. "When I returned and found out what had happened, I was mad with guilt and grief. But in time, that grief resolved itself into a need for revenge. It wasn't hard to find out who murdered my family; there are no secrets in New Orleans if someone really wants to learn the answers. I found out the men's names, all five of them. And though it took years, I tracked them down one by one."

"But why did they kill your wife and child?"

Nathan shrugged and slowly shook his head. "I never asked them why they did it. I suppose it was because they were crazy and drunk, because a woman of color, free or not, had no rights at all. It really didn't matter when I had my hands around their throats. Nothing mattered then but killing them.

"And when they were all dead, I began working for the Underground Railroad. As long as there was slavery, as long as one group of people could dictate the fate of others, there would be tragedies like the one Olivia and my son suffered. That incident turned me into an Abolitionist, but it also taught me that happiness is fleeting. That we should grab and fight for what we have because it may never come again."

Leigh had listened to Nathan's story with tears in her eyes. He had suffered terrible losses, been through so much. He deserved Delia's sweetness and all the happiness she could give him.

"Leigh, please," he continued after a moment, "realize what your love for Hayes means. There must be a reason why he hasn't written. Don't let it change what you feel for him. And don't let the things that happened last spring in Vicksburg undermine your feelings."

"It's odd, Nathan, but, in a way, losing the baby has made me understand what Hayes felt when he learned that Charles was in Vicksburg. I've begun to understand that special bond between a parent and his child."

Leigh made a little helpless gesture before she continued. "I was crushed by the loss of the baby for many reasons: because I wanted the child so much, because I had hoped it would mend the rift between Hayes and me, because it was part of him. But, most of all, I wanted it because it was a part of me, part of my bone and body. I felt connected to that child in a way I have never felt connected to another human being. I would have done anything to save it, anything at all."

"Don't you think Hayes needs to hear that; that you loved that child as a part of him, as a part of yourself? That you understand his motives for going into Vicksburg in ways that were impossible a few months ago?"

It was what they had fought over the night before she left St. Louis, Leigh reflected sadly. Hayes had been desperate to make her understand his bond to Monica and her son. Now she knew what the intangible tie of blood could mean, had learned its significance in the most painful way possible.

Nathan was right. Hayes did need to hear that she understood, to realize that she had been changed by the child she had carried.

Leigh nodded slowly. "But I still don't know where Hayes is. I'm not even sure where to send the letter."

"Where have you been mailing them until now?"

"To the military headquarters at St. Louis with the expectation that they would pass them on."

He nodded. "Let me make some inquiries about where he's been assigned."

"Oh, Nathan, I'd feel so much better if I just knew what Hayes is doing."

He patted her hand and rose to go. "You write that letter, Leigh. You tell him that you've come to understand his feelings, let him know what you've been through. Then tell Hayes that you love him; no man can hear that often enough."

"Nor can any woman," she pointed out with a slow, wry smile.

Nathan smiled too, a smile that made his angular face almost handsome. "You write that letter, and I'll see about the rest."

"Yes, I will," Leigh promised.

"And you won't change your mind about going out to dinner with us?"

"Not tonight. I think writing this letter is too important."

Nathan nodded in agreement.

"I'll see you and Delia in the morning. And, Nathan, thank you for everything."

November 10, 1863—Chattanooga, Tennessee

Vicksburg had been the high place on low ground, while Chattanooga was a low place surrounded by mountains. The city on the bluffs was at the apex of a turn in the Mississippi, while Chattanooga curled protected in a wide meander of the Tennessee. Yet in 1863, both cities shared a common fate. They were dominated and overwhelmed by the military presence; beset and besieged by armies in the throes of war. They were helplessly embroiled in the bitter conflict that would decide the future of a nation.

Surrounded by the river on the north and the Confederate encampments on the south, the Union Army lay weak and gaunt after the privations of the siege. From the heights of Lookout Mountain and Missionary Ridge, the Rebels commanded the whole city with score upon score of guns. Until only a week before they had held the clear advantage, and even now appeared to be in the far stronger position. But the Federal troops had Grant in their camp and would soon have Sherman as well, and the Union had won battles with little more.

To reach the beleaguered city Leigh, Delia, and Nathan had followed the same trail that the supplies traveled: over Raccoon Mountain from Bridgeport, Alabama; across the pontoon bridge to the north bank of the Tennessee; across the river again and into Chattanooga. It was a long, circuitous route, but it was the precious "cracker line" that had given the Union Army hope.

Once they were in the city, accommodations were provided for Nathan and Delia in one of the town's empty houses, while Leigh elected to stay at the military hospital near the edge of town. There she was given a cursory welcome by the head surgeon and assigned a small, unheated tent for her use. Unpacking a few minutes later, Leigh prepared for a long stay. As she had followed an orderly across the hospital compound, she had seen men desperately in need of care. Some must have been the remaining wounded from the battle at Chickamauga back in September, but there were others in the hospital tents who were succumbing to the worsening weather and privations they had suffered.

During the days Leigh and the Travises had spent at the railhead in Bridgeport watching the supplies come in, it had become evident that the Union was preparing for another battle. Grant was stocking weapons and ammunition and waiting for Sherman and his troops to arrive. When they did, there would surely be a confrontation with the Rebels, and, judging by the odds the Union troops would be facing, the need for medical personnel would be dear.

It would be good to feel useful again, Leigh thought as she hung her two calico dresses on the tent post. She had missed nursing during her convalescence and was anxious to assume her new duties.

From the bottom of the carpetbag she took the carefully folded letter she had written to her husband and tucked it between the pages of a book of sonnets Lucas had given her years before. It was odd, she reflected as she stood fingering the dog-eared volume, how her feelings for the two men in her life had become reconciled. Lucas's love had been tender and devoted, but a thing of childhood. Hayes was the passion of her life.

The letter to Hayes had taken a long time to write, with many false starts and pauses to brush away tears. In it she had explained all that had transpired since the end of September and the changes in her feelings. It had expressed her new, hard-won understanding of what had occurred in Vicksburg and of Hayes himself. In it she had opened herself to her husband, and instinctively she knew that would convince Hayes of her sincerity as nothing else could. With Nathan's assurance that the letter would reach

Hayes directly, Leigh felt more optimistic than she had been in months.

She fell quickly into the routine at the Chattanooga hospital. Leigh was no green girl and knew immediately what needed to be done, as if she had worked in military hospitals all her life. She made beds, dressed wounds, and soothed the men with fevers, things she had done a thousand times before. She cooked and cleaned and washed, taking charge of the meager accommodations to make the men as comfortable as possible. It felt good to be back at nursing: to see grateful faces and know she had earned that appreciation; to see relief and know she had soothed the pain. It was late in the afternoon several days later when a wiry young corporal sought her out in the hospital kitchen.

"Mrs. Banister," he began, with a stiff, self-conscious bow, "General Grant would like to see you in his office, if you please."

Leigh was baffled by the summons, and paused only long enough to tell someone where she was going and grab a shawl before she followed the corporal to a carriage. The drive to Grant's headquarters was accomplished quickly and in complete silence. Why on earth would General Grant want to see her? Leigh wondered, and patted her hair into place as best she could. What could the commander of the Army possibly want with her?

Then she was being ushered down a hall and into a room where General Ulysses Grant awaited her. She had seen him from a distance at Vicksburg on many occasions, riding the line of fortifications on his little black horse with his son Fred slung up behind him in the saddle. He was a small man, with an unruly growth of whiskers and eyes that seemed to have seen far too much for his years.

He glanced up as Leigh entered and indicated a chair on the near side of his cluttered desk. "I hope you'll excuse me if I don't rise, Mrs. Banister, but a recent riding accident has left me a little lame."

"Certainly, sir," Leigh answered with appropriate deference as she took her chair.

"You were one of Mrs. Bickerdyke's women at Vicksburg, weren't you?" he asked. "Or was that at Shiloh, Mrs. Banister?"

"It could have been either, General. I was with the nurses at both battles."

"What you women have been able to do to help my men has been nothing short of miraculous, and all of you deserve to be commended for your splendid work."

"Thank you, sir," she acknowledged. "I'm looking forward to welcoming Mother Bickerdyke to Chattanooga, as soon as General Sherman arrives."

"Yes," the general agreed wryly, a smile creeping to tweak his lips. "We're all looking forward to Sherman's arrival."

Then Grant's momentary levity was gone. He pulled thoughtfully at his beard before he continued, changing the subject abruptly. "Mrs. Banister, are you married to Captain Hayes Banister, Captain Banister of the First Missouri Engineers?"

Leigh caught her breath. It hadn't occurred to her that this audience with General Grant could have anything to do with her husband. "Yes," she replied, sucking in a deep draught of air. "Hayes Banister and I are married."

Grant hesitated for a moment longer, watching her. "Then, Mrs. Banister, it is my unpleasant duty to inform you that your husband is missing and presumed dead. General Smith sent a letter to inform you, but when it came to my attention that you had arrived to work at the hospital here, I felt I should break the news to you personally."

For an instant Leigh turned the general's words over in her mind, feeling stunned and shaken. It was as if this man had given her a gift, the knowledge of where her husband was, then immediately snatched it away.

Leigh swallowed hard. "What happened?" she asked unsteadily.

"You knew, of course, that your husband had been here in Chattanooga since September, through the battle at Chickamauga and the siege."

"Here?" Leigh murmured, barely breathing.

"Captain Banister and the other engineers who laid the pontoon bridge were responsible for the survival of the Army of the Cumberland. If it hadn't been for their courage and daring—"

"How did it happen?" Leigh interrupted.

Grant looked across the desk at the determined young woman before him, reading pain and grief, but no uncertainty, in her eyes. "As the engineers were lashing the pontoons into place, they were under constant fire. Your husband's section was hit by one of the shells. Captain Banister and several others were blown off the bridge and into the river."

"But Hayes is a very strong swimmer," Leigh began hopefully. "Surely there's a chance he was able to make it to the bank."

"I think you should realize that he may well have been wounded by the ball or gone into the water unconscious. The men caught one glimpse of him before he disappeared, and there was no sign of him along the riverbank. No sign of him as far downstream as we dared search."

"But your men may have missed him somehow," she argued.

Grant nodded in agreement, but she could read denial in his eyes. "I suppose that is possible," he conceded, "but I doubt it's likely. I'm sorry, Mrs. Banister. I think your husband is dead, and it's probably better if you accept rather than challenge the Army's findings."

Leigh sat staring for a moment, trying to take in all she had learned. Until just a week before, Hayes had been here in Chattanooga, assigned to an engineering company. He had walked these streets, looked out across these hills just as she had. Somehow it seemed so unfair that they should miss each other by inches when they needed so much to see and touch and talk. Nor would she ever see or touch or talk to Hayes again, if she believed what General Grant was telling her. If she took what he said as true, she must believe Hayes was dead, gone from her forever.

"Mrs. Banister?" General Grant's tone was gentle. "I'm terribly sorry about your husband."

The words of consolation were kind, but they also spoke of dismissal. Leigh came unsteadily to her feet, feeling as if her bones had turned to jelly. "Yes," she managed to murmur. "Thank you for taking time to tell me what happened, General."

"Your husband was a very gallant soldier to risk his life

to break the siege. We're all grateful for his sacrifice, and yours.''

"Yes . . ." Leigh made her way to the door. She felt the coolness of the knob beneath her fingers, moved forward as the panel swung outward.

The hall was filled with dozens of civilians and officers waiting to talk to Grant. She moved through them like a sleepwalker.

Hayes, dead. It was impossible, impossible.

The young corporal came to where Leigh stood. "Are you all right, ma'am?" he inquired, his words reaching Leigh from a distance.

"Of course I'm all right," she heard herself assure him. Then, without warning, a golden mist swirled around her until the corporal, her surroundings, and her despairing thoughts were swept away.

20 ↶

Winter 1863—Chattanooga, Tennessee

"Got any more panado ready?" Mother Bickerdyke asked as she crossed the hospital compound to where
Leigh was stirring a huge pot of the steaming, fragrant
gruel. Panado was the mixture the older woman had invented as nourishment for the sick and injured. The for-
mula varied with the ingredients at hand, but for the most
part it was a combination of hot water, whiskey, brown
sugar, and crumbled hardtack. Its restorative properties
were legend among the wounded, and as the stretcher-
bearers brought in more and more casualties from the
fighting at Lookout Mountain, the nurses had made up
gallons of the stuff.

"This pot is ready," Leigh offered, swinging one iron
kettle away from the flames.

Delia joined them at the fire. "Lord, it's cold," she
muttered, and set to work doling out cups of the steaming
panado. "I wish we had just one wagonload of blankets to
give out. The tents are completely full, and there are
wounded lying everywhere without a shred to cover them."

Leigh shivered as an icy blast of wind swept through the
encampment, fully in sympathy for the men lying on the
ground around her. In spite of the months the Union troops
had been in the city, the hospital at Chattanooga was the
most primitive one she had ever seen. There were far too
few tents to shelter the wounded. The cooking facilities

were almost nonexistent, and the supply of medicines, warm clothes, and blankets was critically short.

After the siege was broken, it had been military stores, not sanitary supplies, that had been brought into the town. Grant had been intent on capturing the Confederate strongholds around Chattanooga, and weapons and munitions had taken priority over all the rest as the wagons came rumbling into the town from Bridgeport. And while it was not Leigh's place to question the general's decisions, she fervently wished that he had seen fit to provide the nurses and doctors with better facilities and more supplies.

Soon another kettle of panado was ready, and as Leigh ladled the thick mixture into cups, she glanced across the compound to where the surgical tent stood. The doctors were hard at their grisly work by the wavering light of lanterns. As she watched, one surgeon cut into a soldier's ravaged flesh, then paused to warm his stiffened fingers in the vapor that rose from the man's body. The scene was like a vision of hell, completed by the number of disembodied limbs piling up outside the surgery. Still the wounded continued to arrive, brought in by stretcher-bearers who staggered with weariness. All that any of the nurses could do was tend the fire and make panado to warm the survivors, bathe and dress their wounds, and offer comfort to the patients who had felt the Army surgeons' knives.

The "Battle in the Clouds" was the romantic name the newspaper reporters gave the conflict on Lookout Mountain, because of the thick mist that shrouded the peak's rugged terrain. But there was nothing romantic about the brutality of the fighting or the casualties who continued to arrive all the following day. When the fog cleared on the third morning, the Union flag waved from the summit, and Grant had claimed his victory. But the true price for Lookout Mountain and for Missionary Ridge to the east was paid by the hundreds of dead and two thousand wounded who were in dire need of care.

The weeks that followed the victory were cold and grim for the Federal troops and nurses in Chattanooga. Until the Sanitary Commission managed to have some supplies delivered just before Christmas, the hospital existed at a subsistence level. With the shipment came a good supply of baker's yeast. Using that and the flour confiscated from a nearby mill, Mother Bickerdyke set up a bakery. Bricks from the chimney of a ruined house were used to build an oven, and in the weeks that followed she baked as many as five hundred loaves of bread a day. From the dried fruit that came, she made pies to tempt the most feeble appetite and cookies miraculously concocted from hardtack crumbs and sugar. Of necessity Leigh learned to bake too, adding the accomplishment to the list of others she had learned at Mother Bickerdyke's elbow.

Christmas came to Chattanooga like an unwelcome guest: dreaded and empty-handed. None of the packages from families in the North were allowed to take up vital space on the transport wagons, and the rumor was that they stood in head-high piles at the Bridgeport depot. Morale at the hospital and in the Federal camp fell dangerously low. But on Christmas Eve the nurses made batches of molasses taffy for sick and well alike, and the men spent the evening pulling taffy and singing songs around the campfires.

The winter dragged on in the city with subzero temperatures that gave lie to the Union conviction that the Southern climate was warm and mild. Storms roared down from the mountains, starching the canvas hospital tents with a coating of ice, turning the footing rough and treacherous in the encampments, and making warmth an impossible dream. The fuel the pioneering companies cut was used up with unbelievable speed, and the men were hard-pressed to keep up with the demands of the camp and hospital. Nor was the rest of the country being spared the bad weather. Some newspapers proclaimed this the winter of the century, and Bran wrote that the Mississippi at St. Louis had frozen solid.

The cold weather brought more nurses from the North to help with the burden of caring for the sick. Mary Livermore and Annie Wittenmyer arrived on New Year's Day, and women from other parts of Tennessee came to help, too.

One cold February afternoon, Mother Bickerdyke assigned Leigh one of these newcomers, and Leigh set out to show her the hospital. Sarah was a slight, spare woman only a few years Leigh's senior, and they took to each other instantly. Bundled in a heavy coat against the frigid weather, Leigh took the other woman around the camp and through the hospital tents, pointing out where supplies and medicines were kept and introducing her to the other nurses, doctors, and patients.

When they had completed their rounds, Leigh led Sarah to the relative warmth of the cook tent, and they settled down at the end of one long table to visit over a cup of tea.

"What brings you to Chattanooga, Sarah?" Leigh asked, shrugging out of her coat and stripping off the fingerless gloves many of the nurses had taken to wearing.

"After my husband was killed," the other woman began, staring down into her cup, "I was very despondent. I had my son to keep me occupied, it's true, but that wasn't enough somehow. Our men were giving so much in this war that it seemed only right that we women should do something, too. So I began to go to one of the local hospitals. I found I enjoyed the work, enjoyed being able to help. And when I heard there was such a desperate need here at Chattanooga, I felt compelled to come and help. My mother is looking after David while I'm away."

"What unit was your husband with?" Leigh asked conversationally.

"Justin was with the Confederate Artillery," Sarah admitted with a tilt of her chin.

Leigh did her best to hide her surprise at the other woman's words. Most of their volunteers harbored Union sympathies, but this woman had admitted strong ties to the Confederacy.

In response to Leigh's silence, Sarah continued. "It seems to me that people in trouble need whatever help we can give them, and I've nursed men from both the North and South."

Leigh nodded in agreement. "So have I."

"Then you understand how I feel?"

"Yes, I do, though you are likely to meet others here who won't," Leigh warned. As she spoke, she picked up a spoon and reached across the table for the container of sugar.

As she did, Sarah drew a sharp breath and caught Leigh's left hand between both her own. "Where did you get this ring?" she demanded suddenly.

For an instant Leigh looked down at the signet ring shining in the lantern light. It would have seemed almost delicate on a man's hand, but on Leigh's it was broad and substantial with the wide, gold band melding into the upper surface where three initials were entwined. Since she had come to Chattanooga, there had been little time to grieve for Hayes or dwell on the past. But as she stared down at the ring, a kaleidoscope of memories spun through her brain: of Hayes placing the ring on her finger, of what she had discovered marriage could be, of the way they had parted and the months of painful silence before she had learned that he was dead. Involuntarily Leigh snatched her hand from Sarah's grasp.

"Where did you get it?" Sarah demanded again, her voice growing harsh with the need for a reply.

Leigh swallowed around the lump in her throat, wondering why this woman wanted to know about the ring, her last tangible bond to her own dead husband. "It is my wedding band," she said softly. "My husband took it from his cousin's body on the battlefield at Shiloh and gave it to me when we were married a month or so after."

"Hayes?" Sarah murmured, the single word hardly more than a whisper.

"Yes, Hayes, Hayes Banister." A chill of premonition touched Leigh's heart as she realized who this woman must be. "And you are Sarah Dean, Justin's widow."

For a moment the two women stared at each other in stunned silence. As was often Mother Bickerdyke's way, they had been introduced by first names only, and there had been no reason to ask for more than that.

"Yes, I am. But how . . ."

Quickly Leigh sketched the story Hayes had told her of sitting with his cousin the night he died. It brought back other memories Leigh could not share with Sarah: of Hayes coming to find her at Savannah, of the pain and anger he had felt at his cousin's death, of the need for care and comfort she had seen in his eyes.

"Hayes wrote you about Justin, but the letter was intercepted, and after that he dared not write another," Leigh finished.

"Oh, Leigh, you don't know what it means to me to

know that Justin didn't die alone." There were tears in
Sarah's eyes. "It has haunted me that he fell and died and
was buried in a common grave with no one to mark his
passing. I feel so much better to know Hayes was there."

"Hayes was glad he had been able to make Justin's last
hours more comfortable, but he was surprised to find any
Deans with the Confederate Army."

"I didn't want Justin to go. To me there seemed no
reason, but he was convinced that the Tennessee units
could not go into a fight without him. It was a man's
vanity, I suppose. But it cost him his life and David a
father." Sarah paused. "But how did Hayes come to give
you Justin's ring as a wedding band?"

"We were married in something of a hurry a few months
after Shiloh. Hayes didn't have the time to buy a wedding
band, so he gave me Justin's ring, just until he could get
another. Somehow he never did."

As the two women talked, it became increasingly obvious to Leigh what she must do about the keepsake. She
had known all along that Justin's signet ring had been a
loan, and, as much as it meant to her, it was time to return
it to its rightful owner. She had memories of Hayes to
carry her through a lifetime, memories to cling to for all
her days. She had stored away Hayes's laughter and his
tenderness like a treasure; she had cherished the wondrous
contentment she had felt in his arms. She knew Sarah must
have her memories of Justin, too. But David had nothing
of his father, and it seemed wrong to keep something
Hayes had intended for Justin's son.

Slowly Leigh took the golden ring from her own finger
and laid it in Sarah's palm. "Hayes meant to bring the ring
to David when the war was over, and I think he would
want me to pass it on now that I have the chance."

Sarah hesitated for a moment before her fingers closed
around the bit of gleaming metal, holding it tightly in her
palm. There were tears spilling from her bottomless brown
eyes when she spoke at last. "Oh, Leigh, you can't know
what this means, to have some part of Justin for David. I
realize your sacrifice, and I thank you with all my heart."

The two women sat silent for a long time: Sarah caught
up in memories the other woman could not share, and

Leigh trapped in a torment of her own. She had done the right thing, the thing Hayes would have wanted her to do, but she felt bereft and lost at forfeiting her last link with her husband.

Finally Sarah slid the signet ring onto her finger and brought out a handkerchief to dry her cheeks.

"Leigh, I thank you. You'll never know what this ring means to me and to David."

Leigh smiled sadly and reached across to squeeze the other woman's hand. "Returning the ring was what Hayes intended, and I was glad to carry out his wishes."

"And Hayes," Sarah asked, after a moment. "Where is Hayes serving now?"

Leigh had known the question was inevitable, and she had tried to steel herself to give the answer. "Hayes died here at Chattanooga, several days before I arrived."

November 29, 1864—St. Louis, Missouri

St. Louis had changed since Leigh had left the city, but perhaps no more than Leigh had changed herself. That soft summer morning a year and a half before, she had left the man she loved sleeping soundly in her bed, never suspecting as she had stood silently watching him that it would be the last glimpse she would ever have of Hayes. She carried the memory with her still: of his beard-shadowed face half-hidden in the pillow, of the web of his silky lashes lying dark upon his cheeks, of the strong lines of his body clearly outlined by the bedclothes. Then she had been confused and frightened by the snarl of emotions she had not been able to reconcile. But these last months had brought her the understanding she was seeking and with it a regret that would haunt her all her days. She had carried a child and lost it, sought enlightenment and found it. She had come face-to-face with her weaknesses and turned them into strengths. It was only now that she believed herself worthy of the man Hayes Banister had been, only now that she was ready to give all the love Hayes had craved and deserved. But Hayes was dead, and the loss had marked her deeply.

In the last months, she had accompanied Mary Ann Bickerdyke to Atlanta in the wake of Sherman's army. She had endured the hardships the soldiers had faced and done what she could to help the civilians innocently caught up in the backlash of the war. She had seen men die and had saved the lives of others. She had immersed herself in nursing and had been readily absorbed. Since that day in June of 1863, she had known happiness and pain, conviction and cowardice, generosity and loss. It had made Leigh wholly a woman of her times, determined and unbowed. She had come to grips with the shadows from the past and was ready to start her life anew.

On the morning she had left, the St. Louis waterfront had been silent and deserted, symbolic of a languishing city that had been vanquished by the war. Today it was alive with steamboats and activity, as if the city had a new lease on the future just as Leigh did herself. Her spirits rose as she looked out across the bags and barrels, the boxes and crates, and the mobs of busy people who made the city thrive.

The war in the West was over now that Sterling Price had been driven from Missouri, and though battles were still being fought in the East, every day brought the inevitable Federal victory closer. Sherman was marching to the sea, Grant had Petersburg under siege, and the Shenandoah Valley was being swept of Rebel soldiers. There were still battles left to fight, victories to win, and men to nurse, but far ahead she could see an end to the nation's suffering, and Leigh was infinitely glad.

As the steamboat pulled into its dockage, she caught sight of her father's carriage parked on the rise at Wharf Street. Simultaneously, Bran caught sight of her, and the joyous wave he gave spoke of a welcome that warmed her heart. Minutes later Horace met her at the end of the gangway and swept her up in a warm embrace. Bran and Felicity had waited in the carriage, but their greeting was no less exuberant.

Back at the town house in Lucas Place, they ate a celebratory dinner as they shared stories of their recent activities. Horace was still working with the Quartermaster Corps, though on a much less active level than he had been earlier in the war. Bran, though hampered by his crutches, had taken up helping at the Confederate prisons. Of them all, it was only Felicity who life had not appreciably changed.

Bran once more looked like the young man Leigh had always known, though his natural exuberance was tempered by a serious side that Leigh had never seen.

The change in her father was more startling and pronounced. Horace seemed at least a decade older than he had been at the start of the war. The clothes that had once flattered his robust physique now hung in folds around him, and the light in his eyes that had marked him as a man of power had been extinguished by the hardships he had seen. It was upsetting for Leigh to see the toll the war had taken on her father, as if her memories of childhood had somehow been betrayed. As she watched Horace and noted the subtle changes in his voice and manner, she wondered if it was the war or something much more personal that had been the cause.

"Well, Leigh," Horace addressed her when Bran and Felicity were gone, "what are your plans now that your stint at nursing is done?"

"It's not over, Father, just as the war has not yet reached its conclusion. Sherman sent Mrs. Bickerdyke and me home from Atlanta, but once he reaches Savannah, we'll be joining him again."

"And when will that be?" he inquired.

Leigh gave a lazy shrug. "Come spring, perhaps. It depends on how much resistance he meets cutting across Georgia, I suppose."

Horace took a seat on the settee opposite her. "Though the Confederacy is all but defeated, I doubt the Rebels will give up without a fight."

"No," Leigh agreed.

"But what then? What will you do? Will you return to St. Louis?"

"Father," Leigh began, voicing the plans she had been pondering for months, "I'm going to take the money Grandfather left me and go to medical school back East." At Horace's stunned expression, Leigh hurried to explain. "I've spent the best part of four years living and working in Army hospitals, and I know my capabilities. Even before the war I wanted a career in medicine, but I was afraid. Now that I've seen the worst men can do to each other and proved myself as a nurse, I think it's time to learn all the things battlefield experience could not teach me.''

"But, Leigh, medicine is no place for a woman. You need a home, a family—"

"What I need is for Hayes to turn up alive," she finished sadly.

"There's no hope of that, is there?"

Leigh shook her head. "They never found his body, but it seems useless to pin my hopes on the possibility that he got out of that river somehow. He's been missing for over a year, and I have to go on without him. Hayes would have understood about medical school; he understood about everything I wanted to do.''

Horace fell silent, and the sound of the fire crackling in the grate and the ticking of the ormolu clock seemed loud in the opulent parlor.

"Your mother would have understood too, wouldn't she?" he asked after a few moments.

"Yes, she does understand. I had a letter from her just before I left Atlanta.''

"And how is she? I haven't had word of her since she left St. Louis.''

Leigh looked across at her father. "Why don't you go to see for yourself? She's at Uncle Theo's plantation, and I think she'd be pleased to see you.''

"If she wanted to see me, she should never have left St. Louis." Horace's voice was filled with pain.

Leigh paused before she spoke, measuring her words with care. "She said you wouldn't understand her reasons for leaving; that even though she loved you, she had to go away.''

"Why?" he croaked. "Why did she go?"

"Because she had to prove her strength before she had anything of herself to give. Because you were destroying each other and any love you'd ever had.''

"Oh, God, yes," Horace admitted after a moment, his face softening with the memories. "We did love each other once. I was in love with Althea the first moment I laid eyes on her on the street in New Orleans. She was so beautiful, Leigh, and you are so much like her. I followed her into a millinery shop, drawn as if we were joined by some invisible thread. At first I was afraid to approach her. It was obvious that she was from an old Southern family, and though I had done well myself, I was essentially a self-made man.

"Still, I couldn't help myself." He smiled gently as he remembered. "She was trying on a bonnet, some frilly thing with feathers and pink ribbon. It made her look so soft and fragile, and I knew right then I wanted to hold her and protect her. The proprietor had begun to watch me suspiciously, so I had to take my courage in my hands and talk to her. I finally said—"

" 'Even the brightest plumage is no match for your beauty, madame.' " Leigh laughed. "Yes, Mother told me. She also said you left the store without even taking time to ask her name."

In spite of the years that had intervened, a faint flush rose in Horace's cheeks. "Yes, I did run like a scared rabbit, but I was not so much of a fool as to put her out of my mind. I found out who she was and I married her, in spite of her family's objections. And I did my best to make her happy."

"She still loves you, you know."

"Does she?" Horace asked almost hopefully. "If she loves me, why did she go away?"

Leigh sighed. "We both did Mother a great disservice," she began slowly. "Mother was a diamond, and we treated her like glass. She was far stronger and more capable than either of us let her be, and the problems arose from her idleness, her own dissatisfaction. Hayes understood that long before I could."

Horace sat frowning, digesting Leigh's words.

"Father, why don't you go to her?" she urged. "Mother loves you, and you still love her. The war is no longer keeping you apart. Why don't you go to Louisiana and see if you can't find a way to work things out. It's foolish for you both to be unhappy when there's a chance to mend the rift."

"Did she say she was unhappy? Did she say that she was ready to come back?" Horace inched forward on the settee, intent on his daughter's answer.

"I think you need to talk to her and ask her those questions yourself."

Leigh came to her feet and went to rest one hand on his shoulder. "Take your courage in your hands and approach Mother as you did that day in the millinery shop. Go to Louisiana and see if you can make things right between you."

"Do you really think she'll listen to me after all that's happened?"

"I think you will have to learn to listen to her, too. And if you do, Father, I doubt you will be sorry."

Horace's eyes were narrowed speculatively, as if he were seeing other days. "Perhaps I will go to Louisiana, Leigh," he said slowly. "Perhaps I will go after all."

December 27, 1864

Leigh Banister puttered around the Penningtons' spacious parlor, plucking dead leaves from the plants and straightening the antimacassars. She was too preoccupied to read or sew, and with her father away in Louisiana the house seemed silent and oppressive. Earlier in the day, she had gone with Bran to the Gratiot Street Prison and found that the stories Althea had told were true. The men confined there were filthy and vermin-infested, their cells overcrowded and freezing cold. There were no blankets or clean clothes, and the meager amount of food allowed the inmates was often spoiled and inedible. Nor could she find comfort in believing that the Gratiot Street Prison was the exception to the rule, not when conditions at Camp Douglas near Chicago and at the prison in Elmira, New York, were the scandal of the North.

"They say the Southern prisons are even worse," Bran had told her as they drove home, "and it's small wonder, since the Confederacy can barely feed and clothe its army."

Since she had returned to the house, Leigh had not been able to banish the Confederate prisoners from her mind or drive the chill of their plight from her bones. As she shivered with the memory of the things she'd seen, she worried about the care these men would need when the war came to an end. Surely they could not be expected to find their way home by themselves without food, transportation, and places to rest. These men would be marked by the war in a far different way from the men who had fallen in battle and would need at least as much patience and care to heal their invisible wounds. Perhaps she should talk to someone at the Sanitary Commission about her concerns, Leigh mused as she added coal to the fire in the grate and stirred the winking embers to life.

As she bent over her work she became aware of a commotion in the hall, and a man suddenly burst through the double doors into the parlor. Whirling at the sound of his approach, Leigh dropped the poker with a clatter and stared in disbelief at Major Aaron Crawford.

"I tried to keep him out, Miss," the maid began, "but he forced his way in."

Aaron's heavier voice cut across the servant's explanation. "I was afraid you wouldn't see me if I simply gave her my card, and since I leave for the Eastern theater of the war tomorrow, I was determined to see you."

"Shall I call one of the men, miss, to see this gentleman out?" The maid stood her ground in spite of Crawford's intimidating presence.

Leigh paused to consider the major's words, feeling both curious yet profoundly uneasy. Why did Aaron want to see her? What business could be so pressing that it had brought him here? "It's all right, Matty," she conceded. "I'll see Major Crawford and find out what he wants."

With a frown of disapproval on her face, the girl turned to do her mistress's bidding.

"Thank you for seeing me, Leigh," Aaron began, as the maid closed the doors behind her. "I would hate to leave the city without the latest word on Althea and a chance to say good-bye."

Graciously Leigh indicated a chair for her guest and settled herself on the edge of the long, horsehair settee. She knew that her mother's friendship with this man had cooled in the months before she had gone away, but he still seemed as concerned for her welfare as one of Althea's dearest friends. The inconsistency made Leigh wary, but she gave Crawford his answer anyway.

"Mother's well and happy in Louisiana, Aaron. As a matter of fact, my father has gone to visit her, and they have reconciled." The news that had arrived by letter Christmas Eve had made Leigh's holiday an especially joyous one.

Crawford's eyebrows levered upward at the news. "Reconciled, you say? What a surprise!"

That her mother had spoken to this man of her relationship with Horace startled Leigh. It seemed too intimate and personal a thing to discuss with a mere acquaintance.

"Well, whatever makes Althea happy," Crawford conceded with a shrug. Pausing a moment, he regarded her candidly. "And how are you, Leigh? Although there was no love lost between us, I was sorry to hear about your husband's untimely death."

Unexpected tears sprang to Leigh's eyes. It was odd how she could go for weeks without crying for Hayes and then suddenly want to weep over his death like a broken-hearted child.

"I'm fine, really," she assured him, though the catch in her voice betrayed the state of her emotions.

As she spoke, Crawford shifted from his chair to the opposite end of the settee as if he were intending to soothe and comfort her. Even so, his movement flustered Leigh, and she knew a tremor of unease.

Yet, unwilling to be intimidated, she continued. "I'm working several days a week in the Sanitary Commission offices and awaiting word from Mother Bickerdyke about our next nursing assignment."

"Always useful, always dedicated, always altruistic." Crawford characterized her with his usual air of mockery.

"Surely there are worse things you could accuse me of," she countered coldly.

"Yes," he agreed after a moment, a predatory glow in the depths of his eyes, "I think there are, at that."

She noticed suddenly that his hand had crept along the back of the settee and lay behind her shoulder, that he was

looming near enough for her to smell the whiskey on his
breath.

"I could accuse you of being a tempting minx and a
horrible tease," he murmured, "of being the most desirable woman in St. Louis and the most inaccessible."

She was startled by his whispered words and tried to
move away, but his hands had come to curl around her
shoulders, holding her immobile.

"Unhand me, Aaron," Leigh threatened. "Unhand me
and get out of here before I'm forced to call the servants!"

But the words had hardly left her lips when Crawford
wrapped his arms around her and lowered his mouth to
hers. As she struggled to break free of his unwelcome
caress, recollections of another night almost three years
before skittered across her mind. She had been alone in the
library during a party when Aaron had come in, and,
taking advantage of her solitude, had forced himself upon
her. That night Hayes had been her protector and champion: challenging Aaron; staking his own claim to her,
though Leigh had not realized it at the time. But Hayes
was gone now, and she must see to her own defense.

Though she struggled valiantly, the kiss Crawford forced
upon her was hot and wet, as steamy and rank as summer
heat. With a wicked, probing tongue he explored the
contours of her mouth, and as he ravaged her with kisses,
he bore her down on the divan.

"I want you, Leigh," Aaron growled, subduing her
roughly. "I've wanted both you and your lovely mother
since the first moment I saw you together. You are both so
beautiful, so passionate and ripe. And though your mother
managed to elude me, I intend to make a conquest of the
other Pennington woman before this night is over."

Leigh twisted furiously within his grasp as the meaning
of his words came clear to her. Had Aaron really wanted
carnal knowledge of both her and her mother? Leigh wondered dizzily. What wild, perverted fantasies had he been
entertaining on the many occasions when they had been
together? And how could both she and Althea have considered themselves safe in this man's company?

Images filled her mind that left her shaken and sick, and
her opposition became more violent and determined. But

instead of breaking free, her movements launched them off
the slippery sofa and onto the carpeted floor. They landed
heavily, with Aaron's crushing weight subduing her, and
for a full minute Leigh lay beneath him, stunned and
gasping for breath. Immediately Crawford took advantage
of her weakness and gathered both her hands into a single,
viselike grip.

Covering her mouth with his again, his free hand came
to stroke her breast through the deep gray bombazine of
her simple daytime dress. His fingers tightened cruelly
over the pliant mound of flesh, and she murmured helpless
protests in pain and humiliation. Then he was tugging
impatiently at the neckline of her gown until, with a rasp
of tearing cloth, the bodice came away. Her breasts were
bared where they billowed above the top of her chemise,
and taking advantage of the lavish display, he kneaded her
silken skin.

She fought in vain until Aaron's attention strayed to
more interesting parts of her anatomy, and then she finally
managed to wriggle one wrist free. Frantically, her hand
flailed over her head, seeking some weapon to use in her
defense. There was the woolly roughness of the rug beneath her fingers, the coolness of the tiles at the edge of
the hearth. As she stretched even farther, the round wooden
handle of the fireplace poker found its way into her palm,
and she clung to it desperately as if it were indeed her last
hope of salvation. Gasping with the effort, she raised the
metal wand as high as she could and brought the shaft
down across the breadth of Crawford's back.

Even delivered without much leverage, the blow must
have hurt, and Aaron reared back to capture her wrist with
his free hand. He claimed it easily, and his fingers tightened over her forearm, sending pain coursing to her shoulder. But Leigh held on, thrashing her weapon wildly in the
hope of forcing him to let her go.

When Aaron had burst into the room, Leigh had dropped
the poker into the fire so that now the C-shaped tip was
glowing brilliant red. As they grappled, the wrought-iron
end of the poker flashed past their faces, radiating heat that
gave a new dimension to their battle.

Leigh fought stubbornly, ignoring the growing weakness

in her arm and her waning strength, knowing that if she lost this struggle, Aaron Crawford would extract a price from her that went far beyond simple rape. Leigh rolled suddenly to the right, and as he moved to follow her, the combination of their movements brought the poker's red-hot tip against Aaron Crawford's cheek.

There was a faint sizzle and the smell of seared flesh rising in the air; then Crawford suddenly retreated to cover the left side of his face with his hand.

"Bitch!" Crawford snarled at her. "Vicious, cold-hearted bitch!" Through his half-open fingers she could see the stark white shape of the poker branded into his flesh, and she knew it was a disfigurement he would carry all his days.

"You'll pay for this," he threatened, "as you've never paid before! I'll get even for this, too, as I did for all the rest."

Crawford came to his feet, then staggered toward the door, leaving Leigh weak-kneed and trembling on the floor by the divan.

It was there that Bran found her a few minutes later, shaken by what had transpired and the scope of Crawford's threats.

"Where is he?" he demanded as he gathered Leigh in his arms. "Where's Crawford?" Bran's eyes were blazing with self-righteous fury, and, in spite of the missing leg and his crutches, he looked more than capable of defending her.

"Oh, Bran!" she cried, her tears and laughter suddenly mingling. "How is it you always know to come when I need you?"

"This time Matty sent for me when Crawford arrived. She was far more frightened and suspicious of his errand than you."

"I was a fool to let him in."

"Probably," he agreed grimly. "Now tell me what went on."

In the next minutes, Leigh tried to sketch the events of Crawford's visit, and Bran listened, intent on her wavering explanation.

"By God, I'll kill him!" he muttered when she had

finished. "I'll fight that bloody bastard any time or place he chooses."

"Please, Bran, let it be. There's nothing to be gained by challenging him."

"It's what Hayes would do," he argued.

"And I'd like it no better then. Crawford's leaving St. Louis tomorrow. Please, Bran, let it be."

Though Bran looked plainly unconvinced, he nodded in assent, accepting the situation more for Leigh's sake than his own.

The next months passed in a blur of normality, and Leigh did what she could to put Crawford's threats from her mind. She worked several days a week at the Sanitary Commission offices and visited the Confederate prisons with Bran. She wrote letters and made arrangements for the future she was planning and, in preparation, began to sort through her clothes and belongings.

There were very few keepsakes from her days with Hayes, but among them were some chestnuts and two pretty stones they had found one afternoon at Castlewood, a program from a play they'd seen, and a dance card from a ball. Leigh packed away the magnificent sapphire pendant Hayes had given her for Christmas and the tiny belligerent bulldog he'd whittled while he was ill. But somehow she could not put away the letter she had written Hayes and never mailed, the letter where she had been forced to tell him she had fallen and miscarried their baby. It was odd that a single sheet of paper had come to mean so much to her, but somehow she considered the words and sentiments she had expressed as proof that she had grown worthy of Hayes's love. She read it often until the page was smudged and tattered, drawing comfort from what might have been.

In February, Nathan and Delia came to stay. With the war all but over in the West, Travis had resigned his position, and they were headed for Delia's family's farm in central Illinois. It was good land, though isolated, but Leigh suspected they would not be lonely for Delia was already expecting the first of the "passel of children" she wanted to raise.

On the second evening of their visit, Nathan sat up with

Leigh long after Delia retired. He had seemed particularly silent and preoccupied through dinner, and he clearly wanted to discuss something serious with her.

"Leigh," he began in a grave tone, swirling the brandy in his glass, "have you ever found out why you never received letters from Hayes while you were in Vicksburg?"

His question, straightforward and unvarnished as Nathan's questions always were, sent a strange feeling of foreboding swirling through her. "I suppose I never heard from him because Hayes never wrote."

Nathan sat forward in his chair, his elbows braced against his knees and his coal-black gaze focused on her face. "I think he did write you, Leigh," he said at last. "I have reason to believe he wrote often."

"But how can that be, Nathan?" she demanded in confusion. "No letters ever came."

"A few months back I came across the company clerk from Hayes's outfit at Chattanooga. It seems he posted letters to you at the rate of two or three a week. And while the clerk could not be sure, he said he didn't think Hayes ever heard from you."

"But that's impossible!" Leigh protested. "Delia knows how often I wrote."

With a nod, Nathan acknowledged her words. "It's not impossible if someone was tampering with your mail."

It was obvious that Nathan had given this matter much thought, and though Leigh surmised that he had drawn some conclusions about what had happened, she could not stop the question that sprang to her lips. "But who would do that?"

"It would have to be someone with a good deal of authority," he speculated, "someone with suspicions or a grudge against one or both of you."

Leigh was silent for a moment before she spoke a single name. "Aaron Crawford."

He glanced across at her, his narrow features contracting. "How did you know?"

"It was only a guess, really. Aaron came to the house several months ago, and when I refused his advances, he made threats and said he'd pay me back as he had for refusing him before. But how did he do it? Isn't disrupting the mail illegal?''

''Not as provost marshal, in seeking out a spy.''

''So Aaron never gave up the idea that Hayes was working for the Confederacy.''

''Whether he gave it up or not isn't the point. He used his power as provost marshal to sever the flow of letters between you. I spent this afternoon at the Sanitary Commission offices and found that before you returned to St. Louis, Crawford made a point of looking over all your mail.''

Leigh nodded slowly. ''And because I was not sure where to send Hayes's letters, everything I wrote came to the military headquarters here!''

''You couldn't have known what Crawford was up to,'' Nathan offered consolingly. ''There was nothing you could do.''

''Oh, but Nathan, when I think of the time we wasted, time we could have used to resolve the problems keeping Hayes and me apart. Hayes died not knowing that I loved him, not knowing that I had carried his baby, not knowing of our loss.'' There was despair clearly written on her face, the overwhelming knowledge that because of one man's cruelty she and Hayes had missed so much.

Nathan had no way to change what he had discovered, no way to make right the terrible wrong that had been done. But he believed that there was power in truth, and that, for all it hurt Leigh now, the truth would help her build her life anew.

Yet fate did seem to work in strange and mysterious ways, and the major had paid a price for his deception. ''Crawford was killed last week at Petersburg,'' Nathan said softly. ''He will never be able to hurt or threaten you again.''

Though Leigh felt vaguely guilty for her response, she accepted the news of Crawford's death with a marked sense of relief, glad that the man who had caused so much pain would never return to haunt her.

The Travises stayed in St. Louis for a few days more before heading up the river to their new home. How Nathan would accomplish the transition from wanderer and spy to father and farmer, Leigh could only guess. But if anyone could beat Nathan's sword into a plowshare, it was Delia with her sweetness and joy, her tenderness and love.

Now there was only Leigh's own future to resolve, and when Mother Bickerdyke's telegram arrived summoning her to Philadelphia, Leigh was packed and more than ready to go.

21 ⌖

March 30, 1865—Wilmington, North Carolina

The town was at the end of the long finger of
water that probed deep into the North Carolina coast, and
as Leigh stared out across the expanse of blue, Wilmington's church spires began to appear, rising above the treed
banks of the Cape Fear River. Then slowly, commercial
and civil buildings came into view, followed by a knot of
homes and warehouses. The ship General Sherman had
provided for their use was putting into Wilmington only
long enough to take on fuel and water before heading to
Savannah, but Leigh welcomed the break in the routine.
After traveling most of her life on riverboats where there
was much to see along the banks, she had found her week
on the ocean-going steamer dull, and welcomed a diversion.

When she had arrived in Philadelphia in mid-March, she
had found Mary Ann Bickerdyke in the midst of fund-
raising. It was not an activity the older woman particularly
enjoyed, but it was one of the things she did for the sake
of "her boys." Though Mother Bickerdyke was not an
eloquent speaker, she was an effective one. Her sincerity
and compassion were evident when she told of the hardships and tragedies of battle, and she wrung her listeners'
hearts and pocketbooks as more articulate speakers could
not. Leigh had been asked to talk about her experiences
too and had done so gladly. But both she and Mother
Bickerdyke were at their best helping the men in the ranks,
not soliciting donations.

As Leigh watched the sailors tie up at the dock, she heard a gruff voice from behind her. "You going to stand there all morning, or are you coming with me to get a look at the town?"

Mother Bickerdyke was obviously as tired of the ship as Leigh, and less than five minutes later they set off to explore Wilmington. They passed the customs house, where at the height of the war the blockade runners had unloaded their cargoes of contraband, then strolled by sprawling warehouses and up a street lined with tiny shops. Just six weeks before, the town had been evacuated by General Bragg, and though a Federal occupation force was in evidence, life seemed to have been comfortably reestablished since the surrender.

As they continued up the main street, they came upon the Union headquarters set up in a fine old mansion. But instead of the usual few sentries around the place, there were hundreds of men in the yard. For all the tattered threads of Union uniforms they wore, it was clear that they were not regular soldiers. These men were bearded, unkempt, and dressed in rags. They looked half-starved, and many were sick and covered with running sores.

Mother Bickerdyke approached the sentry at the gate. "What's going on here?" she demanded. "Who are these poor beggars, and what's being done to help them?"

"I can't see how that's any of your business, ma'am—" the corporal began.

But before he could finish the sentence, Mother Bickerdyke had taken out the pass General Grant had given her in the early days of the war and waved it beneath his nose. "I'm General Grant's representative here in Wilmington, and I want to see someone in charge!"

Once the man recovered himself, Leigh and Mary Ann Bickerdyke were ushered up the stairs and into the Union commander's office. "Please, ladies, sit down," the gray-haired colonel murmured solicitously, as impressed by General Grant's pass as the young corporal had been. "What may I do to help you?"

Mary Ann Bickerdyke eyed him. "I want to know who those men are in the yard!"

"They're a sorry lot, ma'am," the commander began,

shaking his head. "They're some of the men released from Andersonville Prison. They were brought into town shortly after the place was liberated."

"And what's being done to help them? They look to me as if their needs are being ignored!"

Mother Bickerdyke was an intimidating woman at the best of times, and she seemed especially formidable now.

"Two of our doctors have begun to take over some of the churches and private homes and set up hospitals," the officer explained, "but we're a small force, and we haven't the supplies or manpower to do more."

"Well, I can!" Mother Bickerdyke informed him. "Mrs. Banister and I were on our way to Savannah with a shipload of sanitary stores for General Sherman's men, but it looks to me like these boys here have been given short shrift too long."

She ignored the colonel's exclamation of surprise and went on characteristically. "Now I'll need a couple of wagons and a detachment of men to bring our things from the ship. And if you can tell us where we can set up, Mrs. Banister and I will get down to business."

The house the officer assigned Leigh and Mother Bickerdyke was several doors from the headquarters building, a tall Greek Revival temple built in the epitome of the Southern style. A few of the worst cases from the yard were taken there directly and were laid out in the downstairs rooms on pallets of straw. As soon as supplies began to arrive, beds were made up in earnest: real cots with soft mattresses and cool, inviting sheets. But before any more men were assigned sleeping quarters, Mother Bickerdyke insisted that they be bathed and dressed in the clean clothes she provided.

In the small orchard next to the mansion, a bathhouse was set up where, within the relative privacy of rope-strung blankets, the men could bathe. They could scrub with a brush and strong soap until they were clean and the vermin were washed away. Then they were given soothing balms to apply to the sores that marred so many skins. These sores, caused by dirt, starvation, and rat bites, could fester and putrefy and, left untreated, had claimed large numbers of lives in the prison camps.

While the men were being bathed and the beds made, Leigh and Mother Bickerdyke set to work providing the thing that would raise morale most quickly: good, nourishing food. In the summer kitchen behind the house, they made soup by the kettleful, lemonade by the gallon, tapioca pudding thick with dried peaches and apricots. To the table outside the kitchen door where Leigh doled out the food came a line of heartbreaking wretches: thin, haggard, and ill with fevers or wounds that had not healed. Their delight at a bowl of thick soup and a piece of hardtack, their overwhelming thanks for a dollop of tapioca and a cup of strong coffee, touched Leigh and made her wish there was more she could do.

When the meal was over, the men came back, seeking Mother Bickerdyke's kindness and good sense or Leigh's compassion and beauty. They were men anxious to talk to a woman after years of loneliness, men quiet and shy after all they had endured. They needed medicines, bandages, and care, but most of all they needed to be drawn out by someone who had the patience to listen to their tales. Some men had borne the ravages of war better than others and had retained a semblance of strength and vitality when others had not. Leigh knew, as she tended her patients, that some of them would die before reaching home or would never be truly well again. But large numbers would survive, thanks to the care they were receiving.

It was the mental wrecks who were the most difficult for Leigh to bear. These were the men who had been driven into their own private world by the prisons and the war, the men who had ceased to deal with the dismal realities of their lives. They sat alone at the back of the compound or moved like sleepwalkers under their comrades' care, their faces blank, their eyes hollow and haunted. Their suffering tortured Leigh, and she ached for all those men had lost.

Toward the end of the first day Leigh paused at her post by the kitchen door to take note of everything she, Mother Bickerdyke, and their helpers had accomplished. Through the house's lighted windows, she could see freshly made beds lined up neatly and orderlies carrying the evening meal to the men too weak to serve themselves. Before her the dinner line wove halfway around the yard, and the men

awaiting their evening meal looked far better than they had
this morning. Though painfully thin, they were clean and
dressed in new clothes, with their wounds tended and their
dinner awaiting them. Thanks to the Christian Commission's generosity, the men would sleep tonight warm, well
fed, and beginning to regain their strength. It filled a
woman with satisfaction to know that she had been a part
of something so worthwhile.

With a contented sigh, Leigh went on ladling stew for
the soldiers' dinners, but as she worked, she caught sight
of a single man emerging from the bathing area. Dressed
as all the other men were in dark trousers and a muslin
shirt, she could not say why this particular man drew her
attention. Perhaps she had noticed him because he was
taller than the others around him or because, for all his
thinness, he still looked powerful and strong. Then the
man began to move, and there was something in his
carriage that reminded Leigh of her husband.

"Hayes," she whispered as she stood staring. Her stunned
gaze crept slowly over the man on the far side of the yard,
seeking some clue to his identity. His height and build
were much the same as Hayes's had been, but in the
fading light she could not seem to make out the cast of his
features or the color of his eyes. By some miracle, might
this be Hayes? she found herself wondering. Could this be
the man she had given up for dead?

Moving with rigid precision, she placed the ladle in the
kettle of stew and slowly stepped around the end of the
table. Her eyes were riveted on the tall stranger as she
started across the yard, her feet moving faster, eating up
the distance between them. As she came closer, she saw
that the soldier's hair and beard were the color Hayes's
had been, and there was something achingly familiar about
the way he held his head.

"Hayes?" she ventured in a whisper, the word like
cotton on her tongue.

"Hayes?" She spoke his name aloud and prayed for
some response. There was hope rising in her chest, but it
was tempered by the desperate fear that this man might not
be the one she sought.

There was a start of recognition at his name, a shudder

of response at the sound of her voice, and slowly he turned
to face her, looking startled and unsure.

Leigh went tingly with the shock as she recognized
those harsh, familiar features: the high forehead and narrow nose, the heavy brows and the sensual curve of his
mouth, half-obscured by the chest-length whiskers.

"Hayes! Oh, Hayes! Thank God, you're safe!" Leigh's
arms came around his neck, and she pressed her body
close to his. The scent of him was in her nostrils, and there
was the taste of his lips against her own. Oblivious to
where they were and to the men around them, Leigh clung
to her husband, reveling in a reunion she had never dreamed
could be. In that moment nothing mattered except that Hayes
was safe, alive after all the months of thinking him dead.
Her tears wet both their cheeks, and his name became a
breathless litany, murmured softly against his skin. Her
joy was so all encompassing that it was a full minute
before she realized that Hayes was not responding to their
reunion with the same abandon she was feeling. Confused,
Leigh looked up at her husband.

Hayes stood staring at her, his expression stark and his
eyes as flat and empty as polished mirrors. Fear stabbed
her as she searched for some sign of recognition in his
face. Then slowly his hands came to rest against her waist,
and he whispered a single syllable: "Leigh."

April 3, 1865

"Have you got a blanket to sit on, Leigh, and
the directions I got from that nice sergeant?" Mother
Bickerdyke nagged as she bustled around the summer
kitchen beginning preparations for the noon meal. The
number of Union soldiers who found their way from prisons in the South to Wilmington was growing, and with it
the need for food and lodging. Already Leigh and Mother
Bickerdyke had filled the empty house next door and the
church across the street.

"I tell you," Leigh answered truculently as she loaded
things into the basket, "I'm not at all sure this picnic is a
good idea. It's been the best part of a week since Hayes

wandered in here, and he has hardly said a dozen words to me since then. I can't imagine how you even convinced him to say he'd go.''

''Oh, he wants to go,'' Mother Bickerdyke snapped, stirring ferociously at the concoction in the bowl before her. ''When it comes to you, Leigh, he's eaten up with wanting. He wants to hold you and talk to you, but he doesn't know how.''

The subject of their conversation sat within sight of the cookhouse on the wide veranda of the antebellum mansion. Conversing easily with two other soldiers, he looked very much the man Leigh had married. In the past days the color had returned to his face, and he seemed to have picked up a bit of the weight he had lost during his months at Andersonville. That Hayes had been held at Libby Prison in Richmond until the previous November explained why he was in better condition than many of the men they saw. Still, he bore that strange, unmistakable stamp of a man who had been a prisoner of war.

Leigh sighed unhappily as she recalled the frustrations of the last days. Her sheer delight at finding Hayes safe had gotten them through the first minutes of their reunion. It was only when she had begun to realize that Hayes was not reciprocating her feelings that she regained control of her emotions. Looking up into his impassive face, she had simultaneously become aware of the catcalls from the men around them and the apathy in her husband's eyes. Frightened and confused, Leigh had tightened her grip on Hayes's arm and drawn him to the relative privacy behind a pile of supply boxes.

''Hayes,'' she had begun, watching him intently, ''Hayes, are you all right?''

''Of course I am,'' he had assured her. But his carefully controlled voice belied the reassuring words.

''But where have you been? The Army told me you were dead.'' The flutter in her voice had been the antithesis of Hayes's icy monotone, and her compulsive need to touch him was in sharp contrast to the way his hands dangled at his sides.

''I've been in Andersonville,'' he had answered, admitting the obvious, ''and before that at Libby.''

"But how did you get there?"

"I was captured." When she would have demanded details, he went on. "After falling off the pontoon bridge, I lost consciousness, and when I came to myself again, I was washed up on the riverbank. I tried to find my way back to Chattanooga, but I was captured by a Rebel patrol."

Prying a pearl out of an oyster would have been easier than getting Hayes to tell her more about his experiences. Giving up for the moment, Leigh had led him back to the kitchen, made sure he had a plate of stew, a biscuit, and some tapioca for dessert, and assigned him a cot in the big bedroom below her own. Perhaps when he'd had a bit to eat and time to rest, he would be more forthcoming, Leigh had reasoned. Leaving Hayes to his own devices, she had gone back to her work with the other men who needed care.

But as the days passed, Hayes continued to be every bit as reticent as he had been that first night. Observing him from across the compound, Leigh noticed that he chatted easily with the other men and seemed to enjoy their company, but he stringently avoided anything that put him in contact with his wife.

For herself, Leigh could not get enough of him. Without looking, she knew whenever he was near and spent more time than she should staring like a lovesick schoolgirl. Even from a distance, she could see the changes the war had made in him: the new lines that webbed from the corners of his eyes, the deepening creases around his mouth, the sprinkling of gray in his walnut-brown hair. The second day he had been shaved and barbered, taking years from his appearance, and though his actions still made him a stranger, he looked very much like the man she loved.

Leigh had watched him with a growing fascination, hungering for the sight of him and listening for the sound of his voice. Dreams of happier times plagued her sleep and the knowledge of what they had once shared sharpened her frustration. She found herself entertaining secret fantasies of leading him to her pallet in the attic, stripping off his clothes, running her hands along his body, and making him a part of herself. But she kept a tight rein on her emotions and tried to content herself with the furtive glances she could steal.

She quickly came to understand the reasons for the change in him. From the other prisoners she began to learn what the conditions had been at Andersonville, with no shelter, no sanitation, and little food. She heard tales of brutal punishment, the cruel guards, and the inhuman treatment. Life in the stockade must have been hell on earth, and it would have deeply scarred a man like Hayes.

Whether he had built his wall of reserve to protect himself from those hardships or from the hurt Leigh herself had caused, she could only guess. Guiitily she remembered how they had parted in St. Louis and the months that had passed without contact between them. Hayes did not know about Aaron Crawford's interference or that they had conceived and lost a child. He had no idea that Leigh had grown into a different woman, capable of understanding and tenderness, or that from loss she had learned a great deal about love.

How much she had to tell him. How much there seemed to be to say, but until now she had not been able to make Hayes listen. Well, perhaps the picnic was a good idea, she conceded, tucking the last few items into the basket. If she and Hayes were alone together, he would be hard-pressed to ignore her.

"Haven't you got everything packed up yet?" Mary Ann Bickerdyke prodded her.

"Yes, all ready," Leigh replied, a faint tremor in her voice.

The older woman came to where Leigh stood. "Scared?" she asked perceptively.

"A little, I guess. You know how I feel about Hayes, but unless I can convince him that I still love him, what chance do we have for a future together?"

"Now, you listen to me, girl," Mother Bickerdyke offered. "Hayes needs you as much as you need him. After what he's been through, he's uncertain and confused. He doesn't know what tomorrow will bring, and, what's worse, he's not even sure about the past. You haven't had a chance to tell him about the baby, have you? Or explain about all the letters that never arrived?''

Leigh shook her head as tears rose in her eyes.

"No, I thought not. And there's no sense crying over something you can fix.''

"I love him, Mother Bickerdyke. I only want a chance to show him how much.''

"Yes, I know you do, and that's why I think you'll find a way to make things right. You go to him, Leigh,'' Mother Bickerdyke said, turning to gaze at the tall, lean man who sat waiting on the veranda. "You're twice the woman you were when you came to me at Cairo. You've got the strength to make that man whole and happy, and I believe you can.

"You tell him all the things he needs to hear: that you understand what he's been through, that you love him. You give Hayes a child to make up for the one you lost. You give him a future to live for that's better than what's past.''

"I don't know if that's what he wants—'' Leigh began.

"It's what he wants,'' the older woman insisted sagely. "You mark me well. It's what every man wants: a little warmth and tenderness, a chance for happiness with the woman he loves. Give Hayes all the care and loving you've spent four years lavishing on other men. Why are you questioning what he needs when you have never questioned what you gave the others?''

"All the others wanted,'' Leigh began thickly, "was comfort and compassion. I've never had to give them what Hayes wants. I've never had to give them myself.''

Mother Bickerdyke nodded and glanced speculatively at Leigh. "Comfort and compassion? A part of yourself?'' she asked softly. "Isn't it all the same thing in the end?''

        It had turned out to be a beautiful day, alive with the sudden warmth of spring. Newly leafed trees rustled overhead, and the green grass flirted with the wind, undulating in the fields like rolling velvet waves. The wild jonquils that splashed across the hillsides were a brilliant complement to the blazing azure sky, and the scent of freshly turned earth lay heavily on the air.

Yet, for all she tried to enjoy the beauty around her, Leigh's attention was on Hayes. He sat hunched forward on the buggy seat, a foot braced against the dashboard, one wrist draped negligently over his knee as he guided the horse with practiced hands. He had been frustratingly uncommunicative since they had left Wilmington, and Leigh sat, trying to ignore the press of silence around them. It was not an easy task when she had so much she wanted to say, so many questions she needed to ask. But each of her attempts at conversation had been politely but firmly rebuffed.

Surreptitiously she watched her husband, noting his quiet but determined intensity. He seemed wary but not apprehensive, guarded but not uneasy, and she wondered at his thoughts. She was fully aware of the nudge of his shoulder against hers as they jolted over the narrow country road. On the breeze she caught the subtle, citrus tang of his skin and saw the sinewy strength of his hands. Never in her life had she been more aware of a man, nor had any man seemed less receptive to her charms.

"We're to take the fork to the right," Leigh instructed, reading the last of the directions from the paper Mary Ann Bickerdyke had given her. "The spring should be just ahead."

With a murmur of acknowledgment, Hayes guided the buggy down the less traveled road, then clucked softly to the horse, urging it to a trot. The vehicle bounced along half a mile farther before Hayes drew on the reins and pulled to the edge of the road.

"This must be the place," he observed.

Down a slight slope lay a pool of silver blue, shining like a mirror in the sun. The pond was surrounded by a grove of willow trees trailing their branches in the water. It was a perfect place for a picnic, serene and isolated. Mother Bickerdyke had obviously known what she was about when she had sent them here.

"Isn't it lovely?" Leigh said softly after a moment. "Shall we look for a place to spread our blanket?"

Hayes swung out of the buggy and turned to help her

down, taking her hand gingerly as if to avoid more intimate contact. While he unhitched the horse from the traces, Leigh gathered a well-worn quilt and a basket of food from the back of the borrowed buggy. Strolling past where Hayes was hobbling the horse, she moved down the path to the pond.

Hayes followed at a more sedate pace, appreciatively noting the swing of his wife's wide skirts as she passed before him. He had no business coming here with Leigh, he chided himself, no business coming here at all. Being alone with her was making him want things he knew he could not have, making him wish he could change things that could not be altered. Back at the house in town it had been hard enough to keep his distance, but here, without the protection of her duty and the men who envied him his wife, he was uncertain of his ability to keep his emotions in check. He found himself in the unenviable position of a man parched with thirst forced to deny himself a drink.

Nor was Leigh making self-denial any easier to bear. In the pink mull gown and scooped bonnet she looked delectable, touchable, soft, and willing. His senses clamored for him to take what she seemed so ready to give, but he knew he dared not weaken.

"Is this all right?" Leigh asked, setting the basket aside and flapping the quilt into place in a sun-spattered clearing at the edge of the pool. Without waiting for his reply she settled herself on the ground and stripped the bonnet from her head.

Hayes came to the edge of the blanket and stared down at her. She was like some pale, exotic blossom spread out before him, her skirts furled wide like opening petals, her smiling face turned up to his. He could feel her enticing him closer, promising ease and pleasure with her eyes. But he was terrifyingly aware of the danger in accepting the things she offered and the unutterable pain that yielding could bring.

When he hesitated, Leigh reached up to catch his hand, pulling him down beside her as if it were where he belonged. He went reluctantly, knowing there was no help for it, fighting the spiral of excitement that wound through him at her touch.

"The pond is pretty, isn't it?" she began quietly, trying not to notice the way he had settled at the very edge of the blanket.

He nodded in agreement. "Very pretty, indeed."

"I wonder if there are ducks."

"It seems a likely place for some."

The silence that had plagued their ride into the country threatened again, and Leigh continued almost compulsively, anxious to fill the void with conversation. "Mother Bickerdyke found someone who knew the countryside around Wilmington and got directions," she explained unnecessarily. "She thought we needed time alone."

Hayes gave a gust of bitter laughter. "Now, why would she think that?"

For a moment Leigh stared at him, stung by his tone. "I suppose it's because we're married, because we're husband and wife."

The spectrum of their relationship was suddenly laid bare, and in spite of himself Hayes had a need to mock the vows they had made. "Oh, I hardly think there's enough left of our marriage for her to be concerned about providing us solitude."

Before Leigh could think of a reply, he continued, plucking a blade of grass and fingering it thoughtfully. "I just hope my untimely 'resurrection' won't prove inconvenient for you."

Leigh paled visibly at his words. What on earth was going through his mind? she wondered. Did he think she had been relieved when he was reported missing, that she preferred to be free? Since he had come into Wilmington, he had been the one avoiding her. And his indifference hurt when she cared so much.

With an effort she kept her voice steady. "Inconvenient? Why, no. I'm quite glad you've turned up here."

"Are you?" he asked skeptically. "I was under the impression you had given up being my wife."

"What?" she gasped. "Why would you think that?"

He pointed to the hand lying lax in her lap. "You've stopped wearing your wedding ring," he noted. "That seemed a clear indication to me."

Leigh glanced down at the third finger of her left hand,

thinking of the signet ring she had worn so long and
faithfully. He had no way of knowing how precious that
ring had become to her, even more when she thought him
dead than when he had made her his wife. But from
something he said, she had gleaned a flicker of insight and
sensed the doubt behind his accusation. Perhaps this was a
chance to show her husband just how much she had changed.

"I gave the ring to a woman I met in the hospital at
Chattanooga," she began softly. "Somehow, I thought
you wouldn't mind."

"Not mind?" Hayes's voice was incredulous. "What
made you think I wouldn't mind?"

"Because the woman was Justin Dean's widow."

"Sarah?" he murmured the name.

"Yes, Sarah. That's what you'd always intended, wasn't
it? You'd always meant to give the signet ring to Justin's
wife and son."

"Yes, but—"

"When I met her," Leigh went on, watching her husband's face, "it seemed the only right thing to do. I had
memories of you, and Sarah had her memories of Justin,
but David is too young to have known his father."

Hayes paused before nodding. "Yes, you're right; he
would have been. How old is David now, anyway?"

"He must be all of five. Sarah brought him to the camp
not long before Mother Bickerdyke and I left for Atlanta.
David is a fine, strong boy, and Sarah has every right to be
proud of him. He looks a bit like you, you know?"

One corner of Hayes's mouth lifted. "Does he? Does he
really? They always said I was more a Dean than a
Banister."

Hayes had smiled as they talked of his cousin's wife and
son, and that spark of sincere emotion drew Leigh to him.
For in that moment, he was not the cool, distant stranger
who had wandered into Wilmington seeking shelter, but
the man she loved. He was not the confusing enigma
whose presence filled her with misgivings, but someone
with whom she had shared the joys and trials of life. Driven
by an urge she could find no way to deny, Leigh reached
across to touch him, desperate for a bit of reassurance.

Hayes watched her approach as if mesmerized, anticipating her touch with eagerness and trepidation. She came slowly, tentatively, but even before he felt the brush of her hand, her essence had begun to envelop him. He was aware of the sweet orange and spice scent in his nostrils, saw the fire spun through her cinnamon hair, heard the breath of his name on her lips like an audible caress. The touch came gently, the lingering stroke of her fingers drifting from his cheek to where his throat lay bared and vulnerable. At even that simple contact his palms went wet, his mouth went dry, and his heart began to thunder.

As if sensing the welcome he could not deny, Leigh seized the moment and crept nearer, brushing her lips across his mouth. The kiss was soft, tender, gentle, but it overwhelmed Hayes, loosing emotions in him he had vowed to deny. Of their own volition his arms swept around her, drawing her close in a gesture of desperate longing. His mouth took hers, crushing, tasting, pressing, seeking the sweep of remembered rapture. A rush of desire came to swamp his senses, and he was helplessly beguiled as Leigh fluttered a wave of eager kisses over the surface of his skin. She kissed his temples, his eyes, and the lobe of his ear, his dimples, his chin, and the line of his jaw. She dipped lower, nibbling down the curve of his throat, sending waves of shivers skimming along his spine.

Then Hayes claimed her mouth again, forcing her lips apart under the scalding onslaught of his own. He felt her tremble and knew that he was trembling, too. She sighed, and he felt the brush of her breath against him. There was excitement and consolation in the deepening fervor of their kiss, and Hayes drank in all her sweetness, feeling at once deprived and satisfied.

But somehow Hayes knew he could not succumb, could not let her magic engulf him. There was danger in mindlessly accepting all she had to give him when so much lay unresolved between them.

"Leigh, wait," he said, his voice husky and low. "Leigh, please. Please stop. I don't want this to happen."

As she raised her head, he could see her face was marked with confusion. "Why, Hayes? Why can't we come together? We're man and wife, and I love you so."

He went totally still at her words, watching her intently

as he searched for truth or insincerity in the shadowed depths of her eyes. "Do you love me, Leigh?" he demanded. "Do you care? And if you do, why weren't there ever any letters, none in all the months we were apart."

She saw in him the disillusionment and hurt she had come to know so well, the mistrust and pain another man had caused. "I did write," she assured him, "and I know now you did, too."

"Of course I wrote, as often as I could. But you never answered. You never sent me any word at all."

"Yes, I did write! I wrote you to say how much I loved you, to tell you I was going to have your child—"

"My child?" Hayes was plainly shaken by her revelation and seemed suddenly paler than before.

"And I wrote when I miscarried it. But Aaron Crawford intercepted our mail."

"Crawford? What reason would Crawford have for doing that?"

"Think, Hayes! Think of the suspicions he had about your loyalty; think about his reasons for hating both of us."

There were emotions warring in Hayes's face, and she knew she was expecting him to assimilate more in these few minutes than anyone could take in. Still, she felt compelled to continue, compelled to tell him everything while she had the chance.

"Hayes, please! I never meant to hurt you. I know that much of what you're feeling is based on how we parted in St. Louis. But please, Hayes, believe me; so much has changed since then. I understand things now that I never expected to understand. I can accept things now that I thought were unacceptable. When I lost the baby, I came to realize what you felt for Monica's son, realize that your actions at Vicksburg were honorable and based in nobility. I care for you, Hayes. I love you more than I can say. I want for us to be together. Now that the war is all but over, we can start again."

He closed his eyes to shut out the sight of her, tried to deafen himself to her words. She was offering him everything a man could wish for, a future sweet with promise, a lifetime of security and love. But he was terrified of caring, of the pain loving her could bring.

Too much was happening too quickly. Her revelations about Crawford and the letters, the news of the child she had carried and lost filled him with doubt and hope and uncertainty that seemed impossible to reconcile. If he allowed himself to believe what she promised, if he let himself accept that she cared, he would be yielding everything, surrendering the last of his reserve.

There was so much trapped inside him, things he did not want to remember or share. If he relinquished his self-control, those memories would surface too, returning to hurt and haunt him. He felt helpless, buffeted, lost. He needed time to consider all she had revealed. He needed time to think about all she wanted and assess his ability to give.

As if sensitive to his turmoil, Leigh was suddenly withdrawing, rising to stand over him, her expression both tender and marked with concern.

"For all this sunshine," she remarked off-handedly, "the wind is surprisingly cool. I'm going to get the shawl I left back in the buggy."

Without waiting for a reply, Leigh turned away and headed up the path. It was not difficult to discern what Hayes was thinking. She had told him too much, expected him to accept in one afternoon things it had taken her months and months to grasp. Patience was in order, and she meant to give Hayes all the time he needed, just as he had given her.

While she had wrestled with her guilt and doubts, Hayes had maintained his faith in what they shared. He had kept his love burning bright to help her find her way. Now it was Hayes who was lost and uncertain when she was sure, his needs that must be satisfied while hers were set aside. It was what Mother Bickerdyke had tried to make her understand this morning, what her own mother had tried to tell her nearly two years before. Because she loved Hayes, because she believed they were meant to be together, she would give him all the time he needed. It was her turn to be strong. With a sense of purpose, she took the shawl from the carriage seat and threaded it through her arms.

Hayes had watched Leigh's retreat into the trees with a strange sense of relief. He needed to be alone to sort out his jumbled feelings. He desperately wanted to believe what she had told him: that in those terrible, lonely months there had been letters for him somewhere, that she had carried and lost his child.

His child, the idea astounded him. It must have been conceived that last night in St. Louis, that night so filled with sweetness and conflict. How had Leigh felt about carrying his baby? he wondered. Had she wanted the child of a man she said she loved but could not trust or understand?

Never in his life had Hayes felt so shaken and unsure, as if all he'd known as truth were now like shifting sand. Absently he noticed the neck of a bottle protruding from the picnic basket and delved inside, hoping it contained something stronger than lemonade or cider. It was a bottle of vintage wine, perhaps one of the last in the Confederacy, but fastened around the bottle was a dog-eared piece of paper. Curious, he slipped the string that bound it and glanced at the closely written page. It was a letter addressed to him.

Bridgeport, Alabama
November 4, 1863

Dearest Hayes,

This may prove to be the most difficult letter I will ever write, and as I pen these words, I am aware of the fullness of my emotions. When I wrote that I was carrying your child, I was filled with excitement and joy. But now I must tell you of our loss. After a fall at Vicksburg, I miscarried our child. And though we all tried very hard to save it, there was nothing we could do.

I had such hopes for that child, and I so longed to hold it in my arms. I had wanted with all my heart to find a way to prove my love. I thought a baby might help to mend the rift between us and give us a reason to resolve our differences. The miscarriage is the end to those dreams, and I mourn their passing just as I do the child's.

But from the miscarriage has come some good; now I understand as never before what a tie of blood can mean. I know how you must have felt when you thought your son was in danger, and I think I can understand the emotions that drove you into Vicksburg to see to his safety.

Please forgive me for all I said that last night in St. Louis. I know now how wrong I was. My most fervent wish is to see things resolved between us.

I love you, Hayes; I want to spend the rest of my life with you. I want to bear you children and grow old at your side. Let's end the estrangement between us; I crave word of your safety. I need your strength as never before and urge you to break your silence.

I will be at Chattanooga after tomorrow and will mail this from there. I am sorry for the news I have been compelled to send you, but I have hope for our future together.

I love you, Hayes, with all my heart.

Leigh

There was no question of the letter's sincerity, no question that she had meant every word, and somewhere deep inside Hayes a knot of doubt and tension eased.

Leigh's footsteps made no sound as she approached the clearing, and she froze where she stood when she saw the paper in her husband's hands. She recognized it instantly and knew that as she watched him, Hayes was reading the painful words of love and loss that had been inscribed upon her heart. In the year and a half since she had penned those words, she had read the letter a thousand times, sometimes as a penance for having come to the understanding of her husband too late and sometimes as a reward to remind her of all the sweetness she'd known. There was no question in her mind about how the letter had come to be in the basket. Mother Bickerdyke had known about the letter and had put it there for Hayes to find.

Leigh waited silently, studying her husband, waiting for his reaction to the sentiments she had written at a different juncture in her life. His head was bowed and his shoulders hunched so she could not read his expression. But when he did not move, when the edges of the page began to flutter in the wind, Leigh moved closer, drawn by burgeoning hope and devastating uncertainty.

"Hayes?" she asked softly. "Hayes?"

There was no response to the sound of her voice, and as the thread of anticipation tightened, she stroked one hand along his cheek to turn his face to hers. It came up slowly, torturously, and as it did, she saw the sheen of tears in his eyes.

With a soft cry she sank to her knees beside him, drawing Hayes close and tangling her hands in his hair. His arms came around her too, crushing her fiercely to his chest.

"Oh, God, Leigh, I'm so sorry," he murmured, his words muffled and harsh against her ear.

"Oh, Hayes, I'm sorry, too."

"I'm sorry you went through the miscarriage alone. I'm sorry that you doubted I loved you."

"Hush, Hayes, hush."

"I'm sorry for the way we parted in St. Louis. That estrangement was as much my fault as yours."

"It doesn't matter now," she told him. "Nothing matters as long as you're safe and here with me."

They clung tight, breast to breast and thigh to thigh, hugging with the vicious tenacity of those who had suffered long separation. This was the true reunion of their lives, going beyond love, beyond need, to the very core of their emotions. They had been separate and now were one, had been divided and had rediscovered unity.

They clung close for a very long time, bound fast in defiance of all that had conspired to keep them apart. But as the need for security was gradually satisfied, another need arose. The touching became more tender and less desperate, more sensual and less binding. Their physical proximity brought awareness of other desires long denied, and a warmth began to envelop them. Strokes became caresses, expressions of sorrow became words of love, kisses fluttered to hair and eyes, lips brushed and brushed again. Mouths merged, tongues played, bodies pressed until they sank down onto the quilt together, the expression of their love burning bright and hot between them.

Side by side they lay beneath the blaze of the cerulean sky, their intimacy as natural and right as the spring alive around them. They kissed, and Leigh thrilled Hayes with the ease of her surrender; they touched, and she offered him the balm of true affection. From the well of her secret longings, Leigh gave more than he could ask. She whispered words of provocation soft against his skin and assuaged his devastating loneliness with tenderness and love.

He sought the corners of her mouth, nibbled the deeply indented bow, lavished care on the pouting lower curve, before he dipped between her lips to tease her tongue with his. He took what she so willingly gave, accepted the fervor of her kiss, tasting the sweet nectar of her femininity deep within his mouth.

He retreated to brush her collarbone with a kiss, tracing a delicate, tingling line to where her neckline barred his way. His hand skimmed across her bodice to trap her swelling breast, spanning the fullness with his palm as his thumb found and pressed the peak.

"I've dreamed of touching you like this more nights than you know," he told her. "I've wanted to see that warm, sleepy glow in your eyes, hear your voice go hushed and deep with longing. In the prison camp the thought of you was my salvation, even when wondering if you loved me defined the scope of my private hell."

"Oh, Hayes, I do love you—" she began, but he silenced her with an eager caress, feeling as he did the subtle, provocative press of her hips against him. Their lips brushed, pillowed, merged. Their hands stroked and aroused, giving inarticulate proof of all their reassurances.

Beneath the ruffled hem of her gown, he stroked up her fabric-covered thigh, to find the opening of her underclothes and probe tenderly inside.

"Hayes."

"Yes, love," he answered her, touching deep, sending billowing waves of languor seeping through her limbs.

"Oh, Hayes."

She was drifting, sinking, succumbing to the sensual world he had wrought, but she generously wanted to share her pleasure with the man who lay beside her. She needed to show Hayes the tenderness he'd been denied, needed to satisfy his passions as well as her own. Her hands moved over him, running along his throat and down his arms, opening the buttons on his shirt and touching the warmth of his skin. She loved the vitality of his flesh beneath her fingers, the brush of the hair on his chest against her palms. She pressed her mouth to the sensitive place at the base of his throat, swirling her tongue against it.

"I've wanted this too," she told him, "wanted to have you beside me, wanted to make you ache with wanting me."

Her eyes were cloudy, hungry, hot, and he moved above her restlessly. "I do want you, Leigh," he whispered at last. "Dear God, I want you more than you can know!"

"And I want you. I want you to be a part of my body, as you are of my heart and life."

Driven by needs they could no longer deny, by the separation they had endured, they undressed each other tenderly and made love beneath the sky.

"Slowly," Hayes whispered as they began to come together. "Slowly, because we've waited so long; slowly, so we can savor each moment."

Their gaze held as their bodies merged, green eyes meeting blue, the simple magic of their love welling up between them. The union was bliss couched in rapture, sweetness pure and true. It was delight that blazed into ecstasy, binding them as close together as two lives could ever be. In this moment, the culmination of their love, there was no other world, only the one of affection and selflessness, of truth and wondrous unity. They shuddered as the crest began to build, felt the madness and the frenzy take them. They ascended to a realm of pure sensation: whole, unafraid, and strong, their hearts and souls inseparable through all eternity.

After a time reality drifted back. It was too soon for them to stir, too soon for them to part. But because they were lying tangled and bared to the world, Hayes pulled one of Leigh's petticoats to cover them.

"This is a peculiar coverlet," she observed drowsily, still luxuriating in the sensual world they'd explored.

Hayes brushed a kiss along her brow, then tucked the ruffled hem around her. "Still, there were plenty of nights last winter," he whispered wryly, "when I would have sold my soul for this."

With the half-teasing comment Hayes began to talk, urgently, volubly, helplessly, suddenly needing to ease the snarl of conflict inside him. A flood of words was coming, bursting the restraints he had tried to impose, pouring from his mouth in a never-ending tide. He told Leigh about the day he had been captured, about a prisoner's life in the Rebel camp, of being marched to Libby Prison in Richmond and the conditions there. He had thought Libby was as near to hell as a living man could come, but then he had been sent to Andersonville, and Andersonville was worse than hell. Being bigger and stronger than most of the prisoners had saved him from the marauding gangs of inmates that preyed upon the weak, but it also drew the attention of the guards who seemed to take sadistic pleasure in their power over the prisoners.

From the other men who had come to Wilmington, Leigh had heard stories of the cruelties, the lack of food and shelter in the prison compound. Now Hayes spoke of those things, holding nothing back, letting the strings of unencumbered words sear away all that haunted him. Sometimes his voice went angry and sharp or soft and deep with pain. Still, the words seemed to purge a festering mass of memories that lost their threatening power once they saw the sun.

He talked as they dressed and ate, talked as they drank their wine, and Leigh stubbornly held her tongue, never once interrupting.

She shed tears of anger for all he had suffered, tears of pain for the inhumanity he had known. She wept with fury, loss, and outrage as Hayes himself could not. Finally, he held her close and dried her eyes with a ruffled, threadbare handkerchief he produced from the pocket of his trousers.

"Why, this is mine!" she noted in astonishment, looking down at the sodden cloth.

"I found it wrapped around the note the morning you left St. Louis," he offered quietly, "and I've kept it with me ever since."

There was no need for him to tell her that there were times when clinging to that piece of cloth was all that kept him sane. It had represented memories of something beautiful and a future he hoped to claim. She seemed to know what the handkerchief meant to him, to understand without a word a hundred things she had not known before.

At last, they lay back on the quilt together, contentedly watching the clouds drift by, enjoying the sunshine and the solitude, the silence and their unity.

"What about the future, Hayes?" she asked in an uncertain tone. "What shall we do now that the war is ending, now that the armies will be going home?"

There was no question that they would be together; he knew just as she did that after this they would never part.

"I don't know, Leigh," he murmured. "For so long there were no possibilities, and now there are so many." He drew a long breath and frowned thoughtfully, considering the future that was theirs. "I think going back to Cincinnati and the shipyard makes some sense, or had you made plans of your own?"

Leigh smiled and touched her husband's cheek in a gentle, soothing caress. "Yes, I've made a few plans of my own, but they fit quite nicely with yours. There is a very good medical school in Cincinnati, and I have been accepted for classes there come fall."

Hayes nodded slowly. "You told me you wanted to be a doctor that first night on the porch."

"It was the first time I admitted to anyone what I'd dreamed of all my life."

"Then I'm glad that you told me, glad you trusted me with your dreams. I've known from that first afternoon how good you are with the ill, and I think you'll make a fine doctor after all the experience you've had. But why did you choose Cincinnati when there are medical schools in St. Louis you could attend?"

"I did it because of you, because when I wrote your

mother to tell her you were missing, I realized I wanted some kind of bond. I needed to keep contact somehow, and I hoped your family would accept me, if not as your wife, then as a friend.''

''Oh, they'll accept you, all right.'' His voice was deep and warm. ''Especially my mother. She likes determined women, and my sister Rose does, too.''

''And how about you, Mr. Banister?'' she teased him gently. ''Do you like determined women, too?''

Hayes grinned and rolled above her. ''They're my favorite kind.''

And then the brief moment of humor passed, and he lowered his mouth to hers. ''Oh, Leigh, this is all I've ever wanted, a life for us together, a life that we can share.''

She knew that there were still things she needed to tell him, questions they both would need to ask. But they had time: time to talk, time to love, time to live. They had the future. They had a lifetime, a lifetime filled with love.

Author's Note

After researching *Let No Man Divide*, I would like to credit as my main source of both information and inspiration the work by Agatha Young, *The Women and the Crisis: Women of the North in the Civil War*. Reading not only this book, but others from her bibliography, gave me an understanding of the trials and triumphs of women in the Civil War era and especially women involved in military nursing. In writing *Let No Man Divide*, I adopted one of Young's premises as my own: that the Civil War was the beginnings of the women's movement as we know it (the convention in Seneca Falls, New York, in 1848 notwithstanding). That until women were forced out of the home to care for the wounded and raise money for relief, they did not realize either how repressed or how capable they really were. The character Leigh represents a pioneer of sorts, a woman who because of her wartime experiences would go on to a field that was then, and is to this day, dominated by men. In truth, many of the women who organized the North's relief agencies became women's rights activists and suffragettes.

After reading a novel as grounded in history as *Let No Man Divide*, I always want to know which characters were real and which were figments of the author's imagination. While Leigh and Hayes were fictitious, they were both based on actual people or amalgamations of people I read about. On the other hand, Mary Ann Bickerdyke was a living, breathing person, remarkable and even stronger and more flamboyant that I could make her. Stories about her experiences during the war are legend, and I drew most of my information from Nina Brown Baker's biography *Cyclone in Calico: The Story of Mary Ann Bickerdyke*. The other nurses mentioned by name, with the exception of Delia, were all real people and left records of their experiences in wartime.

James Eads, too, was a prominent man in St. Louis at the time of the war. He did start out as an urchin selling apples on street corners, and by 1861, he had made his fortune and retired. He came out of retirement to build the ironclads and, after the war in 1879, built Eads' Bridge, which is still in use and has become a St. Louis landmark.

Researching any period and then reproducing it in fiction is a business fraught with peril, and a period of history like the Civil War is particularly difficult because there is so much written about it. Yet there are things that fall through the cracks. In researching the hospital-ship section of this book, information was frustratingly sketchy. Young makes her first mention of them after Fort Donelson. A recent article in *Civil War Times* credits the *Red Rover* as the first U.S. Navy hospital ship. According to the records of the Western Sanitary Commission here in St. Louis, the first ship designed for that purpose was *The City of Louisiana*. As much as we would like it to be, history is not absolute.

In addition to the other books I have credited, I would like to cite *The American Heritage Short History of the Civil War, The Civil War Almanac,* and the Time-Life Civil War Series as my basic sources. I also read a number of delightful journals, newspapers, guidebooks, and narratives of the various campaigns in making *Let No Man Divide* as accurate as possible.

By way of additional research I walked the streets of St. Louis. Camp Jackson is now covered by a railyard, the Planters' House is a bank, Busch Stadium is built over the Lynch slave pen, and Checkerboard Square is on the site of the Gratiot Street Prison. One lone example of the town houses in Lucas Place remains, and I would like to thank Thoren Ware, the curator of the Campbell House, for the time he spent with me.

The Mississippi has changed, too: through both nature and man's design. But there is still a magnificence to it that the years cannot alter. One needs only to stand on the levee and watch the ceaseless flow of water to understand its permanence and hear the echoes of the past.

Elizabeth N. Kary
St. Louis, Missouri
February 1, 1986

Bestselling Books
from Berkley

The nationally bestselling author

CYNTHIA FREEMAN

Cynthia Freeman is one of today's best-loved authors of bittersweet human drama and captivating love stories. With ILLUSIONS OF LOVE she achieved her most magnificent triumph to date.

Now, with SEASONS OF THE HEART she takes us to an even greater height of compelling romance.

"Glossy settings, spunky women, steamy love scenes."
—*New York Times Book Review*

The eternal saga of a woman strong before her time, who must choose between her career, her weak but adoring husband, and a passionate lover whose embrace she cannot resist. . .

A New York Times hardcover bestseller, soon to be a Berkley paperback.

____ **ILLUSIONS OF LOVE** 0-425-08529-5/$4.50